*A story of a different America . . .*

**SILENT HONOR**

PRAISE FOR
DANIELLE STEEL'S
SILENT HONOR

"AN EXTREMELY MOVING BOOK . . . a realistic
portrayal of the Japanese Americans at this period in
our turbulent history." —*Canyon News* (Tex.)

"A POIGNANT STORY." —*Publishers Weekly*

"WELL RESEARCHED AND SOLID."
—*Kirkus Reviews*

"EXTRAORDINARY . . . OUTSTANDING
FICTION." —*Wahpeton News* (N. Dak.)

"AN AMBITIOUS STORY SUCCESSFULLY TOLD
. . . Danielle Steel is an accomplished storyteller."
—*Telegraph Journal* (Canada)

"A reminder of a shameful episode in American history
that should not be forgotten."
—*Library Journal*

A MAIN SELECTION OF
THE LITERARY GUILD
AND
THE DOUBLEDAY BOOK CLUB

## By Danielle Steel

IN HIS FATHER'S FOOTSTEPS • THE GOOD FIGHT • THE CAST
ACCIDENTAL HEROES • FALL FROM GRACE • PAST PERFECT
FAIRYTALE • THE RIGHT TIME • THE DUCHESS
AGAINST ALL ODDS • DANGEROUS GAMES • THE MISTRESS
THE AWARD • RUSHING WATERS • MAGIC • THE APARTMENT
PROPERTY OF A NOBLEWOMAN • BLUE • PRECIOUS GIFTS
UNDERCOVER • COUNTRY • PRODIGAL SON • PEGASUS
A PERFECT LIFE • POWER PLAY • WINNERS • FIRST SIGHT
UNTIL THE END OF TIME • THE SINS OF THE MOTHER
FRIENDS FOREVER • BETRAYAL • HOTEL VENDÔME
HAPPY BIRTHDAY • 44 CHARLES STREET • LEGACY • FAMILY TIES
BIG GIRL • SOUTHERN LIGHTS • MATTERS OF THE HEART
ONE DAY AT A TIME • A GOOD WOMAN • ROGUE • HONOR THYSELF
AMAZING GRACE • BUNGALOW 2 • SISTERS • H.R.H. • COMING OUT
THE HOUSE • TOXIC BACHELORS • MIRACLE • IMPOSSIBLE • ECHOES
SECOND CHANCE • RANSOM • SAFE HARBOUR • JOHNNY ANGEL
DATING GAME • ANSWERED PRAYERS • SUNSET IN ST. TROPEZ
THE COTTAGE • THE KISS • LEAP OF FAITH • LONE EAGLE
JOURNEY • THE HOUSE ON HOPE STREET • THE WEDDING
IRRESISTIBLE FORCES • GRANNY DAN • BITTERSWEET
MIRROR IMAGE • THE KLONE AND I • THE LONG ROAD HOME
THE GHOST • SPECIAL DELIVERY • THE RANCH • SILENT HONOR
MALICE • FIVE DAYS IN PARIS • LIGHTNING • WINGS • THE GIFT
ACCIDENT • VANISHED • MIXED BLESSINGS • JEWELS
NO GREATER LOVE • HEARTBEAT • MESSAGE FROM NAM • DADDY
STAR • ZOYA • KALEIDOSCOPE • FINE THINGS • WANDERLUST
SECRETS • FAMILY ALBUM • FULL CIRCLE • CHANGES
THURSTON HOUSE • CROSSINGS • ONCE IN A LIFETIME
A PERFECT STRANGER • REMEMBRANCE • PALOMINO • LOVE: *POEMS*
THE RING • LOVING • TO LOVE AGAIN • SUMMER'S END
SEASON OF PASSION • THE PROMISE • NOW AND FOREVER
PASSION'S PROMISE • GOING HOME

## Nonfiction

PURE JOY: *The Dogs We Love*
A GIFT OF HOPE: *Helping the Homeless*
HIS BRIGHT LIGHT: *The Story of Nick Traina*

## For Children

PRETTY MINNIE IN PARIS
PRETTY MINNIE IN HOLLYWOOD

# DANIELLE STEEL

# SILENT HONOR

*A Novel*

Dell • New York

*Silent Honor* is a work of fiction. Names, characters, places, and incidents are the products of the author's imagination or are used fictitiously. Any resemblance to actual events, locales, or persons, living or dead, is entirely coincidental.

2018 Dell Mass Market Edition

Published in the United States by Dell, an imprint of Random House, a division of Penguin Random House LLC, New York.

DELL and the HOUSE colophon are registered trademarks of Penguin Random House LLC.

Originally published in hardcover in the United States by Delacorte Press, an imprint of Random House, a division of Penguin Random House LLC, in 1996.

This book contains an excerpt from the forthcoming book *Beauchamp Hall* by Danielle Steel. This excerpt has been set for this edition only and may not reflect the final content of the forthcoming edition.

ISBN 978–0–440–22405–1

Ebook ISBN 978–0–307–56682–9

Cover design: Lynn Andreozzi
Cover illustration: Alan Ayers,
based on image © Lee Avison/Arcangel

Printed in the United States of America

randomhousebooks.com

24  26  27  25  23

Dell mass market edition: November 2018

To Kuniko, who has lived it,
   and is a remarkable lady.

And to Sammie, who thought of it, and
   is very special, and whom
   I love dearly.

With all my love,

d.s.

# Chapter 1

MASAO TAKASHIMAYA's family had searched for five years for a suitable bride for him, ever since his twenty-first birthday. But in spite of all their efforts to find a young woman who suited him, he rejected each of the girls as soon as he met them. He wanted a very special girl, a young woman who would not only serve and respect him, as the go-between promised each would, but he also wanted a woman he could talk to. Someone who would not only listen to him, and obey, but a girl he could share his ideas with. And none of the girls he had seen in the past five years had even come close to fulfilling his wishes. Until Hidemi. She was only nineteen when they met, and she lived in a *buraku*, a tiny farming village, near Ayabe. She was a pretty girl, delicate, and small, and exquisitely gentle. Her face looked as though it were carved of the finest ivory, her dark eyes were like shining onyx. And she scarcely spoke to Masao the first time she met him.

At first, Masao thought she was too shy, too afraid of him, she was just like the others that had been pressed on him before her. They were all too old-fashioned, he complained, he didn't want a wife to follow him like a dog, and look at him in terror. Yet, the women he met at the university didn't appeal to him either. There were certainly very few of them. In 1920, when he began teaching there, the women he met were either the other professors' daughters or wives, or foreigners. But most of them lacked the total purity and sweetness of a girl like Hidemi. Masao wanted everything in a wife, ancient traditions mixed with dreams of the future. He didn't expect her to know many things, but he wanted her to have the same hunger for learning that he did. And at twenty-six, after having taught at the university in Kyoto for two years, he had found her. She was perfect. She was delicate and shy, and yet she was fascinated by the things he said, and several times, through the go-between, she had asked him interesting questions, about his work, his family, and even about Kyoto. She rarely raised her eyes to look at him. And yet once, he had seen her glance at him, with excruciating shyness, and he thought her incredibly lovely.

She stood beside him now, six months after the day they met, with her eyes cast down, wearing the heavy white kimono her grandmother had worn, with the same elaborate gold brocade obi. A tiny dagger hung from it, so she could take her own life, should Masao decide that he did not want her. And on her carefully groomed hair, she wore the *tsunokakushi,* which covered her head but not her face, and made her seem even tinier as he watched her. And hanging just below the *tsunokakushi* were the *kan zashi*, the delicate hair ornaments that had been her mother's. Her mother had also given her a huge princess ball, made of silk threads, and heavily embroidered over the course of Hidemi's lifetime. Her mother had started it when Hidemi was born and added to it through the years, always praying that Hidemi would be gracious, noble, and wise. The princess ball was the most treasured gift her mother could give her, an exquisite symbol of her love and prayers, and hopes for her future.

Masao wore the traditional black kimono with a coat over it, bearing his family's crest, as he stood proudly beside her. Carefully, they each took three sips of sake from three cups, and the Shinto ceremony continued. They had been to the Shinto shrine earlier that day for a private ceremony, and this one was the formal public marriage that would join them forever, in front of all their family and friends, as the master of the ceremony told stories about both families, their history and importance. Both of their families were present, and several of the professors Masao taught with in Kyoto. Only his cousin Takeo was not there. He was five years older than Masao, and was his closest friend, and he would have wanted to be there. But Takeo had gone to the United States the year before, to teach at Stanford University, in California. It was a great opportunity for him, and Masao wished he could have joined him.

The ceremony was extremely solemn and very long, and never once did Hidemi raise her eyes to look at him, or even smile, as they became man and wife, according to the most venerable Shinto traditions. And after the ceremony, at last she hesitantly looked up at him, and the smallest of smiles lit her eyes and then her face, as she bowed low to her new husband. Masao bowed to her as well, and then she was led away by her mother and her sisters to exchange her white kimono for a red one for the reception. In wealthy city families, the bride changed her kimono six or seven times in the course of her wedding, but in their *buraku,* two kimonos had seemed enough for Hidemi.

It was a perfect day for them. It was a beautiful summer day, and the fields of Ayabe were the color of emeralds. They spent the entire afternoon greeting their friends, and accepting the many gifts offered them, and the gifts of money carefully wrapped, and handed to Masao.

There was music, and many friends, and dozens of distant relatives and cousins. Hidemi's cousin from Fukuoka played the koto, and a pair of dancers performed a slow and graceful *bugaku.* There was endless food as well. Especially the traditional tempura, rice balls, kuri shioyaki, chicken, sashimi, red rice with nasu, nishoga, and narazuki. There were delicacies that had been prepared for days by Hidemi's aunts and mother. Her grandmother, *"obaachan,"* had overseen all the preparations herself; she was pleased that her little granddaughter was getting married. She was the right age, and she had learned her lessons well. She would be a good wife for anyone, and the family was pleased with the alliance with Masao, in spite of his reputation for being fascinated by modern concepts. Hidemi's father was amused by him; Masao liked to discuss world politics and speak of worldly things. But he was also well versed in all the important traditions. It was a good family, and he was an honorable young man, and they all felt certain that he would make her an excellent husband.

Masao and Hidemi spent the first night of their marriage with her family, and then left for Kyoto the next day. She was wearing a beautiful pink-and-red kimono her mother had given her, and she looked especially lovely as Masao drove her away in the brand-new 1922 Model T coupe he had borrowed for the occasion. It belonged to an American professor at the university in Kyoto.

And when they returned to Kyoto they settled into his small, spare home, and Hidemi proved everything he had believed about her from the moment he met her. She kept his house immaculate for him, and observed all of the familiar traditions. She went to the nearby shrine regularly, and was polite and hospitable to all of his colleagues whenever he brought them home for dinner. And she was always deeply respectful of Masao. Sometimes, when she was feeling particularly bold, she giggled at him, particularly when he insisted on speaking to her in English. He thought it was extremely important that she learn another language, and he spoke to her on many subjects: of the British running Palestine, of Gandhi in India, and even about Mussolini. There were events happening in the world that he thought she should know about, and his insistence on it amused her. He was very good to her in many ways. He was gentle and kind and considerate, and he told her often that he hoped they would have many children. She was deeply embarrassed when he spoke of such things, but when she dared, she whispered to him that she hoped she would bring him many sons, and great honor.

"Daughters are honorable too, Hidemi-san," he said gently, and she looked at him in amazement. She would have been deeply ashamed to give him only daughters. She knew the importance of bearing sons, particularly coming from a farm community like Ayabe.

She was a sweet girl, and in the ensuing months they became good friends, as they learned to love each other. He was gentle and thoughtful with her, and always deeply touched by her myriad delicate gestures. She always had wonderful meals waiting for him, and flowers, perfectly arranged, particularly in the toko-noma, the alcove where the painted scroll was kept, which was their home's most important and honored decoration.

Shé learned what he liked, and what he didn't, and was careful to shield him from the most minor annoyance. She was the perfect wife for him, and as the months wore on, he was ever more pleased that he had found her. She was still as shy as she had been at first, but he sensed that she was growing more comfortable with him, and more at ease in his world. She had even learned a handful of phrases in English to please him. He still spoke to her only in English at night when they shared dinner. And he spoke to her often of his cousin Takeo in California. He was happy with his job at the university, and had just married a *kibei*, a girl who had been born in the States of a Japanese family, but had been sent to Japan to complete her education. Takeo had said in his letters that she was a nurse, her name was Reiko, and her family was from Tokyo. And more than once, Masao had dreamed of taking Hidemi to California to meet them, but for the moment, Masao could only dream of going there. He had his responsibilities at the university, and despite a very respectable career, he had very little money.

Hidemi did not tell her husband when they were expecting their first child, and according to tradition, and the instruction she had had, the moment it began to show, she bound her stomach. And it was early spring before Masao even knew it. He discovered it one day when they were making love, very discreetly as always. Hidemi was still very shy. And as soon as he suspected it, he asked her. She couldn't even bring herself to answer him. She turned her face away in the dark, blushing scarlet, and nodded.

"Yes, little one? . . . Yes?" He gently moved her chin so that she faced him, and smiled down at her as he held her. "Why didn't you tell me?" But she couldn't answer. She could only look at him, and pray that she wouldn't disgrace herself by giving him a daughter.

"I . . . I pray every day, Masao-san, that it will be a son," she whispered, touched by his gentleness with her, and his kindness.

"I would be just as happy with a daughter," he said honestly, as he lay beside her, dreaming of their future. He loved the idea of having children, her children especially. She was so beautiful and so sweet, he couldn't imagine anything lovelier than a little girl who looked just like her mother. But Hidemi looked shocked by what he had just told her.

"You must not say that, Masao-san!" She was afraid that even thinking about a girl just now might

bring one to them. "You must have a son!" She looked
so adamant about it that it amused him. But he was a
rare man in Japan, he truly didn't care if they had a son
or a daughter. And he thought that the traditional ob-
session with wanting only sons was extremely foolish.
He actually liked the idea of having a daughter whom
he could educate with new ideas and new views, unfet-
tered by the weights and chains of ancient traditions.
He loved Hidemi's sweet, old-fashioned ways, but he
also loved the fact that she seemed amused by his
passion for modern ideas and contraptions. It was one
of the things that had drawn him to her. She happily
tolerated all his newfangled ideas and fascination with
modern developments and politics the world over. She
wasn't deeply involved in any of it herself, but she
always listened with interest to the things he told her.
And the idea of bringing those same ideas to a child,
and bringing him or her up with them from the first,
absolutely enthralled him.

"We will have a thoroughly modern child, Hidemi-
san." He smiled as he turned over to look at her, and
she looked away from him, blushing in embarrassment. Sometimes when he was too direct with her, it
made her feel shy again, but—more than she would
ever have been able to tell him with words—she loved
him deeply. She thought him fascinating and intelligent and sophisticated beyond anything she had ever
dreamed. She even liked it when he spoke to her in
English, no matter how little of it she understood. She
found him completely enchanting. "When will the
baby be born?" he asked, realizing that he had no idea.
The year was already off to an interesting start, particularly in Europe, where the French army had occu-

pied the Ruhr, in a reprisal for delayed reparations payments owed them by the Germans. But world news seemed far less important now, in relation to the arrival of their first baby.

"In early summer," she answered him softly. "I think, July." It would be exactly a year since they'd been married. And it was a nice time of year to have a baby.

"I want you to have it in the hospital," he said as he glanced over at her, and he instantly saw a stubborn look in her eyes. He knew her well, after only eight months of marriage. Even though his more modern ways seemed to amuse her, on some things she had no intention of moving an inch in honor of more modern inventions. And when it came to family matters, she clung to all the old ways with dogged determination.

"I don't need a hospital. My mother and my sister will come to help me. The baby will be born here. We'll call a priest if we need one."

"You don't need a priest, little one, you need a doctor."

She didn't answer him. She had no desire to be disrespectful, nor to heed him. And when the time came, she cried bitterly as he argued with her fiercely. Her mother and oldest sister arrived in June, as planned, and stayed with them. Masao didn't mind, but he still wanted her to see a doctor and have their baby in the hospital in Kyoto. But it was obvious to him that Hidemi was afraid. She didn't want to go to the hospital, or to see a doctor. Masao tried in vain to reason with her, and to convince her mother that it would be better for her. But Hidemi's mother only smiled and treated him as though he were eccentric.

She herself had given birth six times, but only four of her children were living. One had died at birth, and another from diphtheria when still a baby. But she knew about these things, and so did Hidemi's sister. She had two babies of her own, and she had helped many women when their time came.

As the days passed, Masao realized that he wasn't going to convince any of them, and he watched with dismay as Hidemi grew larger and more tired in the heat of the summer. Each day, her mother made her follow the traditions that would make her delivery easier. They went to the shrine, and they prayed. They ate ceremonial foods. And in the afternoons she went on long walks with her sister. And at night when Masao came home, he would find Hidemi waiting for him, with tasty delicacies prepared, always anxious to be with him, and serve his needs, and hear whatever news he told her. But the only news that interested him now was about her. She seemed so tiny, and the baby so large. She was so young and so frail, and he was desperately worried about her.

He had been so anxious to have children with her, but now that the moment had come, he was terrified that a baby might kill her. He spoke to his own mother about it eventually, and she assured him that women were made for such tasks, and that she was sure that Hidemi would be fine, even without the benefit of a modern hospital or a doctor. Most women throughout the world were still having their babies at home, despite Masao's insistence on the advantages of being different.

But he grew more uneasy each day, until finally, late in July, he came home in the afternoon to find the house seemingly deserted. She wasn't waiting for him outside, as usual, nor was she in their room, or at the small brick stove in their kitchen. There was no sound anywhere, and he knocked gently on the room occupied by his mother- and sister-in-law, and there he found them. Hidemi had already been in labor for hours, and she lay there silently, in agony, with a stick between her teeth, writhing in pain as her mother and sister held her. There was steam in the room, and incense, and there was a large bowl of water, and Hidemi's sister was trying to wipe her brow as Masao glanced into the room and then backed away, afraid to enter.

He bowed low, turning away, reluctant to offend any of them, and asked politely how his wife was. He was told that she was doing very well, and his mother-in-law came swiftly to the shoji screen that served as a door, bowed to him, and closed it. There had been not a word or a sound from Hidemi, but from the little he had seen of her, she looked awful. And as he walked away, he was tormented by a thousand terrors. What if she was in too much pain? If she died of it? If the child was too large? If it killed her? Or if she lived, and she never forgave him? Perhaps she would never speak to him again. Or what if she hated him for what she'd been through? The very thought of it dismayed him greatly. He was so much in love with her, so desperate to see her sweet, perfectly carved face again, he almost wished he could enter the room where they were and help her. But he knew that all of them would have been hysterical at the mere thought of anything so outrageous. A birth was not a place for a man. Anywhere in the world, a woman in labor was not to be seen by her husband, and surely not in his world.

He walked slowly through their garden, and sat down, waiting for news of her, forgetting completely to eat, or do anything. And it was dark when his sister-in-law came quietly to him, and bowed. She had prepared sashimi and some rice for him, and he was startled when she offered it to him. He couldn't understand how she had left Hidemi to take care of him, and even the thought of eating repulsed him. He bowed to her, and thanked her for her kindness, and then quickly asked about Hidemi.

"She is very well, Masao-san. You will have a handsome son before morning." Morning was still ten hours away, and he couldn't bear the thought of her being in pain that much longer.

"But how is she?" he pressed her.

"Very well. She is full of joy to be giving you the son you desire, Masao-san. This is a joyful time for her." He knew better than that and couldn't bear the pretense of what she was saying. He could imagine Hidemi in unbearable pain, and the thought of it was driving him crazy.

"You'd best go back to her. Please tell her that I am honored by what she is doing." Hidemi's sister only smiled and bowed, and then disappeared back to her bedroom, while Masao strolled nervously through the garden, and completely forgot the dinner she had made him. There was no way in the world that he could have eaten. And what he had wanted to say to her, but of course couldn't, was to tell Hidemi that he loved her.

He sat alone in the garden all night, thinking

about her, and the year they had shared, how much she meant to him, how gentle and kind she was and how much he loved her. He drank a fair amount of sake that night, and smoked cigarettes, but unlike his peers, he didn't go out with his friends, or go to bed and forget her. Most men would have retired, and been pleased to hear the news in the morning. Instead, he sat there, and paced from time to time, and once he snuck back to the room where she was, and thought he could hear her crying. He couldn't bear the thought of it, and when he glimpsed Hidemi's sister again later on, he asked if he should call a doctor.

"Of course not," she snapped, and then bowed, and disappeared again. She looked distracted and busy.

It was dawn before his mother-in-law came to find him. He had had quite a lot to drink by then, and he was looking slightly disheveled as he smoked a cigarette and watched the sun come up slowly over the horizon. But he was frightened instantly when he saw the look on his mother-in-law's face. There was sorrow there, and disappointment, and he felt his heart stop as he watched her. Suddenly everything seemed to be moving in slow motion. He wanted to ask about his wife, but just seeing the look on his mother-in-law's face, he knew he couldn't. He just waited.

"The news is poor, Masao-san. I am sorry to tell you." He closed his eyes for an instant, bracing himself. Their moment of joy had turned into a nightmare. He had lost them both. He just knew it.

"Hidemi is well." He opened his eyes and stared at her, unable to believe his good fortune, as his throat tightened and his eyes filled with tears that many men would have been ashamed of.

"But the baby?" This time he had to ask her. Hidemi was alive. All was not lost. And how he loved her.

"Is a girl." His mother-in-law lowered her eyes in grief that her daughter had so badly failed him.

"It's a girl?" he asked excitedly. "She's well? She's alive?"

"Of course." Hidemi's mother looked startled by the question. "But I am very sorry. . . ." She began to apologize, and Masao stood up and bowed to her in elated excitement.

"I am not sorry at all. I am very happy. Please tell Hidemi . . ." he began, and then thought better of it. He hurried across the garden as the sky turned from peach to flame, and the sun exploded into the sky like a bonfire.

"Where are you going, Masao-san? You cannot . . ." But there was nothing he could not do. It was his home, and his wife, and his baby. He was law here. Although seeing his wife at this point would have been highly improper, Masao had no thought of that at all, as he bounded up the two steps to their second bedroom, and knocked softly on the shoji screens that shielded her from him. Her sister opened them instantly, and Masao smiled at her, as she looked at him with eyes full of questions.

"I'd like to see my wife."

"She cannot . . . She is . . . I . . . Yes, Masao-san," she said, bowing low to him, and stepping aside after only a moment's hesitation. He was certainly unusual, but she knew her place here, and she disappeared, and went to the kitchen for a moment to prepare tea for him, and join her mother.

"Hidemi?" he asked softly as he entered the room, and then he saw them. She was lying peacefully, wrapped in quilts, and shivering slightly. She was pale, and her hair was pulled back off her face, and she looked incredibly lovely. And in her arms, tightly wrapped so only the tiny face showed, was the most perfect child he had ever seen. She looked as though she had been carved out of ivory, like the tiniest of statues. She looked just like her mother, although, if possible, she was even more beautiful, and he gazed down at her in wonder as he saw her. "Oh . . . she is so beautiful, Hidemi-san. . . . She is so perfect. . . ." And then he looked at his wife, and saw easily how much she'd been through. "Are you all right?" He was still worried about her.

"I am fine," she said, suddenly looking very wise, and a great deal older. She had crossed the mountains from girlhood into womanhood that night, and the journey had been far more arduous than she'd expected.

"You should have let me take you to the hospital," he said anxiously, but she only shook her head in answer. She was happy here at home, with her mother and her sister, and her husband waiting in the garden.

"I'm sorry she is only a girl, Masao-san," Hidemi said with genuine emotion, and her eyes filled with tears as she looked at him. Her mother was right. She had failed him.

"I am not sorry at all. I told you. I wanted a daughter."

"You are very foolish," she said, daring for once to be disrespectful.

"So are you, if you do not think a daughter a great prize . . . perhaps even far greater than a son. She will make us proud one day. You will see, Hidemi-san. She will do great things, speak many languages, go to other countries. She can be anything she wants to be, go anywhere she chooses." Hidemi giggled at him. He was so silly sometimes, and it had been so much harder than she'd thought, but she loved him so dearly. He reached out and took her hand in his, and bent low to kiss her forehead. And then he sat for a long moment, looking with pride at their daughter. He meant everything he had said to her. He didn't mind at all that they had had a daughter. "She is beautiful, like you. . . . What shall we call her?"

"Hiroko." Hidemi smiled. She had always liked the name, and it was the name of her dead sister.

"Hiroko-san," he said happily, looking from his wife to his child, and engulfing them in the love he felt. "She will be a thoroughly modern woman."

Hidemi laughed at him then, beginning to forget the pain, and then she smiled, looking suddenly a great deal older. "She will have a brother soon," she promised him. She wanted to try again, to do it right for him the next time. No matter what he said, or how wild his ideas were, she knew she owed him more than this girl, and that there was nothing more important in life than bearing sons for her husband. And one day, he would have one.

"You should sleep now, little one," he said softly, as his sister-in-law brought in a tray with tea for them.

Hidemi was still shaken from the loss of blood and the shock of all she'd been through.

Hidemi's sister poured tea for both of them, and then left them alone again. But Masao left the room a few minutes later. Hidemi was very tired, and her sister needed to tend to the baby, who was stirring.

His mother-in-law went back into the room then too, and pulled the *fusama* screen to divide the room and give Hidemi privacy. Masao walked through his garden, smiling to himself, prouder than he had ever been in his entire life. He had a daughter, a beautiful little girl. She would be brilliant one day. She would speak English perfectly, and perhaps even French, and German. She would be knowledgeable about world affairs. She would learn many things. She would be the fulfillment of all his dreams, and just as he had told his wife, she would be a completely modern young woman.

And as the sun rose in the sky, he smiled up at it, thinking what a lucky man he was. He had everything he wanted in life. A beautiful wife, and now a lovely little baby daughter. Perhaps one day he would have a son, but for now, this was all he wanted. And when he finally went back to his own room to sleep, he lay on his futon and smiled, thinking of them . . . Hidemi . . . and their tiny daughter . . . Hiroko. . . .

# *Chapter 2*

THE EARTHQUAKE that leveled Tokyo and Yokohama in the first week of September that year rattled Kyoto as well, but not as badly. Hiroko was seven weeks old by then, and Hidemi clung to her, terrified, when the quake struck, and Masao hurried home to find them. There had been considerable damage in the town, but their house withstood the shock fairly well. And it was only later that they learned of the total devastation of Tokyo. Most of the city had been leveled, fires blazed, and for weeks people wandered the streets, starving, and desperate for water.

It was the worst earthquake in Japan's history, and for weeks afterward Masao talked about leaving Japan and moving to California like his cousin Takeo.

"They have earthquakes in California too," Hidemi had reminded him quietly. She had no desire to leave Japan, no matter how great the risk there. Besides, Masao had just been promoted. But he didn't want to risk his family, now that he had one. To him, they were far more important.

"They don't have earthquakes as often there," Masao had snapped at her, unnerved by everything that had happened. He had been terrified for her and the baby. And for weeks they were horrified to hear stories about what had happened to relatives and friends in Tokyo and Yokohama, and the surrounding towns around them. His cousin Takeo's wife, Reiko, had lost both her parents in Tokyo, and other friends had lost relatives as well. It seemed as though everyone in Japan was affected.

But eventually, after the initial excitement died down, Masao turned his attention to world news again, and forgot about moving to California. The war in China was continuing. There was trouble in Germany in October and November, which fascinated him too. And in November, the young National Socialist leader, Adolf Hitler, tried to effect a coup against the German government, failed, and was arrested. Masao was greatly intrigued by him, and taught several of his more advanced political science classes on the subject of the young German radical, whom he felt certain would change the course of Germany before much longer.

In January, Lenin died, which provided further fodder for discussions among the political scientists. And in February, Masao discovered that once again Hidemi was pregnant. The baby was due in June this time, and Hidemi was going to the shrine daily to pray for a son, although Masao again insisted that he would be just as happy with another daughter. Hiroko was seven months old by then, and Hidemi had already started making the traditional silk princess ball for her, just like the one her own mother had given her for her wedding. And when Hiroko wasn't strapped to her mother's back, she was crawling everywhere, and laughing and giggling, and thoroughly enchanting her father. He spoke English to her, and although his own English was not totally without flaws, he was fairly fluent, and even Hidemi could now manage a simple conversation in English. Masao was proud of her. She was a good wife to him, a wonderful friend, and a loving mother. She was everything he had hoped for, and in letters to his cousin in America, he always told little stories about her, and praised her. And he often included photographs of their baby. She was a pretty little girl, tiny for her age, and even more delicate than her mother. But what she lacked in size, she made up for in energy. And at nine months, she started walking.

Hidemi was seven months pregnant when Hiroko walked for the first time. And Hidemi was even bigger this time than the last time. Masao was once again insistent that she go to a hospital and not attempt to have their baby at home without benefit of a doctor.

"It went very well last time, Masao-san." She stood firm. Her sister was pregnant again as well, so she would be unable to come and help her, but her mother was planning to be there.

"People don't do that anymore, Hidemi-san," he insisted. "This is 1924, not the dark ages of the last century. You will be safer in a hospital, and so will the baby." Masao loved reading American medical journals, as well as the material that related to political science for his classes. And after reading about obstetrical complications a number of times, the idea of giving birth at home again appalled him. But Hidemi was far less modern than he, and extremely stubborn.

Just as scheduled, her mother arrived at the beginning of June, and planned to be there for three or four weeks before the baby. She helped Hidemi with Hiroko every day, and it gave Hidemi a little more free time to spend with her husband. They even managed to spend a day and a night in Tokyo, which was a treat for them, and it fascinated them to see all the reconstruction after the earthquake.

Five days after they returned, Masao and Hidemi were lying on their futons late one night, when Masao noticed that Hidemi was moving around restlessly, and finally she got up and went to walk in the garden. He joined her after a little while, and asked her if the baby was coming. And finally, after hesitating, she nodded. A year earlier she wouldn't have said anything to him, but after two years of marriage, she was finally a little less shy, and a little more open with him.

He had long since lost the battle for the hospital, and as he watched her, he asked her if she wanted him to go and get her mother. And for an odd moment, she shook her head, and then reached for his hand, as though she wanted to tell him something.

"Is something wrong, Hidemi? You must tell me if there is." He always worried that out of modesty she would fail to tell him if she was ill or if there was something wrong with her or the baby. "You must not disobey me," he said, hating the words, but knowing that they were the key to making her tell him if there was a problem. "Is something wrong?"

She shook her head as she looked at him, and then turned away, her face filled with emotion.

"Hidemi-san, what is it?"

She turned back to look at him then, with the huge dark eyes he loved so much and which always reminded him of their daughter. "I am afraid, Masao-san. . . ."

"Of having the baby?" He felt so sorry for her, his heart went out to her, momentarily sorry that he had helped her do this. He had felt that way the last time, when he had glimpsed her pain. He hoped that this time it would be easy for her.

But she shook her head, and then looked at him so sadly. She was twenty-one years old, and there were times when she looked like a little girl, and other times when she seemed totally a woman. He was seven years older than she, and much of the time, he felt protective of her, and almost old enough to be her father.

"I am afraid it will not be a son . . . again. . . . Perhaps we will have many daughters." She looked at him despairingly and he gently put his arms around her and held her.

"Then we will have many daughters. . . . I am not afraid of that, Hidemi-san. I only want you to be well, and not suffer. . . . I will be happy with daughters or sons. . . . You must not do this for me again, if you don't wish it." There were times when he thought she had rushed into having another child just to please him and give him the son she felt would bring him honor. Her gift of a son for him was the most important thing she could give him.

And when her mother came to lead her away, Hidemi looked at him reluctantly. She liked being with him, and odd as it seemed, she didn't want to go away from him to have their baby. She knew that in some ways, their relationship was different than that of most Japanese couples. Masao liked being with her, and helping her, and spending time with her and Hiroko. Even now, in pain, she wanted him to be with her, although she knew that her mother would have been shocked to hear her say it. But she would never say it to anyone. They would never have understood her feelings, or the way Masao treated her. He was always so kind and so respectful.

For hours she lay in her mother's room, thinking of him, and this time she knew from the way the pains came that the baby would come before morning. She had felt the pains all afternoon, but hadn't wanted to say anything. She didn't want to leave Masao, and she had liked lying next to him, and being close to him, and all that day being with Hiroko. But now she knew she had work to do, and she lay silently as her mother gave her something to bite on so she wouldn't make a sound. She would do nothing to disgrace her husband.

But as time wore on, the baby didn't seem to move, and when her mother finally looked, she could see nothing. No head, no hair, no movement at all. There was just endless pain, until Hidemi was almost out of her mind with it by morning.

And as though he sensed that something was wrong this time, Masao came to the shoji screens several times and inquired how she was doing. His mother-in-law always bowed politely and assured him that Hidemi was fine, but at first light, he noticed that even the old woman was looking frightened.

"How is she now?" he asked, looking haggard. He

had been worried about her all night, and he wasn't sure why, but he somehow sensed that this time was different. Last time, there had been an atmosphere of calm about the two women bustling in and out of the labor room. This time there was only Hidemi's mother, and he could feel throughout the night that she wasn't pleased with her daughter's progress. "Is the child not coming?" he asked, and she hesitated, and then shook her head, and then he horrified her with his next question. "May I see her?"

She was about to tell him that he couldn't come in, but he looked so determined that she didn't dare say it. She hesitated in the doorway for a moment, and then stepped aside, and what he saw in the room behind her terrified him, as he hurried toward Hidemi. She was only half conscious, and moaning softly. Her face was gray, and she had bitten down so hard on the stick her mother had given her that she'd bitten through it. He pulled it gently out of her mouth, and felt her belly tighten beneath his hand, as he tried to ask her some questions. But she couldn't hear him. And when he looked more closely, after another minute or two, he saw that she had slipped into complete unconsciousness and she was hardly breathing. He had no medical degree, and he'd never been at a delivery before, but he was certain, as he looked at her, that she was dying.

"Why didn't you call me?" he snapped at his mother-in-law, terrified by what he was seeing. Hidemi's lips were faintly blue and so were her fingernails, and he wondered if the baby was even still alive within her. She had been in labor for hours, and she was obviously in serious trouble.

"She is young, she will do it herself," her mother

explained, but even she didn't sound convinced, as he hurried out of the house and ran to the neighbors' house. They had a telephone. He had long since wanted to put one in, but Hidemi always insisted they didn't need one, and in an emergency they could always get a message at the neighbors'. He ran to them now, and called the hospital, which he knew he should have taken her to despite all her protests. They promised to send an ambulance for her as soon as possible, and Masao berated himself for not insisting she go there in the first place.

When he got back to the house, it was an interminable wait for the ambulance to come, and Masao simply sat on the floor, rocking her back and forth in his arms like a baby. He could feel her slipping away from him. And through it all, the terrible tightening of her belly continued. Even her mother seemed helpless now. All the little tricks and old wives' tales had been useless. When the ambulance came for her, her eyes were closed, her face was gray, and her breathing was the merest thread to life. The doctor who had come for her was amazed that she had come this far.

They put her quickly into the ambulance, and Masao asked his mother-in-law to stay with Hiroko. He didn't even take the time to bow, he just left with Hidemi and the doctor. The doctor said very little to Masao in the ambulance, but he checked her constantly, and finally just before they got to the hospital, he looked up and shook his head at Masao.

"Your wife is very ill," he said, confirming Masao's worst fears. "I don't know if we can save her. She has lost a great deal of blood, and she's in shock. I believe the baby is turned the wrong way, and she has worked for many hours. She's very weak now." Nothing that he said came as a surprise, but it sounded like a death sentence to her husband.

"You *must* save her," he said savagely, looking like a samurai and not the gentle soul he was. "You *must*!" He refused to lose her.

"We'll do everything we can," the doctor tried to reassure him. Masao looked half mad, with his hair disheveled and wild eyes full of grief for Hidemi.

"And the baby?" He wanted to know it all now. They had been so stupid to stay at home. It was so old-fashioned and ignorant, and he didn't know why he had let her convince him. And now look at what had happened. More than ever, he was certain that the old ways were dangerous, or even fatal.

"I can still hear a heartbeat," the doctor explained, "but only a faint one. Do you have other children, sir?"

"A daughter," Masao said distractedly, staring at Hidemi in wild-eyed desperation.

"I'm sorry."

"Is there nothing you can do now?" Masao asked. Her breathing seemed even fainter and more labored than it had when the doctor arrived. She was slowly losing her grip on life, and there was nothing he could do to stop her. He felt rage and despair wash over him, as the doctor answered.

"We must wait until we get to the hospital." If she lived that long, the young doctor thought. He doubted now if she'd even survive the operation she needed to save her life and the baby's. It was almost hopeless.

They careened through the streets in the ambulance, and finally reached the hospital after what seemed like an interminable journey, and Hidemi was rushed away from him, still unconscious on a gurney. He wondered if he would ever see her alive again, and he waited alone for what seemed like hours, as he thought of the two brief years of their marriage. She had been so good to him, so loving in countless ways. He couldn't believe that it might all end now, in a single moment, and he hated himself for getting her pregnant.

He waited two hours before a nurse finally came to him. She bowed low before she spoke, and he had a sudden urge to strangle her. He didn't want obsequities, he wanted to know how his wife was.

"You have a son, Takashimaya-san," the nurse told him politely. "He is very big and very healthy." He had been a little blue when he was born, but he had recovered very quickly, unlike his mother, who was still in a grave state in surgery. The outcome did not look hopeful.

"And my wife?" Masao asked, holding his breath in silent prayer.

"She is very ill," the nurse said, bowing again. "She is still in surgery, but the doctor wished you to be informed about your son."

"Will she be all right?" The nurse hesitated, and then nodded, not wanting to be the one to tell him that it was unlikely.

"The doctor will come to see you soon, Takashimaya-san." She bowed again and was gone, as Masao stood and stared out the window. He had a son, a little boy, but all the excitement, all the joy, was dispelled by the terror of losing the baby's mother.

It seemed an eternity before the doctor came to him. In fact, it was almost noon, but Masao didn't know it. He had completely lost track of time. The baby had been born at nine o'clock, but it had taken another three hours to save his mother. But they'd done it. She had lost frightening quantities of blood, and the doctor explained with regret that this would be her last child. There wasn't even the remotest possibility that she could have another. But she was alive. They had saved her, though barely. He explained that she would have to rest for a long time, but he felt certain that eventually, as young as she was, she would be healthy, and useful to him.

"Thank you," Masao said earnestly, bowing low to him, as tears stung his eyes and filled his throat. "Thank you," he whispered again to the doctor, and to all the gods he prayed to. He would have been lost without her.

Masao never left the hospital all day, although he called his neighbors to tell his mother-in-law that Hidemi was all right and they had had a little boy. And after he'd done that, he went to see his son. He was a fat cherub of a child, and Hidemi had already told him months before that she wanted to call him Yuji. She hadn't even chosen a girl's name this time, for fear that picking one might mean she would need one.

And then finally, at the end of the day, they let him see Hidemi. He had never seen a living woman look so pale, and they were still giving her transfusions, and assorted medications intravenously. She was groggy from the painkillers they'd given her, but she recognized Masao the moment she saw him, and she smiled as he bent to kiss her. He almost wished she would blush so he could see some color in her cheeks again, but at least she was alive, and so was their baby, and she was smiling.

"You have a son," she said victoriously. At what price glory.

"I know." He smiled at her. "I have a wife too." To him that was far more important. "You frightened me very badly, little one. No more of your old ideas. It's too dangerous to be so old-fashioned." He had realized more than ever that day how much he loved her.

"We'll have the next one here," she said amiably, and he didn't contradict her. It was still too soon to tell her everything that had happened. But having only two children was no tragedy to him. They had a boy and a girl, she had done her duty by him, and she could retire with honor.

"I have enough with you, and Hiroko, and Yuji." It felt sweet saying his name. He was so new to them, but it felt good to include him.

"Who does he look like?" she asked softly, clinging to Masao's hand, unaware of how close to death she had come. But he was well aware of it and he knew he would never forget the terrors of the night before and that morning.

"He looks like a little samurai, like my father," Masao said, grateful again that they had both been spared.

"He must be handsome and wise like you, Masao-san," she said, drifting slowly back to sleep, still holding on to him, very gently.

"And sweet and kind like his mother," Masao whispered, smiling at her. He knew that he would cherish her forever.

"You must teach him English," she said softly, and

he smiled, laughing at himself for once. "And we will take him to California to visit his cousin," she went on, woozy from the drugs, but busily planning their son's future.

"Maybe he'll go to college there," he said, playing the game with her. "Or maybe Hiroko will. . . . We'll send her to Takeo at Stanford." But this time Hidemi smiled as her eyes fluttered open again.

"She's only a girl. . . ." Hidemi corrected him. "You have a son now."

"She's a modern girl," he whispered as he bent close to his wife. "She will do everything Yuji can," he said, with eyes filled with dreams, and she laughed at him. He was so crazy with his modern ideas and plans for all of them, but she knew just how much she loved him.

"Thank you very much, Masao-san," Hidemi said awkwardly in English as she drifted off to sleep, holding her husband's hand.

"You're welcome, little one," he answered her more fluently, and settled down in a chair to watch her.

# Chapter 3

"No!" HIDEMI said forcefully. It was an old argument between them, and one she absolutely refused to give in on. "She's a girl, not a man. She belongs here, with us. What good will it do to send her to California?" Hidemi adamantly refused to send her daughter away to college.

"She's almost eighteen years old," Masao explained patiently for the thousandth time in a year. "She speaks English very well, but she will benefit enormously from at least a year in the States, if not longer." He wanted her to do all four years of college there, but he knew that for the moment, Hidemi was not ready to let her do it. "It will improve her education, open up her ideas, broaden her horizons. And my cousin and his wife will take good care of her." They had three children of their own, and lived in Palo Alto.

But Hidemi knew all of that, and she still didn't want to do it.

"Send Yuji next year," she said stubbornly, as he looked at her, wondering if he'd ever win the argument. It was really something that he wanted for Hiroko. She was very shy, and very traditional, in spite of her father's revolutionary ideas, and he thought it would do her good to leave Japan for a while. It was Yuji who really wanted to go, who was dying to spread his wings, and who was so much like him.

"We can send Yuji too, but this would be an unforgettable experience for Hiroko. She'll be safe there, she'll be in good hands. And think of all that she'd learn."

"A lot of wild American habits," Hidemi said disapprovingly, and Masao sighed in despair. She was a wonderful wife, but she had very definite, and very traditional, ideas about their children, particularly their daughter. Hiroko had been schooled in every possible ancient tradition before her grandmother died the year before, and Hidemi herself continued all of them with meticulous precision. They were important, certainly, but there were other things Masao wanted Hiroko to learn, that he thought were more important, particularly for a woman. He wanted her to have all the same opportunities as Yuji, and in Japan, that was far from easy. "She can learn English here. I did," Hidemi said firmly as Masao smiled at her.

"I give up. Send her to be a Buddhist nun. Or call a go-between and find her a husband. You might as well. You're not going to let her do anything with her life, are you?"

"Of course I am. She can go to university here. She doesn't have to go all the way to California."

"Think of what you're depriving her of, Hidemi. I'm serious. Can you really live with yourself, doing that to her? Think of the experience she would have there. All right, never mind four years of college. Send her for a year. One school year. It would be a year she would treasure for the rest of her life. She'll make friends, meet new people, get new ideas, and then she can come back and go to university here. But she'll never be quite the same again, if she goes . . . or if she doesn't."

"Why do you have to make it my responsibility for cheating her out of an opportunity? Why is it my fault?" Hidemi pouted.

"Because you want to keep her here. You want to keep her comfortable, hidden in your skirts, safe in our little world, shy, and old-fashioned, and totally tied up by all the useless traditions your mother taught her. Set her free, like a beautiful little bird. She'll come back to us. . . . But don't clip her wings, Hidemi, just because she's a girl. It's not fair. The world is hard enough for women." It was a fight he had long championed, and one his wife didn't entirely agree with. She was perfectly satisfied with her lot in life, in fact, as his wife, she enjoyed a great many freedoms. But she also knew it, and she wasn't entirely deaf to what he was saying, or the voice of her own conscience.

It took another month of soul-searching and arguments, but eventually Hidemi conceded. One year, or more if Hiroko truly loved it, but she only had to go to San Francisco for a year. And Takeo had gotten her into a small but academically excellent women's college in Berkeley called St. Andrew's, and Masao swore she would be safe there. It was a long time to be away, but Hidemi had to agree, though grudgingly, that it was an exciting opportunity for her—though why women had to go to university, and one that far away, was beyond her. She never had, and she had had a wonderful life with her husband and children.

Even Yuji thought it was a great idea, and he could hardly wait for the following year, when he was hoping to apply to Stanford. But in the meantime, he thought his sister was really lucky to be going to California. The only one who didn't share his enthusiasm, other than Hidemi, was Hiroko.

"Aren't you pleased your mother agreed?" Masao asked her confidently, thrilled with his victory when Hidemi finally capitulated and agreed to let Hiroko go to San Francisco. It had been a year-long battle. But Hiroko was silent and hesitant, though she assured him that she was very grateful. She looked like a little doll, with tiny features and graceful limbs. She was even lovelier and more delicate than her mother. But she was also even shyer than her mother had been, and unlike her father, with all his forward ideas, Hiroko was naturally old-fashioned. She took great comfort in it, and had a genuine fondness for all the old ways and traditions. Her grandmother had given her a deep respect for them, but beyond that she was just very comfortable with domestic pursuits and the most ancient of traditions. She was traditional Japanese to her very core, far more so than even her mother. Over the years, Hidemi had developed a deep respect for a number of Masao's modern concepts. But Hiroko showed no interest in any of them. She was just a very old-fashioned girl, and the last thing she wanted was to spend a year in California. She was only doing it to please her father. And it seemed a terribly high price to pay to show her respect for him, but she would never have defied him.

"Aren't you excited?" he asked again, and she nodded, trying to look enthused, but failing. And as he looked at her, his heart sank. He knew his daughter well, and loved her deeply, and he would rather have died than make her unhappy. "Don't you want to go, Hiroko?" he asked sadly. "You can be honest with me. We're not trying to punish you. We want to do something important for your future." It was also a considerable financial drain on them, with his professor's salary, but they really felt it was a worthwhile sacrifice to make for their children.

"I . . ." She struggled with the fear of being disobedient to him, as she lowered her eyes and battled her emotions. She loved them so much, and her brother too, that she hated to leave them. "I don't want to leave you," she said with big eyes filled with tears. "America is so far away. Why can't I just go to Tokyo?" She raised her eyes to his, and he almost cried as he saw them.

"Because you will learn nothing there you can't learn here. In fact, it is better for you here than in the big city. But America . . ." he said, his own eyes filled with dreams. He had never been there, but he had wanted to go all his life. For twenty years he had read his cousin Takeo's letters and wished he could have been there. Now it was a gift he wanted to give his children, the ultimate gift, the only one he would have wanted. "You only have to go for a year, Hiroko. One school year. That's all. If you hate it, you can come back here. A year isn't such a long time. You can do that. And maybe you'll like it. Yuji might even be there your second year, if you stay. You'd be together."

"But you wouldn't be there . . . or Mama. . . . What would I do without you?" she asked as her eyes filled and her lip trembled, and she lowered her eyes in respect for him, and he came to put his arms around her, always startled by how slight she was. She was barely an armful.

"We'll miss you too, but we'll write to you, and you'll have Uncle Tak and Aunt Reiko."

"But I don't know them."

"They're wonderful people." Takeo had come back for a visit nine years before, but Hiroko scarcely remembered him, and Aunt Reiko hadn't been able to make it, because she was expecting their last little girl, Tamiko. "You'll love them, and I know they'll take care of you like one of their own. Please, Hiroko, please give it a chance. I don't want you to be deprived of this opportunity." He had saved for years for it, and it had taken him almost as long to convince his wife, and now Hiroko made him feel like he was punishing her, and he wanted this so much for her. If only she would do it.

"I will do it, Papa. For you," she said, bowing to him, and he wanted to shake her. He wanted her to give up the old ways. She was too young to be so steeped in tradition.

"I want you to do it for yourself," he said. "I want you to be happy there."

"I will try, Papa," she whispered, as the tears slid down her cheeks, and he held her. He felt like a monster, forcing her to go, and yet until the moment she left, he was certain that once she was in California she would love it.

But the morning she left, a pall fell over all of them, and when they left the house, Hiroko just stood outside and cried at the thought of leaving her home and her parents and brother. She stopped for a moment at their little shrine and bowed, and then she followed her mother to the car, and slid into the backseat beside her to begin the drive to Kobe. Yuji and her father chatted quietly in the front, and Hiroko sat in total silence. She just sat and stared out the window as her mother watched her. Hidemi wanted to say something to her, to tell her to be brave, to tell her that she was sorry if they were wrong, but she didn't know what to say to her, so she said nothing. And as Masao glanced at them in the rearview mirror from time to time, he was dismayed by the deafening silence behind him. There were no little girlish sounds, of excitement or amazement. She said nothing about the ship, or America, or her cousins. She said nothing at all. She just sat there, feeling as though her heart would break, as she was torn from her homeland. And each house, each tree, each blade of grass she saw only heightened her anguish.

Her mother had packed all of her things in one trunk, which they had sent ahead to the NYK Line in Kobe. And now the brief hour and a half ride to their pier seemed endless. Even Yuji's attempts to lighten the moment barely brought a smile to her face. She was extremely serious, and she rarely made the kind of jokes or got into the mischief that he did. Yet despite their natural differences, they were extremely close, and it was obvious that they loved each other deeply.

He spoke to her in English now, which he spoke surprisingly well, better than she did. He had a natural gift with languages, as he did with many things, especially music and sports, and in spite of his fondness for having fun, he was an excellent student. Hiroko was slower and more serious about things. She didn't leap into projects, and friendships, and new ideas the way he did. She approached things carefully, with a great deal of thought, and a great deal of precision. But what she did, she did well. She played piano and violin, which she practiced constantly. She had worked considerably less on her English, and although she spoke it well, she always felt awkward. Unlike Yuji.

"You'll be learning to jitterbug in California," he said valiantly, proud of his knowledge of American culture. He also knew all their baseball stars, and he loved learning American slang. He could barely wait to get to Stanford. "You'll have to teach me when I get there," he teased, and Hiroko smiled at him in spite of herself. He was so silly. But they were such good friends. They were less than a year apart, and she couldn't imagine how she was going to live without him. She knew that their cousins had a son nearly his age as well. He was sixteen years old, and his name was Kenji. And they had two younger daughters. But she knew that no one would ever take Yuji's place in her heart, and as they reached the dock, Hiroko felt her legs tremble and her heart sink.

They located the NYK Line pier easily, and the *Nagoya Maru* stood waiting, as passengers arrived and well-wishers went aboard to join them in their cabins. People were laughing and talking all around them as they boarded the ship and looked for Hiroko's cabin.

She had a berth in second class, and her parents were pleased to see that she was sharing a cabin with a much older woman. She was American, and had been studying the art of Japan for a year, and now she was going back to Chicago. She chatted pleasantly with them, and then went out on deck to look for friends, and left Hiroko alone with her parents. She had sensed that this was not an easy moment. And as Hiroko looked at them, her face grew pale, and her father could see that she was about to panic.

"You must be very brave, my little girl," he said gently, as Yuji moved her trunk, and his mother told him where to put it. "Be strong. You will only be alone on the ship, and after that, you will be with your cousins." He had purposely chosen a ship that would sail directly to San Francisco. It made for a very long crossing, but they felt it was safer than having her stop over in Honolulu. She didn't want to go ashore alone, and she was nervous even now about being on the ship without them. She had never gone anywhere alone before, she had never left home, and now she was going so far from everything familiar. "You will be home again very soon," her father said kindly as she looked around the cabin. It was tiny, and more than a little claustrophobic. "The year will pass very quickly."

"Yes, Father," she said, bowing to him, silently begging him not to send her. She was only deferring to his wishes out of respect for him. She would have given anything not to go to California. Like her mother, she didn't understand what it would do for her, and why it was to her advantage. She knew that it was important to see the world, but she wasn't really sure why. It seemed so much better to stay at home, among familiar people and places. In fact, she had never become the modern young woman he had dreamed of. But Masao was certain that this trip would make all the difference.

The whistle blew, and the gong sounded for them to get off almost before Hiroko had had time to get settled, and Masao thought it was just as well. He knew from looking at her that if they stayed much longer, they would never leave her. She looked so terrified and pale, and her hands shook pitifully as she handed her mother a single flower from the tiny bouquet the NYK Line had sent her. Her mother took it in trembling hands too, and then reached out to her daughter and held her. They said not a word, and as the bell sounded again, Masao gently touched his wife's shoulder. It was time to go. They had to leave her.

Hiroko followed them quietly outside, wearing the bright blue kimono her mother had given her. Masao had insisted that she take Western clothes too, certain that she would regret it at college if she didn't have them. She had never worn Western clothes before. Like her mother, she preferred to wear her kimono. But she had taken the Western clothes with her, because her father said to.

The entire family stood on deck, and the air was warm and balmy. It was a perfect day to sail, and most of the passengers were excited, as music played and balloons drifted through the air. But Hiroko looked like an orphan standing bereft on the deck when they left her.

"Be good," Hidemi warned her solemnly. "Help your cousins whenever you are with them." But as she instructed her older child, her eyes filled with tears, and the thought of leaving her seemed unbearably painful. "Write to us. . . ." She wanted to tell her not to forget them, not to fall in love far away, not to stay in San Francisco, but all she could do was look at her and long for the days when she was a little girl, safely at home in Kyoto. And all Hiroko could do was cry as she looked at her mother.

"Take care of yourself, Sis," Yuji said to her in English, and she smiled through her tears. "Say hi to Clark Gable."

"Don't run after too many girls," she teased him in Japanese, and then she hugged him and turned to her father. But somehow leaving him was the hardest of all, because she knew he expected so much from her, and he wanted her to do this.

"Have a good time, Hiroko. Learn many things. Open your eyes and see everything, and then come home and tell us all about it."

"I will, Father," she said, bowing low to him, promising him silently that she would be everything he wanted. She would be brave and wise and inquisitive. She would learn many things, and come back speaking perfect English. But when she stood up and looked at him again, she was stunned to see that there were tears in his eyes too, and he held her very tight for a moment, and then slowly he pulled away, squeezed her hands for a last time, and then turned and led his wife and son to shore, as Hiroko watched them in terror.

She stood at the rail, waving at them, feeling lonelier than she ever had in her entire life, and desperately afraid of what waited for her in California.

And as she watched them fade away, she thought

of each of them, and how much they meant to her, and prayed for the next year to fly by very quickly. She watched the mountains of Japan slowly drift away, and she stood for hours on the deck, just watching her homeland shrink on the horizon.

When Yuji and his parents returned home, the house seemed painfully empty without Hiroko. She had always moved among them so quietly, so efficiently, as she went about her chores, and helped her mother without saying anything, but one always sensed her presence. And now suddenly without her, Yuji realized how lonely it was going to be, and he went out to meet his friends so he didn't have to think about it.

Masao and Hidemi stood looking at each other then, wondering if they'd been wrong, if she was too young, if they'd made a terrible mistake sending her to California. Masao particularly had second thoughts, and at that moment, if he could have, he would have brought her home to them and told her to forget St. Andrew's College. But this time it was Hidemi who was sure, who knew that they had done what they had to do, that it was best for her. Hiroko was only a year younger than she herself had been when she married Masao. Hiroko would learn many things, make many friends, and then she would come home to them again, and dream of the year she had spent in California. Masao was right. It was a different world, a world in which one needed to know more than just traditions, a world in which arranging flowers and pouring tea would no longer be important. It was a world that, one day, would belong to the young, to people like Hiroko and Yuji. She had to be prepared for it, to learn the lessons she would need when she came home again. It would be a year well spent, and as Hidemi thought of it, she looked at her husband and smiled.

"You did the right thing," she said generously, knowing that he needed reassurance. He was feeling terrible. All he could remember was the agony in his child's eyes when he left her on the ship and hurried down the gangplank.

"How can you be sure?" he asked unhappily, but grateful that she had said it.

"Because you are very wise, Masao-san," Hidemi said, bowing to him, and he reached out and took her hand and pulled her slowly to him. They had shared nineteen years, and they had been happy ones. They respected each other, and loved each other deeply. It was a love that had strengthened over the years, and that had weathered storms. And in their time together, they had shared many different decisions, but none as hard as this one. "She will be happy there," Hidemi said, wanting to be sure of it, and believing everything Masao had told her.

"And if she isn't?" he said, feeling old, and suddenly very lonely. But no lonelier than his daughter.

"Then she will grow strong. It will be good for her."

"I hope so," he said softly, as Hidemi took his hand in her own, and they walked slowly out to the garden. They couldn't see the sea from where they were, but they stood in the direction they knew it was in, and as they thought of her, Hiroko stood on the deck of the *Nagoya Maru* and bowed low to the horizon.

# Chapter 4

$T$HE *NAGOYA MARU* docked in San Francisco on August first, after a two-week voyage. The sea had been smooth, and the weather had been good, and for most of the passengers the crossing had been uneventful.

The *Nagoya Maru* had carried mostly families, and a number of older people who didn't want the livelier route via Honolulu. The passengers were primarily Japanese, and many of them were going on to Peru and Brazil. But there had been a number of Americans as well, like the woman who had shared Hiroko's cabin. She had kept to herself, and spoke very little to the other passengers, and only to Hiroko when they were both getting dressed or passed each other on the way to the bathroom. Hiroko had nothing to say to her. She had nothing to say to anyone. She was numb with grief and homesickness all the way to San Francisco, and more than a little seasick.

Several young men had tried to speak to her, all of them Japanese, but she had been extremely polite, and avoided all attempts at conversation. By the time they docked in the States, other than a brief "good morning" or "good night," she had spoken to no one since they left Kobe. She had eaten her meals in the dining room, and even then didn't speak to the other people at her table. She kept her eyes lowered, and appeared absolutely unapproachable, and she wore only her darkest and most serious kimonos.

And just before they docked, she locked her trunk, closed her small case, and stood for a moment looking out the porthole. She could see the new Golden Gate Bridge just ahead of them, and the city was perched on the hills, sparkling white in the sunlight. It looked very pretty, but to her, even from here, it looked and felt completely foreign. And she couldn't help wondering what she would find there. She was going to cousins she didn't know, but whom she had heard about for all of her eighteen years. She only hoped that they were as kind as her father believed, and remembered.

The immigration officers came on with the tug, and they looked over her passport and stamped it, as others stood in line in the main dining room for the same reason. And then she went out on deck, and smoothed down her long black hair. She had worn it in a neatly combed knot, and she was wearing a pale blue kimono. It was the prettiest one she had worn since they left Kobe, and it looked like a piece of summer sky, as she stood at the rail, looking very small and very lovely.

The ship sounded its great horn, and the tugboat eased them in, as the *Nagoya Maru* came to rest at pier 39. And a moment later, the passengers who had been cleared by immigration began disembarking. Most of them were in a great hurry to get off, to meet relatives and friends, to end the two-week voyage. But Hiroko moved down the gangplank very slowly. She moved gracefully, her feet seeming barely to reach the ground, and she was not sure if she would recognize her relatives, or where to find them. It was terrifying just being here. What if they had forgotten to come? If they didn't recognize her, or once they did, if they didn't like her? A thousand thoughts flew through her mind, as she reached the pier, and saw a thousand unfamiliar faces. People were jostling and hurrying everywhere, identifying trunks, and looking for bags and hailing cabbies. And she stood feeling lost in the midst of the excitement. There was almost a party atmosphere and a Dollar Line ship was setting sail nearby in a blare of music. You almost couldn't hear amid the shouting and the noise, with the strains of "Deep in the Heart of Texas" all around them. And just as she despaired of finding anyone, she suddenly looked into a face that reminded her of her father. He was a little older, and not quite as tall, but there was something vaguely familiar about him.

"Hiroko?" he asked, looking down at her, but he was sure of it. She looked exactly like the photograph her father had sent them, and as her eyes rose to his, he saw a shyness and gentleness that touched him deeply. All she could do was nod silently in answer to his question. She was completely overwhelmed by everything that was happening around them, and she had been so afraid not to find them at all, that she couldn't even express her relief to him that he had found her. "I'm Takeo Tanaka. Your Uncle Tak." She nodded again, startled that he was speaking to her in English. He spoke it perfectly, with no trace she could detect of an accent. "Your Aunt Reiko is in the car with the kids." But as he explained it, Hiroko bowed low to him, as low as she possibly could, to show her deep respect for him, and that of her father. And he was as surprised as she had been to hear him speak English. For an instant he hesitated, and then he bowed briefly to her, realizing that not to would have been an offense not only to her, but to her father. But it was only with elders that he ever bowed, never among young people, or even people his own age. Somehow, knowing Masao, he had expected her to be less steeped in tradition. But he remembered that in his brief single meeting with her, Hidemi had been very formal.

"Do you know where your bags are?" he asked quietly, a calming force in the storm all around them. The trunks were being delivered to areas on the pier alphabetically, where customs officers explored their contents, and she pointed at the T, as he began to wonder if she spoke English. As yet, she had not said a word to him, all she had done was bow, and glance up at him once cautiously, though she averted her eyes shyly.

"I think they will be over there," she said carefully, answering his unspoken question about her English. She spoke it deliberately and clearly, although it was obvious that she was not very comfortable with it. "I have only one trunk," she said, sounding even to her own ears very much like Hidemi. Her father and Yuji had an ease with languages, and spoke English as though they used it constantly. Hidemi's English was far less fluent, as was Hiroko's.

"How was the trip?" Takeo asked as they went to the area she had pointed to, and they found her single trunk already waiting. A customs officer was standing nearby and gave her clearance surprisingly quickly.

Then Takeo waved at a porter and indicated where his car was, as he led Hiroko away from the ship, to meet her new cousins. He had driven there in a new Chevrolet station wagon he'd bought that year. It was dark green and carried the whole family with ease, even the dog, who went everywhere with them. But they had left her at home this time so they could put Hiroko's bags in the back, and drive back to Palo Alto. But all of his children had come, and they were all excited to meet her.

"The trip was very smooth," she said in studied answer. "Thank you." She still couldn't understand why he was speaking English to her. He was Japanese, after all. She could only imagine that her father had asked him to make her practice her English. But she was aching to speak Japanese with him. It seemed foolish to be conversing in English. He wasn't any more American than she was, but he had lived in the States for twenty years, and his wife and children had been born here.

He walked ahead of her through the crowd on the pier, and the porter followed behind them with her trunk, and it was only a few minutes before they reached the car, where Reiko and the children were waiting. Reiko, in a red dress, hopped out of the car quickly, and embraced Hiroko warmly while Takeo helped put the trunk in the back of the Chevy.

"Oh, you look so beautiful," Reiko said, smiling at her. She was a pretty woman, of about Hidemi's age, but her hair was cropped short, she was wearing makeup, and she had a red dress on that looked very glamorous to Hiroko. Hiroko bowed low to her, to show her respect for her, just as she had to Uncle Takeo. "You don't have to do that here," Reiko said, still smiling at her, and holding her hand as she turned to her children and introduced them. She called them Ken, Sally, and Tami. Hiroko had always heard of them as Kenji, Sachiko, and Tamiko. Ken was sixteen, and surprisingly tall for a Japanese boy, and Sally was fourteen but looked very grown-up in saddle shoes, a gray skirt, and a pink cashmere sweater. She was a pretty girl, and she looked very much like her mother. And Tami was adorable. She was eight years old, small and lively, and before Hiroko could say a word to her, she threw her arms around Hiroko's neck and kissed her.

"Welcome home, Hiroko!" Tami smiled happily at her, and then commented immediately on how tiny Hiroko was. "I'm almost as tall as you are." Hiroko laughed, and bowed to them, and they watched her do it with interest. "We don't do that here," Tami explained to her. "Only people's grandmothers do stuff like that. And you don't have to wear a kimono either. But yours is really pretty." She looked like a little Japanese doll to them, and Tami insisted on sitting in the back with her and Ken, while Sally got into the front seat with her parents.

In a few minutes they were on their way, and Hiroko was instantly overwhelmed by them, as they chatted and laughed and the kids explained to her about their schools and their friends, and Tami told her all about her dollhouse. Reiko tried quieting them down, but they were much too excited about the arrival of their cousin to listen to her. Hiroko was beautiful, and so small, and she had lovely hair, and Sally said that she looked like a doll her father had given her once, and she wanted to know if Hiroko had brought any Western clothing with her.

"Some." She explained, "My father thought I would need it for college."

"Good idea," Reiko said. "And Sally can lend you anything you need, Hiroko." Hiroko was fascinated by her. Aunt Rei, as she wanted to be called, although they were actually cousins, seemed completely American; she had no accent at all, and in fact, she had been born in Fresno. Cousins of her father's had a flower-growing business there, and her parents had come over before she was born to join them. She had been born in the States, and then sent to school in Japan for several years, which made her a *kibei*. But she had never felt at home in Japan. She was American to her very core, and she had come back to the States and gotten a scholarship to Stanford, where she met Tak, and a year later they were married. A year after that, her parents had retired and gone back to Japan, and they had both been killed in the big earthquake, just after Hiroko was born. The family business in Fresno was still run by her cousins. They were Reiko's only living relatives, except for Takeo and her children.

"I know how you feel, Hiroko," she explained. "When my parents sent me to school in Japan, I felt like I had been sent to another planet. Everything was so different there from what I was used to. My Japanese wasn't very good then, and none of our relatives spoke English at all. I thought they were all strange and old-fashioned."

"Yeah, just like you." Sally pointed at Ken as she interrupted, and they all laughed.

"But I know it's not easy. We probably all seem pretty strange to you." Reiko smiled at Hiroko then, and Hiroko looked down at her lap and smiled shyly. She had scarcely the courage to look at any of them, and the moment they spoke to her, she looked down, and seemed deeply embarrassed. She was the shyest person Sally had ever seen. But more than anything, Hiroko couldn't believe how American they all were. If it weren't for their faces, she would never have known they were Japanese. They didn't speak like real Japanese, act like them, move like them. It was as though they had no tie whatsoever with Japanese manners and culture.

"Do you like American food?" Sally asked, curious about her. They were going to share a room, and Sally was dying to ask her if she had a boyfriend. Ken wondered the same thing. He was going steady with Peggy, their next-door neighbor.

"I have never eaten them," Hiroko answered hesitantly, and Tami giggled. She'd been answering Sally's question.

"It, not them. You mean you've never had hamburgers and milk shakes?" Tami looked at her as though she were a Martian.

"Never. I have read about them. Are they very tasty?" Tami groaned again. They were going to have to do something about her English.

"They're great," Tami said. "You'll love them." They had planned a real American dinner for her that night, a barbecue in their backyard, and they had invited a few of their neighbors, both American and Japanese, to meet their cousin. Takeo was the barbecue chef, and they were going to be cooking hamburgers and hot dogs, and steaks and chicken. Reiko was planning to make corn on the cob, and mashed potatoes, and salad. And Sally made great garlic bread. And Tami had spent a whole morning helping her mother bake chocolate chip cookies and cupcakes, and make homemade ice cream.

The drive to Palo Alto took an hour, and Uncle Tak drove her down University Drive, past the university, so she could see it. It was beautiful, but very different than what she'd expected. The architecture seemed Spanish or Mexican, and the lawns were smooth and green and beautifully tended. Hiroko had been hearing about it for years and it was exciting to finally see it.

"Yuji wants to go there next year," Hiroko said, unconsciously slipping into Japanese, and her younger cousins all looked startled. And from the look on their faces, she realized that they didn't understand her. "Don't you speak Japanese?" she asked in English, as she stared at them in amazement. How could their parents not teach them Japanese?

"I never speak it anymore," her Aunt Reiko explained. "And I'm afraid that now that my parents have been gone for so long, I'm pretty rusty. I keep promising myself I'll try and speak it with Tak, but we never do. And the kids only speak English," she explained, as Hiroko nodded, trying not to look as shocked as she was. There was absolutely nothing Japanese about them, not even Uncle Tak. She couldn't imagine losing her own culture to that extent—he had been born in Japan. At least in Reiko and the children's case, they'd been born in California. But still, it seemed strange to abandon an entire culture. It made her feel even farther from home than she was, and she wondered what her parents would have said if they could have seen them. Her cousins were lovely people, obviously, but they were no longer Japanese in any part of them. They were Americans to their very souls. And Hiroko felt like a total stranger.

"You speak English beautifully," Uncle Tak praised her, and although Tami didn't entirely agree with him, she didn't contradict him. "That must be your father's doing." He smiled. He knew Masao had always had a passion for American language and culture. Takeo had wanted him to come over years before, but Masao had never wanted to risk his job at the university, and the years had rolled along, and it had just never happened.

"My brother speaks much better English than I do," Hiroko told them, and they all smiled. She was doing pretty well, it was just that she still sounded very foreign. Just as they would have, with the exception of Tak, if they had tried to speak Japanese. But for Hiroko, it made being with them a lot harder. She really had no option. She had to speak English with them.

When they left Stanford University, Tak drove them down a pretty, tree-lined street, and Hiroko was surprised to see how large their house was when they reached it. It had been smaller to begin with, but when

Tami came, they had finally outgrown it and Takeo had added on to it. They loved the house and the convenient location. Takeo taught at the university, and like his cousin, he was a full professor of political science. And in his case, he was the head of the department. Reiko worked at the university hospital. She was a nurse, although she only worked part-time now.

The house was well tended, with a generous spread of lawn in both front and back, a number of large trees, and a patio they had put in the previous summer. There was going to be plenty of room for the friends they had invited to meet Hiroko. And when Sally showed her their room, Hiroko was impressed with the large four-poster bed, and all the pink-and-white ruffles. It looked like something in a magazine to her. Sally didn't seem to mind sharing her big bed with her, and she had already cleared a small portion of her closet.

"I do not have many things," Hiroko explained, pointing at the small trunk, which held not only her school clothes but her kimonos. She carefully took out a pink-and-red floral one to wear that night, just as Tami bounded into the room and asked her to come and see her dollhouse.

"Do you want to borrow anything for tonight?" Sally called after her as she disappeared into the hallway. Sally didn't want to say anything to her, but she thought she'd look a little silly at the barbecue in her kimono. And she said as much to her mother when she went downstairs a little later. Reiko was busy making mashed potatoes for their dinner.

"Give her a chance," Reiko said understandingly. "She just got here. She's probably never worn anything but kimonos. You can't expect her to jump into saddle shoes and a pleated skirt in the first five minutes."

"No, but won't people think she looks weird if she goes around in kimonos all the time?" Sally said persistently.

"Of course not. She's a beautiful girl, and she's from Japan. Why don't you give her a chance, Sally. Let her get used to us before you expect her to give up all her old ways for new ones."

"Oh, boy," Ken said, walking in on them and hearing the last of their conversation. "What do you want from her, Sal? Pin curls in her hair, and a jitterbugging contest tomorrow night? Give the kid a chance. She just got here."

"That's what I was just saying to your sister." Ken made himself a peanut butter sandwich as he listened to his mother and sister.

"I just think she'll look weird tonight at the barbecue in a kimono," Sally said again. To Sally, at fourteen, fitting in was important.

"She won't look as weird as you would, goofball." Ken grinned at her, and poured himself a glass of milk to eat with his sandwich. And then he looked at his mother with an air of concern. He had just thought about their dinner. Food was important to him, mostly in large quantities, and usually covered in ketchup. "You're not making anything Japanese tonight, are you, Mom?" He looked genuinely worried as she laughed at him.

"I don't think I'd remember how," she admitted ruefully. "Your grandma's been gone for eighteen years. I never really did know how to make it."

"Good. I hate that stuff. Yuk. All that raw fish and stuff that wiggles."

"What wiggles?" Tak had come in from the back-yard to get the charcoal for the barbecue that night, and was intrigued by their conversation. "Anyone we know?" he asked with interest, as Reiko smiled at him and raised an eyebrow. They were a happy pair. She was still very pretty at thirty-eight, and he was a very handsome man at fifty.

"We were talking about raw fish," Reiko explained to her husband. "Ken was afraid I was going to cook some Japanese dishes for Hiroko."

"Not a chance," his father said, opening a cup-board and pulling out a bag of charcoal. "She's the worst Japanese cook I know. Stick to hamburgers and pot roast, and she's the greatest." He leaned over and kissed his wife, as Ken finished his second sandwich, and Tami and Hiroko came upstairs from the base-ment playroom. Tami had been showing Hiroko the dollhouse her father had made for her. And Reiko had hand crocheted all the carpets and made all the cur-tains. They had even used tiny bits of wallpaper. And Tak had made tiny little paintings, and they'd ordered an exquisite little chandelier, which worked, from En-gland.

"It is so beautiful," Hiroko exclaimed, watching them all go about their tasks in the comfortable kitchen. It was a very handsome house, and provided enough room for all of them. And the playroom down-stairs was enormous. "I have never seen a dollhouse like yours. It is fine enough for a museum," Hiroko said. Ken offered her the other half of his last sand-wich, and she was obviously afraid to take it.

"Peanut butter," he explained, "with grape jelly."

"I have never eaten this before," she said cautiously, and Tami told her in no uncertain terms that she should really try it. But when she did, she made a polite, but startled, face. It was clearly not what she had expected.

"Good, huh?" Tami asked, as Hiroko wondered silently if her mouth would be glued together forever. Sally realized what was happening and handed her a glass of milk, but Hiroko's first taste of American food had not impressed her.

Takeo returned to the backyard with his charcoal then, and as he did, the dog came bounding into the kitchen. And as soon as she did, Hiroko smiled. This was at least a familiar breed. She was a type of Japanese dog called a Shiba. And she was obviously very friendly.

"Her name is Lassie," Tami explained. "I loved the book."

"Not that she looks anything like her. The real Lassie was a collie," Ken said, and reminded Hiroko instantly of Yuji. It was the kind of thing he would have said. Ken reminded her a lot of Yuji, and in some ways it was comforting, but in others it made her even more homesick.

Ken went next door to visit his girlfriend, Peggy, that afternoon, and Sally disappeared quietly down the street, to a neighbor's. She would have offered to take Hiroko with her, but she was afraid Hiroko might tell her mom. She didn't know her that well yet. And Sally wanted to visit her friend because she had a particularly handsome sixteen-year-old brother she liked to flirt with.

Only Tami stayed home with them, but she was busy in the backyard with her dad, and Hiroko stayed in the kitchen to help her Aunt Reiko. Reiko was impressed with how quickly and competently Hiroko did everything. She said very little, and she expected no praise, but she moved around the kitchen, preparing things, like lightning. She understood quickly how the mashed potatoes were made, although she'd never seen them before, and she helped prepare the corn and make the salad. And when Tak asked his wife to marinate the meat for him, Hiroko was quick to learn that as well, and then she went outside with Reiko to help set the enormous buffet table. She was the quietest, most efficient girl Reiko had ever seen, and in spite of her obvious shyness, she knew exactly what she was doing.

"Thank you for all the help," Reiko said quietly to her when they went upstairs to change. She was a lovely girl, and Reiko knew they were going to enjoy her. She only hoped that Hiroko would be happy with them. But she had seemed happier that afternoon, once she had things to do. And it was only now, as they stood on the stairs, that she looked wistful again, and Reiko sensed without Hiroko saying it that she missed her parents. "I really appreciate it," she said gently. "We're glad you're here, Hiroko."

"I am very glad too," Hiroko said, and bowed low to her older cousin.

"You don't need to do that here." Reiko put a gentle hand on her shoulder.

"I do not know another way to show you respect, and thank you for your kindness," she said, as Reiko walked her to Sally's bedroom. Hiroko's things were all neatly put away, and the only visible mess was Sally's.

"You don't need to show us respect. We understand how you feel. Here you can be less formal." Hiroko began to bow again, and then stopped herself with a small smile.

"Here everything is very different," Hiroko admitted. "I will have many things to learn, many new ways." She was just beginning to understand what her father had meant when he said that he wanted her to see the world and learn new customs. She had never imagined for a minute that it would all be so completely different, especially in the house of her cousins.

"You will learn very quickly," Reiko reassured her.

But as she stood at the barbecue that night, Hiroko wasn't so sure. She felt surrounded by a sea of chattering strangers. They came to meet her, they shook her hand, they greeted her, she bowed to them, and they talked about how adorable she was, how pretty her kimono was. But even though many of their faces were Japanese, all of them spoke English and were either nisei or sansei, first- or second-generation Americans. But most of them had lost their Japanese customs and traditions long before, and only their grandparents would have seemed familiar to Hiroko. There were lots of non-Japanese at the party too. And she felt lost amid all of them. She barely even knew her cousins. And after she had helped clear the buffet, she stood alone in their backyard for a time, looking up at the sky, and thinking about her parents.

"It must seem like a long way from home," a voice said softly just behind her, and she turned in surprise to look at the man who had spoken to her. He was tall and young and had dark hair, and by Western standards he was very handsome. And then, just as quickly as she had looked up, she put her head down so he wouldn't see that she was crying. She was homesick, and so lonely.

She stood looking down in mortified silence as he introduced himself. "My name is Peter Jenkins," he said, holding out a hand to her, and she shook it. And then she slowly looked up at him again. He was even taller than Kenji. He was very long and lean, with soft brown hair, blue eyes, and an air of solidity about him. He seemed very young, but he was actually twenty-seven, and Tak's assistant. He was an assistant political science professor at Stanford.

"I went to Japan once. It was the most beautiful country I've ever seen. I especially liked Kyoto." He knew that was where she was from, and he really meant it. "This must all seem so foreign to you," he said gently. "Just coming back from Japan was a shock for me. I can't even imagine what it must be like for you, never having been here." Seeing his own culture through her eyes made it all seem very odd even to him, and he smiled at her warmly. He had a friendly face and kind eyes, and even without knowing him, she liked him.

But Hiroko lowered her eyes again in embarrassment, and smiled hesitantly. He was right. It was a shock. She had been trying to wrestle with all the new impressions and experiences that had assaulted her since that morning. Even her cousins had been different than she expected. And there seemed to be no one here that she could really talk to, at least not for the moment.

"I like it very much," she said softly, staring at her feet, and feeling that she should have bowed to him, but Reiko seemed to think that she shouldn't. "I am very lucky," she whispered, trying to look up at him, but unable to do it. She was simply too shy to look at him again, but he knew that. She was like a little girl, and yet very much a woman. And despite her age, she was nothing like any of his students. She was so much more delicate, so withdrawn, and yet at the same time, one sensed something quietly strong about her. She was an interesting girl, and apparently a bright one, but she had all the exquisite delicacy and gentleness of her culture, and just looking at her in the backyard, Peter Jenkins was bowled over by her. She embodied everything he had loved about Japanese women when he'd visited Japan. And all he could do now was stare at her, as she stood trembling before him.

"Would you like to go back inside?" he asked gently, sensing that he had cornered her there, and she was too embarrassed to flee him. She nodded, and barely glanced up at him through dark lashes. "I hear from Tak that you're going to St. Andrew's in September," he said as they walked slowly back to the house, and he silently admired her kimono. It was lovely. A moment later he found Reiko chatting with two friends, and he left Hiroko there with her cousin, who smiled at him and introduced her easily to the two women.

Hiroko bowed low to them, showing her respect for the Tanakas' friends, and the women looked faintly amused as they watched her. Across the patio, Peter was telling Tak that he had just met their cousin.

"She's a sweet girl, poor thing, she must feel so

lost here," Peter said sympathetically. There was something about her that made you want to take her under your wing and protect her.

"She'll get used to it." Tak smiled, holding a glass of wine. The barbecue had gone well, and everyone seemed to be enjoying the party. "I did." He grinned. "You're just fascinated with Japan, ever since that trip you took." It was true. Peter had been completely enamored with the entire country.

"I can't understand why you don't miss it."

But Tak always said he loved the United States, and it was obvious he would have been a citizen if he could have become one, but he couldn't. Despite twenty years of living in the States and having married an American, it was against the law for him to become an American citizen.

"I was stifled there. Look at her." Takeo glanced at his young cousin. To him, she embodied everything he had hated about Japan, and had fled from. "She is strangled and bound; she is afraid to look at us. She is wearing the same garment they wore five hundred years ago. She'll bind her breasts if she has any, and if she gets pregnant, she'll bind her stomach, and she probably won't even tell her husband she's expecting. When she's old enough, her parents will find her a husband she's never met before. And they'll never have a single real conversation. They'll spend their entire lives bowing to each other, and hiding their feelings. And it's exactly the same thing in business, only worse. Everything is run by tradition, everything is appearances and respect and custom. You can never just speak out and say what you feel, and go after a woman simply because you love her. I'd probably never have been able to marry Reiko in Japan, if we'd met there. I would have had to marry the woman my parents selected. I just couldn't live with it. Seeing Hiroko brought it all back to me today. She's like a bird in a cage, too frightened even to sing. No, I don't miss Japan," he smiled ruefully, "but I'm sure she does. Her father's a good man, and somehow he managed to keep his spirit alive in spite of all that repression. He has a lovely wife, and I think they really like each other. But when I see Hiroko, I see it all again. Nothing ever changes there. It's oppressive," he said, and Peter nodded. He had seen the repression there, and the traditions too. But he had seen so much more. He couldn't understand why Takeo didn't love it as he did.

"You have such a sense of history in Japan, just being there, knowing that nothing has changed for the last thousand years, and hopefully nothing will for the next thousand either. I loved it. And I love watching her. I love everything she stands for," Peter said simply, as Tak looked at him in amusement.

"Don't let Reiko hear you say that. She thinks Japanese women never get a fair shake, and they're completely dominated by their husbands. She's as American as apple pie, and she loves that. She hated going to school there."

"I think you're both crazy." Peter smiled, and then he got pulled away by two of the other professors from Stanford, and he never got to speak to Hiroko again. But he saw her bowing as she said good night to some of the Tanakas' friends, and despite everything Tak had said, Peter thought she looked dignified and graceful. It was a custom he found touching, and not in any way degrading. And as he prepared to leave, their eyes met for a single moment, and for an instant he could have sworn that she looked right at him, but within a fraction of a second her eyes were lowered again and she was talking to one of her cousins.

No one had spoken Japanese to her that night, and she smiled when Peter bowed slightly to her before he left, and said *sayonara*. She looked up at him to see if he was making fun of her. But his eyes were warm, and he was smiling at her. She bowed formally to him then, and kept her eyes down when she told him that it had been an honor to meet him. He said the same, and then left with the attractive blonde he had come with. Hiroko watched him for a moment, and then took Tami upstairs to her bedroom. She was yawning and it was late, but she had had a good time. They all had. Even Hiroko had enjoyed it, although she didn't know anyone, and everything she touched or tasted or encountered was so different from everything she knew and everything she had expected.

"Did you have fun?" Reiko asked as Hiroko came down to help in the kitchen again, after putting Tami to bed. They had invited several students her age, but she had been too shy to speak to them. She had spent most of her time alone, or with Tami. Peter Jenkins was the only adult guest she had actually talked to. But that had been his doing and not hers. It had been difficult for her to speak to anyone, even him. She was just too shy, but she had found the evening interesting and the guests friendly.

"I have fun," she confirmed, and Reiko smiled at her. She knew that Tami would take care of Hiroko's English. Lassie was lying on the floor wagging her tail as they spoke, waiting for scraps from the party. Ken and Tak were outside cleaning up the barbecue, and collecting abandoned glasses. Only Sally seemed not to be helping. She was in the downstairs closet, on the phone with a friend, and had promised half an hour before that she'd be off in a minute, but there was something she *had* to tell her.

"You were a big success," Reiko said, and meant it. "Everyone loved meeting you, Hiroko. And I'm sure it wasn't easy." The young girl blushed, and went on helping with the dishes in silence. She was so shy that it still surprised all of them, and yet Reiko had seen her talking to Peter. He had come to the party tonight with his new girlfriend. She was a model in San Francisco, and she had noticed Ken eyeing her with approval.

"Did everyone have a good time?" Tak inquired as he came in from the patio with a tray full of glasses. "I thought it was a really nice evening," he complimented his wife, and smiled at Hiroko.

"I too," she said softly. "Hamburgers are great," she paraphrased Tami, and they all laughed, as Ken helped himself to some leftover chicken. He ate constantly, but he was the right age for that, and he was going to start football practice for school at the end of August. "Thank you for a very nice party," Hiroko added politely, and a little while later they all went upstairs to their respective bedrooms.

Sally and Hiroko undressed quietly, and then slipped into bed in their nightgowns. And as they lay there, Hiroko thought of how far she had come, the long journey she'd had, the people she'd met, and the warm welcome she'd had from her cousins. Even if they weren't Japanese anymore, she liked all of them. She liked Ken, with his mischief and his long limbs, and his insatiable appetite, and Sally with her fascination with clothes and boys and telephones and secrets, and especially little Tami with her remarkable dollhouse and determination to make Hiroko American, and their parents who had been so kind to her, and even given her a party. She liked their friends too . . . and even Lassie. She just wished, as she lay there, thinking about all of it and what an adventure it had been, that her parents and Yuji could have been there too. And maybe then she wouldn't have been so homesick.

She turned on her side, with her long black hair fanned out behind her on the pillow, and she could hear Sally already snoring softly. But Hiroko couldn't sleep. Too much had happened to her. She had spent her first day in America. And she had more than eleven months ahead of her, before she could go home to her parents.

As she drifted off to sleep, she first counted the months, and then the weeks . . . and finally the moments. . . . She was counting in Japanese as she began to dream, thinking that she was home again, with them. . . . Soon, she whispered as she slept. . . . Soon . . . home . . . And in the distance she heard a young man say *sayonara*. . . . she didn't know who he was, or what it meant, but she sighed as she turned over and put an arm around Sally.

# Chapter 5

HIROKO SPENT her second day in America pleasantly with her cousins. They drove to San Francisco in the station wagon in the afternoon. They went to Golden Gate Park, had tea in the Japanese tea garden, and went to the Academy of Science. They drove her downtown, and she got a glimpse of I. Magnin from the car before they returned to Palo Alto.

Lassie was waiting for them at home, in the yard, and she wagged her tail when she saw Hiroko.

And as soon as they got home, Sally disappeared again, as did Ken, and Hiroko went to help her Aunt Reiko cook dinner. After she had set the table for them, Tami ran downstairs to play with her dollhouse. Reiko had told her to set the table for seven, and Hiroko wondered who was coming to dinner. She thought maybe it was one of the children's friends, but Reiko said casually that it was Tak's assistant.

"I think you met him last night, at the barbecue. His name is Peter Jenkins." Hiroko nodded and lowered her eyes. He was the young man who had spoken to her outside, and told her how much he liked Kyoto.

And he was just as pleasant, and she was just as shy with him as she had been the night before, when he arrived carrying a bottle of wine for Tak, and a bunch of flowers for Reiko.

He asked how they'd spent the afternoon, as he sat down easily in their living room, and Hiroko disappeared immediately to cast an eye on dinner in the kitchen. As she had the night before, she had bowed low to him, and he had bowed to her, which Tak thought was amusing.

"She's incredibly shy, poor little thing," Tak said, once she'd left the room. He hadn't seen women behave that way since he'd left Japan twenty years before. And he hoped she'd get over it during her year in California. Even with him, as a relative, she barely dared look up at him, and with a young man like Peter, she barely dared say a word to him.

Hiroko was quiet during dinner that night, and she seemed thoughtful about their conversation. Ken and Sally were arguing about a movie they had seen, and Tami was just daydreaming. But Peter and Tak and Reiko were having a serious discussion about the war in Europe. The situation was obviously escalating, and the poor British were taking a terrible beating, not to mention the frightening situation between the Germans and the Russians.

"I think we're going to have to get into it eventually," Takeo said quietly. "Roosevelt apparently admitted it privately. There's just no other way."

"That's not what he's saying to the American public," Reiko said firmly, looking worried. Her husband was too old to be called into it, if America entered the war, but Ken was young enough to get drafted in two years, if it continued. And that prospect frightened both Tak and Reiko.

"I thought about volunteering for the RAF last year," Peter admitted seriously, as Hiroko glanced at him cautiously from under her lashes. None of them was paying any attention to her, and it was easier to look at him now, and concentrate on what they all were saying. "But I didn't want to leave the university. There's a real risk I might not get my job back." Everything was seniority and tenure, and he had a great job in the political science department as Tak's assistant. He didn't want to give that up, even for a worthwhile cause, but he knew that maybe eventually he'd have to. But for the moment, he was still thinking about his future. At twenty-seven, he didn't feel as though he could just throw it all away to go and fight someone else's battle.

"I don't think you should go unless we do get into it," Takeo said thoughtfully, although he knew he might have been tempted himself if he were younger. And then, as they finished the meal, the conversation turned to other subjects, the lecture Tak was preparing with Peter's help, and some changes he wanted to make in the department. And it was only then that Peter realized Hiroko was following their conversation very closely.

"Are you interested in politics, Hiroko?" he asked

quietly. He was sitting across from her, and she lowered her eyes again before she blushed and answered.

"Sometimes. My father speaks of these things too. But I do not always understand them."

"Neither do I." He smiled, wishing that she would look at him again. She had eyes that seemed bottomless in their shiny blackness. "Your father teaches at the university in Kyoto, doesn't he?" Peter asked. She nodded, and then got up to help Reiko with the dishes. She could barely bring herself to speak to him, although he seemed very pleasant, and she found his conversation with Takeo both interesting and enlightening.

He and Takeo went into the study after that, to do some work, and when the dishes were done Hiroko went downstairs with Tami to help her work on her dollhouse. She made some tiny origami flowers and birds for her to put in it, and the smallest of drawings to hang on the walls, including one of the mountains at sunset. Reiko was amazed when she came downstairs and saw what she had done. She was not only a girl of gentle manners, but one with many talents.

"Did your mother teach you how to do that?" Reiko was fascinated by the minuscule origami birds she had made for Tami.

"My grandmother." She smiled. She was wearing a green-and-blue kimono as she sat on the floor, with a bright blue obi, and she looked very lovely. "She taught me many things . . . about flowers and animals, and how to care for a house, and weaving straw mats. My father thinks these things are very old-fashioned and quite useless," she said sadly. It was all part of why he had made her come here, because he thought she was too much as her grandmother had been, too old-fashioned, and not modern, as he was. But it was what she felt in her soul, she loved the old ways, and the ancient traditions. She loved helping her mother run their home and do the cooking, and tend the garden. And she loved being with children. She would make a good wife one day, though perhaps not a modern one. Or maybe in America she would learn those things that her father felt were lacking in her. She hoped so, so that she could go home again, and be with them. After two days in America, she liked being there, but she was still terribly homesick.

Tami showed her mother the drawings Hiroko had done, and eventually, the two women went upstairs and put Tami to bed, and then came back down to find Takeo and Peter. They were finished with their work by then, and were sitting in the living room with Ken and Sally. They were playing Monopoly, and Hiroko smiled as she watched them, and they laughed, and Ken accused Sally of cheating.

"You did *not* have a hotel on Park Place. I saw you, you took it."

"I did not!" she squealed at him, and then accused him of stealing Boardwalk. And the fight went on as everyone laughed, and Hiroko tried to understand the game. It looked like fun, but mainly because they were having such a good time at it, and Peter played with them just like one of the children. He offered to give his place to her, but she declined. She was too shy to play with them, although it reminded her of when she had played *shogi* with her brother. He often cheated too, and they got into endless arguments over who had really won, and no one ever seemed to agree on the winner.

It was after ten o'clock when Peter finally left, and Reiko promised to have him to dinner again that week. They wanted to get to know his new girlfriend. But Takeo reminded her that they were leaving for Lake Tahoe the following weekend. They were going to be gone for two weeks. As they did every year, they had rented a cabin. Takeo and Ken loved to fish, and Sally loved to water-ski, although they all agreed that the lake was freezing.

"I'll call you when we get back," Reiko said, and Peter waved as he left, and thanked her for the evening. He and Tak had a big week ahead of them, mapping out the curriculum for the coming term. They both wanted to get it done before Takeo left for his vacation.

And as he left, Peter's eyes met Hiroko's face for just a fraction of a second. There was a moment of understanding there, and then he was gone. She had barely spoken to him all evening. She didn't dare. But she thought him very intelligent, and very interesting. She was intrigued by his ideas, but she would never have dared to enter the conversation. In spite of all her father's efforts to draw her out over the years, she still couldn't bring herself to speak up with strangers.

The time at the lake was easier for her. The things that they did were the same things her family did when they visited the mountains in Japan. They had gone for many years to a *ryokan* on Lake Biwa for their summer vacations. She liked going to the seashore too, but there was something very peaceful about the mountains. She wrote to her parents every day, and played with her cousins. She played tennis with Ken, and he taught her how to fish, although she had always refused to do so with Yuji. She teased her brother about it, and told him she had caught an enormous fish when she wrote to him in a letter.

She tried water-skiing with Sally too, but the water was so icy cold that her legs kept getting numb, and she never seemed to be able to get her arms straight enough to get out of the water. She tried valiantly, but she must have fallen a hundred times before she finally gave up. But she tried again the next day, and by the end of the vacation she managed a short run, and everyone in the boat shouted victoriously as her Uncle Tak laughed, proud of her.

"Thank God. I thought she'd drown, and I'd have to tell her father." He found he really liked the girl, she had lots of spunk and a bright mind. It just seemed a shame that she was so shy, but by the time they left the lake, she seemed considerably more at ease with them. She spoke without being spoken to first, and she made little jokes with Ken, and she had even worn a skirt and sweater once, just to please Sally. But she still wore her kimonos most of the time, and Reiko had to admit that they looked lovely on her, and she would be sorry to see her wear Western clothes once she went to college.

But the real change in her showed when Peter came to dinner again. He had promised to bring his new girlfriend with him, but she had a modeling job in Los Angeles and couldn't come, which was just as well. The evening was more relaxed without her. He was just like family, and the children all greeted him with hugs and squeals and insults when he arrived for Sunday dinner the day after they'd returned from Lake Tahoe. Hiroko bowed to him as usual, and she was wearing a bright orange kimono with pale pink flowers on it, which looked fabulous with her suntan. Her hair was down, and shone like black satin as it hung down her back, but this time she looked at him and smiled. She had grown much braver in two brief weeks in the mountains.

"Good evening, Peter-san," she said politely as she took the flowers he had brought for Reiko. "You are well?" she asked, and then finally looked down again. But for her, it had been a very bold statement.

"I am very well, thank you, Hiroko-san," he said, bowing back to her formally. And he smiled as their eyes met again. "How did you like Lake Tahoe?"

"Very much. I caught many fish, and learned to ski on the water."

"She's a liar," Ken said casually as he strolled by. They were like brother and sister now, after two weeks at the cabin in the mountains. "She caught two, and they were the smallest fish I've ever seen. She did get up on skis though."

"I caught seven fish," she corrected him, looking very much like an older sister, not taking any guff from him, as she grinned, and Peter laughed. She had blossomed in the two weeks they'd been gone, and it touched him to see it. She was opening up like a rare flower, and her face shone at him as she told him about the water-skiing and the fishing.

"It sounds like you all had a great time."

"We did," Reiko confirmed as she kissed him and

thanked him for the flowers. "It always does us good to go up there. You should come with us next year."

"I would love it. . . . That is"—he glanced at his boss with a rueful grin—"if your husband doesn't leave me the entire course to reorganize again." He hadn't really done that, they had sorted out most of the work before he left, but Peter had tied up most of the loose ends for him, and he'd done a good job. Takeo was very pleased with the work that Peter had accomplished in his absence.

Peter brought him up on developments at the university while he'd been gone, and at dinner they once again discussed the situation in Russia. And eventually Peter turned and asked Hiroko if she'd had news of her parents. She was still startled by how easily they all expressed their opinions, especially Reiko. It seemed remarkable to her that a woman should speak her mind so freely. Looking down shyly, she told Peter that she had heard from her parents, and then, as though forcing herself, she looked up at him and smiled and thanked him for asking. She told him about a storm her parents had said they'd had, but other than that, everything was fine. And just talking about them suddenly made her homesick again for Kyoto.

"When do you start school?" he asked quietly. He always felt as though she were a doe, about to dart away from him into the forest, and he had to move ever so slowly, and speak very softly. He almost wanted to put a hand out to her, to show her he wouldn't harm her.

"In two weeks," she answered bravely, forcing herself not to be afraid of him. She wanted to be polite, and to be American, and not hide from his eyes the way a Japanese girl would. In her heart of hearts, she wanted to be like Sally, or her Aunt Reiko. But it was far from easy.

"Are you excited about it?" he asked, excited himself that he was actually having a conversation with her. It meant a lot to him to make her comfortable. He wasn't sure why, but it did. He wanted her to feel at ease with him, and to get to know her better.

"I am afraid, perhaps, Peter-san," she said, astounding him with her honesty. In spite of her timidity, she was very direct sometimes, but he hadn't yet learned that about her. "Maybe they will not like me, if I am so very different." She looked up at him with wise eyes. She was enchanting with her beautiful manners and graceful ways. He couldn't imagine anyone not liking her, particularly not a group of eighteen-year-old girls, and he smiled at the suggestion.

"I think they will like you very much," he said, barely concealing his own admiration for her, as Takeo watched them. For an instant he wondered if Peter was unusually interested in her, and then decided he was just being foolish.

"She's going to wear regular clothes when she goes to school," Tami said, and Hiroko giggled. She knew that Tami was still worried that her cousin would go to college with her kimonos. "Right, Hiroko?"

"Right, Tami-san. I will wear clothes just like Sally." But she realized now that the Western clothes she had brought looked out-of-date and somewhat old-fashioned. Neither she nor her mother had known what to select when they went shopping in Kyoto. But seeing the clothes that Sally and Reiko wore, she realized how ugly her new clothes were.

"I like your kimonos, Hiroko-san," Peter said quietly. "They suit you."

But Hiroko was so embarrassed by his words that she looked down again and did not answer.

After dinner, they played Monopoly again, and this time Hiroko joined in. She had played with them at the lake, and had gotten good at it. She understood the game, and when Sally or Ken cheated she always caught them, as she did that night, and there were wild squeals and laughter as Takeo and Peter dropped out and went to get a cup of coffee in the kitchen. Reiko was still there putting away the dishes. She smiled at them and poured them each a cup of coffee, and the three adults looked back into the living room and watched the antics of the four children. Not that Hiroko was a child anymore, or even Ken, but there was still a wonderful innocence about them.

"She's a lovely girl," Peter said wistfully, as Takeo nodded. He couldn't help remembering his cousin Masao's admonitions to him before she came, not to let her get romantically involved with anyone during her year at St. Andrew's College, and there was something in Peter's eyes now that suggested to Tak that he liked her. But on the other hand, Peter had a girlfriend and Takeo told himself he was being too protective. Hiroko was barely more than a child, although she was certainly very beautiful, and her sweetness and innocence were very alluring.

"She is lovely," Tak agreed quietly. "But she's a child," and then he realized, as he said the words, that she was the same age Reiko had been when he met her. He was thirty and Reiko was one of his students. It wasn't inconceivable that the same thing could happen to Peter. Tak and Reiko had married six months after they met, but Hiroko seemed so childlike in comparison to the girl Reiko had been that Takeo felt foolish for what he'd been thinking. But still, there was a look in Peter's eyes, whenever he looked at her—although Peter would have denied it, if Tak had asked him. What Tak had sensed remained unspoken between them. Takeo glanced at his wife and smiled. They had been happy for two decades. And then he glanced back at his young cousin, still cavorting with their children.

Hiroko was so Japanese, in so many ways. And she was going back to Japan in a year. And although her father had modern ideas, having his daughter marry an American had never been one of them. Masao did not want her dating anyone, not even a Japanese boy, for the moment. He wanted her back in Japan long before her thoughts turned to romance, or marriage.

"I really like Carole," Peter said suddenly, as though trying to convince himself, but even to his own ears he didn't sound entirely sincere. He was far more impressed by Hiroko's beauty and gentleness than by his striking blond girlfriend with the modeling career. She was beautiful, but she was also shallow, and he knew it. Oddly enough, comparing the two women made him uncomfortable. And as they walked back into the living room to observe the Monopoly game again, he reminded himself of how young Hiroko was and how silly he was to be so enchanted by her. It was just that she looked so like a doll, and he loved her discreet manners and fascinating traditions. And as he watched her, he couldn't help noticing again how gentle she was, and how pretty she looked when she laughed. She was teasing Ken, and her laughter sounded like wind chimes. And it disturbed him to realize that as the game wore on, he couldn't take his eyes from her. He hoped no one else noticed it, and took comfort in the fact that whatever he felt for her could be stopped even before it began. Peter had no intention of falling in love with a girl her age, or causing her, or her family, any problems.

He seemed quiet that night when he finally went home. And despite all the laughter that had come before, Hiroko bowed seriously to him, and he bowed back to her. But this time, he said nothing when he left them. And as he drove back to his own house in Menlo Park, he was lost in thought. He felt as though he had been slowly carried away by tides that were so subtle he hadn't even noticed. But at least he was aware of it. He would not allow himself to be swept away by her, no matter how appealing she was. Absolutely nothing was going to happen between him and Hiroko.

After Peter left, Hiroko asked her cousin if Peter-san had been angry. She had noticed how quiet he was, and how little he had said to them when he left.

"Angry? No. Why?" Reiko looked surprised, but Takeo understood the question. He had noticed it too, and it concerned him. Something had been bothering Peter, and Takeo had seen him watching Hiroko very closely. It seemed awkward to object, and yet he had wanted to warn Peter not to let himself get carried away by his emotions.

"He was very serious when he said good-bye," Hiroko explained, and her Uncle Tak nodded.

"He has a lot of work to think about, Hiroko. So do you. You will be starting school soon." And as he said it, she wondered if he was angry at her too, if she had behaved improperly somehow with Peter. But her aunt was smiling at her, and she didn't seem disturbed, so perhaps her uncle's tone meant nothing. But as she went to bed that night, she was worried. Had she done something wrong? Had she offended him? Did they think her too modern or too forward? This new world of hers was so confusing. But by morning, all her concerns seemed to be forgotten, and she decided that she had been foolish. Her uncle had explained Peter's silence satisfactorily. He had a great deal of work to think about. So much so that he didn't come back to dinner during the next two weeks, and on the seventh of September, the entire family drove her to St. Andrew's College in the green Chevy wagon.

It was a beautiful school. The grounds were carefully tended, and there were just over nine hundred students. Most were from San Francisco, or Los Angeles, or elsewhere in California, and a handful were from other states, or Hawaii. There was a girl from France, and another one from England, who was spending the war in the States, having been sent there by her parents. But Hiroko came from by far the greatest distance.

A senior greeted her when she arrived, and she was assigned a room with two other students. She saw their names on the bulletin board—Sharon Williams from Los Angeles, and Anne Spencer from San Francisco—but neither of them had arrived yet.

Reiko and Sally helped her unpack her things while Ken and Tak waited downstairs with Tami. She had been miserable all day. She didn't want her cousin Hiroko to leave them.

"Don't be silly," Reiko had said. "She'll come to us on weekends whenever she can, and for all her vacations."

"But I want her to stay with us," Tami had said unhappily. "Why can't she go to Stanford with Daddy?" Her parents had thought of it, but St. Andrew's was a small, exclusive women's school, and probably a better place for a girl who had lived as sheltered a life as Hiroko's had been. In comparison, Stanford seemed enormous, and it was coed, which Hidemi had absolutely refused to agree to. This had seemed the perfect compromise solution.

But now even Hiroko had her doubts, as they unpacked her things in one of the room's three tiny closets. They were actually lockers. Suddenly she felt as though she were losing her family again, and she looked as glum as Tami when she came back downstairs. She didn't want to leave them.

She was wearing a brown skirt that her mother had bought her, and a beige sweater set that had come with it, and she was wearing the small string of pearls her parents had given her for her eighteenth birthday. She was wearing silk stockings and high heels, and a little brown hat tilted at a rakish angle. Sally had helped her put it on, and she thought she looked great, a lot better than she looked in a kimono, but Hiroko missed the comfort of the familiar garment and the bright silks she had worn all her life. In her new clothes, she felt naked.

Another senior escorted them around the grounds, and showed them the dining room and the library, and the gym, and eventually there was nothing left for her cousins to do, and Tak said they should get back to

Palo Alto. Peter and his friend Carole were coming for dinner. And even hearing that news made her heart sink. She felt as though she were being deserted by all of them. Her life had been nothing but good-byes for the past two months, and this one was almost as hard as the last one.

Tami cried as they left, and Sally hugged Hiroko tight and made her promise to call whenever she could. She wanted to know all about Hiroko's room-mates, and any boys she might meet. And Ken told her that if she needed him to beat anyone up, let him know and he'd drive right over. Aunt Reiko reminded her to call if she needed anything, and looking at Uncle Tak only made Hiroko think of her father, and the lump in her throat grew so large that she couldn't even speak as they left her. She just waved as they drove off, and walked slowly back to her dorm room to wait for her roommates.

It was five o'clock by the time the first one arrived. She had come by train from Los Angeles, and she had bright red hair, and a personality to go with it. She was full of life, and she took photographs of a dozen movie stars out of her suitcase, and started putting them up all around the mirror. Even Hiroko knew who they were, and she was deeply impressed when Sharon said casually to her that her father was a producer. According to her, she had met them all, and she told Hiroko which ones she liked and which ones she didn't.

"Is your mother a movie star?" Hiroko asked with wide eyes, enormously impressed by the people Sharon claimed as old friends of her parents. She was obviously someone very important. Hiroko knew her parents would have loved that.

"My mom is married to a Frenchman, and they live in Europe. She's in Geneva now, because of the war," she said offhandedly, artfully covering up the fact that the divorce had not only been a public scandal in Los Angeles, but also very painful. She hadn't seen her mother in three years, although on Christmas and birthdays she sent Sharon lovely presents.

"What's Japan like?" she asked, hopping onto her bed after she'd unpacked. She was obviously intrigued by Hiroko. The only Japanese she'd ever met had been gardeners and maids, but Hiroko had said her father was a professor in Kyoto. "What does your mom do?" she asked, intrigued. "Does she do anything?" Hiroko looked faintly puzzled by the questions. Reiko was a nurse, but that was here. In Japan, most women did not have professions.

"She is only a woman," she explained, hoping that that covered it. Sharon got up, stared out the window, and whistled.

"Zowie," she said admiringly, as they both stood and watched a staggeringly pretty girl climb out of a limousine, with the assistance of a liveried chauffeur. She had long, slim legs, and blond hair, and she was wearing a straw hat and a white silk dress that looked like it had been made for her in Paris. "Who do we have here? Carole Lombard?"

"A movie star?" Hiroko's eyes grew wide in astonishment, as Sharon laughed.

"I don't think so. Probably just one of us. My dad has a car like that. But he didn't want to drive me up here. He and his girlfriend went to Palm Springs for the weekend." She didn't want to tell Hiroko how lonely her life had been. For all intents and purposes, given who her parents were, hers was a life anyone would have envied. But the truth was far from what she was describing to Hiroko. And Hiroko was far too naive to understand the implications of all that Sharon was saying.

But as they contemplated who the new arrival might be, there was a knock on the door, and the liveried chauffeur they had just seen entered the room carrying a bag, just two steps ahead of Miss Anne Spencer. She was very tall and very cool. She had white-blond hair, and ice-blue eyes, and she looked them both over without hesitation.

"Anne Spencer?" Sharon asked her boldly. When she nodded, Sharon pointed out the closet to the chauffeur.

"Yes?" She didn't look impressed by either of them, and she dismissed Hiroko from her attention the moment she saw her.

"We're your roommates," Sharon said, as though she and Hiroko had been friends forever. "I'm Sharon, and this is Hiroko."

"They told me I'd have a private room," she said with a marked chill, as though the mistake was Sharon's fault, or Hiroko's.

"Not till next year. I asked too. Freshmen sleep in threes or fours. The upperclassmen get all the doubles and singles."

"Not if they promised me one too," she said, and strode out the door as the two girls and the chauffeur watched her. He walked discreetly outside and waited for her, as Sharon shrugged, hoping she *would* get a single. She looked like a real beast to live with. And

Hiroko had no idea what to make of her. They were both part of a mysterious new breed to Hiroko.

Anne Spencer came back twenty minutes later, looking anything but pleased, and she gave curt instructions to the chauffeur to open her bag and leave it just outside the closet. She had thought about bringing the maid with her to unpack for her, but she had decided it was better not to. She had wanted her parents to come with her too, but they were in New York, visiting her sister, who had just had her first baby.

She took off her hat and tossed it on a chair, and then glanced at the mirror where Sharon had put up her photographs of movie stars, and it was obvious that she didn't like them. "Whose are those?" She looked accusingly at Hiroko, still unable to believe that they were forcing her to share a room with some gardener's daughter. She had had plenty to say about that, when she'd gone downstairs, but the woman in charge said she would have to discuss it with the dean of housing on Monday, and for the moment she'd just have to make do with her existing roommates. Anne was outraged. "Are those yours?" Her tone told them everything she thought of her Japanese roommate.

"They're mine," Sharon said proudly. "My father's a producer." Anne only raised an eyebrow. As far as she and her family were concerned, show business people were no better than Orientals. With all the girls she knew who were coming here, she had drawn two complete duds as roommates, and she couldn't believe it.

She dismissed the chauffeur eventually, and unpacked her suitcase in silence, as Hiroko tried not to disturb either of them, and sat down at the desk to write a letter. But it was easy to feel the tension in the room, and the lack of harmony between the roommates. Sharon was at least pleasant to her, but after a cursory attempt at impressing her, she moved on to other rooms, to meet other girls and tell them about her father, the producer. Anne would have said something in total disgust once she left, except that, as far as she was concerned, Hiroko was even worse, and not worth wasting time with in conversation.

"Dearest Mama, Papa, and Yuji, I like it very much here," she wrote in the elegant characters she'd been taught in Japan as a child. "St. Andrew's is very beautiful, and I have two very nice roommates." She knew it was what they wanted to hear, and it would have been impossible to explain the exact tone of Anne's voice, or the nature of her prejudice against Hiroko. It was something Hiroko had never encountered before, but she sensed that even Sharon was not pleased to have a Japanese roommate. It was something she wanted to discuss with Reiko or Tak, but she would never have worried her parents. "One of them is from Los Angeles," she went on. "Her father works in Hollywood, and the other is very beautiful. Her name is Anne, and she is from San Francisco." And as she labored on, Anne glanced at her in disgust, and slammed the door on the way to dinner.

And Anne's attempts to change rooms the next day proved fruitless. The administration was sorry to hear that she didn't like her room, and of course they were well aware of her family's donations, and that her mother had graduated from St. Andrew's in 1917, but they simply didn't have another room to give her. She had insisted, to no avail, that she had been promised a private room, without roommates. After she'd been told she would not be moved, she stormed back to the dorm, and was pacing the room furiously when Hiroko came into the room to get a sweater.

She was always cold in Western clothes, and they always made her feel so naked.

"What do you want?" Anne Spencer snapped at her, still furious that they had refused to move her.

"Nothing, Anne-san," she apologized, bowing before she thought of stopping herself. "I am very sorry if I disturbed you."

"I just can't believe that they'd put us in the same room." Anne stood glaring at her, unaware of how rude she was, or that she had no right to speak that way to Hiroko. She could be very charming when she wanted to be, but she didn't think Hiroko was worth it. "What are you doing in this school?" she asked, sitting down on her bed in total frustration.

"I came here from Japan because my father wished it," Hiroko said simply, still unclear as to why Anne was so angry that they were roommates.

"So did I, but I don't think he had any idea who I'd be going to school with," she said meanly. She was a pretty girl, but she was spoiled, and she had all the prejudices of her class, against all Orientals. In her mind, "Japs" were all servants, and far beneath her.

To Hiroko, this was something new, and she didn't completely understand it. But that day she had felt the same cool reception from other girls at school, and no one seemed anxious to include her. Even Sharon, who had been effusive to her at first, didn't go to meals with her, or offer to sit next to her, although they were in many of the same classes. Unlike Anne, she was friendly to her in their room, but beyond that, she always acted as though she didn't know her. Anne was truer to her feelings and never spoke to her at all, and in some ways her persistently chilly ways wounded Hiroko less than Sharon's hypocrisy, and sudden unpleasantness, when they were around others.

"I don't understand," she said sadly to her Aunt Reiko the next time she went to Palo Alto for the weekend. It was very puzzling. Everyone seemed to keep their distance from her, and Anne and her friends were outright rude to her, and looked right through her. "Why are they angry at me, Reiko-san? What have I done to them?" Tears filled her eyes as she asked, because she had no idea how to fix it. And Reiko sighed in dismay. She knew Hiroko would have had the same problem anywhere, but at least Stanford was bigger and less exclusive. St. Andrew's was a very small world to exist in, although it was a wonderful school, and Reiko knew that she'd get an excellent education. But she was wondering if Tak should write to Masao and suggest that Hiroko transfer to Stanford, or even to the University of California at Berkeley.

"It's about prejudice," Reiko said sadly. "It has nothing to do with your school. This is California. Things are different here. There are negative feelings about the Japanese. It's not easy to overcome. You can keep to your own kind," she said, hating what she was saying, and the fact that she even had to explain it. But the poor girl looked distraught, and she was completely undone by the rejection of her fellow students and roommates. "It'll stop eventually. If you're lucky, they'll get to know who you are, and forget their prejudice. They can't all be like that there." She looked at

Hiroko, and reached out to hug her. She looked like a child with a broken heart, and as Reiko looked at her, she reminded her of Tami.

"Why do they hate me so much, Reiko-san? Only because I am Japanese?" It was incredible, but Reiko nodded.

"Snobbism, racism, prejudice. It sounds as though the Spencer girl thinks she's too important to room with you, and the other one probably thinks the same thing and won't admit it. Are there any other foreign students there?" It would have been nice if there was another girl from Japan, but that was too much to hope for.

"One from England and one from France, but I don't know them. They're both juniors." It was going to be a long year, living with Anne Spencer and being shunned by the others.

"Have you said anything to anyone? Maybe you should tell one of your advisors."

"I am afraid it will only make them more angry. Perhaps it is my . . ." She looked for the right word, and then settled for the next best one. "Perhaps it is my responsibility that they do not like me." She meant *fault*, but Reiko knew better than that, and thought it unlikely. She had run into the same thing when she'd gone to school in Fresno, and times didn't seem to have changed much. As long as they were in a large Japanese community, they were comfortable and safe, but when one moved into other worlds, there were always people who were threatened by it. It was remarkable to realize that despite all the changes around the world, and modern developments, it was still against the law for a Japanese to marry a Caucasian in

California. But it was all a little too insidious to explain to an eighteen-year-old girl from Kyoto.

"It's their loss, Hiroko. You'll make friends there eventually. Just be patient. And try to stay away from the ones you know don't like you." It was what she had told Sally and Ken. They both went to schools where there were Caucasians as well as Japanese, and now and then each of them had encountered prejudice among their peers, or friends' parents, or their teachers. It always hurt Reiko terribly when she heard about it. And in some ways it seemed simpler to her when her children had Japanese friends, especially now that they were older, and romance had entered the picture. What Reiko didn't know was that the boy down the street that Sally was so enamored with was half Irish and half Polish. "You can come home every weekend if you want to," she said to Hiroko. But it was a sad lesson for her to learn, and Hiroko insisted that she had to face it with *gambare,* to endure quietly and bravely. She had promised to persevere no matter how unfriendly the girls were at St. Andrew's. But despite Hiroko's determination, Reiko was still upset about it when she told Tak that evening after dinner.

"She could have run into the same thing at Stanford," he said honestly, when Reiko insisted that he write to Masao and ask him to let her transfer. "The problem is by no means exclusive to St. Andrew's, Rei. After all, this is California."

"And that makes it all right?" She was furious that he was so willing to accept it.

"That makes it what is. They want to keep us segregated from them. They want to believe we're different. And all the differences in our culture, all the little traditions, all the things that our parents and grandparents cling to, are what scare them. It's all part of what makes us different." It was old news to him, but he was sorry for Hiroko anyway. She was a sweet girl and their reaction had come as a shock to her. But Takeo knew, as Reiko did, that there was nothing they could do to change it. "She hasn't been wearing her kimonos at school, has she?" he asked. That certainly wouldn't help her be accepted, but even in Western clothes, she was so totally Japanese, and so obviously unlike the other students.

"I doubt it. I think she left them all here."

"Good. Keep it that way." But he promised to talk to her, and he did the next day. But he had no more advice to offer her than Reiko had. She would simply have to live with their prejudice, and try to find some friends who didn't share those views. She would meet girls in time who felt differently, and in the meantime, she was always welcome in Palo Alto.

But it was easy to see that the problem hadn't improved when, a month later, she was still coming home to them every weekend. Every Friday afternoon she took the train back to them, just as every Friday the chauffeur with the limousine came to pick up Anne Spencer. In the past three weeks she had spoken to Hiroko exactly once, and only then to tell her to move her suitcase.

"That's outrageous," Peter said, when Tak explained it to him.

"It's not the school. It's just the girls, and probably no more than a handful at that, but I guess there are enough of them to make her life miserable, and she's so shy, I don't think she knows how to handle it. She's getting great grades, but she can't be having much fun. And she's here every weekend. Not that we mind, of course. I'm just sorry for her." But Hiroko was happy coming home to them every weekend. She was completely at ease with them now. She played with Tami for hours, knew all of Ken's friends, and Sally had even confided in her about her sixteen-year-old boyfriend. Hiroko was worried about her. She thought the boy was too old, she was concerned because he wasn't Japanese, and the situation was far too clandestine, but for the moment she had promised not to tell her Aunt Reiko.

"Do you think Hiroko will transfer?" Peter inquired. He hadn't seen her since she'd left for school. On Sundays, when he often dined with them, Hiroko had already left to go back to St. Andrew's. So they kept missing each other until late October.

And then one Saturday afternoon he ran into her at the dry cleaners in Palo Alto. Ken had taught her how to drive the station wagon, and she was out doing errands for Reiko. She was staggering under a load of their clothes, wearing a lavender kimono and wooden geta. He knew instantly who it was, although he could scarcely see her concealed behind the load of clothes.

"Hiroko?" he asked. As she peeked around and looked at him, a small smile escaped her.

"Here, let me help you." He took the clothes from her, in his own arms, and smiled as she bowed to him. She was happy to see him. And this time, unlike the other times they'd met, she looked him in the eye for several moments. She had grown braver at St. Andrew's, and Peter couldn't help wondering if things had improved for her since the last time he'd talked to Takeo about her.

"How are you?" he asked very gently as they walked to her car, and he helped her put the clothes in the back of the wagon. He was surprised himself at what he felt seeing her. Suddenly all he wanted to do was sit and talk to her, and admire the way she looked in the pale lavender kimono. "How's school?" he asked, as he looked at her, and saw a look of sadness cross her eyes, and he thought he saw a shimmer of tears there.

"It is very well. How are you, Peter-san?" she asked softly.

"Busy. We've got midterms." She'd been preparing for them too, and as he looked down at her, he found himself wishing that she was one of his students. He wanted to ask how her problems with the other students were, but he didn't want to upset her, or admit that Takeo had told him. "I hear you've been home a lot on weekends. But I seem to miss you every Sunday." She smiled and looked down again. It still embarrassed her to talk to him, especially alone, but she liked being with him. In spite of the differences in their ages, he was easy and comfortable to talk to. "Do you like St. Andrew's?" he inquired, trying to draw out the conversation, and she hesitated for a moment before she answered.

"Perhaps I will like it better soon," she said honestly. In truth, she hated going back every Sunday. She had only seven and a half more months now, and she was counting every moment.

"That doesn't sound very encouraging," he said, watching her. He wished he could take her somewhere, and really talk to her, or walk through the woods or on the campus. He didn't know why, but he would have liked to be alone with her. And as he watched her, he remembered the look in Tak's eyes as he had reminded Peter of how young she was, how innocent, and how unlike American girls. Hiroko was no ordinary young girl, she was from a totally different world from his, and she was very special.

"It is very difficult to be from another place," she said sadly. "I did not know that in California, it would be like this." She had expected to like school, and to make friends. She hadn't expected to be an outcast.

"I felt that way in Japan," he said gently, with eyes that reached out to hers with unspoken compassion. "The way I looked, the way I dressed, the way I moved, everything set me apart. I felt completely out of place the whole time I was there, but I liked it anyway. It was so beautiful, and so fascinating, after a while I didn't mind being different." He smiled at the memories he still cherished. "Sometimes children followed me. They just looked up and stared at me. . . . I gave them candy, and they loved it. And I took lots of pictures." She smiled, remembering other foreigners she'd seen with small armies of children following them. Perhaps if her parents had ever let her, she might have done it as well, but of course they never had.

"I did not know, Peter-san, that I would be one of those people . . . someone odd to be stared at. At college, everyone finds me very strange. . . . It is very alone for me," she confessed with huge, dark eyes that spoke volumes of the loneliness she had felt ever since she'd left Kyoto.

"I'm sorry," he said sadly. He wanted to change things for her, to shield her from the pain, to help her sail home again. He couldn't bear the sorrow he saw in her eyes as he watched her. "Perhaps you're right," he said, not knowing what else to say. "Perhaps it will get better." But there would be no changing Anne, or Sharon, or the others. And Hiroko knew that.

"I am happy here," she said philosophically, "with Uncle Tak and Aunt Rei. They are very kind to me. . . . I am very fortunate to have them."

"They are very fortunate to have you too," he said kindly, and then regretfully, she bowed to him, and told him she had to get back to help Reiko. "I hope things get better at school soon," he encouraged her, wishing that she would be there on Sunday when he came for dinner. But maybe it was just as well she wouldn't. He felt something much too powerful between them each time he saw her. It still haunted him as she drove away; it was like an irresistible force pulling him toward her. He couldn't understand why or how it had happened. She was a young girl, she had come here to go to school. And he was a man, with his own life, his own ways, and a woman of his own kind to keep him involved and busy. What did he need with this child, this girl-woman with the velvet eyes whose face haunted him each time he thought of her? What could possibly ever come of his feelings?

He was annoyed with himself when he got into his car and drove away. It was time to stop it, before it began. It wasn't like Takeo falling in love with Reiko when she was a young student and he was a young professor. This was not 1922, he wasn't Takeo, and she wasn't Reiko. He was American, and she was Japanese.

He had a life and a job, and a girlfriend. And no matter how fiercely Peter was attracted to Hiroko, or how remarkable she was, or even if he fell in love with her one day, they had no future. He put his foot on the gas, and drove away, promising himself he'd forget her. There was no point even dreaming about her. So he wouldn't, he said to himself firmly, as his mind drifted back to the lavender kimono.

# Chapter 6

NOVEMBER WAS slightly easier for Hiroko. Sharon started having trouble in school, and Hiroko volunteered to help her with her studies. Sharon hesitated at first, but in the end she was grateful for Hiroko's help, and as they sat together for hours at night, poring over their work, Hiroko had the illusion of friendship.

Anne still made no bones to either of them about her feelings. She was still outraged to be rooming with Hiroko, and she was almost equally unhappy about Sharon. Show business people were not her kind, she had said in no uncertain terms to the dean of students, and neither were Orientals. They had her rooming with the trash of the school, as far as she was concerned, and after all the money her parents had donated, she honestly felt she deserved a lot better. She

felt personally affronted by them, and her parents had
even come to discuss it with the dean, and the head of
the housing committee. They had been assured that at
the first opportunity, Anne would be given a single
room, but there were simply none available at the moment, and it would have been unfair to the other girls
to make exceptions and heroic efforts for her. And
after all, they reminded the Spencers, as they had
Anne, that Hiroko was a lovely young woman, from a
respected family in Japan. And although the Spencers
conceded that perhaps she was a nice girl, they
pointed out that this was California, not Japan, and the
Japanese were not highly regarded. In fact, Charles
Spencer had assured them that there would be no
further donations to the school until Anne was moved.
But the administration only dug in their heels. They
did not wish to be blackmailed.

And to underline her unhappiness, Anne went
home two days early for the Thanksgiving holidays.
She was threatening to transfer to another school, and
the dean had told her to think it over before doing
anything hasty. And all of this because of poor little
Hiroko. She didn't tell anyone about the continuing
maelstrom. It had been humiliating enough when she
complained at first. And at least Sharon was civil to her
now. Ever since Hiroko had been doing more of her
work for her, Sharon had been a great deal nicer to
Hiroko. She still wasn't overly friendly publicly, but
she was always nice when they got back to the room,
and she even bought her a box of candy to thank her.
Hiroko was particularly good at physics and chemistry,
and she had an easy time with math too, and she was
always well prepared in Latin. Sharon was good in

none of those. The only subject she seemed to do well in was Spanish. But Hiroko didn't take it, so Sharon had very little to offer.

She was going to her father's to spend Thanksgiving in Palm Springs, and Anne had already said that they were flying to New York to be with her sister. She was going to miss a week of school, but as Hiroko stood at the window and watched her get into the limousine, she wasn't sorry. It would be a lot easier for her without Anne.

This time, because of the holiday, Ken drove down to pick Hiroko up at school, and she drove back with him to Palo Alto in high spirits. No one had said anything to her when she left. Even Sharon had forgotten to say good-bye to her, she was in such a hurry to catch the train to Los Angeles to meet her father. She had told Hiroko that Gable and Lombard might be spending Thanksgiving with them, but Hiroko wasn't at all sure she could believe her.

"So how's school?" Ken asked her honestly, and she glanced out the window before she answered, and then turned to look at him.

"Pretty lousy," she said in perfect slang, and he burst into laughter.

"Boy, is your English improving!"

She started laughing too, he always reminded her so much of her brother. "Yuji will be pleased. He speaks American slang very beautifully. I have many things to learn about it."

"Sounds like you're learning to me," Ken said with admiration, but he wasn't surprised to hear what she had said. He had heard his parents talk about her problems. He was sorry for her, she was still so shy, and it seemed unfair for the girls at school to be giving her a hard time. He couldn't even begin to imagine what it was like living with Anne Spencer.

They talked about Thanksgiving then, and their plans for the weekend. They both wanted to see *The Maltese Falcon* with Humphrey Bogart and Sydney Greenstreet, and he had promised to take Tami skating. Ken had also figured out who Sally was spending so much time with, and although he didn't completely approve, he had promised to double-date with her, if their parents would agree to let Sally go with them. She was, after all, only fourteen, and Ken and the other boy were two years older. And to complicate matters, Sally's beau was not Japanese, and Ken wasn't sure how his parents would feel about it.

"What about you? Have you met any boys yet?" He knew there were occasional dances at the school, with boys from U.C. Berkeley, but she had never said anything about going, and he didn't think she did. She was much too shy, and she seemed to have no interest whatsoever in dating.

"I have no time, Kenji-san," she said, calling him by his Japanese name. "I am too busy with my studies." And Sharon's. In the last week she had done all of Sharon's work for her too, so she wouldn't have to tackle it over Thanksgiving. It had kept Hiroko up past lights out every night, and she had sat in the bathroom with a flashlight to complete it.

"Don't you like boys?" he teased. She was almost old enough to be married. Some girls were married at her age, particularly if they didn't go to college.

"My mother says that when I go back to Japan, they will go to a go-between and find a husband for me." She said it without concern, as though she found it not only acceptable but of greater comfort, not to have to choose one's own husband, and her cousin stared at her in amazement.

"Are you serious? That's uncivilized! It's right out of the dark ages." He was horrified, and he couldn't believe she'd do that.

"My parents were married that way," she said with a smile, amused by his reaction. It didn't seem shocking to her at all. Her grandmother said it was better that way, and she believed her. She completely trusted her parents' judgment.

"So were my grandparents," he said as they drove along, "but my parents met each other and fell in love and got married."

"Perhaps they were very lucky. Perhaps in America it is different." Everything else was, so why not marriage? But she liked the old ways, and she preferred to let her parents find her husband when the time came.

"Would you really marry someone you'd never even met?" He was stunned by what she was describing. He had heard about it, but he couldn't conceive of someone wanting to do that now, and certainly not his cousin. She was gorgeous and she could have had any guy she wanted.

"I would meet him, Kenji-san. You meet him, and you decide if you would like him. My father met my mother." Her father also didn't believe that they should go to a go-between for her, but Hidemi had always told Hiroko that she would convince him.

"I think you're crazy," he said, shaking his head as they neared San Mateo.

"I am not crazy, Kenji-san. I do not eat peanut butter, which will close my mouth forever." He laughed at what she said. He knew how she hated it, and how horrified she had been the first time he gave her a taste of it. Later, she had said that she'd been frightened her mouth might never open. "You are crazy, Ken-san. You listen to crazy music." He loved the sound of the big bands, but he also loved jazz as well as boogie-woogie, and Sally was completely nuts over Frank Sinatra. Hiroko liked him too, but she still preferred to listen to Japanese music. And when she did, Ken always made fun of her, and Tam put her hands over her ears and howled. She said it was awful.

But it was always fun for Hiroko to go home to them. She was completely comfortable in their midst, and she was less shy now. She gave her Uncle Tak a warm hug when they arrived, and she went straight to the kitchen to help Reiko. Thanksgiving was the next day, but she was already busy making apple and mince pies, and doing some of the advance preparations. Sally had helped for a while, but after an hour of rolling dough, she had gone outside to meet some girlfriends.

"Hi, Hiroko, how's school?" Reiko asked as she looked up. Ken stood looking longingly into the refrigerator, and finally settled on a leftover lamb chop.

"She says it's 'pretty lousy,'" he answered for her. "I'd say our cousin's English is improving." All three of them laughed, and Tami came downstairs to show Hiroko a magazine ad for the new doll she wanted for Christmas.

She was planning to ask Santa Claus for it, and Reiko already had it hidden in a box in her closet.

"You'll have to be a very good girl," Reiko inspired her.

Ken laughed as he poured himself a glass of milk, and teased his little sister. "Looks like you can forget that one," he said blithely.

Tami glared at him, and Hiroko pulled her close to her and hugged her. It felt so good coming back to them, she loved being with them, and the warmth of their family. To her, they were real Americans, and wonderful people.

After dinner that night, Ken and Sally went out, but Hiroko decided to stay home with Tak and Reiko. They listened to the news for a while, and Tak was particularly interested in the talks between the United States and Japan, which had resulted in the termination of certain trade agreements between them. Relations between Japan and the United States had been deteriorating for a while, and the news from Europe was worse than ever.

"The world's in a hell of a state, Rei," he said quietly, deeply concerned about what he was hearing. Roosevelt was still promising to stay out of the war, but Takeo hadn't believed him in months, and he knew that there were people in Washington who were concerned about Japan eventually becoming a serious aggressor. It seemed unlikely to Tak, but anything was possible, given the state of the world at the moment. Only the week before, a British carrier had been sunk by an Italian torpedo. "I'm really getting worried about what's going on with Japan, and the war in Europe. And the poor Brits can't hold on forever. It's amazing they've held on this long." Reiko nodded, concerned about the same things, although politics always seemed more remote to her than they did to Takeo. But political science was his business. It was his job to analyze what was happening in the world, and it just wasn't very encouraging at the moment.

But world politics were forgotten the next day, when they celebrated two holidays in one: Thanksgiving, and the Japanese holiday Kinro Kansha-no-Hi, which fell on the same day that year. In Japan, it was the opportunity to give thanks for a successful harvest.

"So I guess this year we're doubly thankful," Takeo said lightheartedly as he made a toast, and began to carve the turkey. "Triply thankful," he added, looking down the table. "We have Hiroko to be grateful for too. A wonderful new addition to our family." He raised his glass again, and Peter Jenkins joined him. He was spending Thanksgiving with them, as he did every year, and he was relieved that Carole was spending the long weekend with her family in Milwaukee. He liked coming to the Tanakas' by himself, especially when he knew he'd see Hiroko. But in spite of that, he had made a careful effort to sit at the opposite end of the table from Hiroko. She was down at the other end, between Ken and Tami. He hadn't seen her in a month, but the last time he had seen her had unnerved him. It seemed that each time they met, something about her haunted him, and he found himself thinking about her for days afterwards. And this time, he had promised himself not to let that happen. She was just a very young girl, and it was ridiculous to be attracted to her. He decided it was probably her timidity that appealed to him, and the romance and mystery of her kimono. And just acknowledging that seemed to diffuse it.

She was wearing a bright red kimono that afternoon, with autumn leaves scattered over it. It was a spectacular piece, with a heavy red brocade obi, and she moved about gracefully in her geta and tabi. She looked remarkably beautiful, and her dark hair shone as it hung down her back. She seemed completely unaware of how she looked as she helped Reiko serve dinner. The turkey and stuffing were delicious, and the pies Reiko had made were exceptionally good too. Even Peter agreed that it was the best Thanksgiving dinner she'd ever made, and she smiled at Hiroko and said it was because she'd had so much help this year; Hiroko lowered her eyes in embarrassment, and then smiled at them all a moment later.

In spite of her natural shyness, she seemed completely at ease with them, and she even glanced at Peter several times, and initiated conversations with him when she wasn't interrupted by Tami. It made Peter's plan to ignore her even more difficult, and by the end of the afternoon he looked more than a little distracted. He wanted so desperately to be oblivious to her, to be completely unaware of how she moved and looked, or of how her hand felt next to his when she took his plate, or her hair as it brushed his cheek when she moved past him too quickly. He almost couldn't bear looking at her, just seeing her stand next to him made him want to hold her. He was actually sorry he had come to dinner this year. Just seeing her so close, with all her graceful gentleness, was torture.

Even Tak could see what was happening, and he actually felt sorry for him. It was obvious that he was completely smitten with Hiroko.

Only she was unaware of the effect she had on

him. She moved around him like a summer breeze, barely touching him and yet turning him from hot to cold and back again, totally beyond his control, and almost beyond bearing.

"May I get you something else, Peter-san?" she asked him carefully. He looked very serious and disturbed that afternoon, and she wasn't sure why. She almost wondered if something unpleasant had happened with his girlfriend. But the only thing that had happened was that he was falling in love with Hiroko, and he had no idea what to do about it. She was too young, all wrong, and totally inaccessible to him, but his heart seemed not to know what his head did.

"No . . . thank you, Hiroko-san . . . I'm fine. . . ." But later he let Reiko get him a cup of coffee, and Hiroko saw the look in his eyes and misinterpreted everything he was feeling. She thought he was angry at her, and instead he was in agony, having Hiroko stand so close to him, or lean down, as he smelled the delicate perfume she wore whenever she brushed past him. He felt sure that at any moment it might drive him crazy.

After she helped Reiko clear the dishes away, Hiroko looked up at her sadly.

"Is something wrong?" Reiko asked. Her face was so easy to read, and so open in all its emotions.

"I have offended Peter-san, he is very angry at me, Aunt Rei."

"I don't think he's angry," Reiko said quietly. She had seen the troubled look in his eyes too, but she understood it better than Hiroko. "*Confused* might be a better word." She wasn't sure how much she should say. It was really up to Peter. And in some ways Reiko didn't want to see what was happening. It was easier not to.

"Confused?" Hiroko obviously didn't understand her.

"I think he has a lot on his mind," Reiko said kindly.

Hiroko nodded then, not only reassured, but relieved that Reiko did not appear to know of any unpardonable offense that she had committed against Peter.

Hiroko brought fresh coffee to the study, where Tak and Peter were discussing the British and the Germans. She had brought a small plate of cookies as well, and Peter glanced at her unhappily as she served them. After offering the cookies to both men, she set the plate down and bowed to each of them, as Peter tried to steel himself and listen to what Tak was saying.

But the older man looked at him wisely once she left. Better than Peter, he realized it was hopeless. "You didn't hear a word I said, did you?"

"Yes, I did. I was just thinking it over," he lied, and Tak smiled gently at him. In his own way, Peter was a child too, and he was so in love with Hiroko he couldn't see straight. Tak hadn't wanted this to happen, and yet he recognized that there were times when plans and warnings meant nothing. There were times when what happens was dictated by destiny, and not one's cousins or parents.

"I said that Churchill and Hitler were getting married on Saturday and were you going to the wedding?" Peter grinned sheepishly. Tak had got him.

"Okay, so I'm half out of my mind. Now what?" he asked miserably, all his pain and attempted restraint showing. He had battled his feelings valiantly, but to no avail, and they both knew it, as Peter sat there and stared anxiously at Takeo. Peter didn't want to anger him, or insult him, or create a difficult family situation, and yet in light of his feelings for Hiroko, he felt helpless.

"Have you said anything to her?" Takeo asked cautiously. Somehow he had the impression that Hiroko had no idea what was happening. She seemed oblivious to everything Peter was feeling.

"I didn't want to frighten her," Peter admitted. "I don't know what to say to her. It's not fair, Tak. I have no right to do this." Peter knew it only too well and had reminded himself of it a thousand times since he met her.

"I suppose you've tried to ignore it," Tak said hopefully, and Peter nodded.

"I've done everything I could except be downright rude to her. I've even avoided coming here at times when I knew she'd be here for the weekend. But it doesn't seem to change anything. Every time I see her, it gets worse . . . or better." He smiled ruefully. "I guess that's the trouble." Tak looked at him sympathetically. It was easy to see everything he felt. He was obviously head over heels in love with Hiroko. "I don't suppose your cousin, her father, would be pleased," Peter said, almost in a whisper. Tak watched him, wishing he had a simple answer, and that it were twenty years earlier, and things were as simple for them as they had been for him and Reiko. But the world was a more complicated place now, and his cousin in Japan had entrusted him with his only daughter.

"I don't suppose he would be," Takeo answered honestly. "But on the other hand, he is a very wise, unusually modern man for a Japanese. In an odd way, I think he'd like you. That's not to say that I'm approving of this," he was quick to add, but in all honesty, he couldn't condemn him either. He liked Peter too much, and respected him deeply. He was intelligent, and had integrity, and he was honorable in all the ways that would have mattered to Masao. But he also wasn't Japanese, and he was almost ten years older than Hiroko. There was no easy solution, to put it mildly.

"Are you going to say anything to Hiroko?" Takeo asked, looking worried.

"I don't know yet. She'd probably be horrified and never speak to me again. I don't think she's ready for this, Tak. I'm not sure I am either." The thought of reaching out to her terrified him. What if she was furious, and never saw him again? He knew he couldn't bear it. "Not to mention Carole. I have some things to work out there. I've been meaning to for a while, we've kind of been going our own ways. I was actually relieved when she told me she was spending Thanksgiving in Milwaukee."

"So now what?" Takeo asked, not condemning him for what he felt, or forbidding him to pursue the matter further, although he thought he probably should have. But more than anything, he was worried about both of them, and what might lie ahead for them in the future.

"I just don't know, Tak. I'm too scared to do anything." But he looked relieved as he watched his friend's eyes. He saw compassion there and not anger. He had been desperately afraid of Tak's reaction.

"I never thought you were a coward," Takeo said calmly. It was not a flag of his approval, but it was a sign that he would not stop Peter from moving forward, and Peter felt relief flood over him as he listened. "I think you ought to tread carefully, though, and think seriously about what you're doing. She's not someone to take lightly, and whatever you do now could affect both your lives forever." But his respect for the younger man kept him from forbidding it completely.

"I know," Peter said solemnly. "That's just what I've been telling myself since this summer."

"I know you won't do anything to hurt her," Takeo said pointedly, and Peter nodded. They talked around the subject then for a while, and finally went back to politics briefly, for some relief, before going back to the living room to join the others. Hiroko barely glanced at him, and had no inkling of what the two men had been discussing. She would have been utterly shocked if they had told her, which of course they didn't. They looked quiet and relaxed as they sat down, and listened to the debate as to whether or not the young people wanted to go to the movies.

In the end, Ken and Sally went to see *The Wolf Man*, with Lon Chaney, Jr. They wanted Hiroko to go with them too, but she said she was too tired. She had helped Reiko all afternoon, and she was happy to stay home and work on her needlepoint, and chat with Peter. She was making half a dozen tiny rugs for Tami's dollhouse, and she wanted to finish them before Christmas. And as soon as Tami went to bed, Hiroko took them out and began working on them, just as Tak followed Reiko back to the kitchen. She said she was going to make more coffee, and Takeo went with her to keep her company, and there was something he wanted to tell her. He was concerned about his conversation with Peter, and yet he was sympathetic to him too, and he wanted to know what Reiko thought about it. She was a very wise woman. And she was far from surprised as they talked in hushed tones over the coffee she was making. But what worried Tak was that he felt he had tacitly given Peter permission to pursue Hiroko, and he didn't think he should have.

"It's not up to you, Tak," Reiko said quietly, with loving eyes as she looked up at her husband. "It's up to them," she said softly, and he nodded, wondering if he had failed Masao by not protecting Hiroko from Peter. Yet he knew he couldn't.

And in the living room, Peter watched Hiroko's careful stitching. They sat in silence for a little while, and then Hiroko startled him with her next question.

"Have I offended you, Peter-san?" In spite of Reiko's reassurances, it had troubled her all evening.

"No, Hiroko, you could never offend me," he said as he sat down next to her, and felt his whole body shiver with her nearness. She was completely unaware of what she did to him, and of all that he had felt for her since the day he met her. "You haven't done anything. It is I . . . I have been very foolish." He didn't know what to say to her. He just sat and looked at her, wondering if she would ever forgive him.

"I cannot come here anymore," he said, and she looked horrified. In her mind, he was part of the family, and she would have missed him terribly if he hadn't been there. But she had felt it too. She had no idea what he had been experiencing, but each time she was near him, she felt a tremor. And she lowered her eyes as she listened to him, knowing that her cousins would be very angry with her for chasing away their closest friend, and Tak's assistant.

"I have behaved very badly, Peter-san," she said without looking up at him. "I have been too forward with you, it is only," she said softly, looking up at him, "it is only that I think of you as a cousin." But he only shook his head as he listened.

"You have done nothing wrong, Hiroko . . . nothing. . . . The only trouble is, I do not think of you as a cousin."

"I am deeply sorry," she said, her head bowed so low, he couldn't see her face. "I have been badly behaved, and presumed much. I have been rude to you." She looked up at him with tears on her face, and he wanted to cry himself when he saw her. "Forgive me—"

"Oh, Hiroko, you little fool." He smiled, and pulled her close to him. It was like holding butterfly wings, she seemed so fragile. "You haven't been rude to me, or 'presumed' anything. . . . I don't think of you as a cousin," he said breathlessly, wondering if he could even say the words to her, and yet knowing he had to. "I think of you as someone much, much more important. . . . Perhaps it's wrong of me," he went on anxiously. "I . . . have tried to stop myself, but, Hiroko, each time I see you . . . each time . . ." He faltered, and without saying another word he pulled her closer and kissed her. Her lips were like silk on his, and he couldn't believe how exquisite it felt to be holding her. He wanted to take her in his arms and run away with her, to a place where they both would be safe forever. "I may be crazy," he said when he finally pulled away from her, drunk on the heady wine of her kisses. She had kissed him too. She had never kissed anyone before, but she had felt all the same things he did. "I may be crazy," he said again in a whisper in Reiko's living room, "but I love you. . . ." He kissed her again, and completely forgot where they were as she kissed him.

"You are crazy, Peter-san," she said finally. "We cannot do this."

"I know that," he said unhappily. "I've tortured myself. I've promised myself I wouldn't come here anymore, but each time I do, I realize again what I feel for you. How can that be so wrong? Tell me that." But they both knew it was, and he would have been willing to die before he hurt her. "I want you near me all the time. I want to take care of you. . . . I'll go back to Japan with you, if I have to."

"Oh, Peter," she said, overwhelmed by what he was saying. She had no idea what her father would say. She couldn't imagine him approving of this, and yet all her life he had told her to be modern. And falling in love with an American was certainly very modern. She could only begin to imagine what her mother would say. She would be appalled at Hiroko's behavior. And even her cousins would be shocked, but Peter read her mind as he took her hand in his and kissed it.

"I think Tak saw this coming almost before I did. I told him how I felt earlier this evening," he said honestly.

"Was he very angry?" she asked, looking worried and panicked that Takeo might tell her father.

"Not angry, concerned. I can't blame him. But he didn't seem surprised. I think he's known for a while. At first I think he compared you to Reiko. She was a student when they met, and he was a young professor, and he was older than she was too. But it's different for us, Hiroko. I think you know that," he said sadly. She had already had a taste, at school, of how people reacted to the Japanese, let alone Japanese women involved with Caucasians. In the state of California, they wouldn't even have been allowed to get married. They would have had to go to another state, not that they were planning a wedding. But it was a measure of how hostile other people's sentiments might be to their innocent romance. "I don't want you to get hurt, Hiroko, least of all by anything I do. That's the last thing I want for you," he said, kissing her again, and feeling his head reel as he did it. No woman had ever made him feel as she did, and she was just a wisp of a girl, and her kisses were like whispers, they were so timid. But as they kissed, it was impossible not to think of the challenges they were facing. What would they do now? Or could they simply do what anyone else did, and let chance take them where it would, and enjoy the scenery while they got there? They had no idea where they were going yet, but what they both felt was so powerful, it swept them away on a tide of tenderness and longing.

"We must think about this very seriously, Peter-san," Hiroko said, looking older and wiser than he felt at the moment. Peter felt like a child in her arms, and at the same time like a man filled with passion. He would have married her at that moment if he could have. "We must be very wise, Peter-san . . . and perhaps"—her eyes filled with tears as she said it—"perhaps we must be very strong, and give up what we want most. . . . We cannot hurt anyone, Peter-san. . . . I cannot do that," she said as tears rolled down her cheeks slowly, but as he held her close again, she knew how much she loved him.

"Are you two all right in there?" Takeo called from the kitchen, with an edge of worry in his voice. And neither of them were sure what to answer. Peter answered him and said they were fine, and Reiko said she'd be out with the coffee in a minute. She was still talking to Tak about them in the kitchen. Reiko thought they ought to let them be young and follow their feelings. And Tak was trying to tell himself it was harmless, but he wasn't convinced yet.

"Will you go for a walk with me tomorrow afternoon?" Peter asked nervously. "Perhaps we can talk about this some more. . . . Maybe we could even go to a movie." Hiroko looked at him, unable to believe what was happening to them, and she nodded. She couldn't even imagine going to a movie with him, and being alone with him frightened her. Yet, although she had never been alone with any man, except her father in Japan, she knew she could trust Peter Jenkins.

Reiko arrived with the coffee then, finally. The foursome talked for a while about Christmas plans, and the university, and a little while later, Peter left them. He thanked Reiko for another wonderful Thanksgiving. This one had been a special year for him. He knew that something had happened there that would change his life forever.

Hiroko bowed low to him, as she always did, but she seemed even more solemn this time. He had already promised to come the next afternoon to walk with her. There was suddenly so much to say and think about. And yet she was silent after he left. She said nothing to either of her cousins once Peter was gone. She simply walked upstairs, thinking of him, as they watched her. She had no idea what would happen to them now, and neither did Peter as he drove home, but they both knew that without even planning to, they had left safe shores, and set sail on an extraordinary journey.

# *Chapter 7*

$P$ ETER CAME to pick her up the following afternoon, and as it turned out, no one else was home. Hiroko was wearing a dark green kimono, which was a serious color for her, but she was in a serious mood as they walked along slowly together. Peter explained again how he felt about her, and when he had realized for the first time that he loved her. She had known it too. She had tried not to, and she was still a little taken aback by her own emotions, and the fact that he felt the same way toward her. But each time she had seen him, she had been aware of an irresistible pull in his direction. And now they had both given in to irrevocable forces.

"What are we going to do, Peter-san?" she asked him then, looking deeply troubled. She didn't want to hurt anyone, or betray her ancestry. She had not come to America to disgrace her family, or damage their honor. Yet a part of her told her that she had come here to find him, and she could no longer turn away from what had happened.

"We have to be very sensible, Hiroko-san. And very wise. You will be here until July. Many things can happen between now and then. Perhaps I can come to Japan to see your father next summer." The fact that he scarcely knew her was the one thing that didn't trouble her at all. She would have been prepared to marry a man found by a go-between, and she would have known him even less than she knew Peter Jenkins. The problem they shared was that he was not Japanese, and that was potentially an insurmountable one. "What do you think your father will say?" he asked, looking anxious.

"I don't know, Peter-san," she said honestly. "It will be a great shock to him. Perhaps Uncle Takeo can speak to him also next summer." And then she looked at him with a womanly smile that surprised him. "And until then?"

"We see where life takes us. Perhaps by next summer you won't want to see me again." He smiled, but the way they both felt, it seemed unlikely.

He had driven her to a small lake, where they'd been walking, and they sat on a bench for a while and kissed. He took her breath away, and she had never known anything so exciting.

"I love you," he whispered into her hair, completely inebriated by her. She was the most wonderful woman he'd ever met, the best thing that had ever happened to him. And suddenly, he didn't even want to tell her cousins what had happened between them. Even sharing it with Tak and Reiko might spoil it.

But on the way home, they discussed whether or not to tell her cousins about all their plans and their feelings. In the end, they decided to wait for a while, to see what happened, and to keep the importance of it to themselves, at least for the moment. There was something especially delicious about not sharing it yet, and keeping their precious secret. Takeo already knew how Peter felt; but what no one knew, and Peter cherished, was how Hiroko felt about him.

"I think they know anyway," Peter said honestly, smiling down at her, he was so much taller. "But your little cousins would drive us crazy." Hiroko laughed at the thought, and then wondered what her own brother would say. He liked everything American, but it had never occurred to any of them that she would fall in love with one. It was the remotest thing on her mind when she had sailed on the *Nagoya Maru* from Kobe. And she knew they wouldn't have let her come, if they suspected for a moment that this would happen.

Peter left her at the corner, after the drive home, because they wanted to be discreet. He watched her walk the short distance to the house, and then started the car again, thinking about her every moment. He couldn't help thinking about Tak too, and prayed that he would be able to accept what had happened. He and Hiroko had been pulled toward each other irresistibly. They had no desire to hurt anyone, or break any rules, or defy her family. They just wanted to be together, and hoped that eventually everyone would come to understand it. But for the moment, it was going to be awkward, in more areas than one. He still had to talk to Carole and break off their affair. He knew she wouldn't be heartbroken, but she wasn't going to be happy either. And despite all his good intentions to go into the city the next day after work, he went to see Hiroko instead, and hung around in the afternoon, until Reiko invited him to dinner. She knew what was happening, but she didn't say anything. In a way, the visible pull between them was very touching. Peter was so solicitous of her, and Hiroko was so respectful of him. She seemed to be even more attentive to him these days, and bowing even lower.

But as he watched them, Takeo almost wished he didn't have to see it. It wasn't that he disapproved, but it put him in such an awkward position with his cousin Masao. How was he ever going to explain to him that Hiroko had fallen in love with Tak's assistant? And yet he couldn't help smiling as he watched them. They were so young and so vulnerable. It made Tak's heart ache just to watch them together.

After dinner that night, they all went to the movies, and Takeo invited Peter to go with them. And Tak smiled to himself at the look of complicity between Hiroko and Peter. They thought no one could possibly see what they felt, and Peter thought they were very smooth, which made Takeo turn away and hide his laughter. There was nothing secret about what the two young people were experiencing. Anyone who met them would have seen it. They saw *Suspicion*, with Cary Grant and Joan Fontaine, and all of them loved it, and they went back to the house for hot chocolate, and Peter finally had to tear himself away from her at midnight. Their eyes met and held for a long moment as he left them. She was going back to school the next day, and when they left the movie, Peter had said he would call her at school. Ken was going to drive her back, as he always did, or she might take the train, but neither of them thought it was wise for Peter to do it.

The next day, when she left in her black skirt and white sweater set, her Aunt Reiko looked at her, and a knowing, womanly look passed between them.

"Don't do anything foolish, little one," Reiko said to her, holding her close for a moment, as she would her daughter. "It's easy to get carried away," she warned, and Hiroko nodded. She didn't know much about those things, but her mother had warned her a long time ago to stay away from men. And even kissing Peter as she did, she could see how something terrible could happen.

"I won't dishonor you, Reiko-san," she said, holding her close, and missing her mother.

"Take good care of yourself," Reiko said, and Hiroko knew what she meant. She didn't want her to be foolish.

"I will be back soon, Aunt Rei." She was going to stay at school for the next few weekends, because they had exams, and then she would be off for three weeks over Christmas. She was looking forward to it, especially now. And with his position at the university, Peter would be off at the same time she was.

She was quiet on the drive back to school, and Ken assumed that she was just unhappy to go back there. "It won't be so bad," he tried to encourage her. "You've only got a couple of weeks till Christmas vacation." She could hardly wait, and she smiled just thinking about it. He took her bag into the lobby of the dorm for her, and then he drove back to the house in Palo Alto.

She went upstairs to her room, and Sharon was already there. She looked depressed, and said she'd had a rotten Thanksgiving in Palm Springs with her father. She didn't tell Hiroko, but he'd been drunk for four days, and had a new girlfriend. Sharon hated being with him when he was like that, but now she hated coming back to school more. She'd been getting abysmal grades, and she hated being at the mercy of Hiroko to do her homework. It made her feel so inadequate, and she was tired of school anyway. She was thinking of dropping out at the end of the semester, and trying to become an actress.

"You had a bad holiday, Sharon-san?" Hiroko asked sympathetically, and the redhead shrugged. She was wearing pants and a sweater, and everyone told her she looked just like Katharine Hepburn.

"I guess," she said as she lit a cigarette. They were strictly forbidden to smoke anywhere on campus, but she didn't care. Getting kicked out of school would be a whole lot simpler.

"You must not do that," Hiroko warned. You could smell the smoke easily, and they would both get in trouble.

And half an hour later, when another girl walked in to talk to Sharon and saw the butts, she went to the monitor and told them that the Japanese girl in Sharon's room had been smoking. They didn't question Hiroko about it until the following afternoon, and she didn't want to get Sharon into trouble. They questioned Sharon too, and she didn't confess or tell them it wasn't Hiroko. There was nothing Hiroko felt she could do except take the blame herself, which seemed the honorable thing to do, and she sat in her room and cried afterward at the disgrace of being on probation.

Peter called her that night, and he was horrified at what she told him. "Tell them the truth, for heaven's sake. Don't take that on yourself. Why should you be on probation?"

"But then they will hate me more, Peter-san," she whispered into the phone, feeling as though she had failed everyone, and deeply unhappy. He was furious at what the other girl had done, reporting her, and even more so at Sharon for letting Hiroko take the blame, and not confessing.

"What kind of spoiled brats are they?" He had hit the nail on the head, and he was sorrier than ever that she wasn't at Stanford.

He volunteered to come to see her the following week if she didn't come home to Palo Alto again, but she thought he shouldn't. If he visited her, it was sure to create a stir on campus, and that was the last thing she wanted. So instead, he promised to call her.

And Anne Spencer came back at the end of that week, in time for exams, and she had nothing to say to either of them, neither Sharon nor Hiroko.

Sharon stayed out after curfew the next day, and came back drunk and got into a fight with the monitors, so she wound up on probation anyway, in spite of Hiroko's attempt to save her over the cigarette incident on Monday. And she didn't prepare for her history exam because of it, and she complained bitterly to Hiroko that she had flunked it.

But Anne paid attention to none of it. She didn't want to stoop to listening to their problems and the gossip about them. She had heard about the incident with the cigarettes, and refused to get involved. If they wanted to smoke and get on probation, it was their problem, not hers. She knew Sharon smoked, but she was surprised to hear that Hiroko had joined her.

As always, she kept away from them, studied with her friends, got straight A's, and did all her homework. She had plenty of friends, and lately she had been sleeping in their dorm rooms with them. She went to great lengths to avoid sleeping in the same room with Sharon and Hiroko. And the monitors who found her in other dorms knew why she was staying there, and they always closed their eyes to it and said nothing.

It was a long week for Hiroko after the excitement of the holiday, and on Friday night, she was sorry she hadn't gone to Palo Alto. She had spoken to Peter again, and she had been thinking constantly about everything he had said over Thanksgiving. She still couldn't believe all that he had said to her, or that she had kissed him. And she thought about him all weekend at school, when she wrote her parents a letter. She thought about mentioning him, but then she decided that was ridiculous. It would only worry them, and there was nothing to say at the moment. It would be so difficult to explain it to them anyway, she didn't understand it herself yet. And thousands of miles away, they would be even more bemused, so instead she only told them about Thanksgiving with the Tanakas.

She went to bed early on Saturday. Anne was out, as usual, and Sharon was in another room, smoking cigarettes and sneaking gin with a girl that Hiroko knew but didn't like. Hiroko was just relieved that they didn't do it in her room. She was still on probation for the last time Sharon had been smoking.

On Sunday morning, Hiroko went to play tennis with three girls who had signed up. They were polite and pleasant to her, although one of the girls seemed to hesitate when she arrived. But after a few minutes, she didn't seem to have any objection to playing with Hiroko. It was often that way for her. People reacted to her at first, uncomfortable about how foreign she was, and the fact that she was Japanese, but often they would relax a little bit once they knew her. Some of them were simply unable to overcome their prejudice, particularly the girls from San Francisco. They were notorious for disliking Japanese, and for assuming that they came from uneducated backgrounds. In truth, Hiroko's family was more cultured, and far older, than most of theirs. Her father could trace his family back to the fourteenth century, and her mother even further, but they had no great wealth or aristocratic fortune, like the Spencers.

Hiroko and her partner won the doubles game, and the girls had lemonade in the cafeteria, and chatted amiably about the game. They told Hiroko they'd like to play with her again, and for the first time in three months she felt as though she'd made some friends, and she decided that maybe she'd just had bad luck with her roommates.

It was just after eleven o'clock when she went back to her room to change, and as she stepped out of the shower half an hour later, she could hear someone screaming. She thought there had been an accident, and without hesitating, she grabbed her dressing gown, tied it around herself without even taking the time to get dry, and hurried into the hallway. There were little clusters of girls gathered all along the hall, several people had radios on, and most of the girls were crying, particularly the girl three doors away, from Hawaii.

"What is happening?" Hiroko asked anxiously. She had no idea what had occurred, but everyone looked frightened and frantic, and someone on another floor was shouting down the stairs. Hiroko struggled to understand what they were saying. No one seemed to have heard her question.

"We've been bombed!" the voice said. "We've been bombed!" Someone else shouted, and unconsciously Hiroko glanced toward the window, but saw nothing. Another girl turned to her in tears and all she could say was, "They've bombed Pearl Harbor." She had no idea where that was, and neither did most of the girls, but the girl from Hawaii was deathly pale. She knew exactly where it was.

"It's in Hawaii," she said in answer to someone's question. And then someone else explained further.

"The Japanese have just bombed Pearl Harbor." Hiroko felt her heart turn to stone as she listened, as someone else said, "It can't be."

"What if they come here?" someone screamed, and suddenly everyone was crying and shouting, and running everywhere. There was pandemonium in the halls of St. Andrew's College, and Hiroko was struggling to understand what had happened. It still wasn't clear to everyone. But it appeared that the Japanese had made two bombing runs on United States military bases in the Hawaiian Islands. Supposedly, all of the American planes on the ground had been destroyed, an undisclosed number of ships had been sunk, and still more were burning. Countless men had been killed and maimed, and although the details were as yet unknown, it was obviously an extremely serious assault on American soil, and it was inevitable that within hours war would be declared, if it hadn't already. And the girls' worst fears, mirroring those of the entire West Coast, were that the same planes would head straight for California.

Girls were continuing to shriek in the halls, and as tears streamed down her cheeks, Hiroko slipped slowly back into her room, wondering what this could possibly mean. What had really happened? Were they truly at war? Were her parents safe? Would she have to go home? Would she be arrested by the police? Would she be sent to jail, and then deported? Would Yuji have to go to war? It was all beyond imagining, and suddenly everything she'd heard for months about conferences with Japan, and broken treaties in Europe, and Hitler and Mussolini and Stalin, all came into focus. The world was at war, and she was part of it now. Most horrible of all, she was the enemy in a foreign land, and she was four thousand miles away from her parents.

It was another hour before she ventured back into the hall, after she put her clothes on. Many of the girls had gone back to their rooms, but some were still there, talking and crying, and listening to other girls' radios from their doorways. She was almost afraid to walk among them now, and then suddenly she saw one of the girls with whom she had played tennis. She was also from Hawaii, and she was crying. Two hours before, she had been one of Hiroko's new friends, and

now, through an act of war, they were enemies, and
she turned and looked at Hiroko with raw hatred.

"You! How can you even dare to look at us! My
parents could be dead by now . . . and you're the
one who did it!" It was completely illogical, but emotions ran high that day, and the other girl from Hawaii
ran out into the hall to scream at her, and, sobbing
uncontrollably, Hiroko ran back to her room in terror.

She stayed in her room all afternoon, listening to
the radio and the terrifying reports that continued to
come in, but at least there had been no air attacks on
California. There was panic in the streets, and in the
air, and everyone was being warned to be on the look-
out for enemy planes. Sailors and soldiers were re-
called, and civilians had been pouring into police and
fire stations all afternoon to volunteer for civil defense
jobs. The United States had never been attacked on its
own soil before, and no one had ever seen anything
like it.

Tak and Reiko tried to call her that afternoon, but
no one would put the call through to her. They said
they were keeping the lines open for emergency calls,
and Tak didn't dare single her out for more attention.
He was afraid that she was experiencing exactly what
she was going through, and he was worried about her
all day, but he didn't want to drive there and leave his
wife and children. They were all upset too, and their
only concern was for the United States. They had no
ties left to Japan, except with Hiroko's father. Takeo
tried unsuccessfully to reach him too, and then finally
decided on a telegram, asking him to confirm that all
was well with them, and what he wanted them to do
with his daughter. If the United States declared war on

Japan, which seemed inevitable now, he assumed that Masao would want her kept safe in the States, but on the other hand, Takeo wasn't sure the authorities would let her stay. It was a dilemma that would have to be solved when they had more information.

It was after six o'clock by the time Tak was finally able to get through to Hiroko, and by then she was hysterical. She had stayed in her room all day, afraid to come out and be attacked for what her country had done to Pearl Harbor. And no one had come into the room. She worried why no one from home called her. She had no contact with anyone, as she sat and sobbed, until finally one of the monitors came to tell her that her uncle was on the phone, and escorted her downstairs without further comment. And when she got there, all Hiroko could do was sob, and speak Japanese to him, telling him how terrible it was, how worried she was about all of them, her parents, and Reiko and Tak and the children. She couldn't even remember her English. She was an eighteen-year-old girl, alone in a foreign land, among enemies and strangers. But at least she had them, he reminded her. And she silently remembered that she had Peter. Or perhaps he would hate her now too. Perhaps no one would ever speak to her again. She had waited all day for the police to come, and was astounded when they hadn't. She had waited, too, for someone from the university to ask her to leave, but perhaps all of that would happen on Monday, she told her cousin.

"Now, calm down," Takeo told her on the phone. "None of that is happening. And none of this is your fault. Let's see what the President says tomorrow"—although he also felt war was certain—"and I want to get in touch with your father. I'm not at all sure that you'll be asked to leave. You're a student and you got trapped here, and they'll either get you passage back to Japan or let you stay here. No one is going to put you in jail, Hiroko, for heaven's sake. You're not a foreign agent. And your father may actually want you to stay here, if that's possible—it may be safer." He was making perfect sense, but he wasn't an eighteen-year-old girl, and he hadn't been alone in his room all day, surrounded by hostile female students.

"What about Mama and Papa and Yuji? If there's a war with Japan, they won't be safe either."

"They'll do the best they can. But you'll be better off here, with us. I'll do what I can to find out what's going on tomorrow and I'll call you. Just calm down, and don't panic."

It had been reassuring talking to him, and later that night she got a call from Peter. He wanted to know if she was all right, and if she was staying at school, or going back to Palo Alto. He had spent a frantic afternoon, worrying about her, and trying to get through without success. He hadn't wanted to call her cousins to see if they had reached her, because he didn't want to admit just how involved he was with her, although they certainly suspected.

"Are you all right?" he asked nervously. He suspected from all she'd said that they were being awful to her, and he was afraid she'd get hurt if she stayed there.

"I'm fine, Peter-san," she said bravely.

"Are you coming home? To the Tanakas, I mean."

"I don't know. Uncle Tak wants me to stay here. He's going to speak to some people tomorrow and see what this means for me, if I'll have to leave . . . and he wants to try to reach my father."

"He'd better do it quick," Peter said tersely. "I suspect that after tomorrow we'll be out of touch with them for a long time." And he wasn't sure what this meant for her either. "What about school? Can you really stay there, is it safe?"

"I'm all right. Tak thinks I should stay and see what happens." Peter didn't agree with him, but he didn't want to worry her. After the cool reception she'd had, he doubted things would improve now, and he thought she should go back to Palo Alto. "What is happening there, Peter-san?" she asked. She felt cut off from everything in Berkeley.

"People are going crazy here. Everyone is panicked. They all think the Japanese are going to bomb the West Coast, and they might, but they haven't yet, so that's something." It had been a long day for all of them. No one had any idea what was coming.

What neither of them knew was that the FBI started making arrests that night, of people they suspected of being spies and wanted to question. Many of them were commercial fishermen with shortwave radios on their boats, others were people they had watched for weeks, or suspected of enemy associations.

"I will be back in Palo Alto at the end of this week anyway," she said to him. Friday was the start of her Christmas vacation.

"I'll talk to you before that. And Hiroko . . ." He hesitated, not wanting to frighten her, but he wanted her to know that he would take care of her, no matter what happened. "If anything happens, try to stay calm, and stay there. I'll come and get you." He sounded so serious and so firm. She smiled for the first time all day as she listened to him.

"Thank you, Peter-san."

She walked slowly back to her room then, and that night she slept alone. Neither of her roommates wanted to share a room with her. And no one said a word to her as she went to her room and closed the door. She sat alone on the bed, thinking of Peter. And the next morning, they all had their answer.

At nine-thirty San Francisco time, President Roosevelt addressed Congress. It took him six minutes, and he asked them to declare war on Japan. Not only had the Japanese chosen to ignore "conversations with its government and its Emperor, looking toward the maintenance of peace in the Pacific, but they had deliberately planned, and bombed, not only our military installations in the Hawaiian Islands, but also Malaya, the Philippines, Wake Island, Guam, Midway, and Hong Kong." The attack on the Pacific had been complete and extensive. War had in effect been declared the day before, and Roosevelt only wanted Congress to confirm it. With the exception of one vote, they voted unanimously, and the documents were signed at one o'clock that afternoon. In retaliation, by the end of the day, Japan had declared war on both the United States and Britain. America was in the war at last.

But just before all communication had ended officially, one of the consul's last acts in San Francisco was to call Tak with a message from Masao. He had said he wanted Hiroko to stay in San Francisco if at all possible, if America and Japan declared war on each other. He felt more comfortable with her there, and urged

Tak to keep her with them. And he also sent the message that Yuji had joined the air force, and they all sent their warmest thoughts to their cousins.

In the United States, it was not only a day of infamy, as Roosevelt had said, but also a day of chaos. Japanese-owned banks, businesses, newspapers, and radio stations were seized. Fishing boats were seized as well, and even small businesses were closed. Some Germans and Italians were questioned and held, but mainly Japanese. The borders were sealed, and no Japanese national could buy an air ticket to go anywhere, so Hiroko couldn't have left anyway. The entire West Coast was on alert, and at six-forty that night there was an air raid. There was an unconfirmed report from somewhere of hostile aircraft approaching. People scattered everywhere, women screamed, and in their homes and basements and makeshift bomb shelters, people waited for the attack that never came, and finally, the sirens abated. All the radio stations had gone off the air, and in spite of precautions in the cities, afterward everyone realized that the prison island of Alcatraz had remained lit up like a beacon.

A second air raid siren went off that night, and the radio stations went off the air again. And again, after terrifying everyone, nothing happened.

The third one went off at one-thirty A.M., and yet again the radio stations disappeared from the air, and once again everyone scampered to safety, this time in their nightgowns and bathrobes, holding children in their arms, dragging pets with them.

At two A.M. another blackout was ordered, and at three A.M. the roar of two squadrons of enemy planes was reported. They were never seen or heard from

again, and the next day Lieutenant General John De
Witt insisted that they came from an aircraft carrier,
but no sign of it was found anywhere. The carrier itself
was never spotted, only the phantom planes were
heard but not seen, and the next day the headlines
were full of threats of enemy attacks and imaginary
sightings. By December ninth, the entire city was exhausted.

But the same circus began again that night, this
time not only in San Francisco but also in New York
and Boston. People were terrified everywhere, and the
threat of the Japanese was overwhelming. And no one
could withstand the constant panic of the air raids and
headlines. Particularly on the West Coast, General De
Witt was whipping everyone into a frenzy of terror.

Two days after that, on Thursday, Germany declared war on the United States, as Guam fell to the
Japanese. And in Berkeley, the U.S. Treasury ordered
every Japanese-owned business that had been seized
on Monday to be closed. Japanese-held business in the
United States, such as it was, was over.

It was a difficult time for Hiroko too. She had
scarcely left her room since it all began, and her roommates avoided her more pointedly than ever. On December eleventh, she had a serious meeting with the
dean of students. Hiroko was sure that, given everything she'd been hearing on the news, they would ask
her to leave the school, and she was astounded when
they didn't. The dean of students was extremely kind,
told her that she had no illusions whatsoever that
Hiroko was any part of this, but just like the Americans
who'd been bombed, Hiroko was an innocent victim.
She knew that this was a highly emotional time for all

of them, and she had heard rumors of unkindness to Hiroko by other students, but Hiroko said nothing to her at all about Sharon Williams's sins, or the extreme unkindness of Anne Spencer.

She suggested that Hiroko leave on schedule, like the other students, for her Christmas vacation the next day, and return to St. Andrew's again after Christmas.

"I'm sure things will have settled down a little by then, and you can get back to your schoolwork." Hiroko had only left her room for exams all week. She had even taken food from the dining room to eat in her room so she wouldn't have to face the other students. But she had kept up with her work, as always. She was a topflight student. "This has been a difficult time for everyone, particularly the girls from Hawaii," said the dean. There were only two of them, and they had finally heard that no one in their immediate families had been injured, but one of them looked as though she were going to lunge at Hiroko each time she saw her. "Have you heard anything at all from your own family?" the dean inquired discreetly.

"Only that they wish me to stay here," Hiroko said softly. "My father does not wish me to return to Japan now." The months and the weeks she had counted had been in vain, and she had realized only the night before that it might be years before she was able to return to her homeland. The thought of it brought tears to her eyes again, and she looked at the dean with gratitude for being so kind to her, and letting her come back after Christmas. She was, after all, an enemy alien, and they easily could have asked her to withdraw, but they hadn't. All week she had seen the newspapers raving about the "sneaky Japs" in the headlines, and it was very painful.

"This will be a difficult Christmas for all of us, I'm sure," the dean said solemnly. Everyone had loved ones and relatives who were enlisting. It was rare that anyone was untouched by what had happened. "But you can start fresh in the new year, Hiroko. We'll be happy to have you." She stood up and shook Hiroko's hand, and when she left the office and returned to her room, Hiroko found she was still shaking. She could still go to school. She hadn't been expelled for being Japanese. And she was surprised to realize that it was an enormous relief to her. Unlike the girls, at least the administration was not treating her as though she personally had attacked Pearl Harbor.

She packed her things that night to go back to Palo Alto the next day. And for the first time in four days, Sharon and Anne returned to the room too, and packed their things. And for the first time since Pearl Harbor, they slept there. But twice that night, they all had to go downstairs for air raids. Every night now there were reports of enemy aircraft heading toward the coast, or submarines sighted, ready to torpedo unsuspecting ships in the harbor. But the planes and the carriers never materialized, nor did the submarines, or the torpedoes. The only thing that materialized, until it was almost tangible, was panic.

This time, Takeo himself came to drive her home, and he brought Aunt Rei, and Hiroko was enormously relieved to see them. It had been an agonizing week for her, and none of the girls in her dorm said goodbye to her, or wished her a merry Christmas. And the moment she got into the car with her relatives, Hiroko began to cry. It was such a relief to see them.

"It was just terrible," she said in Japanese. Every time she spoke to them now, she forgot to speak English. Usually they didn't care, but this time, as they drove away, Reiko said sharply that she had to speak English. "Why?" Hiroko looked at her, surprised. She knew she would understand her, and English was such an effort for her, especially now, with everything that had happened.

"It doesn't matter how difficult it is for you, Hiroko. We're at war with Japan," she said bluntly. "You could be picked up as an enemy agent."

"I think that's a little extreme." Uncle Tak smiled at her, thinking that his wife had gone too far this time, but he agreed it was certainly more diplomatic to speak English. "I do think, though, that right now you should make the effort. People are very nervous." The headlines had been incredible, about Jap threats, and Jap planes, and Jap bombs. Commander of the Western Defense Command, General De Witt, was feeding the press an absolute tidal wave of terror.

And by Saturday, Italy, Germany, and Japan, as well as Romania and Bulgaria, had all declared war against the Allies. Hiroko felt as though she'd personally been bombed all week, she was absolutely exhausted from everything that had happened. She slept almost all day Saturday, and only got up in time to help Reiko cook dinner. Tami was particularly worried about her. But her mother just said to let her be. She just hoped they wouldn't have an air raid.

And it wasn't until Sunday that Hiroko saw Peter. He came to see Tak, officially, but he knew she was there, and he was anxious to see her. She came slowly downstairs in a dark gray kimono, with a serious air, and she looked sadder than he had ever seen her, in the somber color. She bowed to him, as she always had before, and this time, her cousin reached out a hand and touched her shoulder.

"Hiroko, don't do that anymore. Right now, it's important that you don't stand out anywhere. Even here. It's better if you stop bowing." She looked shocked by what he had said. She couldn't afford to be different anymore. Everything was changing. He left them alone then, and went to look for some papers, with a small, wintry smile at Peter.

"Are you all right?" Peter asked her cautiously. He had been afraid to ask Tak about her too often, but he had been worried sick about her all week, and he was relieved to see her. She looked tired, and a little wan, and she had clearly lost weight. If anything, she looked even smaller.

"I am fine, Peter-san," she said, starting to bow again, but this time her cousin's words stopped her.

"Tak's right," Peter said softly. "One of my sansei friends told me the other night that her grandmother burned her little Japanese flag on Monday night, she was afraid to get into trouble."

"That's foolish," Hiroko said, sounding even to her own ears like her father.

"Maybe not. People do crazy things in wartime. Are you going back?" he asked worriedly. "To St. Andrew's, I mean." He already knew from Tak that her father wanted her to stay in California, even if she would have been able to return to Japan, which he doubted. "What did they tell you?"

"They said I could go back to school, and they are very sorry if people have been unkind to me."

He was surprised that she had told them, but she hadn't. Others had, and she explained that as he nodded.

"What makes you think they won't do it again?"

"They might. But I cannot live with *chizoku*. I must have Bushido, and go back to face them." She smiled, watching him. There was something very strong about her now. She knew she had to be brave, and she would not let her family down. She would be dignified and proud. She would not live with shame, *chizoku*. And the Bushido she spoke of, he had heard of before. It was the courage of the samurai to walk into battle. "I will go back, Peter-san. I am not at war with them. I am not at war with anyone." She looked luminous and peaceful, and he was drawn to her again, as he had been before, as though a magnet deep inside him pulled him to her.

"I'm glad to hear it," he said softly. "I'm not at war with anyone either." Not yet anyway. He had already spoken to his draft board. For the moment, unless things changed, he was going to finish the school year, and then he would join the army. Stanford had made a special request for him, so they didn't have to close the department.

"It's a shame they will not let you stay longer," she said sadly. "It will be hard for Uncle Tak when you're gone, for all of us," she said, her eyes caressing his, as he touched her fingers. "It will be dangerous for you, Peter-san." And then she told him about Yuji joining the air force. It was a strange time, and she realized suddenly that she would have people she loved on both sides of the war. It was a sad position to be in.

They talked on for a little while, and eventually the others joined them, and Peter stayed for dinner. They went outside for a short walk afterward, and took the dog. The lively Shiba followed them down the street, past the familiar houses of the Tanakas' neighbors. But even here, according to Reiko, there had been subtle reactions. Two of their neighbors had suddenly been chilly toward them. Their sons had already enlisted in the army, as had the older brothers of all of Ken's friends. And one of the patients she'd cared for in the hospital that week had asked her to leave his room. He said he didn't want any damn Jap taking care of him, she might kill him. He'd been very old and very infirm, so she'd put it down to that, but one of the other nisei nurses had had the same experience with a young woman from Hawaii.

"It's not going to be easy for them," Peter said softly about her cousins. "People are bound to react at first. I guess it'll calm down eventually. It can't go on like this forever, but people are upset, understandably. We were attacked, and when they see a Japanese face, it reminds them."

"But my cousins are American," she parried, but he knew that.

"Obviously, but some people don't know that. And I guess others are just too upset to think it through. Your cousins are as American as I am."

"I am the only enemy here," Hiroko said sadly, looking up at him, and without saying a word, he pulled her into his arms and kissed her.

"You're not my enemy, Hiroko-san . . . you

never will be." She affected him as no other woman had before her. And that week, he had finally broken off with Carole, except that the final argument with her had turned out differently than he'd expected. He'd had dinner with her, intending to explain to her that his affections were otherwise engaged. But before he could even tell her that, she told him she thought he should ask for a transfer at Stanford.

"To what? Biology?" he had asked, amused. "Why?" He was completely baffled. But she had gone on to say that as far as she was concerned, the American thing to do was to refuse to work with Takeo, or better yet, to have him fired. "Are you crazy?" he had asked her, wide-eyed, unable to believe she had said those words to him. Takeo Tanaka was a credit to the university, and nothing less than brilliant.

"Maybe, but he's the enemy," she had said flatly. "He ought to be deported."

"To where? He's lived here for twenty years, for chrissake. He'd be a citizen, if he could be." Peter had been furious about what she was saying. And eventually she got around to saying that Hiroko should be put in jail, or maybe shot, in retaliation for the men and women who had died at Pearl Harbor. It was the craziest thing he'd ever heard. But when she mentioned Hiroko, he held back no longer. "How can you say things like that?" he asked, stupefied. "How can you react to all that hysterical garbage they put in the papers? I don't believe for a minute that there were aircraft carriers off the coast every night last week. If there had been, they'd have bombed us. I think people are hysterical, and that goddamn General De Witt along with them. But how you can say something like that, Carole, is beyond me." She'd been adamant with him, and there was no convincing her that her view of American-born Japanese was utterly crazy. He knew there was no point in arguing with her, but he did anyway, out of sheer loyalty to his friends, and then he told her that for her peculiar views, and other reasons that were too lengthy to go into, he no longer wanted to see her.

She seemed almost relieved, and she told him pointedly that as far as she was concerned anyway, anyone that was sympathetic to the Japanese was obviously an enemy agent. He couldn't believe he'd heard her say it, and he actually laughed when he went back to his car, and told Tak a modified version of it the next morning. But Takeo was neither as amused nor as angry as Peter had been. He saw Carole's view as only the tip of the iceberg.

"I think we're going to hear a lot of people saying things like that. There's going to be an inevitable reaction to the panic."

"But that's ridiculous. You're not Japanese anymore, and my working for you hardly makes me a spy. Now, come on, Tak, you've got to admit, it's pretty funny."

"I don't think any of it is funny right now. I think we all need to be very careful."

And he had said as much to Reiko, and they all discussed it again at dinner on Sunday. But Peter thought that Takeo was a little too worried. Telling Hiroko not to bow anymore was probably sensible. There was no point in drawing attention to the fact that she was foreign. But as for the nisei and the sansei, and all of them who were American born, they had no reason to be concerned. This was their homeland.

After dinner Peter and Hiroko took Lassie out for a walk and continued the discussion.

"Uncle Tak is very nervous," she said cautiously to Peter, as they headed home with Lassie. "I suppose he's worried about the war. We all are. We must all try very hard to set a good example." It was the same thing someone else had said, and it struck Peter as he listened to her that all the American-born Japanese seemed to feel the same need to prove that they were good guys, and it wasn't their fault. But all Japanese were being identified visually as enemy aliens, no matter where they'd been born. It was incredibly unfair. And it might even be dangerous for Hiroko, who really was a Japanese citizen. He worried about her going back to college. As emotions rose, and people's brothers and boyfriends went to war, her classmates were liable to get angrier and angrier at Hiroko.

"I don't want you to go back if you'll be in any danger," he said firmly before she left. He was very protective of her, and she was surprised to see, by the look on his face, that he meant it.

"They are only girls." Hiroko smiled at him. They couldn't do anything to her, except what they had before, hurt her feelings.

"Think about it, Hiroko. You don't have to go back there."

"You worry too much." She smiled up at him again. "Like Uncle Tak, I am strong." But she was also young, and very gentle. And she would not dishonor her father by giving up school, or quitting.

"I know, Bushido," he teased, as the Shiba barked

at a dog somewhere. "Maybe you have too much Bushido for your own good, Miss Takashimaya." She laughed at him then. It was so easy to be with him. She was so comfortable and so at ease, there were no national differences between them. Their countries were at war, but it didn't mean anything between them. They were simply two people. It was sad, she said quietly, that the world could not be more like them.

He agreed with her, and they walked slowly back to the Tanakas, and as they did, Peter saw one of the neighbors peeking out their window, and looking at them with an angry expression. He couldn't imagine what their problem was, except that maybe the dog had been barking. And then, when he looked at her, he realized what they saw. A Japanese woman, and a Caucasian. It had come to that then. In truth, it had come to that long before, but now it seemed doubly obvious. He wondered, as they walked along, if there would be much of this, if people with Japanese friends would be ostracized or shunned. It was hard to believe that the girl he had just broken up with was echoing more than her own opinions. But even if people ostracized him for his friendship with them, he didn't care. His relationship with Takeo meant far too much to him for him to sacrifice it, and he would risk anything to be near Hiroko.

"What are you thinking, Peter-san?" she asked gently as they passed the last of the neighbors. "You look very serious." Her English had improved at school, in spite of all the problems and distractions.

"That people are crazy these days. It's dangerous when people get this panicked. You must be careful. Don't go out alone, make sure you're always with

Reiko, or Tak, or Ken, or me." He smiled openly and she laughed at him.

"You will protect me, Peter-san."

"Only if you do everything I tell you," he said, feeling like a boy again, as they walked through the cool air, and into the Tanakas' front garden.

"And what will you tell me to do?" She was teasing him, and he loved it.

"This is what I'll tell you to do," he whispered to her as he pulled her into his arms in the doorway, and then he kissed her. No one was watching them, and they were safe here. And as he had before, he took her breath away, and she did the same for him, and both of them looked slightly disheveled as they walked into the kitchen.

But Reiko and Takeo didn't look as sympathetic to them as they had before, and all Tak would say as he looked at them was that they should be very careful. Peter knew what he meant, nodded, and then left a few minutes later. And her cousins said nothing to her, but she felt their concern as she went upstairs to sleep with Sally.

They were well aware of Peter's relationship with Hiroko by now. No matter how discreet the two young lovers had been, it was obvious that something had changed between them and they had become much closer, particularly since war had broken out. Tak and Reiko hadn't acknowledged it, but they knew, and they didn't disapprove of Peter, but they were afraid for Hiroko. And for the same reasons, they told her the next day to put away her kimonos. This was not a time to draw attention to herself, or to remind everyone that she wasn't a nisei. She didn't argue with them, but she was sad when she put them away. Her kimonos were so beautiful and she felt so awkward in Western clothes. With very few exceptions, she thought that most of them were ugly.

But Sally was delighted to see her in Western clothes, and she bought her a pair of saddle shoes for Christmas.

Christmas was quiet for them that year. Takeo took Ken to chop down their own Christmas tree, as he always did, but somehow the entire Japanese community seemed to be keeping very quiet. And day by day, the news was never good. Two days before Christmas, the Japanese took Wake Island. And on Christmas Day, the Japanese took Hong Kong. Even for the Tanakas, it was a quiet day, and Takeo raised an eyebrow when Peter joined them. He appreciated his friendship, but he thought he was making things difficult for himself. Even at the university, in the past two weeks, for Peter's own good, Tak had tried to keep his distance.

"Don't put yourself on the line for us," Tak said to him quietly that afternoon. "It isn't worth it. Eventually, people will get used to what's happening, but right now tempers are still hot." But it had to do with more than just him, and he knew it. Peter felt constantly drawn to the Tanakas so he could be close to Hiroko. And however unfortunate the situation may have been, or even dangerous for Peter, Takeo knew that he was sincere and that he loved her.

And on Christmas night, after everyone else had gone to bed, Peter slipped the smallest of silver rings on Hiroko's finger. It was only a symbol of what they felt, and a small thing. He had bought her a beautiful silk shawl, and some old books of poetry he had found in Japanese, and he had written her a haiku. But he also wanted to give her the ring, as a symbol of what they had now, and hoped to share one day. It was the narrowest of bands with two hearts entwined. It was Victorian and he had found it in an antique shop, and it was so small, he thought that no one would notice.

"You are too good to me, Peter-san," she said breathlessly, and he kissed her fingers.

"You must not call me that anymore. Tak is right." She had lost her kimonos, and the privilege of bowing to him, and now she must lose yet another sign of her respect for him, but she did not argue.

"Why is everyone so frightened of clothes and words, and even little girls?" Earlier that day she and Tami had been in a store and someone had made an ugly comment. She and Tami had hurried away, but one of Reiko's friends had told her that in a store down the street where they had always been nothing but hospitable to the Japanese, they had refused to serve them.

"We're Americans, we're not 'Japs,'" Tami had said, fighting tears, as Hiroko hurried away with her, and she had looked to her older cousin for an explanation, but at first Hiroko had none to give her. She had been shocked by the man's willingness to hurt a child, and she was very angry.

"It's because you are with me, and I am Japanese," Hiroko had explained to her finally, but even that seemed a paltry explanation. She was barely more than a girl herself, and she was only a woman, not a soldier, or an army.

"People are going to stay frightened for a while,

until they forget some of it, and things start to improve. In the meantime, you all have to be very sensible and very careful," Peter warned her.

"And when they are wise again, may I wear my kimonos?" she asked, amused for a moment by the absurdity of all of it, and he laughed.

"We'll go to Japan one day, and you can wear them all again." But their dream of his going to visit her father next summer, to meet her family, had been shot down in flames at Pearl Harbor. She had no idea when she would be able to go home again, and thinking about that depressed her. At times, she was so lonely for them, and she had no idea when she'd see them. It made her reach out to Peter all the more, and as he kissed her that night, she wondered what would happen. In June, he would go to war. But until then, they had to seize each precious moment. There would be many of them, and she would string them like beads, to finger until he returned again. And he would return, she prayed, as he kissed her again, and she felt the ring, and promised herself that one day he would visit her parents. In the meantime, all they could do was cling to the present, and wait for the future, together.

# Chapter 8

O N DECEMBER twenty-ninth, all "enemy aliens" in the western states were ordered to surrender their "contraband," which included shortwave radios, cameras of any variety and size, binoculars, or weapons. The only confusion came regarding the term "enemy alien," which would have appeared to mean Japanese nationals, but within hours it became clear that the term meant anyone of Japanese descent, whether citizens or foreigners.

"But that can't be," Reiko said, as Takeo explained the term to them. "We're Americans, we're not *aliens*." She looked puzzled.

"Not anymore," he said grimly. Up until now, being a resident alien had never bothered him. And it hadn't even caused him a problem at Stanford.

But suddenly everything had changed, and like

Hiroko, he was an enemy alien. Even more shocking than that, so were his wife and children, all of whom had been born in California.

They collected all the cameras in the family, and he had a pair of binoculars, which he used at Lake Tahoe when they went sailing. They delivered them to the local police station, and he saw several of their neighbors there, and the policeman who took the things from him looked extremely embarrassed.

For Takeo and his family, it was their first taste of reality. And Hiroko began to worry that her staying with them might cause them trouble. She silently decided to stay at St. Andrew's as much as she could. Perhaps it was even dangerous for them to have an "enemy" staying with them. And perhaps even more so for Peter to love one.

But despite their growing fears of reprisals in the area, and panic over attacks from air or sea, Peter asked Tak if he could take Hiroko out on New Year's Eve. It was to be their first official date, and Peter looked extremely formal, and a little nervous, when he asked him.

"You're serious about her, aren't you?" Tak finally asked him, looking worried. He knew he couldn't put off asking him any longer. Peter had acknowledged his own feelings to him long since, but never Hiroko's. And it was time now.

"Yes, I'm very serious about her, Tak." He admitted it almost proudly and without hesitation. "I tried to run away from it . . . but I just couldn't. . . . Every time I saw her I would think about her for days. . . . She haunted me. I've never known anyone like her." His eyes told their own tale. But so did Takeo's. He was deeply concerned about both of them. If nothing else, they were cursed with dismal timing.

"She's a sweet girl, but you're both wading into dangerous waters," he warned. It had only been three weeks since Pearl Harbor, and anti-Japanese feelings were running high. Takeo had already heard of investigations by the FBI, and people he knew being questioned. He didn't want something like that happening to Peter. "You're going to have to be very careful." It was obvious from what he'd seen that nothing was going to stop them.

"I know that. I wasn't suggesting we go to the USO, or dancing at the Fairmont. One of the assistants in psychology is having a little gathering on New Year's Eve; he invited me and some of the other assistants in our department. It'll be very circumspect and very private."

Takeo nodded as he listened. In a way, it was a relief for all concerned to acknowledge their relationship, and although Takeo had had serious doubts about it at first, he wasn't so sure now. He had thought it unwise for her to become involved with an American, and he had been acutely aware of his responsibilities to her father. But somehow he couldn't bring himself to object any longer. So many things had changed, so much pain had been caused. If anything, their involvement was more dangerous now than it had been when she first arrived, and yet they had a right to some hope in their lives, and Takeo sensed how intent Peter was on taking care of Hiroko. And what right did he have to deprive them? But he felt a keen responsibility nonetheless to warn them of the dangers. Takeo was frightened now, not only for them, but for his own wife and children.

"Just be careful, for both your sakes," Takeo urged him again, looking at Peter intently. "And if things don't feel right when you go out, come back home immediately. Don't put yourselves in an awkward position." God only knew what people would do when driven into a frenzy by fear and national emotion.

"I'll be careful," Peter assured him, looking at him sadly. "And Tak, this isn't about politics, for either of us. It's about her. I'm American. I love my country. I'm willing to die for it. This isn't about sympathies, it's just about her, and me . . . and people. . . . I love her. I'll stand by her."

"I know that," Takeo said, looking sorrowfully into the future. Their two nations were at war, it was going to affect the entire world, not just two people. "But it could get more complicated very quickly."

"I hope not. For her sake. It must be very hard for her, she's the one with divided loyalties. She loves her family, her country, but she likes it here too, and she feels loyal to all of you. It must be difficult for her to be here." But fortunately, in spite of her father's, and her cousin's, interest in politics she viewed the political issues from a distance. Like most girls her age, she was worried about the people she knew, and loved, and not the ramifications of decisions made by governments. Her vision was limited, as was most everyone's at that point. "Anyway, will you let me take her out?"

Takeo nodded at him thoughtfully, and repeated himself again. "Just be careful."

But on New Year's Eve, politics were far from everyone's mind. She had borrowed a black taffeta dress that Reiko hadn't worn in years, and she covered it with a little velvet jacket of Sally's. She looked beautiful, with her single strand of pearls, her exquisite face and huge eyes, and her long shining black hair that hung to her waist. And Sally had forced her to learn to walk in a pair of her mother's high heels. According to Hiroko, they were much, much harder to wear than geta.

Peter's eyes grew wide when he came to pick her up, and this time she didn't bow. She simply stood there, looking very shy, and very lovely. It was as though she had suddenly grown up, and everything that had been concealed from him was unveiled now.

"You look fantastic," he said, and he meant it. He had never seen anyone as beautiful, and this time he felt shy with her, as Takeo poured them each a tiny cup of sake.

"No more after this," he said cautiously, but he and Reiko toasted the New Year with them. It reminded Hiroko of important family occasions in Kyoto with her father. And it made her feel homesick again. She hadn't heard from them since he had gotten word to her through the consulate that he wanted her to stay in California. *"Kampai!"* Takeo toasted them, and Reiko smiled at them. They looked so young and so hopeful. And they did remind her of her first days with Takeo, when she was one of his students, and falling in love with him. It was irresistible, watching them. And Hiroko's cheeks glowed pink from the sake.

"Where will you be tonight?" Takeo asked conversationally as they chatted for a few minutes.

"Not far from here, the psych assistant has a house a couple of blocks off campus. We're going to have dinner there, and do a little dancing." He smiled at Hiroko. It still shocked him to realize that he was going out with a freshman. She was far less sophisticated than most of the girls he'd gone out with for the last five years, but in many ways, she was far wiser. "What about you two?" Peter asked. Reiko was wearing the red silk dress Tak had bought her for Christmas, and it was very pretty.

"We'll just be down the street for dinner," Reiko explained. Sally was going to friends across the street. Ken was going to Peggy's house, and Tami was staying home with a sitter. As they left, Peter promised that they wouldn't be home too late. But Tak didn't give them a curfew.

Hiroko giggled as they went out, and Peter smiled at her, admiring her again. It was impossible not to, she looked dazzling, and he knew his friends would be very impressed with her. It was their first official date and they were both excited. "You look very grown-up," he teased, and she laughed again as they ran to his car. It was chilly.

"Thank you, Peter," she said deliberately, eliminating the *san* after his name. She had listened carefully to all her cousin's warnings. No kimonos, no bowing, no foreign terms, no speaking Japanese in public. She had to make an effort now not to be different. He felt it was important for her well-being and her safety.

It was her first date with any man, and she almost trembled with excitement as they drove along the edge of the campus. The house where they went was small, but there was a record on, and there was lots of noise. The house was filled with graduate students and young teachers. And no one seemed to notice when they arrived, although when she took her coat off and moved inside, Peter noticed a few people stare, but no one made any comments. There was a young nisei couple there too. Peter knew them vaguely, and knew that she taught biology, and he was in the language department. But Peter never got close enough to them in the crowded room to introduce them to Hiroko.

There was plenty of food, red and white wine, and cheap champagne, and some of the guests had brought their own bottles of gin and scotch and vodka. Several of the guests were pretty drunk, but most of them were talking or laughing, or dancing in a back bedroom that had been cleared and filled with balloons and streamers for just that purpose. And in the distance, from where they stood, they could hear Frank Sinatra crooning.

Peter introduced her to everyone he knew, and helped her to fill her plate with roast beef and a little turkey. And eventually they set their plates down and danced in the back room to a record of Tommy Dorsey's band with Frank Sinatra singing. Peter held her close to him as they danced, and it was almost midnight. He could feel her warmth next to him, and she felt so delicate in his arms, he was almost afraid to hurt her. There were no words for what he felt for her. It was as though they were there alone, in a deserted world, with no one else around them.

It was the best New Year's Eve he'd had, just dancing with her, and holding her, and when someone shouted that it was midnight, he kissed her. Afterward, she looked up, terribly embarrassed that he had kissed her in public. But she saw that others were doing it too, and Peter whispered to her with a smile that it was the custom.

"Oh." She nodded seriously, and he kissed her again, as they danced slowly around the floor, and ushered in 1942, with dreams of hope and freedom.

"I love you, Hiroko-san," he whispered so only she could hear, and she looked up at him with eyes full of wonder and nodded. She didn't dare say the words to him with so many people around them.

They were still dancing, held close in each other's arms, when the air-raid siren went off, and there was a collective groan. No one wanted it to spoil their evening, and there was a momentary urge to ignore it, but their host insisted that they had to go down to the cellar. Someone turned all the lights off, as the din grew, and people hurried down the stairs carrying bottles of champagne, and wine, and Peter noticed that many of them were drunk. And once they all got to the cellar it was very crowded. It had been built for a small family, and it was jam-packed now with at least fifty people. The young nisei couple were gone, and several of the others Peter knew had left, but it was a jovial group, until people started to get hot and uncomfortable and a couple of the girls complained that they couldn't breathe, and everything was so dusty. It was really miserable in the cellar, but the sirens raged on, and they knew they had to stay there even though there were blackout shades on the windows upstairs. The Tanakas had put them in too; everyone had in the three weeks since Pearl Harbor.

"Christ, you'd think they'd leave us alone on New Year's Eve, damn Japs," someone said in the far corner. It was dark and all they had were flashlights. In one corner a couple kissed, but as Peter stood with his arm around Hiroko, the cellar seemed anything but romantic. All they wanted to do was go upstairs and go home, and so did the others. Half an hour later they were still there, and fed up with it. But the sirens continued for an hour. Finally, at one-thirty, they all went back upstairs, looking dusty and tired, their festive mood destroyed, and one of the men looked at Hiroko and lurched toward her.

"It's goddamn little Japs like you that spoil it for the rest of us, you know," he said to her angrily. "I'll be in the army next week, thanks to you. And by the way, thanks a lot for Pearl Harbor." He looked as though he was going to swing at her, and Peter pushed her swiftly behind him.

"That's enough, Madison." He was drunk, but it didn't excuse what he was saying, and behind Peter, Hiroko was white and shaking.

"Oh, go shove it, Jenkins," the drunk responded. "You're such a Jap lover you can't see straight. When are you going to get smart, and stop kissing ass on Tanaka? The FBI'll get you one of these days, you know. Maybe they'll even grab your girlfriend," he said, and then stormed off, as Peter glared at him, not wanting to start a brawl on New Year's Eve, or upset Hiroko any more than she had been. He could see that she was fighting back tears, and he took her with him to get her coat. The joy of the evening had been shattered.

"I'm sorry," he said as he helped her into it. "He's drunk, he doesn't know what he's saying." But it was upsetting to both of them. They thanked their host, and hurried to the car, as the others watched them. No one had said a word to Madison, and Peter wondered if what he had voiced was silently echoed by the others. Did they all think him a fool? Was everyone willing to turn on the Japanese they knew? But with the exception of Hiroko, none of these people were real Japanese. Takeo was as American as any citizen after twenty years in the States, and Reiko and the children had been born there. What were they talking about? And even Hiroko was hardly responsible for Pearl Harbor. Why take it out on her? What were they thinking? But tempers were running high these days; it was exactly what Takeo had seen coming.

And as Peter drove her home, she began to cry and apologize for ruining his evening. "You should have taken someone else, Peter-san," she said, slipping into her old ways without thinking. "An American girl. It was not wise to take me."

"Maybe not," he said, his jaw firm. "But I'm not in love with an American girl." He glanced over at her, and pulled the car over so he could talk to her. He pulled her close to him, and held her as she trembled. "I'm in love with you, Hiroko. And you must be strong now. This could happen again. Takeo thinks it'll take a while for things to calm down, especially with all this 'enemy alien' nonsense going on, where they're collecting cameras from students, and the army telling us every five minutes that we're about to be attacked." With all the air raids they had had in the past three and a half weeks, there had not been a single attack or a genuine sighting. But the papers were full of mystery ships that were supposedly just offshore, and the phantom planes that some people saw and others didn't, and spies being arrested daily. "You can't listen to people like that jerk at the party. You know who you are. Listen to your heart, Hiroko, and mine, not to people who call you names, or try to hold you responsible for something you had nothing to do with."

"But Japan is my country. I am responsible for their actions."

"That's quite a burden to put on yourself," he said, suddenly looking tired. It had been a long night in the cellar, and they were both still dusty. "You're responsible for you, and no one else. You can't control what Japan does." It pained her to feel ashamed of the actions of her own country. Just as it would have pained him, or her cousins, if America had done something disgraceful.

"I am sorry to you," she said awkwardly, and his heart went out to her again. She looked so dignified, and so gentle. "I am sorry to you that my country has done something so terrible. It is very ugly," she said, filled with shame, as he leaned down and kissed her.

"It is ugly, but it's not your fault. And you're not ugly. You're beautiful. Just be patient, Hiroko. It will get better."

But when they got home, they found that they weren't the only ones who'd had a difficult evening. The parents of Sally's best friend had asked her not to come back again. They were well aware of her crush on their son, and they thought it unsuitable, and their oldest son had just joined the navy. Sally was in her room, drowning in tears when they found her. She had taken off her dress, and she was wearing her mother's bathrobe and when they urged her to come down, she told them all what had happened over cookies Reiko had made. Sally was sobbing as she told them.

"They were so mean to me. They said I couldn't come back to the house again. I've known Kathy all my life, she's like my sister. And she didn't say anything, she just looked embarrassed, and when I left she cried. Her brother wasn't even there tonight, they wouldn't let him see me. Their mother said I was an 'alien,' that the government says so. I'm not an 'alien,' Mom." She cried even harder as she said the word. "I'm just a kid. . . . I'm American. I was born here."

Ken came in from his evening then and heard what she'd said. His girlfriend was sansei, which meant that even her parents had been born in the States, but she'd had trouble at school right before Christmas vacation. And he'd gotten in several fights because of her. People were definitely going crazy.

"How can people be so dumb?" Ken said, looking at his sister angrily. They had known the Jordans all their lives. How could they do that to her? And she was right, she was just a kid. Why punish her for something she had nothing to do with?

Peter told them what had happened to Hiroko then, and they all agreed that they hoped the New Year would be better than the last one. But they also agreed that they had to be more careful. Public emotions were running high, and people were being whipped into a frenzy.

"What I don't like," Peter said honestly, "is this 'enemy alien' stuff. Just because people look Japanese doesn't make them foreign. All of a sudden, it's like no one can tell the difference."

"Maybe they don't want to," Reiko said sadly. Things had been rough at the hospital for her too. Several people had made ugly comments about her or refused to work alongside her, some of those people she'd known for years. It was very painful.

Sally calmed down eventually, and Peter sat with the others for a long time, and then, finally, he left them. Hiroko walked him to the door, and he kissed her, and told her he was sorry it had been such a rotten evening.

"It wasn't rotten, Peter-san," she said, forgetting herself again, but at least here it didn't matter. "It was very good. I was with you. That is all that is important," she said softly.

"That's all that's important to me too," Peter said, and kissed her one last time, and then he left. After Hiroko said good night to Tak and Reiko, they both worried more than ever about her seeing Peter in this atmosphere. But like an express train, surging ahead in the dark of night, it was too late to stop them.

The next day Sally moped around the house, and Ken tried to get her to come out with him and Peggy, but she wouldn't. She missed Kathy, even more than she missed her brother. They had been best friends forever and now she was forbidden even to call her.

Tak and Reiko went to the store and did some errands, and Peter took Hiroko and Tami for a drive, and they noticed with fascination the endless lines of boys lining up to join the navy in Palo Alto. Some looked hungover, some were still drunk, but most looked like they knew what they were doing. People had been signing up in droves for the past three weeks. And among the throng were a number of nisei.

Manila fell to the Japanese the next day, and even more young men signed up after that. But three days later, the Selective Service reclassified all the nisei and sansei. They were put in a class called IV-C, and they were told that they would either be discharged from the service or could hold only menial jobs, like those in the kitchen.

"Second-class citizens, if that," Peter said through clenched teeth.

"It's going to make great teaching one day," Tak said grimly. "I just wonder who'll be here to teach the class. Probably not me, or anyone like me. You'll have to do it, Peter."

"Don't be stupid, Tak." He didn't want to hear it.

"I'm not. Look around you. Read the papers." The emotions against the Japanese were running higher than ever, even against American-born Japanese like Reiko. People seemed to be unable to differentiate between their enemies and their friends, their allies and "enemy aliens," as they called them.

Hiroko went back to St. Andrew's in the midst of all the worries and bad news, and it was easier than she expected. Despite Peter's protests, she took the train to go there.

The Tanakas had all been too busy to take her, and the only surprise she had was that she couldn't get a cab at the station. So she walked the rest of the way, carrying her suitcase, all the way from the station. A few buses went by, but they wouldn't stop to pick her up either. But, warmer and more tired than she'd anticipated, she nevertheless reached St. Andrew's safely.

When she got to school, the head of the dorms told her that they had made a little change. They felt sure that under the circumstances these days, she would prefer a private room, and they had done everything they could to find one for her. But in spite of the appeal of it, Hiroko felt guilty. She knew how vehemently Anne Spencer had wanted a private room, and it didn't seem fair to take this one from her. And she explained that to the dorm mistress, and explained that she would be willing to do without one.

"That's very kind of you, Hiroko," the woman said nervously. "But Anne has agreed to room with some other girls this semester. And Sharon will have a new roommate. So we hope everyone will be happy."

But the "private" room they had found for her was actually nothing more than a broom closet in the attic. She had to go up the back stairs to get to it, and there were no other girls nearby. She had to go down three flights of stairs to get to the bathroom. And when Hiroko stepped inside it, wide-eyed, it was freezing. There was no heating at all, and no view. It didn't even have a window.

"This is my room?" she asked, looking startled, as the woman nodded, hoping she wouldn't object or make any comment.

"Yes, it's small, of course. And we've given you some extra blankets." There were two, and even standing there, Hiroko could feel the bitter chill. And in the warmer weather, right under the roof, with no ventilation at all, it would be stifling. It was lit by a single bulb hanging from a wire on the ceiling, and the only furniture was a bed, a chair, and a dresser. There wasn't even a desk where she could do her work, or a closet to hang her clothes. And everything she had left in her last room had been put in her new one in boxes.

"Thank you," Hiroko said softly, fighting back tears, and praying that she could hold them back long enough for the dorm mistress to leave so she wouldn't see them.

"I'm glad you like it," she said, grateful that the girl had agreed and not created a problem. There had been no choice. The Spencers and several other parents had demanded that they do this. They were incensed that she was coming back at all. But the school had refused to let her go. She was a sweet girl, and an excellent student, and other than the one smoking incident she'd been put on probation for, there had never been a single disciplinary problem. They had refused to expel her for political reasons. "Let us know if you need anything," she said to Hiroko, and then gently closed the door, leaving Hiroko there alone to sit on the bed and cry. She was more than an enemy alien now, she was a pariah.

She went to the library to do her studies that afternoon, but she didn't even bother to go to dinner. She didn't want to see any of them. She had glimpsed Anne coming back from her golf lessons only that afternoon, and she had overheard Sharon bragging to someone about spending Christmas with Gary Cooper. It was probably all a lie anyway, and who cared? She was too hurt by where they had put her to listen to Sharon's stories anymore. She didn't even call her cousins to tell them about the room. It was just too painful.

She went to bed early instead, without eating anything, and the next day she went to class looking pale, and wearing a heavy sweater. It had been freezing in her room all night, and by Thursday she was sneezing. But she didn't say a word to anyone; she didn't speak to a soul all week. And whenever she entered a room, they all acted as though they didn't see her.

She was going to go home on Friday night, but she had a bad cold by then, and wasn't feeling up to it. And she still hadn't told her cousins about the "private room"; she just called and told them she wasn't coming.

And when she went to get a cup of tea in the dining room on Friday night, the nurse happened to see her, and saw instantly that she had a fever.

"Are you all right?" she asked kindly, and Hiroko tried to smile, but her eyes filled with tears. It had been a terrible week, and she was feeling really awful. She had a bad chest cold, and her eyes were red and she was sneezing. In the end, the nurse insisted that she come to the infirmary, and once she got her there and took her temperature, she discovered that she had a hundred and two fever. "You're not going anywhere, young lady," she said firmly, "except to bed, right here. And in the morning, we're going to call the doctor." Hiroko felt so rotten, she didn't even argue, and she let the nurse put her to bed, grateful for a warm room and an abundance of blankets.

In the morning, her fever was down a little bit, but the nurse still insisted on calling the doctor. He came late that afternoon and said that she had bronchitis and a mild case of influenza, but by Sunday she could go back to her own room. Which she did, still feeling ill, but at least a little better.

She walked slowly up the stairs, carrying her few things. She had a lot of studying to do, and she was going to go to the library as soon as she changed her clothes. But when she got to her room, she found that the door wouldn't open. It had been locked somehow, although there was no lock on it, and the door seemed to be jammed, but as Hiroko pushed it open as hard as she could, she was met with a stench that left her breathless, and as the door opened fully a bucket of red paint fell on her and splashed everywhere. She was gasping and crying and trying to catch her breath, as she saw that her few belongings had been strewn everywhere, and someone had used the rest of the red paint to write the word JAP all over her walls, and in smaller letters *go home* and *get out of here.* But the worst of all was the dead cat they had put on her bed. It looked as though it had been dead for weeks, and it actually had maggots.

Hiroko ran screaming out the door, hysterical, and down the stairs as fast as she could, smearing paint everywhere. It was on her clothes, on her shoes, in her eyes, on her hands as she flew down the stairs, touching the walls and the banisters. She didn't even know where she was going. A few girls looked surprised when she got downstairs and others seemed to disappear, as Hiroko screamed in terror. She didn't even know what to say or do, all she could remember was the stench of the cat, and the paint pouring through her hair, and the terror of what they had done to the only haven she had there.

"Hiroko!" The dorm mistress and her assistant came running immediately and were horrified at what they saw as she stood there. "Oh, my God . . . oh, my God!!" The younger of the two women began to cry as she looked at her, and so did Hiroko. She took Hiroko in her arms, oblivious to the paint that covered her, and held her. "Who did this?"

Hiroko was too incoherent to speak, but she had no idea anyway, and would never have told them even

if she did know. But when the two women went upstairs after leaving her in the infirmary, they were appalled at what they saw in her room. It was vicious.
And late that night, both nurses worked on getting the
paint out of her hair, put drops in her eyes to soothe
them, and put her to bed in the infirmary. The school
administration was sick over what had happened to
her, and it was possible that it was just an isolated
incident, but for her sake, and her safety, they felt they
had to make a decision.

They called her cousins that night, and both Reiko
and Tak came in the station wagon to get her the next
day. They were frightened when they got the call, they
thought she'd been hurt. And she had been, but not in
any of the ways they expected.

They were overwhelmed when they saw her room.
The cat was gone by then, but they were told about it,
and janitors were already trying to clean the walls, but
the deans had wanted the Tanakas to see it. They
wanted them to fully understand the situation for her
there, and the basis for their ultimate decision.

"It grieves us to say this to you," they admitted in
their meeting with the Tanakas. "And it is a terrible
condemnation of all of us here. We each share the
shame of what has happened. But because of it, because of the political climate at the moment, and the
way the girls apparently are reacting to it, Hiroko is not
safe here. We cannot be responsible for her, if things
like this can happen in our midst. For her own sake,
we cannot let her stay here." They were terribly sorry,
and they said all the right things, but they did not want
the responsibility of her getting injured the next time.
As it was, she could have been blinded by the paint, or

even killed if the can had hit her. It was just too dangerous, and they suggested that perhaps the wisest course was for her to take a semester off, and see how the public mood had altered. She would be welcome to return at the right time: she had been an excellent student.

The Tanakas sat and listened to them, looking grief stricken, wondering how long it would be before things like this started happening at Stanford.

"Have you said anything to Hiroko yet?" Takeo asked unhappily. He didn't disagree with them, and in a way, he wanted her to leave and come home with them. But he knew she would be disappointed.

"We wanted to speak to you first," the dean said, and then called her in, and said all the same things to Hiroko. And in spite of all her efforts not to, she cried when they told her.

"I must leave?" she asked, looking deeply embarrassed as they nodded. She lowered her eyes, and looked very Japanese. In her view, she had failed dismally. It was all her fault. And then she looked at her cousin. "My father will be so ashamed of me," she said in English. She longed to speak Japanese to him, but she knew she couldn't.

"Your father will understand," the dean said kindly. "This situation is beyond anyone's control. And it does not speak well for our young ladies. They should be ashamed, Hiroko, not you. We are doing this for your safety." First they had had to put her in a broom closet, and now they were dumping paint cans on her head, and putting a dead cat in her room. If that was the way the other girls felt about her, she definitely did not belong there. "Perhaps you will come back someday."

"I would like that," she said sadly. "I must go to college in America. I have promised my father," she said, honoring her promise.

"Maybe you could transfer to the University of California, or Stanford, and live with your cousins." It was a possibility, but as a Japanese national, it was unlikely that anyone would take her.

"You can stay at home with me for a few months." Reiko smiled at her, heartbroken at what the girls had done to her. It was an experience no one should have had, and Hiroko was so gentle and kind that the idea of anyone abusing her turned Reiko's stomach.

"We're very sorry," the administrators said again, and a little while later Hiroko went upstairs to pack her things with Reiko. Some had been stolen, most had been destroyed. The red paint had splashed everywhere; it was still in her hair, despite both nurses' efforts. It would take weeks to get it out. They'd even had to get it off her eyelashes and eyebrows.

Reiko took her bag to the car, while Hiroko stripped her bed and folded her blankets. And as she did, she suddenly sensed a presence behind her, and turned in terror. Maybe this time they would attack her. But the only person she saw standing there, looking hesitant, was Anne Spencer. Hiroko said not a word to her, she just stood there and waited, sure that the tall, aristocratic blonde had come to gloat, or maybe even to hurt her. And yet there was a look of sorrow in Anne's eyes, and they filled with tears as she held a hand out to Hiroko.

"I came to say good-bye," she said in a whisper to

her. "I'm sorry about what they did to you. I heard about it last night." She could still see some of the paint in her hair and around her eyes, and she felt desperately sorry for her. She hadn't wanted to room with her, but she had never wanted anything like this to happen. And she had lain awake all night, thinking about it, after someone told her. It was a sick thing to do and she wanted Hiroko to know how she felt about it. She was outraged. Anne knew she'd had a right to be upset over being asked to room with her. But in her mind, that was different. She felt adamant that no one had a right to do this to another human being. And Japanese or not, Hiroko was very decent. Anne knew it from all she'd seen of her, and in her own way, respected her for it. She didn't want to be her friend or her roommate—she was still convinced that simply because Hiroko was Japanese, she was somehow beneath her. In her world, Japanese were nannies and gardeners and servants. But no matter what else she felt, Anne didn't wish her any harm either. And she felt terrible about everything the other girls had done to her.

"Will you go back to Japan?" Anne was suddenly curious about her. It was too late now, but at least she had wanted to say good-bye, and tell her she was sorry. She wanted her to know that she wasn't part of the attack that had been perpetrated on her by the others.

"My father wishes me to stay here, and I cannot go back anyway. There are no ships now." She was trapped here, with people who hated her as much as those who had vandalized her room, and even ones like Anne Spencer, who openly shunned her. Hiroko didn't comprehend the depths of Anne's sympathy now, nor did she trust her. Yet she sensed something straightforward and honest about her.

"Good luck," Anne said sadly, standing there for a moment, and then she disappeared. And as Hiroko walked slowly downstairs, she thought about her. She had had such high hopes for St. Andrew's. And on her way out, she saw Sharon too. She looked straight at Hiroko as though she'd never seen her before, and then turned on her heel and walked down the hall, laughing with a group of girls, telling them all about the day she had spent with Greer Garson.

Several of the deans shook Hiroko's hand when she left, but none of the girls said anything. And despite the polite words, there was no doubt in Hiroko's mind. She had disgraced her family. She had failed them.

She slipped into the backseat of the car quietly, with her head bowed, and without knowing why, she glanced back as they drove away. The last face she saw at St. Andrew's was Anne Spencer's, watching her from an upstairs window.

# Chapter 9

FOR THE next several weeks, Hiroko flew around the Tanakas' house like a whirlwind. Reiko was busy at the hospital, and Hiroko did everything for her. She cooked, she cleaned, she watched Tami in the afternoons. She even helped the little girl make a whole new set of drapes and bedspreads for her dollhouse. And when Reiko came home in the afternoons that she worked, she found everything immaculate and in order.

"It's embarrassing," she said to Tak. "I haven't cleaned house in three weeks. I feel like a lady of leisure."

"I think she's trying to make it up to us for having to leave St. Andrew's. I'm not sure she really understands that it wasn't her fault," he said sadly. "In her mind, this has been a great loss of honor. She came

here to go to school, to honor her father, and now she
can't. To her, the reason for that is unimportant. She's
paying penance." She said nothing about what had
happened, once she left St. Andrew's, and Tak had
warned the children not to annoy her about it. She felt
terrible and she was trying to make the best of a difficult situation.

They had talked about Hiroko applying to Stanford, but Tak seriously doubted that they'd be willing
to accept an alien at this point. They had been incredibly kind to Tak, but Hiroko didn't want to risk embarrassment, to herself or to him, by applying. So instead,
she made herself useful to everyone in the family. And
the main task she seemed to have set herself was to
become as American as she could. He hadn't seen her
in a kimono in almost two months, she never bowed or
called him "san" anymore, and whenever she had a
minute, she read, or listened to the radio, and she had
seriously begun to improve her English.

Peter spent considerable time with her too, and he
had been devastated for her over what had happened
at St. Andrew's, but he saw the change in her too.
Though at first she seemed filled with shame, she also
seemed determined not to let it defeat her.

But the news still wasn't good. The Japanese had
invaded the Dutch East Indies two days before she left
school, and two weeks after that, the state Personnel
Board voted to bar all Japanese from applying for, or
keeping, civil service jobs. Things were definitely not
improving. And Tak was hearing things he didn't like at
Stanford. There was a certain amount of unrest these
days about his being the head of the department.

But no one was prepared for the army declaring

"restricted areas" all up and down the West Coast, and putting a curfew on "enemy aliens." And Takeo was even more shocked when they were told they could only travel back and forth to their place of employment, and stay within a five-mile radius of their residence. Anything farther than that would require a special permit.

"It's like being in a ghetto," he said darkly to Peter when they heard about it. And at home, when he told his family, Sally was horrified. To her it meant she couldn't even go to a late movie.

"It means a lot more than that," Tak said to his wife later that night when they were alone in their bedroom. But neither of them were prepared when the head of the university apologized deeply to him, but said that Peter was being made head of the department, and Takeo would have to become his assistant. It meant a considerable cut in pay, but a loss of prestige as well—not that Takeo begrudged it to Peter, but it was just more of the same thing. Little by little, all their privileges and rights were being chipped away. And it was only a week after that when the hospital told Reiko they wouldn't need her. Too many patients had complained about being cared for by an enemy alien, no matter how talented a nurse she was, or how gentle with her patients.

"I guess we're lucky they don't make us wear stars, like the Jews in Germany," Takeo said bitterly to Peter over lunch one day, in the office Takeo had relinquished to him, but which still felt like his. It was a painful situation. "But in our case we don't need to. They can see who we are, or at least they think they can. To them, we all look the same, issei, nisei, sansei.

What's the difference?" In his case, he had been born in Japan, which made him issei. But his children, having been born in the States, were nisei. And their children would be sansei. The only real "enemy alien," if you could even call her that on a pure technicality, was Hiroko, because she'd been trapped here.

In fact, a new term had emerged, a truly confusing one. Japanese were being referred to as aliens and non-aliens. The non-aliens were actually American citizens, people of Japanese descent who had been born in the United States. The nisei. But both groups were being lumped together, because they were Japanese. Non-aliens somehow made them sound a lot less friendly. Reiko was actually no longer a citizen, she was a non-alien, a variation of the enemy, and someone not to be trusted.

"I feel like a doctor with a fascinating disease," Takeo said to Peter thoughtfully. "I have this constant urge to put the diseased cells under the microscope and study them, while I'm dying." He had no illusions that things weren't going from bad to worse. The question was, how bad would they get? And none of the answers so far were very reassuring.

"You won't die of this, Tak." Peter tried to comfort him, but he still felt guilty over having his friend and recent boss's job and his office. But at least Tak hadn't gotten fired; many others had. And Peter was grateful that he hadn't.

On Valentine's Day, one newspaper printed an editorial urging the evacuation of all Japanese, regardless of their citizenship status. Singapore fell to the Japanese the next day. And the day after that, the Joint Immigration Committee agreed with the editorial, urging the removal of all Japanese, as the FBI continued to make mass arrests, hoping to catch Japanese spies in California. But thus far, not a single person had been charged or indicted for acts of treason.

On February nineteenth, Executive Order 9066 was signed by the President, in effect giving the military the power to designate areas from which "any and all persons" could be excluded. In effect, it allowed the military to ask the Japanese to leave any area from which they wished them excluded. It was a document of profound importance. And Public Law 77-503 made it a federal offense to refuse to leave a military area when ordered to do so. Failure to obey was a crime punishable by a term in prison.

Some thought these laws would change very little in practice, but others, like Tak and Peter, feared that this was only the first roll of the drums, and the real terror would come later. They already had curfews, limitations, needed special permits to go anywhere, were being referred to as aliens no matter what their history, and now the army had the power to exclude them. And in the ensuing days, the Japanese were asked to evacuate voluntarily, to sell their homes and businesses, and move elsewhere.

To make matters worse, there was finally a real attack on the coast, when a Japanese submarine fired at a Santa Barbara oil field on February twenty-third. There were no deaths or casualties, but the hysteria it caused was the final straw, and exactly what General De Witt needed. The proof was there now. The country was under attack by the Japanese, and every man, woman, and child of Japanese origin was under suspicion.

But even the few who chose to move away voluntarily did not find warm receptions elsewhere. Governors of other states were in an uproar as they began to trickle in. But most of the Japanese in California chose to stay there. They had homes, and businesses, and lives, and nobody wanted to move away for voluntary exclusion.

It was like a rising tide of despair in those days, as Takeo listened to the news, and discussed it with Reiko. She was panicked at the idea of having to move anywhere "voluntarily." She had lived in California all her life, and so had their children. They had never been farther away than Los Angeles. The prospect of going east, or to the Midwest, or anywhere else, upset her deeply.

"Tak, I just don't want to." They'd heard several tales of people who had tried to move away, but been met by such ferocious opposition wherever they went that they came right back to San Francisco. "I'm not going."

He didn't want to tell her that one day she might have to. But he and Peter discussed it constantly. What if they were simply told to leave the state? Much of the hysteria was caused by there being so many Japanese along the coastline. And the prevailing thought was that if they were farther away, they would create less of a danger.

In late March, armed soldiers descended on Japanese communities in the state of Washington, and gave them six days to sell their homes and businesses and report to a local fairground, and they were held incarcerated there, pending "relocation." But no one knew "to where" yet. The army was talking about setting up camps for them, but no one knew where, or if it was really true. It was all gossip and rumor. And the entire Japanese community was stunned into terrified silence.

"Do you think it could happen here?" Reiko asked her husband in bed that night. It seemed incredible, if what they'd heard was true. She still wasn't sure she believed it. But eventually photographs in the newspapers confirmed it. There were images of children standing next to suitcases, with tags attached to buttons on their coats, old people, women crying, and proud locals standing next to signs that said JAPS, GET OUT! WE DON'T WANT YOU! It was a nightmare.

"I don't know," Tak said, wishing he had the courage to lie to her, but he didn't. "I think so, Rei. I think we have to be prepared for anything." But no one ever is in life, and they were no different.

In spite of what they heard, they went about their lives as usual. The children went to school, and Reiko and Hiroko cleaned the house. Takeo went to school and pretended to work for Peter. And Ken spent time with his girlfriend after he did his chores. But no matter how ominous world events were, it was hard to believe that their lives would ever unravel.

Peter spent a lot of time with Hiroko that spring. She had applied herself to studying in every spare moment she had, so as not to let her father down completely. She was reading everything she could about politics, and art, and American history, and always in English. Her English had improved considerably, and she had grown up somewhat. Her experience at St. Andrew's had hurt her a great deal, but it had also taught her something. She had never heard from any of the girls again, nor the school, except for a formal letter telling her that they were sorry that she had withdrawn, but accepted her reasons. She had been given incompletes in everything, and academically her time, and her father's money, had been wasted. She was sensitive to that too, and planned one day to repay him for the time lost, and make restitution. She tried to explain it to Peter once or twice, and he was intrigued by her thinking. She had every intention of making up for the shame of not finishing the year at school, but in her heart of hearts, she considered it an enormous failure.

She had planted a lovely garden that spring, and kept the house immaculate. When she could get the ingredients, she sometimes made traditional Japanese dishes for them. Though the children hated Japanese food, Takeo and Peter loved it. She used all the arts and skills she had learned from her grandmother, and enjoyed teaching Peter as much as she could about her culture. He was increasingly fascinated by it, and even more so by the gentle, capable woman she was becoming. But she was careful to learn his ways too, and she enjoyed discussing his work with him, and the things he taught at the university. They would sit for hours, lost in conversation.

"What do you suppose you're going to do?" Takeo asked him quietly one day in April. It was obvious that Peter was deeply in love with her, but in the present circumstances, and perhaps even after that, there was very little they could do about it. It was not at all like his situation, at the same stage, with Reiko. They had gotten married within six months, but there was no hope of Hiroko being able to marry Peter in California.

"I don't know," Peter said honestly. He had thought of asking her to go out of state with him and get married, but he wasn't at all sure she'd do it. Her father's approval was very important to her, and he knew nothing about Peter. She couldn't even write to her father now, and at times he knew she was still very homesick for her parents. "I wanted to go to Japan to meet her father this summer, and talk to him, to see if he's as modern in his thinking as you all seem to think. But those plans went out the window with Pearl Harbor."

"It could be years before this is over," Tak said sadly.

"She'll never agree to get married without her parents' knowledge and approval," Peter said pensively.

And he was joining the army in June. The Selective Service had agreed to wait until then, so he could finish the term, particularly now that he was the head of the department. But beyond that, he had no special powers. And he didn't like leaving her without some kind of protection, although of course she had the Tanakas. Even without the war, he wanted to marry her anyway. But she kept insisting that they had to wait for the approval of her father. "You don't think they'll ever evacuate anyone here, do you, Tak?" They had all followed closely what had just gone on in Seattle. It was a different state, though not a different army.

"I don't know what to think anymore. I think anything is possible. This whole country's going crazy, about the Japanese anyway. And in some ways, I can't blame them. We're at war with Japan, they have every reason to be suspicious of aliens. What I can't understand though is how they can pretend that American-born citizens are suddenly aliens. That's what's crazy." And all the Japanese boys who had volunteered had either wound up in kitchens or been sent home. None of them were being assigned to fighting units. The country had an immeasurable distrust for the loyalty of the nisei, and for the moment, nothing could persuade them to see anything differently. "I wish I had the answers. I guess if I really thought they'd evacuate us, I'd be packing my bags for New Hampshire. But I keep thinking it's all going to settle down, we'll all get our jobs back"—he smiled at his young friend without malice—"and they'll say they're sorry. But there's a part of me that knows I'm being stupid."

"I don't think you're stupid. It makes sense. The other stuff certainly doesn't," Peter answered, and all he could think about now was Hiroko. He wanted to marry her, to shield her from all this, from the fear and the prejudice and the uncertainty. But even just taking her out to dinner, or a movie, he couldn't protect her. There was always the fear that someone would come up to them, and spit at her, or say something, or shout an obscenity at her. It had happened to them, and to others. It had happened to her at the grocery store just that week, and Tak had told her to patronize only nisei stores, so she wouldn't have a problem. When Peter heard, he told her how worried he was about leaving her when he joined the army. And this time he brought up the subject of marriage, but for her it was impossible until she was in contact with her family again, and even then, they might not agree to it. But the thought of her marrying anyone else almost killed him. He hated the thought of leaving her, of not seeing her face, or her shining black hair, or her lithe, graceful movements. She always seemed to flit around him like a hummingbird, bringing him things, making him tea, smiling at him, telling him a funny story about Tami. She loved the little girl, and children generally, and more and more Peter found himself dreaming of having a life with her, and having her bear his children. He wanted to be with her, for eternity, and no executive order could change that.

Hiroko was so brave about what was happening. She was always quiet, and strong, and peaceful. She never showed her pain, and always tried to reassure Peter, and the others.

Tak was sorry for Peter and Hiroko, whenever he looked at them. He thought it was going to be a long, hard road to their future.

But the following week, they had bad news from Reiko's family. Her cousins in Fresno had been sent to Terminal Island, then within two weeks they had been given notice again, and sent to an assembly center in Los Angeles. When they left Fresno, they had been given three days to sell their things, and they had lost everything. They'd sold their house for a hundred dollars, walked away from their car, and their huge crop of Mother's Day flowers had had to be abandoned.

"But that's impossible," Reiko said, in tears, reading Tak their letter. "Three days? How could they do that?" They'd been evacuated with hundreds of others, and were being held at a fairground. The news had an unreal quality, and none of them had absorbed what it meant when, three weeks to the day, an exclusion order was posted for their area in Palo Alto. They had ten days to sell their houses, their businesses, their cars, store their minor belongings, and evacuate. A "responsible member" of the family had to come to the Civil Control Station nearest them, which in their case happened to be an old Buddhist temple, to get further instructions. But they knew nothing more for the moment.

Takeo heard of it that day at the university, and he saw several of the posters on the way home. He stopped to read one carefully, feeling his heart pound mercilessly, and the next morning it was all spelled out in the papers.

Peter had come to the house to offer them his help, and he and Tak went to the Civil Control Station together. He tried to find out what was going on, but they wouldn't tell him any more than they would tell Takeo. In ten days from the order, nine days now, the entire family had to report to the assembly center at Tanforan Racetrack in San Bruno. Each adult could bring a hundred and fifty pounds of belongings with them, including bedding, toiletries, and clothes for any climate. Children were allowed seventy-five pounds each. But every single person must be able to carry their own belongings, which made the weight allowances ridiculous. A fifty-pound child couldn't carry seventy-five pounds of boxes or valises, nor could Reiko or Hiroko, or even Ken, carry a hundred and fifty pounds. So in effect, the weight allowances meant nothing.

Takeo was given tags for each of them, and asked if there was anyone elderly or infirm in his family, in which case he would have been given special tags, which were larger. He was numb as he listened to them, and stared at the tags in his hand once he had them. There were twenty tags for each person and each suitcase. And their number was 70917. They no longer had a name, just a number. He was told that pets of any kind could not come along, not even small ones. And that they must not bring money, jewelry, cameras, radios, weapons, or any object made of metal. And the United States government was offering to store larger household items like refrigerators and washing machines, heavy furniture, or pianos, in warehouses provided for them, but at their own risk, should anything get damaged.

He couldn't even think as he left the line, holding the tags with their number, and he and Peter left the small temple feeling dazed. They had been forbidden to leave the area. It was too late to flee now.

They had nine days to report to Tanforan, nine days to sell everything. And he had been told that they were going there to be relocated, but no one seemed to know to where, or was willing to tell them. He couldn't even tell Reiko what kind of clothes to bring, for cool or warm weather. He knew nothing. He wasn't even entirely sure they would all be together, or if they would be safe wherever they were sent. The thought of that made him tremble.

There were whispers in the line that the men would be executed, that they would all be shot, that the children would be sold as slaves, and husbands and wives would be sent to separate places. It all sounded like rumor to him, but in fact there was no way of knowing. He could promise Reiko nothing. But the man who had given him the tags had asked if they were all immediate family, or extended, and Takeo had said that one of the tags was for their cousin. He did not say that she was full Japanese, and only here as a student, but they would find out eventually, when they saw her passport. The man's only response was that there was no guarantee they would be relocated together. He realized then that he was still an alien too, and there was always the possibility that his fate would be different than his wife's, or that perhaps he would go to prison.

Peter looked deeply concerned as they drove home and he questioned Takeo. "Did he say she might not be relocated with you?" Takeo nodded in silence, as Peter tried not to panic. "You can't let that happen, Tak. You can't leave her by herself. God only knows what will happen to her." His voice was raised and he was staring at his friend, as the abominable tags lay on the seat between them, and Tak turned to him with tears in his eyes as they stopped at a light.

"Do you think I can change any of it? Do you think I want any of us to go at all, together or separately? What exactly do you think I can do here?" The tears rolled down his cheeks, and Peter touched his arm, appalled at everything that had happened.

"I'm sorry," he said, with tears in his own eyes, and the two men rode back to the house in silence, wondering what they would say to the women. Peter only wished he could go with them. He had been told at the control station that he could assist them when they went to the assembly center at Tanforan, and he could visit them, but he couldn't stay there, and he would have to leave his car a good distance from Tanforan, and bring no contraband with him.

But he was completely panicked at the idea of

leaving Hiroko there. It was like taking her to prison. And if she was separated from her cousins, she would have no protection whatsoever. He couldn't even begin to imagine what might happen.

Takeo stopped the car outside the house, sighed audibly, and glanced at Peter. He knew they were waiting for him, but he couldn't bear the thought of telling them what their fate was. Their worst nightmares had come true, and he realized now that he should have left months before, and gone anywhere. It would have been no worse than what had just happened. And now they were forbidden to leave the area, until they reported to the assembly center at Tanforan for relocation.

There were mysterious little words involved, like *assembly center*, and *relocation*, and *alien*, all of which meant other things than what they were meant to. They were ordinary words in which monsters hid, ready to devour them.

"What are you going to say to them, Tak?" Peter asked, looking anguished for him as they both blew their noses. It was as though someone had just died, their lives, his career, their future.

"I have no idea what to say to them," Tak said grimly. Then he looked at Peter with a pained smile. "Want to buy a house, or a car?" He had no idea where to begin, there was so much to give up, put away, and get rid of.

"I'll do everything I can, Tak. You know that."

"I'm serious about the house or the car." He had heard of other people who had sold hotels for a hundred dollars, cars for fifteen. You couldn't take it with you, or hang on to it, and he couldn't see himself storing things like their washing machine for God only knew how many years in a federal warehouse. He was going to sell everything he could, and give away what he had to. "I guess we'd better go in," he said, wishing he didn't have to, wishing he didn't have to see their faces when he told them, especially Reiko's. The kids would be horrified, but they were young, they'd survive anything as long as their lives and their safety weren't jeopardized. But things weren't all that important. He and Reiko had spent nineteen years building everything, and now they had nine days to tear it all apart, and leave it on the junk heap.

Peter put his arm around his shoulders as they walked inside, and the two men almost cried when they saw Reiko and Hiroko. Hiroko was not yet nineteen, but she looked quiet and dignified in a black skirt and sweater as she stood next to her cousin. Her eyes met Peter's immediately, and it took every ounce of courage he had not to turn away from the questions he saw there. Takeo went straight to his wife, took her in his arms and held her, and without hearing anything, she started to cry. The tags were still concealed in his pocket.

"Do we really have to go, Tak?" she asked, hoping that he had been able to talk them out of it, by some miracle or quirk of fate. She wanted someone to tell them that it was all a mistake and they could stay at home in Palo Alto.

"Yes, sweetheart. We do. We have to go to the Tanforan Assembly Center for relocation."

"When?"

"In nine days," he said, feeling a weight crush his chest, but he stood firm as he told her. "We have to sell the house, and whatever else we can. We can store the rest in government warehouses, if we want to." She couldn't believe what she was hearing. He took the tags out of his pocket then, and she started to cry again, as Hiroko stood wide-eyed, and watched them. She hadn't made a sound, and her eyes went to Peter's, filled with terror.

"Will I go with you, Takeo-san?" she asked, reverting to the old ways. It didn't matter now, no one could hear them.

"Yes," he lied. He wasn't sure, but it was too soon to tell her. He didn't want to frighten her any more than he had to.

The children joined them then and he told them everything, or all that he knew anyway, and everyone cried, even Peter. It was a terrible morning, and Tami sobbed horribly when she heard they couldn't bring Lassie, their Shiba.

"What'll we do with her?" she cried. "They won't kill her, will they?"

"Of course not." Takeo gently touched her hair, feeling the acute ache of not being able to protect his youngest child, or any of them, from what had happened. But there were no miracles for them now. Only sorrow. "We'll give Lassie to friends, people we know will be good to her," he tried to reassure her.

"What about Peter?" She looked at him hopefully, maybe he'd give her back one day, but Peter gently took her little hand in his and kissed it.

"I'm going away soon too. I'm going into the army."

And then Tami turned to Hiroko with fresh terror. "What about my dollhouse?"

"We'll pack it very carefully," Hiroko promised, "and take it with us." But Takeo shook his head again.

"We can't. We can only take what we can carry."

"Can I take my doll?" Tami asked desperately, and this time he nodded.

The two younger girls were both crying when they left the room, and Ken was wiping his eyes, but he sat looking stern and stubborn as he listened, and then finally his father glanced at him, aware that there was a growing problem.

"What's the matter, Ken?" It was an odd question to ask, but the boy looked as though he were going to explode at any moment.

"This country, if you want to know what I think, that's what's the matter. You may not be a citizen, Dad, but I am. I was born here. I could get drafted next year. I could die for them, but in the meantime, they're going to ship me off someplace because of my Japanese ancestors, 'in whatever degree.' " That was the criterion they were using. Japanese ancestry, in any degree. And citizenship or country of origin meant nothing. All his life he had pledged his allegiance to the flag, and sung "The Star-Spangled Banner"; he'd been a Boy Scout and had a paper route and eaten corn on the cob and apple pie on the Fourth of July, and now he was an "alien" and he had to be evacuated like a criminal or a spy. It was the worst thing that had ever happened to him. And as he listened to them, all of his ideals and beliefs and values were being shattered.

"I know, son. It's not fair. But it's what they want from us. We have no choice now."

"What if we refuse to go?" Others had, but not many. Only a handful.

"They'll probably put you in prison."

"Maybe I'd prefer that," he said staunchly, but Tak shook his head, and Reiko only cried harder. It was bad enough losing her home, but not her children.

"We wouldn't want that to happen, Ken. We want you to come with us."

"Will they keep us together, Tak?" Reiko asked, looking frightened as Ken stormed into the kitchen. He wanted to go and talk to Peggy. But the same thing was happening to her family. It was happening to all of them. And no one understood it any better than he did.

Tak looked at his wife, unable to lie to her. He never had, and he wouldn't start now. He didn't want to promise her something he couldn't deliver. "I'm not sure yet. There were a lot of rumors. Maybe because I'm a Japanese citizen, they might keep me separate, but I'm just guessing that. No one said anything. And we all have the same number." But later, when Peter and Hiroko went outside, Reiko questioned him again.

"What about Hiroko?"

"I don't know that either. She really is an enemy alien in their eyes, unlike the rest of you. There could be a problem. I just don't know, Rei. We'll have to wait and see what happens." They were the hardest words he had ever said to her, and as he held her in his arms, he started to cry. He felt as though he had failed her completely. Everything had gone wrong, and they were losing everything, and God only knew where they would go, or what would happen. Maybe the truth would be even worse than the rumors. Maybe they would all be shot. It could happen. But for the moment, they had to do what they could, and have faith that they'd stay together. "I'm so sorry, Rei," he said over and over again, and she held him and comforted him, and told him that none of them could have known. None of this was his fault, but she could tell, looking at him, that he didn't believe her.

And then, as she looked out the window at Peter and Hiroko again, she asked Tak a question. "Do you think they should get married?"

But Takeo only shook his head. He and Peter had talked about it only that morning. "They can't now. They can't be married in this state, and she can't go anywhere now. We're all stuck here. They'll have to wait until he comes back, assuming she's free to move around again by then." But who knew when that would be. And out in the garden, Peter was saying the same thing to Hiroko. He wanted her to promise him that when he returned, and she was free, they would be married.

"I can't promise you that without my father," she said sadly, looking at him, longing for him, wishing that things could be different. But she had failed her father once, by leaving school, she couldn't fail him again, by marrying without his approval. "I want to marry you, Peter. . . . I want to take care of you." She smiled as he pulled her down on his lap on a bench in the garden.

"I want to take care of *you* forever. I wish I could stay longer now. I'd like to be with you at Tanforan. I'll come as often as they let me." She nodded, still unable to absorb what had happened. And although she tried to put a brave face on it for him, he could see that she was very frightened. He held her in his arms for a long time, and he could feel her shaking.

"I feel so sad for Uncle Tak and Aunt Reiko, this is so hard for them."

"I know it is. I want to do everything I can," he said, but there wasn't much he could do. He had promised to bank what little money Takeo saved. And he had offered to buy everything Takeo couldn't sell. But it wasn't easy to unravel a life in nine days. Others had to sell businesses and crops, or simply abandon what they had as they left for relocation.

"I will take care of the children for them, when we get there," Hiroko explained, but Peter couldn't help wondering if she would even be with them. And he agonized again over the fact that he could do nothing to protect her. "Kenji is very angry."

"He has a right to be. What he said is true. He's as American as I am. They have no right to treat him like the enemy; he isn't."

"It's very wrong what they're doing, isn't it?" She was sure of it, but she was still confused about the implications and their reasons. The papers were so full of near-Japanese attacks and threats all along the coast, that sometimes she believed them. It was their justification for relocation of the Japanese, that and the constant accusation that their loyalty was in question. But why would they be loyal to Japan when most of them had no relatives there and had never even been there? It was impossible to explain rationally, and Hiroko shook her head as she listened. "Poor Uncle Tak . . ." she said again. "Poor all of them." She didn't even think of herself as she said it. And then, pensively, "I must give all my kimonos away. They are very heavy, and I cannot carry all of them. And perhaps it is still better, even now, if I do not wear them."

"I'll keep them for you," he said sadly. He would rather have kept her safe from anything that might happen. "We'll be together when this is over, Hiroko. No matter what happens to us along the way. You must remember that always, no matter where all this takes us. Will you remember that?" She nodded in answer, and he kissed her.

"I will be waiting for you, Peter," she said softly.

"I'll come back," he said, with a look of determination, praying that the gods would keep them both safe in the meantime.

They walked somberly inside again, and from then on, they never stopped. They were all busy.

Takeo resigned his job at the university, and Peter took a week's leave of absence to help them. And in comparison to many of their friends, Tak got a good price for the house: he got over a thousand dollars. Many of the others had sold theirs for a hundred, or even less sometimes, if they had greedy neighbors. There were people waiting now to take advantage of the situation. They learned, too, that other people had been given only three or four days' notice to report to Tanforan. Nine days was a real bonus.

But he got only fifty dollars for the car, and five dollars for a brand-new set of golf clubs. He would have given them to Peter, but he was leaving too. He was going to store his own things when he left for the army. They had a huge yard sale, with everything they couldn't pack or leave behind. And Reiko cried when she sold her wedding dress to a beautiful young girl for three dollars. But Hiroko carefully packed Tami's dollhouse in a box, with all the tiny furniture and accessories, and marked it carefully with Takeo's name for the government warehouse.

They weren't storing many things; it didn't seem worth it to Tak. Just boxes of their photographs, the dollhouse, and some special mementos. All the bigger items were sold for pennies on their front lawn, as Peter kept track of the money. By the end of the sale they had made roughly three thousand dollars. It seemed like a lot to them, but not when you considered that they had sold everything they owned. And the worst moment of all was when Tak's secretary at the university came to pick up Lassie. Tami held her and cried, and refused to let her leave, and finally Hiroko just held the child as she keened. The poor woman cried as she led the dog away, and Lassie howled and barked out the window of the car all the way around the corner. It was as though even she knew what had happened. It was a terrible day for all of them, they had each lost something important. Ken had sold his collection of signed baseball bats, and all his old Little League uniforms. And Sally had given up the four-poster bed she loved so much. They had even sold all the beds, and at Hiroko's suggestion, until they left, they were going to sleep on futons.

"That's horrible," Sally wailed as her mother told her. She was giving up everything, her clothes, her friends, her school, even her bed, and now she had to sleep on the floor, like a dog.

"You'd do it if you were in Japan," her mother said, smiling at Hiroko. But that made Sally even more furious.

"I'm not Japanese! I'm American!" she stormed at

them, and then ran into the house and slammed the door behind her. It was hard on all of them, particularly Tami, who was grieving for Lassie and her dollhouse.

"We'll make a new one when we get there," Hiroko promised her.

"You don't know how, and Daddy won't want to." Her parents were in a terrible mood these days, and the only person who ever played with her was her cousin.

"Yes, he will. He can show me how. We'll make it together, you and I."

"Okay." Tami brightened a little. She was nine now. Sally had just turned fifteen, but it had done nothing for her disposition. The only good news was that Ken's girlfriend Peggy and her family were going to Tanforan on the same day they were.

Sally's friend Kathy had never spoken to her again. She had driven slowly by the house that afternoon with her brother, and glanced at the yard sale, but they hadn't stopped, they didn't wave, and Sally turned away when she saw them.

They had only two days left in the house after the yard sale, and there was still a lot to do. The new owners had bought some of the furniture, fortunately, but not much. They had their own things. And Hiroko worked night and day with Reiko to pack for them, and get rid of everything else, leaving it for friends, or taking it to charities. The hard part was knowing what to take for relocation. They didn't know if they'd need country or city clothes, lightweight or warm ones, and they didn't want to weigh themselves down with the wrong gear, since they could take so little.

It was close to ten o'clock on the last night when they finished packing, and Peter was still with them. Tak handed him a beer, and then went upstairs to help Reiko, and Peter and Hiroko sat outside on the front steps. It was a beautiful April night, and it was hard to believe that anything bad was going to happen.

"Thank you for your help, Peter." She smiled at him, and he leaned over unceremoniously and kissed her. She could taste the cold beer on his lips, and she smiled and kissed him again.

"You work too hard," he said gently, and pulled her closer to him. She had been tireless, and Reiko had been so upset, she had been more than a little distracted, so Hiroko had done much of the work.

"You worked just as hard as I did," she said calmly. It was true. Tak had said more than once that they couldn't have done it without him. He had hauled things away, gone through endless boxes with Tak, packed whatever he could, unplugged appliances and moved furniture, and even taken their few boxes to the government warehouse. He had taken a few things of theirs to his house too, to store with his own when he left, and as promised, Hiroko's kimonos.

"We'll make a good couple one day, we're a good team. We both work hard." He smiled at her, with eyes tinged with mischief. He loved talking about getting married one day, and making her blush. She was still very old-fashioned in some ways, and he loved it. "How many children will we have?" he asked conversationally, and chuckled when she blushed darker.

"As many as you wish, Peter-san," she said, sounding very Japanese, but no one could hear them. "My mother wanted many children, many sons, but she got very sick when my brother was born, and almost died. She wanted to have him at home, and my father wanted her in the hospital. My father is very modern, but my mother likes the old ways . . . like me," she added with a shy smile.

"Like us," he corrected. "I want you to take very good care of yourself at Tanforan, as best you can. Conditions may not be good there. Be careful, Hiroko." He was afraid to say more, but he was terrified of what someone might do to her there, and he could only pray that they would let her stay with the Tanakas, and not send her elsewhere. There was nothing he could do now to protect her.

"I will be wise . . . and you too . . ." She looked at him pointedly. He was going away to war, she wasn't. And it was so peaceful sitting there in the warm garden. Neither of them realized how little quiet they would ever have again. She would be living in a relocation center with thousands of people all around her, and he would be in the army. It was a moment to cling to and cherish, one they would both remember forever.

"You'll be careful?" he asked again, looking sadly at her.

"I will. I promise." He looked into her eyes then, and set the beer down. And then he held her tight and kissed her. Holding her like that took his breath away at times, and it was hard not to get carried away, but fortunately they didn't have the opportunity to be other than responsible, but the temptation was always great when he kissed her.

"I'd better go," he said hungrily, wanting to devour her with his hands, and his lips, but he was always afraid to frighten her or to hurt her.

"I love you, Peter-san," she whispered, as he kissed her again. "I love you very much. . . ." In spite of himself, he moaned softly as he held her, and she smiled at him. There was a part of their life that she could not even imagine, yet in a part of her she longed for.

"I love you too, little one. . . . I'll see you tomorrow."

He left her at the gate with another kiss, and then with a wave he drove away, and she walked slowly back to the house, wondering what would happen to them. But fate has only questions, never answers. And she had just reached the door, when she heard someone call her name. She turned in surprise, and saw Anne Spencer walking slowly toward her. At first, Hiroko didn't even recognize her. Her hair was pulled back and she was wearing an old sweater, and carrying a basket.

"Hiroko," she said again, and this time, Hiroko walked toward her. The last time she had seen her was the day she'd left St. Andrew's when Anne had come to say good-bye to her, and then stood and watched her from the window.

They had certainly never been friends, and yet, since that last day, there had been a thin bond of respect between them. Hiroko had understood how much Anne had disapproved of the others vandalizing her room and tormenting her. And yet there had never been any warmth between them.

"Anne Spencer?" Hiroko asked cautiously.

"I heard that you were going." Her words surprised Hiroko.

"How did you hear that?"

"A friend of mine was in your cousin's class at Stanford," she said simply. "I'm sorry." This was the second time she had said that to Hiroko for something she hadn't done, and had nothing to do with. "Do you know where you're going yet?"

"Tanforan Assembly Center. After that, we do not know where." Anne nodded.

"I brought you this." She handed the basket to her. It was filled with sturdy delicacies, like good jams, and some cheese, and tins of soup, and meats, things that would sustain them. Hiroko was surprised, when she looked into it, by how many things there were, and how generous Anne had been. She scarcely knew her.

"Thank you." Hiroko stood holding the basket and looking up at her, wondering again why she had done it.

"I want you to know that I don't believe in what they're doing. I think it's terrible, and I'm sorry," she said again, and her eyes were bright with unshed tears. The two women looked at each other for a long moment, and Hiroko bowed low to her, to honor her, still holding the basket.

"Thank you, Anne-san."

"May God be with you," she whispered, and then turned and ran out of the garden. Hiroko heard a car start, and drive away, and she walked slowly back into the house, holding the basket.

# Chapter 10

THE DAY they left their house was the darkest any of them had ever experienced and one they would always remember.

The dog was already gone, and the car, and the house was almost empty. There was an eerie feeling to it now. The new owners were coming by that afternoon to start moving in, and Tak had left the keys with a neighbor.

They had thrown most of their food away, which seemed a waste, and given the rest to Peter.

But the most painful of all was leaving the house they had lived in for nearly eighteen years. Reiko and Tak had bought it when she was expecting Ken. It was the house all of their children had come home to after they'd been born, the house they had all known and loved, and where they had been happy for most of their marriage. Reiko stood looking around her for a last time, thinking of the happy times, and Tak had come to stand with her for a moment and put an arm around her.

"We'll be back, Rei," he said sadly.

"But it'll be someone else's," she said, as tears streamed down her face.

"We'll buy another house." But they had lives to live, and obstacles to overcome before they could return to do that. "I promise."

"I know," she said, trying to be brave, and as she slowly walked out, holding his hand, she said a small prayer, hoping they would all be home again soon, safe and together.

Peter drove them to the control station with their meager belongings. Everything had been tagged with the tags that had been given to them. Tami wore hers on the button of her sweater. Sally's was on her wrist, and Reiko's, Tak's, and Ken's were on their jackets. And Peter carefully attached Hiroko's to the top button of her sweater. 70917.

Hiroko sat in the car with Anne Spencer's basket on her lap. Reiko had been pleased with the gift and felt sure it would be useful, but no one even thought of it now as they rode along.

The drive to the control station was brief and silent. And as they turned the corner and saw the control station, it looked like pandemonium, as they all stared at the crowds of people, luggage, and buses.

"My God," Tak said, shocked at what he saw there. "Are they sending all of Palo Alto?"

"It sure looks like it, doesn't it?" Peter said, trying to avoid the hordes of people crossing the street to get there. They were all carrying suitcases and boxes, and trying to hold children's hands, and guide old people across the street. And there were at least a dozen buses waiting for them. It was a total mess, and Tak wasn't looking forward to joining the crowd.

The authorities had said that Peter couldn't drive them to Tanforan. They were not allowed to arrive by private vehicle. They had to go by bus from the control station with the others. But Peter had promised to drive to Tanforan himself after he dropped them off, and try to find them. But first he parked the car. He was going to stay with them as long as he could at the control station.

"What a mess," Tak said, and reluctantly, they got out of the car with all their belongings and joined the crowd. They were herded instantly into a larger group, and within a few minutes Peter was told he had to leave them. He asked if there was some sort of gathering point where he could meet his friends at Tanforan, but no one seemed to know, and Tak waved at him through the crowd as Peter disappeared, and Hiroko tried to fight off a wave of panic. Suddenly, this was real. They were about to be incarcerated, or relocated, or evacuated, or whatever they wanted to call it. But she was no longer free, he was no longer there, and she could no longer reach out to him anytime she wanted. What if she never saw him again . . . if he couldn't find them . . . if . . . As though sensing her cousin's fears, and everyone else's, Tami started to cry then. She was clutching her doll, which had a tag on it too, and Hiroko held Tami's hand tight so they wouldn't lose her.

Aunt Rei was looking grim. And Ken was looking

for his girlfriend Peggy while Tak kept urging them to stay close together. They were handed some papers eventually, told to put their things on the bus, and loaded in without further explanation. They spent an hour sitting there after that, and it was almost noon, and they were sweltering as the buses finally left for Tanforan. The ride took only half an hour.

But when they got to Tanforan, the chaos was even greater. There were lines of people for as far as you could see, thousands of them, old people with large tags, infirm people sitting on benches, stacks of suitcases, boxes of food, children crying. For as far as the eye could see there was humanity. There was a tent where they were preparing food, and not far from it was a long line of open toilets.

The entire experience was one Hiroko knew she would never forget. It had rained the day before, and they were up to their ankles in mud, as they stood in a long line, among what must have been over six thousand people. And as she looked at them, she gave up any hope of seeing Peter.

"He'll never find us," she said glumly.

"Maybe not," Tak said, looking around in horror. His new wing tip shoes had just been destroyed by the mud that almost reached his ankles. And Sally was saying that she had to go to the bathroom but would rather die than go in an open toilet. Hiroko and her mother had already promised to hold a blanket up for her, but she refused even to try it. But Hiroko and Reiko both knew that sooner or later they'd all have to use the open toilet, no matter how distasteful.

They were in line for three hours, and Anne's food basket came in very handy. None of them could leave the admissions lines to get in the food lines, and Tami was whining terribly as they stood in the mud, and perched on their suitcases when they got too tired.

When they reached the head of their admission line, they were each given throat exams, and the skin on their hands and arms was examined too, though even Reiko had no idea what they were doing. And then they were all surprised when they were given vaccinations by other "inmates." Reiko wasn't even sure they were nurses. They were just civilians helping out. And she noticed that the people in the cooking tent looked like volunteers too. They were wearing the oddest assortment of costumes. Brown suits, and blue coats, and little hats with pretty feathers. She asked if there was an infirmary, and someone waved vaguely in a distant direction and told her that there was one.

"Maybe they need some help," Reiko said softly to Tak, but who knew how long they'd be there. And by the time they got in the next line, their arms were all sore from the vaccinations, and poor Tami was so exhausted she said she felt like throwing up. But Hiroko was holding her hand, and smoothing her hair back and telling her a story about a wood elf and a little fairy, and after a while, Tami just held her doll and stopped crying, as she listened.

Ken was feeling better too. He had just spotted his girlfriend, which was an absolute miracle in a crowd that size. But there was still no sign of Peter. It was four o'clock in the afternoon by then, and they had been there for hours, and they still hadn't been assigned their quarters.

They stood on that line for hours, and even though they saw people lining up for dinner, they couldn't leave their line again. And finally they were given a number and told where to look for their quarters. They were in 22P, and they picked up their suitcases and headed in the direction they'd been told to go. They were almost home, for the moment. They still hadn't been told how long they would be there, or where they were going after that. And the long lines of stalls were extremely confusing. They went around and around for a while, and finally Ken saw their number. All it was was a horse stall. It had once housed a thorough-bred, but now it stood empty. It was barely big enough for a horse, let alone a family of six people. It was open to the air, and it had a half door that had been enough to keep the horse in. And when they looked inside, they saw that it had been whitewashed but not cleaned. It was filled with manure and debris and straw, and the stench was overwhelming.

This time it was too much for Reiko. She leaned over and piteously retched whatever she had eaten since that morning.

"Oh, God, Tak," she said, more miserable than she had ever been. "I can't do this."

"Yes, you can, Rei. You have to," he said softly. Their children were staring at them, looking to them for direction. "You sit down with the girls. Hiroko will get you some water. And Ken and I will find a couple of shovels and get it cleaned out. Maybe you should line up for some food with the kids. You can bring us some." But the last thing she wanted was to stand in line for dinner, and the children weren't hungry either. Instead, they sat down, as he had told them to, on their suitcases, and they dug into Anne's basket again. It had proven to be a godsend.

Reiko was still looking pale by then, but a little better. They were sitting some distance from the stall, and Hiroko had found large burlap feed sacks, which she and Sally were filling with straw to use as mattresses once the stalls were cleared out. But the best Ken and Tak had been able to find were two old coffee cans, and they were emptying the manure in agonizingly small quantities when Peter arrived, looking hot and disheveled. But he looked like a vision when Hiroko saw him. She ran to him and put her arms around him, unable to believe that he had really found them.

"I've been at the administration building since noon," he said wearily. "I practically had to sell my soul to get in here. They can't seem to understand why anyone would want to visit. They did everything they could to stop me." He kissed her gently, relieved beyond words to have found them at all. He had looked systematically along practically every row of stalls, and on every food line, and as he glanced over her shoulder he saw what Tak and Ken were doing. "That looks like fun," he said wryly, and Tak looked up at him and grinned. He hadn't totally lost his sense of humor, and seeing Peter had done wonders for all of them. They didn't feel so totally deserted.

"Don't knock it till you try it."

"That's a deal," Peter said, dropping his jacket on a pile of straw that Hiroko was using to fill the feed sacks. He rolled up his sleeves, and sacrificing his favorite shoes, marched into the manure to work alongside Ken and Tak. They had found another coffee can, and within a few minutes he was as filthy as they were.

It was an enormous job, and the stall looked as though it hadn't been cleaned in years, and it probably hadn't.

"No wonder the horse left," Peter grumbled as he dumped another can of manure out. It was like emptying the ocean with a teacup. "This place is a mess."

"Nice, huh?" Tak said, and Ken said nothing. He hated being here, hated what it meant, and what they had done to him. He would have given anything at that moment to get even with the people who had inflicted this horror on them.

"I wish I could say I'd seen worse," Peter quipped, as they worked side by side, getting filthier by the minute and getting nowhere. "But actually I don't think I have."

"Wait till you get to Europe with Uncle Sam. They'll probably have you doing jobs just like this."

"At least I'm getting in a little early practice."

Long after it had gotten dark, Reiko and the girls were lying on the straw mattresses Hiroko had made, and the three men were still working. Eventually Hiroko went to get them steaming cups of tea, and brought it to them, and offered to help the men, but they all declined. It was just too rotten a job for a woman.

"Do you have to leave at any particular time?" Tak asked Peter as they took a break, but he only shrugged as he smiled over at Hiroko.

"They didn't say anything. I'll just stay till they throw me out, I guess." And a few minutes later, they went back to work. They finished cleaning the stall at two o'clock in the morning. Ken hosed it down, and Peter helped them scrub the walls. The manure was gone, and they had gotten down to some fairly clean-looking mud, which they also hosed down with water.

"You may need to let it dry for a couple of days," Peter said thoughtfully. "Just hope it doesn't rain again." But once it was dry, they would put straw down on it, and then put their mattresses on it. All they could do for now was sit outside on the straw bags Hiroko had made them. Ken sat down on one of them, exhausted, and Takeo joined him. And Peter let himself down slowly on the one where Hiroko was sitting. She had waited up for them, and she had wanted to be with Peter. Reiko and the two girls were already sleeping. "This doesn't look like it's going to be much of a place," he said to her quietly. His whole body was aching. And the others had worked just as hard as he had.

"It looks awful," Hiroko confirmed to him. She couldn't imagine staying there, or being there at all, let alone spending the day they just had, cleaning two feet of manure out of a horse stall. "Thank you for everything you did. Poor Uncle Tak," she whispered. He looked exhausted.

"I'm just sorry you all have to be here."

"*Shikata ga nai,*" she said softly to him, as he raised an eyebrow for the translation. "It means that this cannot be helped. It must simply be." But he nodded, wishing that it weren't so.

"I hate to leave you here, little one." He put an arm around her and held her close to him. He worried about causing trouble for her, but how much more trouble could there be now? They were already here, and no one was watching them closely. There were families milling about, and old people, and in the daytime, children. He stood out because he was not Japanese, but no one seemed particularly interested in his presence. "I wish I could take you away with me." He smiled, kissing her carefully, not wanting to touch her with his filthy hands.

"So do I wish you could take me away," she said sadly. She realized now what they had, and might have some day, and what they had lost that day. She had lost her freedom, and suddenly every moment with him was even more precious, and she wondered if she had been foolish when she had told him she hadn't wanted to get married without her father's approval. Perhaps she should have gone to another state with him, as he had asked, and gotten married. It was too late now, but it was heavy on her mind as he went to wash with Ken and Tak, and use the open latrines that looked so awful. She couldn't see them from where she sat, but she knew they were there. She and Aunt Rei and the girls had tackled them earlier, taking turns, holding up blankets.

Peter came back with the others a few minutes later, and told her she should try to get some sleep. He said he'd come back the next day, in the afternoon. He had to teach only in the morning. But he couldn't seem to tear himself away, and she didn't want him to. It was another half hour before he finally left her, and she watched him walk away, feeling as though her last friend on earth had disappeared, as her cousin watched her.

"Get some sleep," Takeo said, handing her a blanket, wishing she had never come to America, for her sake. She was going to get hurt here. There was simply no other way. It was too late for them, and they were in love in a hostile world, which would do nothing to help them, only hurt them.

Hiroko lay curled up on her sack of straw, under a coat and a thin blanket they had brought, thinking of Peter, wondering where life would take them.

# Chapter 11

THEY WOKE up with the sun the next day, as the bugles blared, and went to stand on line at one of the camp's eleven mess halls for breakfast. They had to use color-coded ID cards and eat in shifts, and the food looked anything but appealing. There was some kind of thin gruel, and fruit, and powdered eggs, and some stale rolls that tasted as though they'd been around since New Year's. The food was edible, but barely, and all they ate was cereal. And afterward, they all went for a walk, and watched people trying to settle in and do what they had done the night before, shovel manure, sit on their suitcases, fill sacks with straw, and walk around and try to find familiar faces. They found some. Some teachers Tak had known, and a friend of Reiko's. Ken discovered with relief that Peggy's stall was just around the corner. It meant a lot to all of them to see people they knew. And Sally discovered two friends from her old school, and was thrilled to see them. Little Tami talked to anyone, and made friends among the children.

There was an atmosphere of determination evident everywhere, of trying to make the best of things, and a woman in the next row of stalls was planting seeds and determined to start a garden.

"I hope we won't be here that long," Reiko said nervously. They had still heard nothing about when they were going to move on, but Reiko couldn't imagine planting anything, or trying to put down roots here. This was just a matter of survival and existence.

She went to check out the infirmary that afternoon, and it was pretty grim. There were already a number of people there, mostly with stomachaches and dysentery. Two of the nurses told her to be careful of the food, a lot of things were spoiled, and to watch out for the water. And she passed it on to the others when she got back to them. She had promised to go back to the infirmary in the morning and help them.

The mud in the stall was almost dry by that afternoon, and Ken and Hiroko spread straw on it, and then moved their mattresses and valises in. It was clean now, they knew, and yet everything still smelled of horses.

And just as they finished putting their few belongings into the stall, Peter came, and Hiroko's face lit up like a sunburst. He told Tak whatever news there was from the university, and he had brought some chocolate bars and some cookies and fruit for them. He hadn't been sure how much the guards would let him bring in, and he was anxious not to annoy them. Tami reached for the chocolates immediately, and Sally gratefully took an apple and thanked him.

He sat with them for quite a while, and Hiroko stayed at the stall with him, while the others went to line up for dinner. She insisted she wasn't hungry, and she made do with one of his chocolate bars, and some cookies. And as he sat there, chatting with her, it was still incredible to him that entire families were living cramped into one horse stall each. That was all they had been allotted. And all over the state Japanese families were being taken to assembly centers like this, while they waited for relocation.

"Was everything all right today?" he asked with a look of concern, once the others left. Takeo was looking very down, but Reiko was a little livelier than she'd been the day before, and the children seemed to have adjusted. Tami wasn't crying as much, Sally was happy to have found a friend, and Ken didn't look quite as angry.

"We're all right," she said, looking peaceful, and he reached out and took her hand, and held it. It was strange for him without them. He had driven past the house, and was shocked to see children he didn't know and a different dog there. They were already moving in, and to Peter they looked like interlopers as he drove away quickly.

"I don't know what to do without you," he said, looking into the eyes where he found so much comfort. "I just keep coming here. I wish they'd let me stay with you. It's the only place I want to be now." She was relieved to hear it, but it wasn't fair to him in some ways. This was their problem, he didn't belong here. And it would only prolong the agony for them. He was leaving in seven weeks. But she didn't have the courage to tell him to stop coming. She just couldn't.

"I'm glad," she said honestly. She needed him. And she had waited all day anxiously for the moment he would come. She lived now for each of these precious moments. She told him about what she'd seen that day as they walked around, and even about the woman who was planting the tiny garden.

"It's not easy to defeat these people, thank God," he said, watching them around him. They were cleaning stalls, organizing things, hosing walls down and whitewashing them. There were groups of men playing cards, or go, the Japanese checkers, and a few old women chatting and knitting, and everywhere around them there were children. Despite the circumstances they were in, there was an atmosphere of hope and camaraderie that even he had noticed in the short time he'd been there. There were very few complaints, and more often than not, there was a fair amount of good humor. There was laughter here and there, and only the older men looked grief stricken sometimes to have been unable to keep their families from this, while the young men looked really angry, like Kenji. But for the most part, people were just trying to get on with living.

Hiroko smiled as she looked up at Peter. He was her life now. He and her cousins had become even more important, since losing touch with her family. She missed hearing from them, and knowing that they were all right. All she knew of them was that Yuji was in the air force, but she knew nothing more than that. And she knew she would have to live with the silence until the war ended. She thought about them at times, and prayed for them, but there was no possibility at all of further contact. She wasn't even quite sure how much contact she would be able to have with Peter when he left. He said he would write, but she just hoped they would let her have his letters, and vice versa.

"You're an amazing woman," he said quietly, watching her eat an apple, with wide, honest eyes filled with kindness. He loved watching her, always busy, always taking care of things, but saying very little. And he loved watching her with Tami.

"I'm only a foolish girl," she said, smiling at him, well aware of her second-rate status among her own people, although her father had taught her differently. He had told her that she could do anything she wanted, and one day she might do something important.

"You're a lot more than a foolish girl," Peter said. He leaned over and kissed her, as an old woman walked by with a little boy and turned the other way, disapproving. He was, after all, Caucasian.

"Do you want to go for a walk?" he asked, and she nodded, and put her apple core in the coffee can they were using for garbage. They had found three of them when they arrived and kept them.

There were open fields out back where the horses had been exercised, and it was ringed with barbed wire and fences, and there was a guardpost at the gate, but for once there was no one to bother them, as they walked in the tall grass and talked about the past and the future. The present seemed to be hanging in space in front of them, going nowhere, but they could see far ahead of them, to the place where they wanted to be one day, together. And as they walked, her mind drifted back to the places where she had once been, in Kyoto with her family, and in the mountains visiting her father's parents. It was a beautiful place, and it gave her comfort now to think about it as she held Peter's hand and walked in silence. And then as they arrived at the farthest reaches of the camp, they came to a stop together. And without saying anything, he put his arms around her and held her. One day there would be no boundaries, no limits for them, no place where they would have to stop. He longed to share that day with her, and in the meantime, they had each other.

"I wish I could just lift you out of here, Hiroko," he said sadly. "I never realized how lucky we were before. I wish . . ." He looked down at her, and she knew what he wished. She wished it too. "I wish I had taken you away and married you, when I could have."

"I would still be here," she said sensibly, "and they still wouldn't let you stay here. We would have had to go far, far away to have escaped all this." He knew she was right. He would have had to give up his job at the university and go far away with her. And none of them had really understood then how high the price would be for not leaving. They had all waited for the problems to go away, for people's attitudes to improve. But nothing was going to get better for a long time now. And they had missed their chance to flee. All that was left to them was to get through it.

"This will all be behind us one day, Hiroko. We'll be married," he smiled at her, feeling very young and a little foolish, "and we'll have lots of children."

"How many?" She loved playing the game with

him, although it still embarrassed her a little bit. It was odd speaking about their children.

"Six or seven." He grinned, and then pulled her close to him and kissed her. He kissed her hard this time, and he wanted her desperately. They stood in the shadow of a small shed as the sun went down, and he felt the softness of her body against his as he leaned toward her. He wanted to feel her next to him, to touch every part of her, he wanted all of her as he kissed her lips and her eyes and her throat, and his hand drifted to her breasts and she didn't stop him, until finally she pulled away ever so gently. She could hardly breathe with the excitement of him, and he was even more excited than she was.

"Oh, God, Hiroko, I want you so much," he said, aching for her, and for everything that had happened to them. He wanted to make it all better for her and he couldn't. They began walking slowly again, and before they reached the crowds, he stopped and held her once more, out in the open fields. He just stood there with her, and held her. He could feel her breathing ever so gently, and her narrow hips pressed against him. They were moving ever closer to the flame these days, but there was something so compelling about what was happening to them, that neither of them tried to stop it.

"We should go back," she said finally, feeling parts of him that she had never allowed herself to be aware of before, but the eyes that looked up at him were filled with love and trust and not regret or fear. She wanted him as badly as he wanted her. They had just missed the only chance they'd had to seize the moment.

They walked back to the others hand in hand without saying a word, and when they got back, both Reiko and Tak noticed something different about her. She seemed more grown-up these days, and very womanly and sure when she stood next to Peter. It was as though she already belonged to him, and wasn't afraid who knew it. She had committed something to him, silently, without saying a word, and the narrow silver ring with the two hearts he had given her over Christmas was always on her finger.

"How was dinner?" she asked, and they made an assortment of disparaging faces, but Tami seemed pleased. They had actually had dessert, it was green Jell-O, and Tami said she liked it. And at the mention of dessert, Hiroko laughed. She remembered the first time she had ever seen Jell-O at their house, and she had no idea what it was or how to attack it. She had pushed it around her plate while it jiggled ominously at her, and she had watched Tami to see how she ate it, with lots of whipped cream, which looked even worse to Hiroko.

They all laughed when she talked about it, and then Tak told some funny stories about when he'd first come to the States, and the experiences he'd had. And Reiko talked about how strange it had been for her in Japan when her parents sent her there to school. And as they talked, there was singing from a stall down the road. There were gentle sounds everywhere, and the sun set over them all like a blessing.

Peter sat with them until late that night, on wooden boxes outside the stall. Reiko and the girls went to bed, and Ken went to see his girlfriend for a while. And Tak and Peter talked. Hiroko came to check on them occasionally, to see if they needed anything. She brought Tak his cigarettes, and offered the last food from Anne's basket to both of them. Then she left them alone to talk, and went back to Reiko.

"I should have married her months ago," Peter said sadly as he watched her disappear into the stall like a spirit.

"You will one day," Tak said quietly, he was sure of it now, and he no longer objected. They had a right to their happiness, if this was what they wanted. He felt he had no right to keep them from it. He'd been watching them. In essence, they already were married, in soul and spirit. The rest would come later. "Just take care of yourself when you go overseas. You think they'll send you to Japan?"

"They might," Peter said. "I have to report to Fort Ord, but I just got the feeling they'd send me to Europe. There's plenty to do there. And I'd just as soon not be fighting the Japanese. I don't want to have a lot of apologizing to do to her father."

Takeo smiled as he said it. "You'd like him, he's a great guy. He's a real character, he's always been way ahead of himself, with his ideas and his teaching. I'm surprised he never came to the States. I guess he couldn't afford it. His wife looked like a sweet girl too, very traditional. She's a lot like Hiroko." But Hiroko had changed a lot in the past few months, they had all noticed it. She had gotten a lot braver, and less bound by tradition. The incident at St. Andrew's had brought her out of herself a lot, she had seemed stronger and more independent after that, and her relationship with Peter had matured her. "I'm sure you'll meet them all one day," Takeo said thoughtfully. "If they survive the war. I hope they do. Her brother's about Ken's age. I think he's a year older." Tak was worried about Ken too. He was so angry these days, so disillusioned about his country. He had fallen in with a bunch of kids who were very angry. They felt their country had betrayed them and putting them in camps was a violation of the Constitution.

"Maybe he'll be a lawyer," Peter said encouragingly, and Tak smiled.

"I hope so."

At midnight, Peter stood up and stretched. It was uncomfortable sitting on the wooden boxes. And he walked softly to the stall to say good-bye to Hiroko, but when he knocked, and then glanced in, he saw that she was sound asleep on one of their makeshift mattresses, covered by a blanket. She looked so peaceful lying there, he stood for a long moment watching her, and then backed quietly away and returned to Takeo.

"I'll come back tomorrow after class," he told Tak when he left. And he did, every day, and he spent the entire day and evening with them on the weekends. He had no other life now, no place else he wanted to be. And he even brought a bunch of papers past the guards, and Tak helped him correct them. It was the only distraction Tak had had since he'd been there, and he was grateful for it. And having Tak do the work for him gave Peter more free time to spend with Hiroko.

Reiko was working at the infirmary every day by then. They'd been in the camp for two weeks, and several thousand more evacuees had arrived. There were more than eight thousand people in the camp, and it was harder and harder to find a moment of solitude, a place to walk that dozens of others hadn't gotten to first, or a place to sit without having to listen to ten or twelve other conversations.

The only peace Hiroko and Peter got was when they walked far out into the fields, in the high grass, and no one else seemed to care or notice. They walked out there every day, it gave her exercise, but more than that it gave her peace, and a quiet moment with Peter. And when they had walked for a while, they sat in the tall grass, near the fence, and disappeared completely. They sat like children, hiding there, giggling and laughing and talking, like forgotten people. It was almost like a game for them, and Peter was surprised the guards didn't keep a better watch, and no one had noticed, but he was pleased they hadn't. They didn't do anything they shouldn't have, but it was wonderful not being observed, or surrounded by thousands of strangers.

He lay on his side, talking to her for hours sometimes, as they listened to crickets nearby, and wildflowers grew around them. For a short time, looking at the sky, they could pretend that they were free, and life was as it might have been, if things were different.

"What do you dream of, Peter-san?" she asked him one day as they lay side by side, watching the clouds drift by on a Sunday. She had been there exactly two weeks that day, and it was the middle of May, and the weather was warm. The sky was the color of Wedgwood.

"You," he said easily. "And you, what do you dream about, my love, other than me, of course?" he teased her, and she laughed.

"Kyoto sometimes . . . the places I went as a

child. I want to take you to all those places one day."
And then he asked her something he never had before.

"Could you be happy living here, in this country, I
mean?" Maybe after what she was going through, she
couldn't. But she nodded thoughtfully. She had
thought about it before. She wanted to see her parents
again, but she wanted to be with him, wherever he
was.

"I could," she said cautiously, "if they allow me to.
It will be difficult living here after this war," she said,
thinking of St. Andrew's and the girls there.

"We could go east. I had an offer to teach at Har-
vard last year. But I didn't want to leave Tak." Then he
smiled as he looked down at her again, lying on her
side in the grass next to him like a little butterfly,
resting. "I'm glad I didn't."

"Perhaps it was meant to be, Peter," she said seriously. "Perhaps we are destined to be together." It
sounded silly said out loud, but she believed that. And
as she said it, he leaned over and kissed her. He
touched her face gently with his hands, and then her
neck, and slowly he did something he had never dared
do before and knew he shouldn't. But no one could see
them, and she lay so close to him, he couldn't bear it.
They had so little now, so little hope, so little time, so
little future, it made him want to grab what they had
and never let it get away from him, not for a single
moment. He slowly unbuttoned the dress she wore. It
was a lavender silk with tiny buttons all the way down,
and it reminded him of one of her kimonos. He meant
to unbutton it only a short way down, but he just kept
unbuttoning, as he kissed her, and she moved closer to
him, and suddenly he realized he had undressed her.

She had on a peach-colored satin slip, and it was silky beneath his fingers, and like the dress it slid off easily in the warm sunshine, and suddenly she lay there, exposed to him in all her exquisiteness, and he realized with astonishment that she hadn't stopped him. She didn't even think about it, as he lay next to her and kissed her and pulled her still closer to him, and then he felt her unbuttoning his shirt with her tiny, nimble fingers, and he felt them on his flesh, and groaned as he kissed her and pressed her hard against him. He knew he should stop, he wanted to, he promised himself he would, but somehow he couldn't, and she did nothing to push him away. She wanted him there, next to her. She wanted to be his now. She was his in every way, her heart, her soul, and she was giving him the rest of her as they lay beneath the summer sky. It was a perfect moment in time, and it was theirs, and neither of them could push it away as he freed her long black hair, and moved ever closer to her, until he was on top of her, and she made no sound at all as he entered her, and felt his soul soar through the sky with hers. They seemed to hang in space for hours, as he devoured her with his lips, his hands, his body, and she gave as much back to him. It seemed a lifetime before they were spent, and he lay silently holding her, wondering if they were mad or the only sane people left on earth. The only thing he knew for sure was how very much he loved her.

"I love you so much," he whispered, as he heard a bird sing somewhere, and she smiled up at him. There was no little girl there now. She was entirely a woman. "Oh, darling," he said, and held her like a child in his arms, terrified that she'd be sorry. He looked down at her then, and there was no reproach in her eyes, only pleasure.

"I am yours now," she said softly. It didn't even occur to him what would happen if she got pregnant. But there was nothing they could do about it, he had no protection with him. He had known she was a virgin, and he had never thought for a moment that he would make love to her.

"Are you angry with me?" he asked, worried about what she would feel later. He was terrified, he didn't want to do anything to hurt or lose her. "I'm so sorry." But he was only sorry if she was. In his heart, he wasn't.

"No, my love." She smiled peacefully at him, and leaned over to kiss him. "I am very happy. There was no other way," she said simply. "But in our hearts, I know we are married."

He wanted to do more than that for her, especially since he was going away, but he had no idea how to do it. But as they lay there talking afterward, and he slowly buttoned her dress again, he had a thought and shared it with her. He wanted her to make inquiries. Surely, there was someone there who could do it.

"It will not be accepted by them," she said knowingly of the authorities who controlled her life now.

"It will be accepted by us," he said solemnly. "That's all that matters." He told her to see what she could find out, and he helped her to her feet after kissing her again. She was worried that their indiscretion would show, but in spite of the fact that it had been the first time for her, she looked surprisingly respectable as they walked slowly back through the tall grass. They stopped several times and kissed again, and Peter knew that never in his life had he ever been so happy.

Takeo was waiting for them when they got back, and he had finished all of Peter's papers. He looked pleased, and he wanted to talk to him. Peter sat down, and Hiroko disappeared for a while, and when she returned she looked fresh and well combed and her face was shining. Their eyes met briefly over Tak's head and as they did, they each felt an explosion of excitement.

Peter came back to her every day, and they wandered through the tall grass, and disappeared into the mysteries of each other's arms. They could not stay away from each other now, could not get enough of the love they shared, could not in a thousand years be sated. But Hiroko had a plan. And by the following week, she had found what she wanted. She had heard about him in the infirmary, coincidentally from Reiko. And the moment she could, she went to see him.

He told her it would not mean anything, except in the eyes of God, not man. But she told him that that was what they wanted. The rest would have to come later. And he showed no surprise when she brought Peter to him the next afternoon. He didn't seem at all surprised that Peter was Caucasian. And the old Buddhist priest performed the ceremony and married them, holding his prayer beads in one hand, and intoning the same words that had once joined her parents twenty years before, and Takeo and Reiko. They were familiar words to her, and it was brief. He pronounced them man and wife in the eyes of God and man. And when it was over, he bowed low, and wished them many children.

Hiroko bowed low to him, and thanked him, and Peter did as well, and was dismayed to realize that they could not give him anything. Money or any gift at all would only have gotten him into trouble. Peter asked Hiroko to explain that to him in Japanese, since he spoke no English at all, and she did, but he said he understood, and wanted nothing more than their blessing.

They bowed low to him and assured him of it, and as he blessed them yet again, Peter surprised her by bringing a thin gold band out of his pocket. It was so narrow you could barely see it, and it slipped perfectly on her hand, and was the exact size of her finger.

"We'll have that made official one day," he said, deeply moved by what had just passed between them.

"It already is," she said, bowing low to him, and saying the words in Japanese that assured him she would honor him forever.

They thanked the old priest, and asked him to keep their secret for them, and with a smile, he promised, and a moment later they left him. Peter was beaming from ear to ear, and Hiroko stood close to him, feeling like a part of him. It seemed incredible to both of them that the whole camp couldn't see it.

"Wait a minute," he said as they walked quickly past a row of horse stalls. "I forgot something."

"What?" She looked suddenly worried, and without another word, he took her in his arms and kissed her, in plain sight of everyone, and she could hear the children laughing and giggling.

"I had to kiss the bride to make it official," he explained, and she laughed at him, and they walked on. Even old people were smiling at them. They were young and in love, and foolish. And even if he wasn't Japanese, they could see that he was very handsome, and they looked very happy together.

But in spite of the lightheartedness, it was a serious moment for both of them, and they talked about it at length that night, what it meant, and how serious they were about their future. As far as they both were concerned, they were married. She fingered the ring a number of times, and she had slid the silver one next to it, and wondered if anyone would notice. But her wedding band was so narrow it hid easily behind the other.

They continued to go for long walks each day, and to do what came so easily there, and no one appeared to suspect what they were doing, not even her cousins. But the only thing that worried Peter considerably was the fear that she would get pregnant. But in spite of his fears, they always seemed to get carried away, and most of the time passion got the best of them, despite his good intentions.

"We should be more careful," he said, reproaching himself one day. She was so beautiful, so sensuous, he lost his head each time he was with her.

"I don't care," she said, throwing caution to the wind as she lay with him, and then she lowered her eyes and looked shy with him for the first time in a long time, and whispered the words, "I want your baby."

"But not here, sweetheart," he chided her. "Later." But all his good intentions were usually rapidly forgotten, they went nowhere. He lay in the grass with her, and lost sight of everything except his insatiable desire for her, his endless love, and the wonders of her body. "I'm worse than a kid," he laughed as they strolled back to her stall again. But it was the only moment of the day when they were both transported beyond reality, beyond the fears and terrible rumors of what was coming. He was leaving in three weeks and there was still constant talk about where they would all be sent, who would go where, and if they would be safe there.

And a week after their little ceremony, when Peter came to the camp, he was stopped at the gate, and asked to stop at the administration building. He was sure that the old priest had told the guards something. He tried to appear calm as he went inside, and asked if there was a problem. They wanted to know why he came to visit so often, who he had dealings with and why. They wanted to know his political views, and asked to see identification.

Peter showed them everything he had, and his identification from the university, which attested to the fact that he was a full professor. He explained that Takeo Tanaka had worked with him, first as his boss and then as his assistant. And he explained also that he would be leaving for the army soon, and it was important that together they complete the program. He said he needed Tak's help to complete everything to the university's satisfaction before he went into the army in two weeks. But no matter how good his story was, they kept him there for three hours, explaining, describing the program to them. They were impressed by Stanford, of course, but they were particularly interested in the fact that he taught political science. And in the end, the only thing that saved him, he thought, was the fact that in two weeks he was leaving for the army. Whatever threat, or annoyance, he posed, it wouldn't be there for much longer.

And before he left the administration building that afternoon, he tried to find out where and when Hiroko and her cousins were being moved. The man he'd spoken to said he had no idea, that a dozen camps were being set up throughout the western states, but that for the moment they weren't ready. The evacuees would be there for a while yet. But unfortunately, Peter wouldn't.

"Don't feel so bad for them," the lieutenant said to him confidentially. "They're just a bunch of Japs. Your guy may be a smart one, but believe me, most of them aren't. Half of them can't even speak English."

Peter nodded, pretending to be sympathetic to him, but said that he'd heard most of them were Americans.

"If you can call them that. They've got all this garbage about issei, nisei, who's born where. The fact is they're Japs, and you can't trust 'em to be loyal to this country. Watch out for them," he warned, "your guy too. I guess you'll be glad to join the army." He smiled, unaware of how wrong he was. But Peter was immensely relieved when he was allowed to leave and join the Tanakas and Hiroko, who had worried about him all afternoon. But when he told them all about it, he could see from Hiroko's eyes that she'd been frightened, and he shook his head imperceptibly at her to reassure her. The guards knew nothing about them. That night, when he slipped away with her, the grass was damp and the ground cold, but they had never felt as much passion for each other. Each of them had been terrified they'd lose the other. For a moment, sitting there that afternoon, he'd thought they would tell him he could no longer visit. He had never been so grateful in his life as when he left the guard room.

And as she lay breathless in his arms, devouring him, he knew that she had felt the same terror.

"How am I ever going to leave you?" he asked unhappily. He could hardly stand to be away from her for a night now. It was going to be nightmarish when he left, and the army had just changed his orders. He was only stopping briefly at Ford Ord, and then going on to Fort Dix, New Jersey, for training. He'd been right, he was going to Europe, and he wouldn't be back in California before he left. All they had were the next two weeks together, and after that a lifetime of prayers until it was over.

She couldn't leave him that night, nor he her, they had been too terrified that afternoon, and this time when they finally returned to the stall, they looked drained and worried as Takeo watched them. He knew how hard it was going to be for Peter to leave her, and it was already starting to take its toll. But there was nothing anyone could do to help them. And they hugged again, and then silently Tak turned and went to bed, leaving Peter and Hiroko their last few moments together.

And by the following week, General De Witt announced proudly that the removal of a hundred thousand persons of Japanese ancestry from Military Area Number One had been completed. Ten thousand of them were at Tanforan, and they still had absolutely no clue as to where they were going.

Peter had left Stanford by then, and even the battles of Corregidor and Midway didn't interest him. All he could think of now was Hiroko. He had one week left, and he wanted to spend every possible minute of it with her. And fortunately for them, no one interrogated or stopped him again. He left his car far from the gate, and always came in on foot, looking bland and unassuming. He drew no attention to himself, and the lieutenant thought he was his friend now. But Peter managed to spend as many as eighteen hours a day at the camp with Hiroko, and sometimes twenty.

And when no one was looking, she fingered her gold ring, and remembered the day of their wedding. But no matter how tightly they clung, or how many times he said he loved her, or she him, the moment came. The last day, the final night, the last hour. She lay in his arms for hours that night, looking up at the stars, thinking of where he would be, and the memories they had to hold on to. He was leaving for Fort Ord in the morning. There were no words left by the time he walked her back to the stall where she lived with her cousins. The others had gone to bed by then, but Tak was waiting for them. He wanted to say good-bye to him. Peter had been like a brother to him.

"Take care of yourself," Peter said hoarsely to Takeo, barely able to say good-bye as they embraced. The moment was just too painful. "It'll be all over soon. I'll let you know how to write to me," he said, wanting to encourage him to hang on, and not sure how to do it. It had been easy to see in the past month how disheartened Takeo had become. If he hadn't had his family, he would have broken.

"You too, Peter, stay safe. For all our sakes." Peter looked down at Hiroko, who was crying softly. She had cried all afternoon, all night. She had tried so hard to be strong for him, but she couldn't do it. And neither could Peter. As he stood at the end of the row with her, he held her in his arms, and they both cried. Everyone had gone to bed by then, and there was no one to watch them, and by then, Hiroko was sobbing softly.

"I'll be back, Hiroko. Just know that. No matter what happens, or where you are, I'll be there when this is over."

"So will I," she said staunchly. She knew, as young as she was, that he was the only man she would ever love. And she was his now. "I am yours forever, Peter-san," she said, repeating the words of their wedding.

"Take care of yourself, please God . . . take care, I love you," he said, holding her for one last time, and kissing her as their tears mingled on their cheeks. *"Genki de gambatte,"* she said softly, slowly regaining her composure. "Stay well with all your might." He had heard the phrase a lot recently and knew what she was saying.

"You too, little one. Just remember how much I love you."

"I love you too, Peter-san," she said, and then bowed low to him as slowly, he walked away.

They let him out the gate, and she stood there and watched him. She stood there for as long as she could see him. And then she walked slowly back to her stall, where she lay in her clothes, on the straw, thinking of Peter, and each moment they had shared. It seemed impossible that he was gone, that they were here, that this was the end, and not the beginning. She hoped it wouldn't be. . . . He had to come back to her. . . . He had to live. . . . She murmured the words of a Buddhist prayer as she lay there, and Takeo tried not to hear her.

# *Chapter 12*

THE WEEKS after Peter left were exquisitely painful for Hiroko. She went through the motions of activity every day. She stood in line, but seldom ate. She cleaned their stall. She helped carry endless buckets of water. She showered when the water was hot and Reiko told her to. And she played with Tami. But her mind was gone, her soul, her life, her husband. And no one knew he was even that. They thought he was their friend, her boyfriend. Only Reiko suspected how much more he had been. She had been watching them for weeks, and she was afraid that Hiroko would get sick now, from pining for him. Her entire being seemed to be entwined in Peter's. She asked her to work in the infirmary with her, to keep her busy. And they needed help. Ten thousand people had at least as many ailments. There were sore throats and colds, and

injuries, stomach ailments, and a constant flow of new
cases of measles. There was whooping cough, and old
people with heart disease and pleurisy, and several
times a week there were emergency operations. There
were minimal supplies and medicines, but they had
some of the best doctors and nurses in San Francisco,
all of whom had been evacuated with them. They had
been no more exempt than anyone else, and all they
could do now was practice with what was available to
them. But at least the infirmary kept Hiroko busy.

She heard from Peter several times. He was in
training in Fort Dix, but she scarcely knew more than
that. Two of his letters arrived completely blacked out
by censors. All she could read was "my darling" and at
the very end, "I love you. Peter." The rest was gone,
and she couldn't even begin to guess what he had told
her. She wrote to him as well, and wondered if the
same thing had happened to her letters.

Her birthday came and went in July, and the anniversary of the date she had come to the States. The
little vegetable garden the woman had planted in the
next row had begun to grow, and someone had started
both a knitting club and a glee club. There was boxing
now, and sumo wrestling, and several softball teams.
There were lots of activities for the children, and religious groups mainly for the women. And once, Hiroko
had run into the old Buddhist priest who had secretly
married her to Peter. She had smiled at him, and he
bowed, but they said nothing to each other.

And still there was no word of when they were
leaving. They knew that some people had been sent to
a camp called Manzanar in northern California, but
most of the evacuees in Tanforan had gone nowhere.

At the end of August, the Germans laid siege to Stalingrad, and by then Hiroko had caught the dysentery that affected everyone. She was working in the infirmary, but there was never enough medicine, and week by week she got thinner. Reiko worried about her, but she said that she felt fine, and stomach ailments were so ordinary in camp that the doctors paid no attention to her. Still, it worried Reiko to see her look so pale and obviously feel so poorly, but there was nothing they could do about it. And Takeo hadn't been well either. He had had pains in his chest more than once. Most of the time he said nothing about it, but on one occasion he had had to go lie down in their stall. And after Peter left, he always seemed quiet and disheartened. More than anything, he was lonely and had no one to talk to. He had no interest in joining any of the clubs that were proliferating. He kept mostly to himself, and the only one he seemed to want to talk to, other than his wife, was Hiroko.

"You miss him terribly, child, don't you?" he asked one day, and she nodded. It had taken every ounce of strength she had just to put one foot in front of the other since June. Without Peter, there was nothing to live for. And all she could do now was listen to the echoes of her memories and dream of the future. The present held nothing for her. It was empty.

In September, he wrote and told her he was in England, and there were rumors of something big coming up soon, and he'd let her know as soon as he was transferred. All they had for him now was an APO box, and in the next several weeks, his letters to Hiroko became less and less frequent. She wondered, with terror, if the letters would ever find her, if and when they moved her.

Day after day she went to the infirmary, and the combination of monotony and fear was killing. They still didn't know if they'd be separated from their families, or even their children. But at least for the moment, as they waited, things seemed peaceful.

Reiko even had her assisting with their minor surgeries. She was good at it, and the doctors liked her. And the only tragedy was when they lost a ten-year-old-boy during an appendectomy, simply because they didn't have the right instruments or medication. It had depressed Reiko and Hiroko terribly, and the next morning, when she had to go to work, Hiroko was so ill with stomach problems that she couldn't go. But more than anything, she couldn't bear the thought of another child dying, or seeing another operation.

Instead, during the morning, she helped Tami make another dollhouse. They'd been working on it for a while, but it was difficult without the materials or tools, and it was taking forever. And the other one she'd had at home had been so pretty. Tami always looked wistful when she compared them.

Takeo agreed to watch Tami that afternoon, and out of a sense of responsibility, Hiroko went back to the infirmary to help Reiko. And her cousin was pleased to see her.

"I thought we'd lost you forever." She smiled. It had been a rough day for Hiroko the day before, and she knew it.

"I just couldn't take it again." And she certainly looked ill. Much of what they ate was spoiled, and everyone got sick frequently, mostly with food poisoning, and some with ulcers.

"Just take it easy. Why don't you roll bandages for us today?" Reiko suggested, giving her plenty of work to do, and Hiroko was grateful not to have to tackle anything more upsetting.

At the end of the day, they slowly walked back to their stall, still wearing their caps and aprons. They didn't wear full uniforms, there were none available, but their caps helped to identify them as medical personnel, or nurses. But when they got to the stall, Takeo looked even worse than Hiroko had that morning.

"What's wrong? Are you all right?" Reiko asked him quickly, afraid it was his heart again. He was too young to have those problems, but they'd been through a lot in the past five months since April.

"We're leaving," he said quietly with a look of despair. It was late September, it was almost exactly five months since they had been there.

"When?"

"Sometime in the next few days, maybe sooner."

"How do you know?" she asked sharply. There were so many rumors, it was hard to know what was true anymore. And after five months there, she was almost afraid to leave. This was unpleasant and uncomfortable, but at least it was familiar.

He silently handed her a slip of paper. Her name was written on it, and the names of their three children.

"I don't understand," she said. "You're not on this." She looked up at him with frightened eyes, and he nodded, and held up another piece of paper. It bore his name, but showed a different day and time for his departure. He was leaving a day later. "What does this mean?" she asked. "Do you know?"

Takeo sighed. "The man who handed these to me said it must mean we're going to different destinations, otherwise we'd be on the same piece of paper."

Reiko only looked at him, and began to cry silently as she reached out and held him. There were others who had had the same news who were crying nearby. Married children were being sent separately from their parents and younger siblings, uncles and aunts. The administration wasn't worried about who went where. And then she realized suddenly that there was no slip for Hiroko.

"I didn't get one for her at all," Takeo explained, still puzzled. Hiroko spent the entire night terrified, sure that they would be leaving without her, and she would be completely alone at whatever camp they sent her to, without relative or friend or husband. Just thinking about it made her sick again the next morning. But shortly after that, as she prepared to leave for the infirmary, they came to find her. She was leaving even later than the others, obviously to yet another place, the day after Takeo. And there was no time even to think about it. Reiko and the children were leaving in the morning, without them.

Takeo went to the administration building that afternoon along with countless others, and nothing had changed as they explained it to him. He was still a Japanese national, and a greater security risk, and his wife and children weren't. They were non-aliens, the new word for *citizen*. And he was the enemy, as was Hiroko. In addition, his work as a professor of political science concerned them a great deal, and he was going to have to be interrogated with a number of other people who posed a similar, or equal, problem. He was going to a highly secured camp, they explained, where the highest-risk evacuees would be sent. His wife would be sent somewhere with less security. And when he asked if he could join her eventually, they said that it would depend on many things, and they had no idea as to the outcome. As for Hiroko, she clearly was an enemy alien, she had admitted to them that she had family in Japan, and a brother in the air force. Her category was the greatest risk of all, they said without sympathy. And they were also aware through the FBI that she was romantically involved with a highly political Caucasian.

"He's not highly political, for heaven's sake," Takeo argued with them on her behalf. "He was my assistant at Stanford."

"We'll be happy to discuss that with you in the interrogation, sir," they said bluntly, "and with her. We'll have plenty of time to do it."

But when he told Reiko about it that night, he was certain they were sending him to prison. And possibly Hiroko as well. They made her ties to Japan sound extremely ominous. She was a nineteen-year-old girl, and a student, and she was in love with an American. It hardly seemed enough to die for, but none of them were convinced they wouldn't be shot as spies. Not even Hiroko. As she listened to him, and others that night, she felt certain that she would go to prison as a spy, and probably be executed, and even terrified as she was, she tried to force herself to accept it.

When she and Takeo said good-bye to Reiko and the children the next day, it was with the certainty that

they would never meet again. And despite all her years
of hearing about samurai and their dignity, Hiroko
could not contain her grief as she said good-bye to
Tami.

"You *have* to come with us," the child said, wearing her number tag on her coat again. "We can't leave
you here, Hiroko."

"I will go somewhere else, Tami-san, and perhaps
later I'll join you." But she looked pale and ill as she
stood there and embraced their mother, thinking of
her own, and sure that she would never see any of
them again. They had been told that they were going
to a camp for lesser security risks than Takeo and
Hiroko, so perhaps they would be safe there. And
friends came to wave at the bus before it left, and the
shades would be drawn so they could not see where
they were going. For a long time Tak and Reiko just
stood holding each other as they cried and their children watched them. He kissed each of them, sure that
he would never see them again, and told them to take
good care of their mother. And then there was a grim
moment when he said good-bye to his son. There were
few words, but vast emotions. And there were other
scenes around them just like it. It was Ken's second
painful farewell that day. Peggy and her family had
been sent to Manzanar earlier that morning.

And then finally, in a blinding flash of pain, Reiko
and the children boarded. The shades were lowered,
their frightened faces disappeared, and the bus lum-
bered off to a destination unknown, in the North, as
Takeo and Hiroko watched them. And the next day
was no better. She went alone to say good-bye to Tak
this time. He looked gray and tired, and ancient for a

man of fifty-one, who had looked youthful only months before. But the past months had taken an immeasurable toll on him. And like Reiko, Hiroko thought she was seeing him for the last time, and braced herself for it.

"Take care of yourself," he said gently, feeling dead inside from having left his loved ones the day before, but he felt something for her as well. She had a life ahead of her, a future, if they didn't kill her here, which they might still. But he hoped for her sake that Peter would come back for her eventually. They deserved each other. "God bless you," he said, and then got on the bus without looking back at her. But she stood for as long as she could, watching the bus disappear in a cloud of dust, and then she went back to their deserted stall to wait till morning.

And that night she walked over the fields where she had lain with Peter. She sat in the tall grass quietly, and wondered what would happen if she never came out again, if she just sat there till she died, or they found her. What if she didn't leave on the bus in the morning? But they had her name now. And her number. And they knew something about Peter. Apparently the FBI had a file on him, because of her, and his work at Stanford. And she had told them about her brother in the Japanese air force. They would come and look for her if she didn't show up at the bus. And they might do something to Peter, or the others, if she didn't cooperate, so she couldn't let that happen.

She sat for a long time, thinking of Peter, praying for him, longing for him, and then she walked slowly back, as they once had together. And like a vision from the past, she saw the old Buddhist priest on her way back and she smiled at him, wondering if he'd acknowledge her. He bowed to her, and then he stopped her.

"My prayers are very strong for you, and your husband," he said softly. "Walk softly, and always with God beside you." He bowed again, and then walked on, as though his thoughts had moved on to another subject. But seeing him that night had been like a blessing, and she felt stronger.

She had a shower early the next day, before she left, and packed the last of her things in her one small suitcase, and she found one of the origami birds she had made for Tami in the straw beside her mattress. It was like a sign from her, a memory of a friendly face, and someone she loved, as she held the little paper bird in her fingers, picked up her bag with her other hand, and walked to the bus in silence. She saw one of Sally's friends, but the girl didn't acknowledge her, and one of the doctors Reiko had worked with. She shuddered slightly as she boarded the bus, afraid of what they'd do to her wherever she was going. But there was no way to change it now, and the others were gone. Tak and Reiko, the children . . . Peter . . . There was nothing left to do except what the old priest had told her the night before. Walk with God beside her . . . and walk softly . . . and wait for Peter. And if she died now, at their hands, which she thought was possible, and accepted, at least he would know how much she loved him.

The bus filled quickly this time, and armed guards boarded it with them. There were only women on the bus with her, and terrifying thoughts entered her mind, but no one approached her. The curtains were let down so they wouldn't see where they were being taken, and the guards took their places, with the guns pointed at them. And then, grinding through the gears, the bus took off toward wherever destiny would take her.

# Chapter 13

*T*HE BUS ride from Tanforan was surprisingly brief. Barely half an hour after they'd begun, the bus came to a halt and the guards shepherded them off. Hiroko couldn't imagine where they were, but she was told to take her valise, and to leave the bus with the other women.

And as soon as they stepped off, she saw that they were at the train station at San Bruno. A train was waiting for them, and other busloads of people were being ushered off at gunpoint. This was serious now. There were no smiles, no kind words, no explanations, and none of the guards looked friendly. No one looked her in the eye as she was shoved onto the train, ahead of dozens of other women. But on the train there were men in other cars, segregated this time, and she noticed that there were more men than women. As she took her seat, on a hard wooden bench, clutching her suitcase with trembling hands, she felt certain that they were taking her back to San Francisco for deportation.

The trains were very old, and had few comforts, and the windows were all boarded up so they couldn't see where they were going. There were whispers and little cries, there were no children this time, and most of the women thought they were going to prison, or to a camp somewhere for execution. Hiroko only sat there with closed eyes, holding the thought of Peter in her mind, trying not to think of dying. She wasn't afraid to die, but she ached at the thought of never seeing him again, never being in his arms, never telling him again how much she loved him. Perhaps, she thought, as the train lurched to life and several women stumbled, perhaps if they could never be together again, it was better to die. And then she thought of something her grandmother had taught her as a little girl. It was *giri,* the obligation to the dignity of one's name. It was the honor that she now owed her father, to be dignified, and strong and wise, to go willingly to her death, with pride. She thought of *on* as well, the obligation she had to her country and to her parents. And no matter how frightened she was, or how sad, she vowed silently not to disgrace them.

It grew hot on the train after a while, just from all the people pressed in there. She learned later that there hadn't been enough passenger cars, so they used freight cars to transport the passengers. A few women were sick on the train, but Hiroko was too numb to feel anything. She felt only sorrow as she sat there.

And as night fell, it grew cool again, and still they

rode on. Perhaps she would not sail from San Francisco, she realized, but from Washington State or from Los Angeles. She knew that before the war, ships had sailed to Japan from either place. Or perhaps the others were right, and they were simply going to die. Execution was simpler than deportation. The woman next to her cried all night, sobbing for her husband and children. She was a Japanese national, like Hiroko, and she had only been in the States for six months. She and her husband had come here to live with cousins while he worked on a building project. He was an engineer, and they had taken him the day before, just as they had Takeo. And her two small children had been sent earlier with her cousins and their children. Like Reiko, her cousins were nisei.

Hiroko hadn't gone to the bathroom all day, and she was aching to when they finally stopped at midnight. It was dark outside, there were no houses anywhere, and they were shepherded off the train at gunpoint again, and told they could go to the bathroom there. There were no toilets, no trees, no shelter, and there were men watching them. A month before, her own modesty would have caused her to die first, but now she didn't care. Like the others, she did what she had to do. And feeling deeply ashamed, she got back on the train again, and huddled in the corner, still clutching her suitcase. She almost wondered why she even kept it. If she were going to die, she wouldn't need the pair of slacks Reiko had packed for her, or the warm sweaters she had brought, or the photograph of her parents. She had a photograph of Peter too. Takeo had taken it of them just before they had to turn in their cameras as contraband. He was standing next to her, and she was still looking painfully shy in a kimono. It seemed a lifetime ago now, and it was hard to believe that it had been three months since she'd seen him. Harder still to realize that life had ever been normal, that they had lived in homes, and driven cars, gone anywhere, and had friends and jobs, and ideals and dreams. They had nothing now, except the infinitesimally tiny sliver of time that was the present.

She was dozing when the train stopped again. She had no idea what time it was, but the sky was gray when they slid open the freight doors, and the air was freezing when it hit her. She woke suddenly, and they all struggled to their feet. There was shouting outside, and there were more men waving guns at them, and telling them to get off the train, which they all did in a hurry. Hiroko stumbled as she jumped off the train, and another woman steadied her with a small smile. It was like a ray of sunshine in the dark night, a reminder that someone else was there with her.

"God bless you," the woman whispered to her in perfect English.

"God bless all of us," someone else added nearby, and with that, the bayonets were pointed at them, and they hurried forward as they were told to.

Hiroko saw the male prisoners again, and in the distance she could see buildings. It was hard to tell what they were, but she heard a man say that they were barracks. And then, carrying their few things, they walked for two miles, with the soldiers beside them. There were no people to be seen, only the soldiers, and plumes of steam flew from their mouths as they walked in the frigid air. It felt like winter, though it was only September.

"Are you all right?" she asked an old woman, who looked ill. And then she realized from the blank stare that she didn't speak English, and she asked her in Japanese, and the woman only nodded, fighting for breath. She explained that she had two sons in the army in Japan, but she had a son here who was a doctor. He had already gone to Manzanar the week before, but for some reason they hadn't taken her with him. She didn't look well, but she didn't complain, and Hiroko gently took her suitcase and carried it for her.

They reached a large building finally. It had taken them an hour and a half to get there. Some of the women were foolishly wearing high heels, some were old, and none of them could walk very quickly. The men had passed them quite a while before, a long column of them, being marched at a rapid pace by young soldiers. And only a few of the old ones straggled behind, with the bayonets firmly pointed at them.

But there was no sign of the men as the women were ushered into the building and told that they had been brought there for interrogation. For whatever reason, they had been designated as "higher risk," and they were going to be kept there until their future status could be determined. The speech the lieutenant made was brief and dry, and they were led away to cells, their suitcases labeled with their numbers and taken from them. And Hiroko was shocked when she was handed prison garb, and told to take her clothes off.

There was no privacy once again, she simply had to change her clothes while the soldiers watched them. And again she was mortified, as she crouched low and put on the ugly pajamas that they gave them. They

were far too big for her, and she looked like a little girl
as they walked her to a cell with two other women.

There were three steel cots in the room, with
straw mattresses, and in the corner an open toilet. It
was a stockade that was being used for them. And
Hiroko stood and looked out the window in despair, as
the sun came up. It was hard to believe she would ever
have a life again, or be free, or that she would ever see
Peter. And when she turned away from the window,
she saw that the other two women were crying. She
said nothing to them; she quietly sat down on her own
bed and looked toward the mountains she could see
outside. She had no idea where they were, or where
they would go from here, if anywhere. This was her
fate now.

For the next three weeks they were given three
small meals a day. The food was poor, but it was fresh
at least, and none of them had the ravaging stomach
problems they had had at Tanforan. Hiroko felt better
too, and she slept a lot, and wove the straw from her
mattress into mats. Without even thinking, she had
started making tatami. Now and then when she found
scraps of paper, she made little birds. And once, when
one of the other women had found some thread, they
had hung Hiroko's little origami birds from it at the
window. It was October by then, and they had no
news, of their own fate or of the others. Hiroko had
heard of several suicides among the men. The women
seemed to accept their fate more willingly, and most of
them seemed to have no idea why they had been put
in prison. And then, finally, Hiroko was called for interrogation.

They wanted to know about her brother in Japan,

if she had heard from him, if he had gotten messages to her since the war began, and what she knew of his position in the air force. It was easy to answer them. She had no idea where he was, or what he did. And her only message about him had been from her father via the consulate immediately after Pearl Harbor was struck, when all he said was for her to stay and continue to go to school, and he had mentioned that Yuji was in the air force. But more than that she did not know. She told them Yuji's name, and age, and hoped that they would not cause him any trouble. But it was impossible for her even to imagine how they could do that. The two nations were at war, and a young boy in the air force of Japan was hardly accessible to them.

They asked her about her father, what he had taught at the university, and if he had had radical ideas, or was involved with the government in any way. And she smiled quietly as she answered. Her father was a dreamer, filled with new ideas that most of the time seemed far too advanced even for his colleagues. But he was no radical, no political force. She described him as a gentle man, fascinated by history, both modern and ancient, which was a fairly accurate portrayal of her father.

Then they pressed her about Takeo and what she knew of him, his activities, his associations, his politics, and she assured them that as far as she knew, he was only a teacher, and a good person. He was devoted to his family, and she had never heard him express any disloyalty to the United States. And she made a point of saying that he had always wished he could become a citizen, and actually felt as though he were one.

And then, finally, after several days of questioning,

as she knew they would, they came to Peter. Her only fear was that someone might have heard or seen the brief ceremony by the Buddhist priest at Tanforan. She knew that even that symbolic religious ceremony, not recognized by the state, would have gotten him into trouble.

She said that they were friends, that she knew him because he was Tak's assistant, but she gave them nothing more than that, and they did not ask her. They wanted to know if she had heard from him, and they knew she had. They had kept careful records of his letters, and she admitted easily that he had written to her, but all of his letters had been censored. And when they asked, she said that when she had last heard from him he had left Fort Dix, New Jersey, and was in England, serving under General Eisenhower. But she hadn't heard from him since, and she wasn't even sure that she would now.

"Do you wish to go back to Japan?" they asked, writing down what she said. She was being interrogated by two young officers, and more than once they conferred with each other out of her hearing. But she answered them honestly, and without artifice, looking at them squarely.

"My father wishes me to stay in America," she said softly, wondering again if they would send her back to Japan, or simply shoot her. She didn't care anymore, as long as she didn't dishonor the family, or hurt Peter by something she said. She was very careful.

"Why does he want you to stay here?" they asked pointedly, suddenly very interested by what she said. They were getting to the real meat now.

"He sent a message to my cousin that he thought

it was safer, and he wanted me to continue my education."

"Where were you doing that?" They looked surprised, as though they thought she'd been a maid somewhere, or a farmer. But she was used to that.

"I was at St. Andrew's College," she said, and they wrote it down.

"But do *you* want to go back?" They sounded as if they would have shipped her back to Japan if she wanted, but she didn't. They were offering to send those back to Japan who wanted to go, and letting those who had citizenship give it up and go back to Japan, even if they'd never been there. The War Relocation Authority, or WRA, was also offering to find war work in factories in the East, but most people were too afraid to agree to be sent away to unknown locations, to work in factories where they were frightened they'd be tormented. It was almost easier to stay in the camps, with people they knew, or to whom they were related.

"I wish to stay here," she said quietly. "I do not wish to return to Japan," she said firmly.

"Why?" They pressed, still suspicious of her, even though the men kidded among themselves about how pretty she was. She had a luminous quality about her, and there was a sense of peace that would have touched them deeply, if they had let it.

"I want to help my cousins if I can." She also wanted to stay in the States because of Peter, but she didn't say so. But she did say that she loved America, which was true. She did now, for a number of reasons, in spite of the relocation. And she never lost sight of the fact that her father wanted her to stay there, so she had to. She could not disobey him.

Eventually, they went back to asking questions about Peter again, and wanted to know why he had come to see them so often at Tanforan. They had marked down every one of his visits, how often he was there, how long he stayed. What they didn't know, fortunately, was what he had done with Hiroko while he'd been there. But the FBI had asked him plenty of questions, both at the camp and when he went into the army. Apparently, they'd been satisfied at his end, and Hiroko gave them almost the same answers.

"He was trying to finish my cousin's work before he left for the army. He had many papers to correct, many things to do. He was the head of his department at Stanford, and my cousin had been the head before . . . before . . ." They knew what she meant, and nodded. "So he had many things to teach him."

"Was he there to see you as well?" She didn't deny it, but gave them no further information either.

"Perhaps. But we had very little time together, he had much work to do with my cousin."

They nodded and went back to it again, and again, and again during that week, asking her if she was loyal to the United States, or to Japan. She said she had no political views, she was only very sad that the two countries were fighting. For her, there was no real division of loyalties. She loved her country, but she loved her family here as well, and as a woman she had no choices to make, no army to serve in.

She met all their questions quietly and calmly, with simple, direct answers. And a week after they had begun, they put a tag on her again, gave her back her clothes, and handed her her suitcase. She had no idea where she was going, if she had passed or failed, or what she had done, if this meant deportation, or execution. Surely, nothing anymore ever meant freedom. She was simply moving on to the next stage, and leaving the place she was in. She said a brief good-bye to the women who had shared her cell with her, wished them luck, and was led outside wearing her own clothes. She looked deathly pale, but she was not quite as thin as she had been a month before. She had been in prison for a month, and had had no news whatsoever of her cousins.

They walked her outside, with half a dozen other women, and a large group of men, and she heard someone refer to them as the "loyals," whatever that was, and then they were marched along in the freezing cold, down a long, narrow road to a group of dilapidated barracks. It appeared to be a separate camp from the one she'd been in, or perhaps it was the same one, but there was a good distance between the two. This time, as they entered the barbed wire and she saw the guards watching them from towers, she also saw activity and children. She heard them playing somewhere, and saw people walking arm in arm on the dirt road between the buildings. There was more of a look of real life to this, and normal activity. It was more like Tanforan, and there were twice as many people. But this seemed more orderly, and as Hiroko glanced around, relieved to see people smiling again, and children nearby, one of the guards handed her a piece of paper with her number on it, and the additional number of her building. She was in 14C this time, and she had no idea of who she would live with.

"It's down the third row to your right, next to the school building," the guard said pleasantly, and suddenly she wondered if she had passed some test, and passed to a different level. Perhaps they weren't going to send her back, or shoot her. She saw the other women smiling too; it was such a relief after what they'd been through. The men seemed to be taking the change more seriously, and were talking quietly amongst themselves, asking each other questions to which no one had the answers. Everything was a mystery here, from one moment to the next, just as it had been for all of them ever since Pearl Harbor.

She left the others and walked down the road he'd pointed to, without a guard, without any companion. It was the first time she'd been alone for over a month, and it felt wonderful, just walking along, not having to talk to anyone, or answer any questions. She knew the guards in the tower were watching her, and there was barbed wire all around them, but in the context of how they'd lived for the past six months, this was freedom.

She found the building easily, once she realized which barracks the school was in. There were long rows of bleak buildings, with numbers indicating "apartments," as they were called, where whole families lived, no matter how large, but there were little signs on the door, and wind chimes people had made beside them. They were in closed rooms, not in horse stalls like in Tanforan, and as she walked along, she saw a sign that said WELCOME TO TULE LAKE, and for the first time in a month, she knew the name of where she was, not that it made a difference. And yet, it did; in a way, she felt almost human again. And she smiled as she saw a little girl sitting on a step, holding a doll.

The child was wearing a knit hat and a heavy sweater, but she sat dejectedly, looking at the ground and humming to herself. She looked so sad, it touched Hiroko's heart as she approached. Then Hiroko let out a little gasp as the child looked up at her. It was Tami.

"Hiroko!" she screamed, hurling herself into her cousin's arms as the older girl burst into tears. "Hiroko! Mom!" She was shouting, and her mother came running out, wearing a worn brown dress and an apron. She'd been cleaning their "house," on a break from the infirmary. It was lunchtime.

"Oh, my God," Reiko said as she rushed to her, and the two women hugged so tightly it hurt them, and then she pulled away quickly to ask with worried eyes, "Have you seen Tak? Where were you?"

"I was in prison, nearby," she explained, shaking her head about Tak and pointing to the direction from which she had come. Reiko had heard there was another camp nearby for people of high security risk, where they were holding them for interrogation. But she had had no idea that Hiroko was there and she didn't know where Takeo was either.

"Are you all right? What did they do to you?" Reiko asked her anxiously.

"They asked many questions. I never saw Takeo," she said definitely, "but he left in the same kind of bus that we did, so perhaps he was there." There were a dozen possibilities, as they both knew. He could have been at Manzanar, or the camp they'd opened at Minidoka the month before, or out of state at any of the other camps, Gila River or Poston, Arizona; Grenada, in Colorado; Heart Mountain in Wyoming; or Topaz in Utah. He could even have been as far away as Arkansas, at Rohwer. In the past month, five new camps had opened, and they were setting up one more in Arkansas, called Jerome, due to start receiving internees at any moment. There was some communication between the camps, but it was limited and censored, and Reiko had no way of contacting anyone to ask about Takeo. Undoubtedly, in most cases she knew people in different camps, but she had no way of knowing who was where or how to reach them. And every day it was a surprise to see who would appear, and who they knew, even at Tule Lake, where people were still arriving.

Hiroko realized from her number then that she had been assigned to stay with Reiko and the children, and they walked her inside, and she saw that they had two tiny rooms, one in which Reiko slept with Sally and Tami, on narrow cots, and the other which they used as a sitting room, and where Ken slept at night, and Tak would too, if he joined them. There was barely enough room to add Hiroko too, but there were other families that were much larger and they did it. You did whatever you had to do, to make it work, there was no choice. This was what they had been assigned to.

"How are Sally and Ken?" Hiroko asked anxiously, as she searched Reiko's eyes, noticing again how worried and thin her cousin looked. Reiko had been desperate for news of Tak, and anxious too about Hiroko.

"They're all right. Ken is working in the fields here, not that he can do much at this time of year, but there are provisions stored, and they have to handle what's brought in. He could have gone to school," she said with a sigh, "but he refused to." He was still furious at what they'd done to them, and talked all the time about the violation of the Constitution. He wasn't alone, there were other boys as angry as he was, and adults too. Some of the nisei were talking about renouncing their citizenship and going to Japan, although they had never been there in their lives. It was their only choice if they didn't want to stay in the camps, or work in the jobs the WRA got them in factories in distant locations. They didn't want to go to Japan, but the shame and indignity of being in the camps was too much for them, and they preferred to try their fate in the homeland of their ancestors. But Reiko had never even thought of it, and she knew Tak wouldn't either. They were American to the core, and they just had to sit this out until it was over. "Sally's at school, and she's made some friends here." There were several girls' clubs, a friendship club, music groups, art classes, gardening clubs. There was already a plan to put together both an orchestra and a symphony, and there was talk of a recital by Christmas. It was incredible that in the limited world they shared, the people here were determined not to complain, to hold their heads high, and to make it pleasant. It brought tears to Hiroko's eyes when Reiko told her about it. These people were so brave, she had no right to complain, or even to cry for Peter. And as Reiko looked at her, she took her in her arms again, feeling as though she had found one of her daughters, and Tami held both of them, with her doll, so happy to have Hiroko back with them.

"Can we make my new dollhouse now?" she asked, looking nine again, and not worldly-wise and deeply sad, as she had a few minutes before when Hiroko first saw her.

"If we can find the right things." She smiled down at her little cousin, and held her small hand firmly in her own, as Reiko looked Hiroko over. She actually looked better than she had at Tanforan. She'd been so sick with stomach problems and dysentery, that at the end Reiko had been worried.

"How's your stomach?" Reiko asked, sounding like a nurse, and Hiroko looked startled.

"Much better." She smiled shyly. No one had inquired about her health in months, and it made her feel so vulnerable and loved to have someone care about her, and not just by asking her questions and waiting for answers. "Are you well, Aunt Rei?"

"I'm fine." Except that she couldn't sleep at night, worrying about her husband. And she knew from her own nursing experience that she was developing a gastric ulcer. But other than that, they were managing. The conditions were fair, the guards were decent to them, and the other people in the camp were, for the most part, remarkable. There was the occasional complainer, but most of the people her age were determined to make the best of it, particularly the women. Some of the men were having a harder time of it, they felt responsible, and guilt-ridden for not having been able to save their families and businesses, and seen it coming. They felt useless here, doing menial jobs, peeling potatoes, or digging ditches in the frozen ground. It did not compare with being architects or engineers or professors or even farmers. It shamed them deeply to be here. And the old people sat around and talked about old times, touching the past with ancient hands, so they would not be touched by the present. Only the children seemed relatively unscathed by it. Most of them had adjusted admirably, except those who were ill or frail. And the teenagers were almost enjoying it, Reiko sometimes thought. There were so many of them, they were together all the time, and they gathered constantly to sing, or play music, or just talk and laugh, and drive the old ones crazy.

"I'm working at the infirmary," Reiko explained, "naturally. We've had a lot of sick kids here. Some nasty influenzas, even in these few weeks, and more measles." Measles was the bane of their existence. The children got so sick, and the adults even more so. And now and then some of the old people were felled, and more often than not, it killed them. There had already been several deaths in the brief month that Reiko had been at Tule Lake, mostly from problems that would have been minor elsewhere. She hated assisting at surgery here, the conditions were terrible, and they never seemed to have enough ether.

"We're managing," she went on with a resigned smile. Life would have been so much happier for her, if they'd been with Takeo. She couldn't imagine going through the whole war without him, but for the moment it looked like she might have to. She just prayed he was still alive, and would stay that way until they met again. She hadn't liked the way he'd looked at Tanforan before they left, but there was nothing she could do about it now, except pray, and worry. "Just do yourself a favor, and don't get sick here," she said to Hiroko. "Stay warm, eat what you can, and try to stay away from sick children. They pay me twelve dollars a month at the infirmary." She smiled as she helped Hiroko unpack her things, and looked disapprovingly at Hiroko's coat. It wasn't warm enough for Tule Lake. "You'd better join one of the knitting clubs, and make yourself some sweaters." It was hard to get wool, but some of them were unraveling old sweaters to make new ones, particularly for the children, or the women having babies. Reiko had set up something of a maternity ward for them, but they couldn't waste ether on them, or medications. They needed them for the serious surgeries. It was a lot like the old days of medicine.

They went back out into the winter sunshine then, and Tami told her that they were making decorations for Halloween at school. And Reiko and Hiroko dropped her off at school after lunch on their way back to the infirmary. In spite of Reiko's warnings, Hiroko wanted to volunteer to work with her there. She thought it sounded interesting and useful, more so than working in the kitchen.

And when Reiko introduced her to the doctors she was working for, they were delighted to have more help. They gave her an apron and a cap, and had her start by making beds and washing sheets and rags soaked in blood, and pans filled with vomit. She was retching miserably outside when Reiko saw her later that afternoon, and smiled sympathetically at her.

"I'm sorry, it's not pretty work here."

"It's all right," Hiroko whispered hoarsely, just grateful to be out of prison again. She would do anything she had to.

And in the next couple of weeks, she almost got used to it. She did hideous jobs for them, but little by little they also let her talk to the patients. She was such a sweet girl and had such gentle ways that everyone loved her. And her naturally fluent Japanese was a great help with all the old people who were sick in the infirmary. They particularly appreciated her extensive knowledge of their traditions.

Ken was happy to have her back again too, because he could talk to her about some of the things that were bothering him, and she listened carefully. He even admitted secretly that he had heard some of the other nisei talk about renouncing their American citizenship to go to Japan and get out of camp, and more than once he had thought about it. He knew it would break his mother's heart, but every fiber in his being rebelled at the idea of being imprisoned in camp, while other Americans, just like him, fought for their country. But Hiroko begged him not to even consider giving up his citizenship, nor to tell his mother about it. More than anything, he wished he could join the U.S. Army, but that was no longer an option. Those who had, before the evacuation came, were doing K.P. in boot camps and even regular posts around the country. And recently, the draft boards had been classifying nisei as IV-C, "aliens ineligible to serve," so the army was out for Ken, and all the other young men like him. Hiroko was grateful that she was able to reason with him, most of the time. It was only when he talked to his other young male friends that he got so worked up there was no talking to him. He had heard from Peggy at Manzanar once or twice too, but communication between the camps was difficult, and they seemed to be drifting apart. They each had their own troubles.

And Sally was difficult sometimes too. At fifteen, she felt grown-up, and longed for more freedom. She wanted to hang out with the young people there, many

of whom were not as strictly brought up as she was.
And Reiko was particularly anxious to keep her in
check, and it wasn't always easy to do it. Hiroko had
several talks with her, about following the rules, and
listening to her mother, and it really annoyed her when
Hiroko tried to play big sister.

"You're only four years older than me," she complained. "How can you be so stupid?"

"We do not want you to get into trouble," Hiroko
said firmly, and urged her to join one of the girls'
clubs. But Sally thought they were silly. Hiroko joined
the symphony, alternately playing piano and violin.
And in her spare time, she was doing artwork with the
children, mostly origami, and she had promised to do
flower arranging with Reiko's women's club when
there were flowers after the winter.

The news from the war was interesting too. Several people got newspapers, though they weren't always current. But Hiroko was able to learn that
Eisenhower and his men had landed at Casablanca,
Oran, and Algiers with the British, and the Vichy
French in North Africa had surrendered. It was a major coup, and Hiroko could only pray that Peter was
safe and still with them.

And four days afterward, German troops had
moved into occupied France, apparently mainly to
subdue the French Resistance. But that was the only
news they heard before Thanksgiving.

Their Thanksgiving meal was sketchy that year; no
one was able to get turkey. Some people had received
care packages from friends. Others had begun using
their salaries to buy things from catalogs, which were
sent to them at the camps. But it was difficult to get

enough food to cook a real Thanksgiving dinner. They made do with chickens, and hamburger, and in some cases, even baloney. But as usual, they were grateful to be alive, and the children were in high spirits the night before the holiday. A new load of arrivals came by train that day, and another group from the other part of the camp, which was used as a prison. More and more people were being released from there as their loyalty was questioned and eventually found adequate to put them in the camp with the others.

And Reiko had just come home from work on Wednesday afternoon, the day before Thanksgiving, and she was helping Tami with her homework, when someone knocked on the door, and Sally opened it, and then she just stood there, staring. And suddenly there was a scream, as Reiko saw him and flew to him. It was Takeo. He looked tired and worn, and terribly thin, and his hair was much grayer than it had been before, but he was safe, he was well, he was "loyal," and other than over two months' confinement in a small cell, he had not been mistreated.

"Thank God, thank God," Reiko said over and over again as he kissed her, and then he pulled all of his children into his arms, as Hiroko watched them. None of them could believe their good fortune to have him back in their midst after his long absence.

Reiko kept looking him over as a mother would a small child, holding him in her arms, and touching his face and his hair, wanting to assure herself that he was real and not her imagination. But as he sat down with them, she saw that he seemed almost broken by what had happened. It was not what they had done to him, so much as what they hadn't. They hadn't given him freedom or respect, or acknowledged him as an American, or even as a man who had a right to something from them. In two months, he had had a lot of time to think, and like everyone else, he had thought of going back to Japan, but he knew he couldn't do it. He didn't want to be there. He wasn't Japanese anymore. He felt completely American, by adoption. The heartbreak came when he realized that his adoptive country didn't want him.

But he said none of that to Reiko as he sat with her, or as they walked slowly to the mess hall for dinner. He seemed to be moving very slowly, and Reiko was more concerned than ever. She wanted to know if he'd been ill, but he just said he was tired, and she noticed that he had a hard time breathing. He was exhausted and out of breath when they reached the mess hall.

But afterward, he seemed to revive again, and that night, Ken slept in the bedroom with the others, so Tak and Reiko could be alone. They slept in the single narrow cot in the living room, with the straw poking at them, but they were thrilled to be together.

And their Thanksgiving Day the next day was a real celebration. They ate in the mess hall with everyone, and afterward came back to play charades, and eat some cookies that Reiko had been able to get for them. They were all in high spirits, and Tak looked more like his old self again. He was laughing with them, and when he looked around, he teased his wife and said that their house was a dump. He had already talked to some men who had been building furniture, and had agreed to join them. They were using scrap lumber and anything they could find. And there were a number of things Takeo wanted to provide her.

It was hard to believe they'd ever had a real home, with furniture and nice things, some antiques, and curtains that were more than pieces of old dresses. But he promised Reiko that he would do what he could for them. It made him feel better to take care of his family in whatever way he could, and as Reiko watched him, he didn't seem quite as breathless. She tried to discourage him from smoking, but he laughed at her, and she could see in his eyes that there was something different there. He wasn't angry, like Ken, but he was bitter.

"There isn't much else left, is there?" he answered her complaint about his smoking.

"Yes, there is," she said gently. "There's us, and the children. We'll go home one day. This won't last forever."

"Home to where? The house is gone, and I'll be too old to get my job back."

"No, you won't," she said with a look of determination. She was not going to be defeated by this. She had decided that more than ever in the past month, as had so many others. And she wouldn't let him be beaten by it either. "And we'll get another house, a better one. Peter has our money in his account. And we're young enough to make more when we leave here." She looked at him with eyes he had never seen before, and he was so proud of her he almost cried. He felt ashamed by all that he'd been feeling. "I'm not going to let this beat us."

"Neither will I," he promised her. And she was pleased the next day when he told her he had spoken to several of the men about the elections they were going to have, electing community councils. Everyone over eighteen could vote, which was a first for him. For the first time in their lives in the United States, the issei could be part of an electoral process. They had been born in Japan, and until now had been unable to participate in elections. But he was angry afterward when he found out that the camp administrator had announced that only nisei and sansei, who were American born, could hold office. And the nisei and sansei did not object, they were satisfied to have the power. It seemed to Tak as though no one wanted those who were Japanese born. Not the Americans, and not even his own kind. There was no place for them.

"Don't take it so hard," Reiko said to him. "The young ones want their turn too." But he felt disgraced by it, as he did by everything else that had happened, and she didn't know what to do to soothe his wounds anymore. He was quieter than he used to be, and so easily discouraged.

But she said nothing about her worries to Hiroko as they worked side by side in the infirmary. Hiroko was learning many things, and she was beaming on the Monday after Thanksgiving. She had finally heard from Peter. The letter had taken weeks to arrive, and had been blackened by censors at both ends. She had no idea what he'd told her, not all of it anyway. All she knew was that he was in Oran when he wrote, and had been fighting Rommel. He said he missed her terribly. And he said he'd been getting her letters. His letters had been forwarded to Tule Lake from Tanforan, and she had already written him long since with her new address, but he obviously hadn't gotten it yet. She smiled for days after she got the letter, and worked twice as hard for Reiko.

There was a terrible rash of influenza again in the first week of December, when the temperatures went down below zero.

There were several cases of pneumonia too, and two old people died, which depressed Hiroko. She had tried so hard to keep them alive, reading to them in Japanese, bathing them, keeping them warm and telling them stories. But it had been hopeless. And she was even more upset when a little girl was brought in, one of Tami's friends, also in extremis.

The doctors were sure she wouldn't live the night, but Hiroko sat with her tirelessly and refused to go home. For Hiroko, it was almost as if it had been Tami. And Reiko watched her struggling to keep the child alive, as the little girl's mother sat by her side and wept. Hiroko worked with her incessantly for three days, and then finally the fever broke, and the doctors said she would recover.

Hiroko almost swooned when she heard the news. She was so tired she could barely stand up. She hadn't even left the child to go and eat. Reiko had brought her food from the mess hall. But she had saved the little girl, she had done what they couldn't, without medicine or a hospital. She had done it with love and determination. And the child's mother thanked her again, as Hiroko smiled and left the infirmary. She took two steps out the door, with her apron over her arm, and as she looked up at the winter sky, everything swirled slowly around her, and she fainted.

An old woman across the road saw her go down, and watched for a moment to see if she'd just fallen.

But she lay still on the ground and there was no movement at all as the old woman hurried over. She looked at her quickly and hurried inside to call a doctor. Reiko was still there and she ran outside to see what had happened, and Hiroko lay there, still and gray and unconscious.

A doctor came outside as Reiko called, and two of the nurses. He took her pulse, and opened her eyes to look at her pupils, but she didn't even stir. She was totally immobile as they carried her inside, and Tami's little friend started to cry when she saw her.

"Is she dead? Did she die?" the little girl cried. She had been so alive only a few minutes before, although everyone could see she was very tired. But the little girl's mother was quick to reassure her, telling her Hiroko was just sleeping.

The doctor carried her himself into a partitioned area, concealed by blankets, and took her pulse again. He didn't like what he was seeing. She was barely breathing.

"What's wrong?" Reiko breathed, no longer the nurse, but more the mother.

"I'm not sure yet," he said honestly in English. He was sansei, second-generation American, and had gone to Stanford. He could have gone East to relatives when the voluntary order for evacuation came, but he hadn't. And in the end, he had decided to stay here to help his people. "Her blood pressure is very low, and she's hardly breathing." He turned to look at Reiko over his shoulder. "Has this ever happened to her before?"

"Not that I know of."

Her color was terrible, and they were using smelling salts to no avail. If anything, she was getting worse. Reiko wondered if it was influenza of some kind, or perhaps polio. Scarlet fever . . . she couldn't imagine what had struck her. And she wasn't hot, she was cold, as though her circulation were slowing to a disastrous level.

The doctor was slapping her then, shaking her gently, and he glanced at the nurse next to him and gave a rapid order. "Take her clothes off!" He wanted to see her abdomen and her chest, wanted to know why she wasn't breathing. And Reiko worked hurriedly with the other two girls to hastily unbutton the heavy wool dress she wore. It was long and loose and flowing and the tiny buttons down the front seemed to take forever. There was even a small tearing sound as the doctor pushed the dress aside, and hastily pulled her slip up, and then they saw it. She was bound from her breasts to her thighs with long strips of bandaging, tied so tightly that they were literally stopping her circulation. "Good lord, what's she done to herself?" He had no idea what the bandages were for, he'd never seen them, and wondered what she had concealed, but Reiko knew. She hadn't seen them in years. But she knew instantly as he rapidly cut through them. And almost as she did, they could see her flesh come alive again, and her color improve. She had tied them so tightly, she had impaired not only her circulation, but her breathing.

She still hadn't moved, but as he removed the endless circle of bandages, her body grew beneath his hands, and even he understood what she had done, although he'd never seen it.

"The poor kid," he said, glancing up at Reiko and

then back at Hiroko again. She had bound herself to
within an inch of her life, and her baby's. The moment
the bandages fell away from her, they could see that
she was very pregnant. It had been a crazy thing to do,
but her grandmother had told her about it, and her
mother had done it when she was pregnant with her,
and with Yuji. And she hadn't wanted anyone to know
about the baby, not even Peter. She had never told
him. She had only discovered it after he left, in June.
And she hadn't been certain till July. As close as she
could guess, the baby was due at the end of February,
or in early March. She was six months pregnant.

It was fully another five minutes before she
stirred, as Reiko and the other nurse gently massaged
her skin, and felt the baby give a resounding kick in
protest. It was going to be a lot happier now without
the restraints its mother had put on it, but Reiko's
mind was racing as she watched her. She couldn't
imagine when, or how, she had done this. They had
been at the assembly center since April, and the only
man she'd ever seen her with was Peter. And surely,
he wouldn't have been foolish enough to do this. But
someone had. And Hiroko was going to have a baby.

After a few more minutes, she opened her eyes
and looked at them, feeling very far away and a little
groggy. She still hadn't realized that they had opened
her dress, or cut her bindings. Reiko had covered her
discreetly with a blanket, and the doctor looked down
at her with a gentle look of disapproval.

"That was a pretty silly thing to do," he said, taking
her hand and holding it as he looked at her.

"I know." She smiled. "But I didn't want to leave
her. I thought that if I stayed with her, I could help

her." She thought he was talking about the patient she hadn't left for a moment in three days.

"I didn't mean her, I meant you. . . . That's a pretty mean thing you've been doing to your baby. I'm surprised he let you get away with it. You almost strangled both of you just now." She hadn't removed the binding in days, and he wondered if the baby had grown since she'd been home, and so the bindings tightened until she finally fainted. He wondered how she could have borne it. "I don't want you doing that again," he said firmly, and Hiroko turned her face away as she blushed deeply, and he nodded at Reiko. "I'm going to leave you with your aunt right now. But I don't want to see you working this hard for a while. You've got someone else to think about, Hiroko." He patted her arm and spoke softly to her cousin. "Keep her in bed today and tomorrow. She can come back to work after that. She'll be fine." He smiled, and then he left the little cubicle with the other two nurses. Hiroko was alone with her cousin. She turned her face slowly to face her, and she was crying.

"I'm so sorry, Aunt Rei." Not about the binding, but that she was pregnant. "I'm so sorry." She had disgraced all of them, and yet she had wanted this so badly, and she still did. No matter how great the disgrace, she wanted Peter's baby.

"Why didn't you tell me?"

"I couldn't." There was so much she couldn't tell them, and she didn't want to get Peter in trouble. She thought maybe if she'd told them, they wouldn't let her see him again. Or worse, if someone found out and they told the FBI, he might be punished. She had imagined all kinds of terrors.

Reiko hesitated for only a moment before she asked the next question. "It's Peter's, isn't it?" But Hiroko wouldn't answer her, for all the same reasons. She was afraid for him, and even for their baby. What if they took it away after it was born? But they wouldn't. A Japanese ancestor, in any degree, was cause for internment. This baby would be a prisoner, just as she was. No one would take it from her. It was her only comfort. "Why won't you tell me?" Reiko asked.

"I can't tell you, Aunt Rei," she said softly, determined to protect him, no matter what it cost her. And in a way she was protecting Reiko too, by not confirming it to her. And Reiko knew this and didn't press her again, but she knew in her heart it was Peter's.

She helped Hiroko button her dress again, and stand up, when she finally thought she could, although she almost swooned again. But Reiko made her sit down and brought her a glass of water, and she threw away the vicious bindings.

"Don't you ever do that again!" she scolded her. "Even my mother didn't do that, and she was pretty old-fashioned." But she smiled at her then anyway. What a difficult secret she had kept for all this time, all alone, even in prison. She wondered if Peter knew, but even if he did, there was nothing he could do now to help her.

They walked slowly back to their little room, arm in arm, and Reiko talked to her soothingly about not working too hard, eating as best she could, and taking care of herself and the baby. But as she looked at her, she was amazed to realize how pregnant she looked. In a single moment, without the bindings she had worn,

Hiroko's stomach looked enormous. It was in sharp contrast to her tiny frame, and Reiko suddenly worried that she might have trouble giving birth. And this was no place to have medical problems or complications.

They walked quietly inside, and Hiroko went to lie down. Takeo looked up as they came in. He had just finished making a piece of furniture he was particularly pleased with, and that afternoon he was going to work in the mess hall. He planned to start teaching at the school soon. But when he saw Hiroko, his mouth almost fell open, and he managed not to say anything until a few minutes later when he walked back outside with Reiko.

"Have I missed something here? Am I completely blind?" He looked totally bemused. "The last time I saw her, two days ago, she was quite normal. Now she comes back looking about six or seven months pregnant, if memory serves me correctly. What exactly are you doing at that infirmary? Making miracles, or have I lost my mind here?"

"No, not exactly." Reiko smiled ruefully, accepting a cigarette from him. It was so good to have him back again, to share things with him, and have someone to talk to. No matter how disillusioned he was, he was the man she had loved for twenty years, her best friend, her partner. She was sad for Hiroko that she couldn't share the same relationship with the baby's father. "She's been hiding this from us, Tak," Reiko explained, still unable to believe what the girl had been doing to herself. "She was so tightly bound, she almost strangled herself. God only knows what that does to the baby. She was completely unconscious, and we had no idea why until we undressed her. She had almost stopped breathing."

"Poor kid. I suppose I can guess who the father is, or can I? Have I missed something?" Maybe there had been someone else, she was so discreet there was no knowing, but Reiko didn't think so.

"It must be Peter," she agreed, "but she won't tell me. I think she's afraid to. Maybe she's afraid they'll do something to him, or take the baby away. Or maybe she's protecting us. I don't know."

"Do you suppose he knows?" Tak smoked his cigarette thoughtfully. It was one of the few pleasures he still had there.

"I have no idea, but somehow I doubt it. I can't imagine she'd dare to write it to him, even if she wanted to. Not if she's afraid even to tell us." And then she thought of something else that concerned her. This was not an easy situation, but most of all not for Hiroko. "What do you think we should say to the children?"

"There's not much we can say. She's having a baby, and we love her, and we'll love the baby. And that's that," he said matter-of-factly.

Reiko smiled at him, faintly amused by the simplicity of the statement. "I'll remind you of that if this ever happens to Sally."

"That's different." He laughed and shook his head, looking at his wife with appreciation and affection. She always saw the humor in things, and helped him to. He loved that and many things about her, along with her good nature. "If it were Sally, I'd kill her. Hiroko's not my daughter." And then he thought about it. "Poor kid. She's been through an awful lot, and now this. I guess that's why she was always so sick to her stomach at Tanforan. I sure never suspected this."

"Neither did I," Reiko admitted, and then she looked at her husband again. "Do you suppose he'll marry her, if it's his?"

But Takeo was quick to answer. "He would have anyway, Rei. He's crazy about her. And it probably is his. It's funny, I noticed something different about them there. They used to go on those long walks every afternoon, but I couldn't imagine they'd get themselves into trouble. But they were always so close, so bound to each other, the way married people are. I'm surprised he didn't marry her before he left."

"I don't think she wanted to, without her father's consent." Reiko guessed correctly, as Hiroko walked slowly out of the house and stood before them.

"I'm so sorry," she said, her head bowed, aching at having brought shame on them. She had somehow thought that she could keep it a secret forever, which was childish.

"We love you," Reiko said, and put an arm around her, and then she smiled as she looked down at her tummy. It reminded her of her own children when they were born. It had been a good time for her and Tak. She was only sorry for Hiroko that this wouldn't be easy, and she had only them, and not a husband.

"When is it coming?" Takeo asked quietly, turning to look at her as she blushed again. She was still wrestling with the embarrassment and at the same time she was proud, and happy that she had Peter's baby.

"In February," she answered softly, "perhaps March."

He nodded then, looking up at the sky, thinking of

many things, his own life, his marriage, his children
. . . and Peter. And then he smiled at her, and put an
arm around her too. "That's a good time to have a
baby. It'll be spring then . . . a new beginning, a new
life. . . . Maybe a new world for all of us by then."

"Thank you, Uncle Tak," she said, and kissed him
on the cheek, as she closed her eyes and thought of
Peter, and prayed he would still be safe then.

# Chapter 14

THE CHILDREN'S reactions to Hiroko's pregnancy were mixed. Tami was thrilled, Ken was surprised and protective of her, and Sally was less than sympathetic. She was annoyed that everyone was suddenly being so solicitous of her, in spite of what she'd done, and she had more than one argument about it with her mother.

"If I had done that, you and Daddy would have killed me."

Reiko smiled, remembering what Tak had said along just those lines, and agreed with her. "Probably. But this is a little different. She's nineteen years old, almost twenty, she's in a different situation, and she's not our daughter."

"It's still disgusting anyway, that everyone is acting like she's the Virgin Mary waiting for baby Jesus."

"Oh, for heaven's sake, Sally, don't be so unkind to her. The poor thing is all alone, and this is a terrible situation for any girl to be in."

"Does she even know who the father is?" Sally asked rudely, and her mother glowered at her.

"We're not discussing that. All I'm saying is that we need to be nice to her, and help her take care of the baby."

"Well, don't count on me to baby-sit. Just think of what my friends will say." She was mortified, but Reiko was not sorry for her. It had happened to plenty of other girls over the years, and it was not up to Sally to be throwing stones at her cousin.

"A lot will depend on how you explain it to them," her mother said firmly.

"I don't need to, Mom, everyone can see it."

They did, but very few people commented on it. In the difficult life they had led, it almost went unnoticed. And to some, they thought it provided a sign of hope and new life, and they thought she was lucky. No one ostracized her, or said anything. A few asked when the baby was due, but most people said nothing. And absolutely no one inquired about the father.

Reiko and Tak asked her a few more times, but she refused to confirm their suspicions, or even say anything about it. And in the month of December, she had several more letters from Peter. He was still in North Africa, and he was well. He had absolutely no idea what was happening to Hiroko, and his letters were full of declarations of love for her, as hers were to him. She gave him news of Reiko and Tak, and the kids, and said fairly little about the camp, and nothing at all about the baby. He had asked for a photograph of her, but she had none with her, other than the one he had given her of both of them, and no one in camp was allowed to have a camera, so it was easy to ignore his requests for pictures.

The anniversary of Pearl Harbor was a quiet day for all of them, except at Manzanar, where they later heard that tempers had run high and there had been a riot over mess hall administration. Two were killed and ten were wounded, and it sobered everyone at Tule Lake even further. And the guards became suddenly more restrictive.

After that, everyone turned their sights toward Christmas. Takeo was teaching in the high school by then, and Reiko was busy at the infirmary helping the few doctors tend to colds and the occasional appendectomy, and influenza. And Hiroko had gone back to work after two days of rest and she felt fine now. And every night, she and Tak had a secret project. He was helping her make a dollhouse for Tami, he had made the frame, and was making the furniture, and Hiroko was making all the wall decorations, the rugs, and curtains and tiny paintings. In some ways, although it wasn't as expensively made, it was even more elaborate than her old one. And they had been very creative about substituting one thing for another.

He was also working on a Monopoly game for her, and he and Reiko were having a great time putting it together. He was making a chess game for Ken too. And Reiko was knitting a beautiful pink angora sweater for Sally, from wool she'd ordered from Montgomery Ward with most of her salary.

Reiko had knitted a sweater for Tak too, and she'd sent away for a warm jacket for him with the rest of her money. And she and her whole knitting club had been knitting tiny little things to give Hiroko a shower after Christmas. Tak was carving her a little cradle too.

And on Christmas Day, they were all surprised with their presents from each other. Tak had bought Reiko a beautiful dress from the Sears catalog with his meager earnings, and Hiroko had given them both a poem she had written about what they meant to her, called "Winter Storms, Summer Rainbows." And everyone loved their presents.

But the only gift anyone wanted that year was freedom. Regardless of that, it was a lovely day, in spite of where they were, and most people in the camp tried not to think of where they had been the year before, or who they had been with. The old men played go, their checker game, the women chatted and sewed, people ate and talked and dreamed, and visited each other in their little rooms, with handmade decorations. They had been incarcerated and locked up, and almost everything had been taken from them, but it was impossible to take away their spirit. They were all determined to keep going and be strong, for themselves and each other. Hiroko thought of that when she played with the symphony at the Christmas concert.

And on New Year's Eve, there was a dance at the recreation building, and a swing band that Ken had just joined played. Hiroko went to watch for a little while, and one young man asked her to dance, but she blushed and said she couldn't. Under her heavy coat, he hadn't noticed her stomach.

In January, the Germans surrendered at Stalingrad, which was an important victory for the Allies. At

Tule Lake it was a quiet month, except another wave of influenza hit the camp, this one worse than any of the others. It went on for almost a month, and a few of the old people died and others were in grave danger.

And much to everyone's surprise, at the end of January, the Selective Service had reopened for Japanese men and boys and the "privilege" of volunteering for the military had been restored to them. But Ken no longer wanted to go into the army, he didn't see why he should volunteer now to serve a country that had betrayed him. Most of the other young men felt the same, and they were still in an uproar over it when camp officials asked everyone to sign a loyalty oath in the first week of February. To many of the internees, the loyalty oath was not a problem. They were all loyal to the United States, but to Ken, and many young men like him, they felt even more betrayed by the questions they were asked and the answers that were required of them. There were two questions in particular that irked them, one asking if they would be willing to serve in the armed forces of the United States on combat duty, wherever ordered, and the other was if they would foreswear any allegiance to Japan or the Emperor, neither of which should have worried anyone, since so many were Americans or had lived in the States all their lives. But the young men like Ken were particularly outraged to have had all their rights taken away from them, and now be asked if they were willing to die for a country that had treated them so badly. Ken had been desperate to join the army for over a year, but after being betrayed and incarcerated for months, he no longer wanted to serve, or do anything for his country.

And like him, just on principle, many of the young men refused to answer those two questions positively, and as a result got labeled the No-No Boys, for the two questions they refused to say yes to, and they were swiftly sent off to segregation at the higher-security area at Tule Lake, for further interrogation.

It created a huge outcry in all the camps, and Ken still hadn't signed the oath two days after he'd been shown it. Everyone else in the family had, and Ken and his father argued furiously over it. Takeo understood how he felt, and he ached for him and all the young men like him. They had been shunned and sent away, their rights as Americans had been denied them. But now their right to serve had been restored, and other than war work through the WRA, or renouncing their citizenship, there was no other way to leave the camps. This was a chance to prove themselves as Americans, to have their rights restored, to prove that they were loyal citizens, and Tak didn't want Ken to fail to do that. He *had* to sign the loyalty oath, not to would be a disaster.

"I don't even feel American anymore, Dad," Ken said angrily. "I don't feel American. I don't feel Japanese. I don't feel anything," he said unhappily, and his father didn't know what to say to him.

"You have no choice, son. I understand. I respect how you feel. But I am telling you to sign the loyalty oath. If you don't, they're going to put you in prison, and cause you a great deal of trouble. Ken, you have to." They battled about it for days, and finally, not wanting to cause trouble for them, Ken signed, but many of his friends didn't. They didn't because it was the only opportunity they had to object to what had happened to them, but it made them instantly suspect and many of them were considered dangerous. Many renounced their citizenship immediately, and chose to go to Japan as they had threatened to for months. And Ken had threatened too, but in the end, he couldn't do it.

Those who didn't sign were rounded up from the other camps as well, and the No-No Boys wound up in the segregation section at Tule Lake. It was, in fact, at that point being built into a separate camp, for people thought to be disloyal to the United States, and security was immediately increased to deal with the problem. Tak was deeply grateful that, in the end, Ken had agreed to sign the loyalty oath, even if it meant seeing him go off to war and risk his life for his country. At least his loyalty as an American would never be questioned.

Signing the loyalty oath took a great deal of pressure off all of them, and even Hiroko felt relieved when she went back to work at the infirmary during a fresh outbreak of influenza. For Hiroko, as a genuine alien, the loyalty oath had given her a real opportunity to pledge her loyalty to the United States, which was something she wanted, although of course in her case, question twenty-seven was of no importance, since she couldn't go into the army.

A new epidemic of measles kept them busy after that for two weeks, and at the end of the second week, Hiroko stayed late into the night to help Reiko. And for once Reiko looked as tired as she was. Hiroko had been working tirelessly for days, but she wanted to give them all the help she could before the baby came. She knew that in another week or two, she would have to stay at home, at least for a little while, with the baby.

The knitting club had given her the shower by then, and everything was ready. Tami was more excited than anyone, and even Sally had softened a little bit, although she was still fairly vocal with her disapproval. But Hiroko had other things on her mind that night, as she took care of two old men and a woman who were covered with spots from the measles. She knew that she herself had had it as a child, and wasn't afraid of catching it. But their coughs raged, along with their fevers.

"How are they?" Reiko asked softly as she came by to check on her and watched admiringly. Hiroko had a genuine talent for nursing. She was doing everything she could to make them comfortable, and showed no signs of fatigue herself, although it was her second straight shift on duty. Reiko had thought of sending her home earlier, but Hiroko had insisted on staying at the infirmary with Reiko.

"They're about the same," Hiroko said quietly, sponging their brows again, and glancing up at her cousin.

"And how are you?" It was pointless even to ask, she'd been on her feet, off and on, for hours. And Reiko noticed her rub her back a couple of times, later, when she watched her. She came back to check on her again around midnight, and told her she should go home, but Hiroko looked bright-eyed and full of energy. Reiko smiled at her and hurried off to help a doctor with what looked like a perforated ulcer.

It was two A.M. when she came by again, and this time Hiroko looked exhausted. Her patients were finally asleep, and she was helping another nurse change the dressings on a little boy with burns. He had been playing with matches when his straw mattress caught fire, and he was crying while Hiroko held him. Reiko saw her wince several times in sympathy for the child, and when she set him down again and finally stood up, she noticed that Hiroko held on to the table. And then she knew, even before Hiroko did, that she was in labor.

"Are you all right?" she asked, and Hiroko winced again and tried to smile.

"I'm fine. My back is just tired," she said, but she looked distracted, and Reiko smiled at her. It was time. It was the first of March, time for her baby to come.

"Why don't you sit down for a few minutes," Reiko suggested, and knew from the fact that Hiroko did, that she was probably in more pain than she was willing to admit. Reiko got her a cup of tea, and the two women talked softly in the dim light of the makeshift nurses' station. It was freezing outside, and drafty in the barracks where they were working, but there was a cozy feeling between the two women. And as they chatted, and others came and went, Hiroko's face grew more and more strained, and she looked more and more worried. "Are you in a lot of pain?" Reiko finally asked, and this time, Hiroko looked up with eyes filled with tears, and nodded. She had tried to work in spite of it for hours, hoping it would go away, that it was not time. Suddenly she was terrified, and she didn't feel ready to face it. Just sitting there, the pains were becoming unbearable, and she suddenly clutched Reiko's hand and gasped. No one had prepared her for what this would be like. But Reiko was sitting calmly with her, and she put an arm around her and gently helped her to stand up, as two other nurses appeared and Reiko explained that Hiroko was in labor.

"Well, that's good news." Sandra, the eldest of the nurses, smiled at her. She was a small, round, smiling nisei woman whom Reiko had worked with years before at Stanford. "I could use a little good news tonight." She was tired of dying old people with measles. But Hiroko looked like a wide-eyed little girl as she stared at them, not knowing what to expect. "It's all right," the older woman said soothingly, seeing what was happening to her. It was normal for young girls to panic. She was only nineteen, she had no mother at hand, and it was her first baby. But the nurses of the infirmary all took her under their wing, and two of them joined her and Reiko and led her slowly to a little cubicle they'd set aside for deliveries, carefully partitioned with old blankets. And one of them left immediately to tell the doctor they'd need him that night.

As it turned out, it was the same doctor who had been on duty the morning that she'd fainted, and he smiled warmly when he saw Hiroko again, although she could barely smile at him by the time he got there. He asked her when the pains had begun, and she looked sheepishly at Reiko, and admitted that she'd felt the first twinges early that morning, just before dawn. It had been nearly twenty-four hours by now, and the pains were getting more and more powerful with each moment. She could hardly talk as the next one came, and the nurses lay her down gently and helped take her clothes off. Reiko was standing close to her head, and holding one hand, as the doctor examined her beneath a rough drape, and Hiroko turned her face away in mortification. No one had ever examined her before this, except externally and very superficially after she fainted. No one else had ever seen or touched her except Peter.

"It's all right," Reiko said soothingly, and Sandra took her other hand and held it.

The doctor was pleased, but surprised that she had stayed on her feet as long as she had. She was almost fully dilated and he could see the baby's hair. With an encouraging look, he told her it wouldn't be long at all. But as he left the cubicle, he signaled to Reiko, and she joined him. Hiroko was writhing with another pain, but fighting not to make any noise, so no one would hear her just beyond the partitions made of flimsy blankets. The room just beyond them was filled with sleeping patients, and Hiroko would have felt disgraced if she'd made a sound to wake them.

"The baby looks big to me," he said to Reiko. "I don't want to have to section her here. She's going to have to do everything she can to push that baby out. I don't care if you ladies have to stand on her stomach, Rei. I don't want to have to do that kind of surgery here in camp, unless I have to. It's too risky for her and the baby." She nodded, worrying about Hiroko, who still had not confirmed that Peter was the father of her baby. If it was Peter, as it surely was, he was tall and broad, and the baby might be much too big for Hiroko to deliver on her own. But she said nothing to the doctor about the baby's father, as he moved on to check on some other patients.

The other nurse was helping Hiroko breathe and trying to keep her calm when Reiko got back to her bedside. The two women exchanged a knowing look, as Hiroko seized their hands again, and this time she cried out, despite the flimsy blankets around her and the patients on the other side of them who might hear her.

"It's all right, go ahead," Sandra encouraged her. "Don't worry about it. If they don't like it, they can go to another hospital." She smiled, and Hiroko tried not to scream but lost the battle as the next pain engulfed her.

"Aunt Rei," she said hoarsely, "this is terrible. . . . Is there medicine? . . . something . . ." They had given whatever they had to patients for pain ever since she'd worked there, she couldn't imagine surviving this without it. But they needed what anesthesia they had for surgeries, not for delivering babies, and Reiko knew she could not give her anything unless the doctor said so. And he hadn't suggested it when he came by to see her.

He came back several times in the next two hours, and at four-thirty, he told her to start pushing. But the baby was so large it didn't move at all. It just sat trapped where it was, unable to go back, and unwilling to go forward.

"Stubborn little thing," the doctor said, after battling with a pair of forceps that left Hiroko gasping in agony, as three nurses held her. It was six o'clock by then, and they had gotten nowhere in the last few hours. He glanced at Reiko from time to time, and she remembered his warning, but there was nothing they could do to help Hiroko move the baby.

"Try, Hiroko, come on," Sandy told her. "Push as hard as you can." She had, but it was exactly what her own mother had experienced with Yuji. The baby was too big, the mother too small. But this wasn't Kyoto. And there was no hospital to go to. There were only these women helping her, and a minimum of tools and options. The doctor tried the forceps again, and then told Sandy to press as hard as she could on Hiroko's stomach, just above the baby. They were going to try to force the baby out. Hiroko screamed as she thought she felt her ribs breaking, and the baby moved forward a tiny bit, as the three nurses working with her gave a cheer, including Reiko, but Hiroko didn't acknowledge them or smile. She was in too much pain and growing weaker by the moment.

"More!" the doctor said, trying the forceps again, as Sandy pushed harder and this time the other nurse added pressure as well. Hiroko screamed again and looked pitifully at Reiko. But her cousin could do nothing for her.

"No . . . no . . . I can't. . . . No! . . ." Hiroko said breathlessly, fighting them, and then suddenly all she could think of was Peter, and the promises they'd made each other. Suddenly, she knew that if she did not do this for him, she would die, and so would their baby. The agonies she'd been through that night were for him, and she could not give up or stop until she had done what she was there to do, bring his child into the world, and be there for him when he returned. No matter what happened now, she could not fail him. Remembering that gave her a strength she never knew she had. She fought valiantly to help push her child into the world, but still the baby refused to move. It seemed hopeless to her, and to everyone who watched her. And after another hour, both their heartbeats were weakening slowly. The doctor knew he had no choice. No matter what the risk, he had to do it. She was bleeding a lot too, and two women had hemorrhaged to death in childbirth the week before. He wanted to do what he could to control the damage while he still had the option, and to save, if not Hiroko, at least the baby's life.

"Take her to the operating room," he said to Sandy in a tone of somber resignation. "She can't do this anymore." But Hiroko heard him and clutched his hand, looking ghostly pale and very frightened.

"No!" She knew that was how Yuji had been born, and how they had both almost died. Her father had told her the story, to prove to her how dangerous the old ways were, but here they had no choice. There were only the old ways, or death if those methods failed. Feeling demons behind her, she battled the forces of nature with fresh fervor, knowing that what she might lose was her own or her baby's life. She fought with all the terror of what she knew might happen if she didn't succeed in pushing the baby out. The doctor tried the forceps one more time and dared even more than he should have. But he had felt Hiroko's struggle for life. And both nurses pressed on her again, as Hiroko fought with everything she had, and for yet another moment it seemed hopeless. And then it came, moving slowly at first, and then hurtling forward with another pain and then another, and suddenly there was a terrifying scream, and a long thin howl, and then a little shout of fury. He had a bright red face, and soft brown hair, and dark blue almond-shaped eyes, and except for a hint of something faintly

Japanese, he looked exactly like his father, as Hiroko lay staring at him, totally spent and unable to believe she had done it.

"Oh . . ." Hiroko said, almost too weak to speak as she looked at him in wonder. He was so beautiful, so perfect, and very large, just as the doctor had said. They weighed him on a little scale they had.

"Exactly ten pounds," the doctor said, staring at the baby who had defied him for hours, and then smiling at his mother who had refused to give up. "Hiroko, you're a hero. That is just amazing." If anyone would have asked him, he would have sworn he was going to have to do a cesarean section, but he was glad now he hadn't. In the condition Hiroko had been in by then, he was almost sure they both would have died. But by some miracle, he had saved them. And Hiroko had astounded him, by refusing to give up and persevering.

The sun was coming up by then, and the nurses cleaned Hiroko up as she lay peacefully and held her baby. Everyone was touched by what they had seen that night.

"I'm sorry it was so rough," Reiko said softly to her. She had been very brave, and incredibly strong, and given the size of him, none of them could believe she had made it. But Hiroko was an extraordinary young woman.

The new mother whispered proudly to her cousin then, looking happily at her baby. "He looks just like Peter, doesn't he?" As she looked at him, it was all worth it. For a time, it had been like an express train driving through her soul, dragging her down and then up again, and just when she thought she would die, he had been born. She only wished now that Peter could see him, and Reiko realized that it was the first time Hiroko had acknowledged who his father was.

"You have to tell him," Reiko said firmly, but Hiroko shook her head.

"It will only worry him. I will tell him when he returns." She had long since made up her mind. What if he did not wish to come back to her? She would never force him. This way, he was free as the wind, and if he decided to return to her, he would, and he would find them waiting for him, as she had been since the moment he left. She looked at Reiko then, and decided to share some of the secret with her. They had been through so much that night, and Reiko and the others had been so kind. "We were married by a Buddhist priest at Tanforan. I was afraid someone would know and they would punish Peter for it, but they didn't." She picked up her hand and showed Reiko the narrow ring, and Reiko couldn't believe she'd never seen it.

"You're awfully good at keeping secrets . . . and having babies." She kissed her and told her to get some sleep, and when Hiroko and the baby were both sound asleep, she went home to Takeo and told him about the baby. He was just getting ready to leave for the high school. Reiko was shocked to realize it was nine o'clock. The night had flown by like moments.

"I wondered if that was what happened when neither of you came home last night, but I figured you'd send a message if there was anything I could do. Is she all right?"

"She's fine now, but she had all of us scared for a

while, even the doctor," Reiko said, still with a look of wonder. "The baby weighed ten pounds. And he's just beautiful, Tak." And then she smiled sadly, thinking about Hiroko and Peter, and what a long road they had ahead of them, and a hard one. "He looks just like Peter." But that in itself would present problems for Hiroko and the child.

"I thought so." It couldn't have been anyone else, they both knew that. And he was glad for them. They had a bond to hold them together. And knowing Peter as he did, he knew it would mean a lot to him too. "She should tell him. I hope she will," Tak said gently.

"She doesn't want to. She says he'll worry too much," Reiko said, sitting down with an exhausted sigh.

"He ought to know he has a son." He smiled at his wife, remembering what it had meant to them when Ken was born, and the girls too. He was sad for Hiroko that Peter couldn't be there with her. But glad that the child had been born. Perhaps it was an omen of new life to come, of something hopeful.

"She says they were married by a Buddhist priest at Tanforan," Reiko said, taking her shoes off. It had been a very long night. "Apparently, she's been wearing a wedding band since May, and I never even saw it. She wears it with another ring, and somehow I missed it."

"You don't miss much else." He kissed her, and knew he had to leave for school. "I'll go see her this afternoon." He started out the door, and then stopped, looking at his wife with a warm smile. It was a happy moment for them too. A baby was a blessing for them

all, particularly here at Tule Lake. "Congratulations."
He beamed at her.

"I love you," she said, and he hurried out, looking
happier than he had in a long time, as his wife watched
him with a smile, thinking of Hiroko's baby.

# Chapter 15

*H*IROKO STAYED at the infirmary for a week, and then she and the baby came home to the adoring family waiting for them. She called the baby Toyo, and even Ken spent hours playing with him, holding him, and drew the line only at diapers. But Tak was the champion of them all. He was happy to take care of him whenever Hiroko needed a break, or wanted to sleep. He loved doing it, and the baby was completely at ease with him. He never cried. He just slept happily in his arms, until he decided he was hungry, and needed his mother.

Two weeks after he was born, feeling guilty lying around, Hiroko went back to the infirmary, and she took Toyo with her, strapped to her back. One of the older women in the camp had made her the kind of bands her mother had worn, called an *obuhimo*, to hold the baby on her back, and he seemed very content sleeping on his mother as she moved around. She hadn't regained all her strength, and she went back to rolling bandages again. She took it easy at first, and kept away from the more acutely sick people, since she kept the baby with her all the time. But everyone who saw Toyo loved him. He was big and fat and good-natured, and looked just like a little Buddha, except that anyone who looked at him knew that he was not pure-blooded Japanese. More than ever, after he was born, he looked just like Peter. And true to her word, Hiroko wrote to him, but said nothing about their baby.

The army had sent recruiters into the camps by then, many were signing up, but the No-No Boys still held firm for the most part. They even went so far as to threaten the boys who enlisted.

But Ken startled them all with his news three weeks to the day after Hiroko had had the baby. He had gone to the administration building that afternoon. He had turned eighteen two days before, and without even discussing it with his parents beforehand, he had signed up for the army.

"You *what*?" His mother stared at him, unable to believe what he'd just told them. "I thought you had no interest in defending this country," she said, wishing he had kept it that way. She loved her country, but she didn't want to sacrifice her son. They had sacrificed enough already.

"I volunteered for the army," he said again as his parents looked at him in dismay. Despite all of his earlier protests and sense of betrayal, his conflicts seemed to have been put to rest. And suddenly he looked so proud of himself. He was getting out of camp, which was what he wanted.

"Why didn't you discuss it with us first?" Tak asked, looking hurt. He had been so vocal with them about his anger and his sense of betrayal, and now suddenly he had joined the army. But it was one of their few ways out of camp, and the only one palatable to Ken. He just couldn't stay in the camp any longer. Three of them had gone together that afternoon, and the other two boys were, at that exact moment, having the same conversation with their parents. It wasn't that Tak wasn't proud of him, or even patriotic. It was just that it was such a surprise. Nothing he had said had warned them that he was thinking of enlisting. Most of the parents were unprepared, though proud.

Many of the boys left that month. Once the boys signed up, they left within the week, and his last night with them was painful and poignant. They shared a lot of memories and tried not to cry.

They saw him off at the bus the next day, and Tak cried openly. He couldn't believe Ken was leaving them, but in a way he was relieved to know that at least one of them was going to be free now.

"Take care of yourself," he said in a strangled voice. "Don't forget how much Mom and I love you." They were Americans, offering up their son for their country, and yet here they were, behind barbed wire, essentially imprisoned.

"I love you," Ken shouted from the steps of the bus, and then looked embarrassed, as they all stood there. Sally and Tami were crying when he left, and Hiroko fought to hide her tears as she held her baby. She had said good-bye to so many people by then. All of them had. Some of them would be back one day, but others wouldn't. As the bus pulled away, and they watched him leave, Hiroko prayed for his safety, while crying for Ken and his parents. And when they walked back to their tiny home, Takeo cried again as he hung a star in the window for all to see. Some windows had several stars in them. But they all stood there after he'd hung it, and thought of Kenji. It was a painful time. A time of hope, and pride, and terror.

They had a letter from Ken shortly afterwards. He was in Camp Shelby, Mississippi, and he told them he would be joining the 442nd Regimental Combat Team. They were an all-nisei battalion, and most of them were from Hawaii. Interestingly, although they were closer to Japan, there were no relocation camps in Hawaii. And in his letters Ken sounded happy and excited. There had been a big ceremony for them in Honolulu before they left, on the grounds of the Iolani Palace. From everything he said in his letters, which they read over and over, he was thrilled to be out of camp. He was also excited to be doing his patriotic duty. In spite of his initial resistance, he had settled down, and he sent his parents a photograph of himself in his uniform looking very handsome. Reiko put it carefully on a little table Tak had made, and showed the photo to all their friends. It looked like a shrine, and seeing it that way sometimes made Hiroko nervous. She wished that he were there with them, and not just someone they talked about. But she understood his fervor about going to war and serving his country.

She also heard from Peter more frequently. He was still in North Africa, and unfortunately, so were the Germans. And from what she could make out, despite the censor's efforts to keep the news from them, it sounded as though the fighting was ferocious. But at least in June she knew he was still safe, and Ken was fine too.

In July, a serious bout of meningitis hit the camp. Several old people died quickly, and a number of small children were swiftly felled and in critical condition. It was terrible, and mothers sat night and day with them in quarantine, but many of them died. And there were ghastly funerals with tiny little coffins put into narrow graves in the dusty ground. It was more than Hiroko could bear, particularly now with Toyo to worry about, and still a baby. He was only four months old. But it was not Toyo who got it late one hot summer night. It was Tami. She seemed hot when she went to bed that night, but later, Hiroko heard her crying softly when she got up to feed Toyo. She was still nursing him, and he was hungry frequently. Often she got up two or three times a night.

But poor Tami had a frightful fever. Her neck was stiff, and she was almost delirious the next morning when Tak carried her to the infirmary and left her there with Reiko.

The battle raged on for days, and Tami seemed unaware of where she was most of the time. Hiroko left Toyo with Tak and took turns with Reiko sitting with her, and sometimes Takeo came and spent the night with her instead, just putting damp cloths on her head, and talking to her, and singing the little songs she had loved as a baby. If anything, Tak looked worse than he ever had. He had a special bond with her, and Reiko knew it would kill him if they lost her.

"Don't let her die, please. . . . Hiroko, please don't let her die," he said one night as he sobbed, and Hiroko gently put her arms around him.

"She's in God's hands, Tak. He is taking good care of her. You must trust him." But when she said it, he turned on her and surprised her with the vehemence of his anger.

"Like he's taken care of us, and put us here?" he said, and then regretted the words almost as soon as he'd said them. She looked so startled by the force of his fury. "I'm sorry. . . ." he said hoarsely. "I'm sorry. . . ." They all were. And despite their efforts to make the best of it, they all knew that life in camp was grueling.

Things went from bad to worse for a while, and Hiroko sat with Tami every night hoping to relieve her parents. She went home only to feed Toyo, and then she would come back again to relieve Tak or Reiko, and send them home to rest. Both of them looked awful, and the outlook for Tami stayed grim. Hiroko worked tirelessly over the child, bathing her, watching her, forcing fluids into her, and a young paramedic she'd seen before helped her by doing whatever he could to assist her. His name was Tadashi, and he had come to the camp with his family when Tanforan closed. He had a bad limp, and wore a brace, and she knew from something he had said to her that he'd had polio. But she had been struck early on by how gentle he was, and how tireless with the patients. He had graduated from Berkeley the year before, and he had signed the loyalty oath immediately. But because of his limp, the army had refused to take him. He was one of the few young men left, except for the No-No Boys, who had refused to sign the loyalty oath, and the troublemakers, who had taken to marching every morning in military style, in their sweatshirts with their emblem, and their "bozu" haircuts, as symbols of defiance. By then the others, all who were able to, had joined the army. But Tadashi had stayed, and was working as a medic. He was a talented musician too. Hiroko had played with him in the camp symphony, and he had always been very friendly. She had worked with him a few times, and she liked him. He was bright and conscientious and easy to work with, and in a funny way, he reminded her of Yuji.

But he was particularly kind to them while Tami was sick, and did everything he could to help them. He had a tall, lanky look to him, a warm smile, and Hiroko had heard from someone else that in Japan his family was very distinguished. He was *kibei*, he'd been born in the States, but had gone to Japan to study before he went to Berkeley.

"How is Tami?" he asked late one night. It was the eighth night of her illness. Other children had either died or recovered in less time than that, and she'd been delirious again earlier when Tak left in tears with Reiko.

"I don't know," Hiroko said with a sigh, not wanting to admit that little by little they were losing her. He sat down next to Hiroko quietly, and handed her a cup of tea. She looked exhausted.

"Thank you," she said, and smiled at him. He was nice-looking, but he seemed young to her, even though he was four years older than she was. Having Toyo had somehow matured her, and there were times when she felt very old now.

"How's your little boy?"

"He's fine, thank God," she said, smiling, thinking of Toyo, but she was terrified of what was going to happen to Tami.

Even Sally had come to the hospital a number of times, although she and Hiroko had had more than their share of differences lately. It seemed as though they just couldn't get along, ever since the baby. Sally was spending most of her time with the No-No Boys, and Hiroko had scolded her over it repeatedly, and told her how much it upset her parents. And Sally's response was always that Hiroko wasn't her mother and it was none of her business. She was sixteen, and a real handful for Reiko. Coming to camp had not been good for her, her schooling had suffered, and she'd been thrown in with some kids whom she would have been better off not knowing. She wasn't interested in hanging out with the girls, who joined friendship clubs, or bands, or glee clubs. And she didn't want to hear about that from Hiroko either. When Hiroko had tried to tell her she was too young to go out with boys, Sally had said in no uncertain terms that at least she hadn't been dumb enough to have an illegitimate baby. Ever since that encounter, the month before, Hiroko and Sally had hardly spoken. But Hiroko was sorry for her anyway, she knew she was deeply unhappy and afraid about their future. She was also not unaware that her father hadn't been looking well, and that scared her too. And now with Tami so sick, Sally looked panicked. Everything she'd ever counted on seemed to be disappearing. Even her brother had gotten out of camp by going to the army. For Sally, there seemed to be no one left to talk to or rely on, except for a handful of friends she should never have had, including one of the younger No-No Boys, who came to the hospital with her once to visit Tami.

"Your cousin Sally looks like quite a handful," Tad said conversationally after she left. Hiroko smiled at him over her cup of tea.

"My aunt says it's a bad age. It must be," she said charitably. And then she smiled, keeping an eye on Tami's still form. She hadn't even stirred in an hour. "I think I'm lucky I have a little boy," she said. But he couldn't help wondering how lucky she really was. Everyone in camp knew she wasn't married, and having a baby here and no husband to take care of her afterward seemed anything but lucky. But he would never have dared ask her anything about the baby's father, and what had happened. He could see from the few times he'd seen the child that the father was Caucasian. But she had had no visitors, and she seemed to have no plans for marriage.

But as they sat quietly together, talking about their families in Japan, Tami stirred and began to cry. Eventually she got so bad they decided to send for Tak and Reiko. And since he was still there, Tadashi volunteered to get them.

They came running to the infirmary, and sat for hours, watching Tami slip away from them, but by morning she fell into a deep sleep, and the fever broke unexpectedly. It was a miracle. There was no explanation. She had been sick for longer than anyone in the camp, but she had survived. Her father just sat at her bedside and sobbed as he looked at her and kissed her hand, grateful that she had been spared, and that tragedy hadn't struck them. He was so undone that Hiroko took him home, and left Reiko with Tami. But as soon as she got home, and helped put Tak to bed, she could see, from looking at him, that something was wrong with her baby. She had left him with Sally. But he felt hot to her touch, and he was crying and restless. And when she tried to nurse him, instead of guzzling her milk as he always did, he refused to take it, and whenever she moved him, he cried out, as though something hurt him.

"How long has he been like that?" she asked Sally, looking worried, but the teenager only shrugged and said she thought he was fine the night before. "Are you sure?" she asked, and Sally admitted that she wasn't. She said she thought he was asleep, and hadn't really checked him. And Hiroko forced herself not to snap at her cousin. Instead, she scooped him up, and went back to the infirmary with him, to see the doctor. Toyo was only four months old, and probably too little to survive if he got meningitis.

But as soon as the doctor saw him, she felt her heart stop as she heard his words. Toyo had contracted the much-dreaded meningitis. They put him in isolation, just as they had Tami, and Hiroko sat with him, never leaving him for an instant. The fever got worse, and he cried piteously. She could tell from touching him that his little neck was stiff, and all his limbs ached. And her breasts were aching and hard as rocks, while he refused to nurse, and she sat and cried, holding him, praying he would survive, and wondering for the thousandth time if she should have told Peter about their baby. What if he died and Peter never knew him, or about him? Even the thought of it was beyond bearing.

Reiko came and sat with her night after night. Tami was much better by then, eating, and talking and playing. They said she would go home in a few days, but poor Toyo only got worse as Hiroko cried and held him. She never left him for an instant, and would let no one else touch him. And when she couldn't bear it anymore, she lay on the floor next to his crib and slept on the tatami someone had brought from home and put there.

"You can't go on like this, Hiroko. You have to go home and get some sleep," Reiko insisted to no avail. Sandra, the old nurse who had been there the night he'd been born, had come to see them several times, and tried to get Hiroko to leave too. But no one could convince her to leave her baby.

The doctor came and saw him several times a day, but no one could change the course of destiny, or stop the disease that racked him. All they could do was wait and see what happened.

Tadashi came by to see them several times too. He brought her tea, or water, or sometimes a piece of fruit. And once he brought her a flower, but he could see how distracted she was, and ravaged by grief. She knew she wouldn't live another day if her baby died. And she sat praying for him day after day, and silently talking to Peter.

"How is he?" Tadashi whispered one afternoon as he came in from the main ward to see her. As usual, it was hot and dusty outside, and there had been a lot of complaining in the camp. Tule Lake had just officially been designated a "segregation" center, and six thousand "loyals" were going to be moved out in the next two months and sent to other camps while nine thousand "disloyals," or high-security risks, were being moved in, which meant that the camp would be more crowded than ever. And tighter security measures were going to be set up. Tanks had already been placed beyond the fence, and soldiers brought in as guards. People were not pleased as they watched higher fences going up, with more barbed wire. The delusion of freedom was long gone and getting worse now. But Hiroko knew about none of that as she sat with her baby.

"I think he's worse," Hiroko said miserably, and looked up at Tadashi as she declined an apple. She just couldn't eat, except when she absolutely had to, so she could still feed her baby, who occasionally nursed a little. But the doctors couldn't do anything for him, nor could his mother.

"He'll be all right," Tadashi said to her, with a gentle hand on her shoulder, and then he disappeared again, and that night she sat alone and sobbed, as she was convinced her baby was dying. Hiroko was alone in his isolation cubicle, when Tad came back in and watched her. He was afraid to intrude on her misery, but he didn't want to leave her alone either. He had had a married sister Hiroko's age, and she had died two months before, having a miscarriage, and he missed her. And in some ways, it made him feel closer to Hiroko.

He sat down silently next to her finally, and just sat there watching Toyo with her, and not speaking. He was the sweetest little boy, and as they watched him, his breathing grew more and more labored. He was fighting for each breath, and gasping through blue lips, but they had no air tubes to use, no oxygen, for fear it would explode. There was nothing they could do to help him. Hiroko just picked him up and crooned to him as she cried and tried to hold him upright. And Tadashi gently sponged his little face with cool water. He had lost weight in the last few days, and he didn't even look like the little Buddha he had been.

And then suddenly, as she held him, he stopped breathing completely. He had a look of surprise at first, as though he were choking on something, and a moment later, he went limp in her arms as she gasped and stared at him in total panic. But before she could say a word, Tadashi took him from her, and lay him on the tatami, and began massaging his little heart. He was blue by then, and Tadashi knelt over him, and began giving him artificial respiration. He breathed for him methodically as Hiroko knelt beside them and keened for her baby. And after a moment, there was a little sound, and then a cry, and a gurgle. His color improved a little bit, and they bathed his forehead again as the baby watched them. And then Tad went to get a small tub with cool water, and together they bathed him. And in the morning, at last, his fever had broken. The baby looked better than he had in days, and Hiroko looked ashen. She knew they had almost lost him, and it was Tad who had saved him.

"What can I say to thank you?" she asked him in Japanese, her eyes filled with tears and gratitude. Without him, Toyo would have died, and she knew it. "You saved my baby."

"God saved your baby, Hiroko. I just helped. So did you. That's all we can do here. We are only helpers." But without him, Toyo wouldn't have been here. "You should go and get some sleep now. I'll watch him till you get back." But as usual, she refused to leave her son. And Tad went home to get some rest, and came back for his shift at five o'clock, with Reiko. She had heard what had happened the night before from some of the nurses, and she thanked him, and a little while later, he went back to check on Hiroko. He had a proprietary feeling now about Toyo, and he was pleased to see the baby looking pinker than he had in days, and gurgling at his mother.

"You made a miracle," she said with a tired smile, but her hair was disheveled, and stuck to her forehead. It was warm in the small cubicle, and she kept fanning herself, and he saw that her eyes were very bright as he talked to her, and she seemed very nervous.

"You need to lie down," he said, sounding like a medic. "You're going to get sick yourself if you don't get some rest." And he meant it. It amused and touched her when he sounded firm with her. Although they had worked together before, they had become friends in the course of Tami's illness, and Toyo's. She hadn't even seen the little girl since Toyo had gotten sick. She had never left him.

But when Tad came back later that night, Hiroko looked worse, and she seemed very restless, and he said something to Reiko when he saw her.

"I think she's exhausted. You should make her go home before she collapses."

"Any suggestions? Beat her with a broom handle?" Reiko said with a tired smile. They had a lot of sick kids on their hands, and they had had a case of polio that morning. An epidemic of polio would have devastated the camp, and they had the child in another building. "She won't leave that baby."

"You're her cousin. Tell her she has to," he insisted, looking young and determined, as Reiko shook her head.

"You don't know Hiroko. She's very stubborn."

"I know. So was my sister," he said sadly. They were so much alike in some ways. Hiroko even looked like her at times.

"I'll talk to her," Reiko said, trying to appease him, but when they both went back to Toyo's cubicle, they found Hiroko with her blouse open, looking as though she was blazing with heat, fanning herself, and talking to someone who wasn't there. Reiko realized immediately that Hiroko was speaking to Peter. Hiroko looked at them and started to speak Japanese to them, and thought they were her parents. And she kept talking about Yuji. Reiko took one look at her and hurried to get the doctor. And Tadashi talked to her quietly in Japanese as she stood up and began to walk toward him. She looked incredibly beautiful, but confused, as she talked to him in English and said she was sorry she hadn't told him about the baby. And just as she reached him, he caught her as she slid slowly to the floor. She was unconscious instantly. And as soon as the doctor came, and found Tadashi kneeling next to her, cradling her head, he examined her and said she had meningitis.

But this time the miracle was harder won. Toyo had to be weaned, and he was unhappy about it, but he was still recovering, as his mother grew worse each day, and eventually slipped from unconsciousness into what looked like a coma. They gave her what medications they had, but her fever blazed, and she never regained consciousness. And after a week, the doctor told Reiko it looked hopeless. There was nothing they could do for her. She lingered for another week, as they were more and more convinced she was dying. In fact, whenever the doctor examined her, he was always surprised she was still with them. Tadashi looked grief stricken each time he came by to look at her, and even Sally cried, regretting all the horrible things she'd said to her, and the arguments they'd had. And Tami was so upset, Reiko was afraid she'd have some kind of relapse. She wouldn't even eat once she heard how ill Hiroko was. Only the baby was unaware of what had happened.

And Hiroko looked as though she had disappeared, she'd lost so much weight, as she lay on her cot in the infirmary, and Tad watched her. He had worked double duty for the past two weeks, in the hope of doing something useful for her. He barely knew her, but he didn't want her to die like his sister.

"Please, Hiroko," he whispered, as he sat watching her, sometimes late at night when no one else was there. "Please, for Toyo." He didn't dare say "for me." It would have been too presumptuous. And then, finally, late one night, she stirred, and began to murmur in her sleep again. She was calling for Peter, and then she started to cry and talk about the baby. "It was so hard . . ." she kept saying. "I couldn't do it. . . . I'm sorry. . . . I don't know where he is now." But Tad knew what she was talking about. He understood, and he gently took her warm hand in his own and held it.

"The baby's all right, Hiroko. He's fine. He needs you. We all do." He had fallen in love with a woman he barely knew, at first only because she looked like his sister. They were all so lonely, and so confused and so tired. And he was tired of the warring factions. He hated not having been able to join the army. And he was sick of the No-No Boys complaining and making trouble, and of the others complaining about them. And most of all he was tired of living behind barbed wire in a country he loved. And she didn't deserve to be there either. None of them did. But they were here anyway. And she had given him a ray of hope. She had seemed so pure and so alive and so giving, until she fell ill, and he almost lost her. "Hiroko," he whispered her name, but she didn't speak again that night, and when he came back in the morning, she was worse. It was endless. And he knew the doctors were right. She was dying.

Reiko and Tak were with her that night when he came back to the infirmary to work, and they had a Buddhist priest with them. He was talking to them and shaking his head and telling them he was sorry. And as Tadashi saw him, he thought she had died and his eyes filled with tears, but Sandra saw him.

"Not yet," she said softly.

The others left after a little while, and he went back to her partitioned cubicle to see her. He wanted to say his own good-byes to her, although he scarcely knew her. At least he had saved her baby for her. It was something. But now he wished he could have saved her, but knew he couldn't.

"I'm sorry this is happening to you," he said sadly, as he watched her. He was kneeling next to her bed, and her eyes were like deep holes in her face, but she made no sound and no movement. "I wish you'd stay . . . we need a little sunshine here." He smiled. They needed a lot of things, and she was one of them. And then he sat there for a while, already missing her, and a long while later, she gently opened her eyes and looked at him, not recognizing him, and asked for Peter. "He's not here, Hiroko. . . ." And as she closed her eyes again, he wanted to stop her. What if this was the last time? What if she left now? "Hiroko," he said in an arresting voice. "Don't go. . . . Come back here." She opened her eyes again and looked at him.

"Where's Peter?" Her voice sounded stronger.

"I don't know. But we're here. We want you to stay."

She nodded and closed her eyes again, but then she looked at him again, confused, as though she suddenly remembered who he was, and he was interrupting her from something important. "Where's Toyo?" she asked softly after a while.

"He's here. Do you want to see him?" She nodded, and Tadashi raced to get the baby. One of the nurses questioned him, and he told her what he was doing. It sounded crazy to her, but it couldn't do any harm, since they both had meningitis.

Hiroko was sleeping again when he got back to her, but he shook her gently. And Toyo was making little cooing sounds as he held him. She opened her eyes, looking confused again, and he gently set the baby down next to her, so his face was right next to his mother's. And he recognized her instantly, and made happy little sounds, as Tad kept him from falling. And then, sensing him next to her, she opened her eyes, and saw her baby.

"Toyo," she said, as her eyes filled with tears, and then she looked up at Tadashi.

"Is he okay?" she whispered, worried about him again, but Tadashi nodded.

"He's fine, now you need to get better. We all need you."

She smiled then, as though he had said something very foolish, and held Toyo's fingers with her own, and then she rolled over a little bit and kissed him. "I love you," she said to the baby, and Tadashi wished it had been for him. But all he wanted from her was that she not die. It wasn't too much to ask of her, but it was a lot to ask of God at the moment.

He let the baby stay with her for a while, and when one of the nurses came to get him, Hiroko was awake, and she was talking softly to Tadashi. He sat with her all night, and in the morning, she was still very ill, but her fever had broken. It had been a long, long night, and they had talked of many things, her parents, her brother, Japan, her cousins, California, St. Andrew's, but never Peter. But when he finally left her, he sensed, as the nurses did, that she wouldn't leave them.

"You're going to get a reputation around here as some kind of faith healer if you're not careful, Tadashi Watanabe," Sandra teased him as he finally left the infirmary. And Reiko made a point of finding him later that day to thank him.

They had had three miracles in their family. All three of them had survived the dread disease that had killed so many in the camp. But a week later, when Hiroko was sitting up in the hospital, with her baby on her lap, she knew that one more miracle to ask would have been too many. Takeo came to see her, after talking about it all the night before with Reiko. It had happened two months earlier anyway, what difference did it make if it waited some more? But somehow it hadn't seemed right to keep it from her any longer. And the circumstances by which he'd heard the news were so unusual, that somehow he felt they were meant to know it.

He had gotten a letter from a Spanish diplomat he had taught with several years earlier at Stanford, when the Spaniard was on sabbatical from the University of Madrid. But the man also knew Hiroko's father, and had met him in Kyoto. And Masao had somehow gotten the news to him that Yuji had been killed in May in New Guinea, and he felt that Hiroko and his cousins should know it, if Don Alfonso could reach them.

She was shocked when she heard the news, and one of the nurses took the baby from her as she cried in her cousin's arms. Yuji had always been so dear to her. When he was little, he had been her baby. It was like losing Toyo. But at least, Tak reminded her as she grieved, she still had her son.

But she was inconsolable as she lay in her bed that night, and when Tadashi saw her, it reminded him of how he had felt when he lost his sister. It was all so senseless.

"I can't imagine not finding him when I go home again," Hiroko said, and started to cry again, as Toyo slept beside her.

"I feel that way about Mary." His sister had a Japanese name too, but he had never used it. "Her husband enlisted right afterward. I think he was crazy with grief over losing her and the baby. They had just gotten married before the evacuation." So much had happened to all of them. And Peter and Ken were still out there, fighting for their country. It was hard enough surviving here, with all the problems, and the disease and the hardships, let alone with an enemy to fight. Thinking about it made her even more frightened. "The hard thing here," he voiced what they all felt, "is that we don't have a lot of choices." But as he said it, Hiroko realized one that she hadn't thought of.

With her brother gone, her parents would have no one to take care of them. They had lost their son, and now she owed them something as their daughter. For the first time since the option had been offered to her, she thought seriously about going back to Japan to help them. And she said as much to Tadashi as they sat there. But he looked shocked. He would never have gone back in the midst of the war. But it was not his country.

"But it is mine," Hiroko said, thinking about it. "I owe them a lot. I can't just leave them there alone," she said, thinking of what painful choices they all had.

"What about your cousins?"

"I can't help them here. I can't really help anyone."

"I'm not sure getting killed in a bombing raid in Japan would really help your parents, or your baby," he said strongly, hoping to dissuade her.

"I'll have to think about it," she said, and he went back to work, praying that she wouldn't do it. There were so many things to pray for, so many things they all hoped would never happen. It was hard to remember anymore what life had been like when it wasn't filled with grief and betrayal, and terror.

# Chapter 16

THINGS WERE hard for all of them in camp after that. All summer, the Young Men's Organization to Serve the Mother Country, the No-No Boys who had refused to sign the loyalty oath in February, made trouble. They intimidated all those who had signed the oath and were still in camp, particularly the young men who were just reaching draft age. The No-No's turned up in the dark of night, making threats, and hanging around corners calling people names and generally terrorizing anyone who cared to listen. The term *inu*, or dog, was bandied about by them everywhere, labeling all those who had signed the oath as dogs who didn't deserve to live long enough to join the army. They organized work strikes and stoppages whenever possible, and incited many of the unhappy young people to riot. Those who felt they had been betrayed, and badly used by the land of their birth, and were being offered as cannon fodder now, were easy prey to the No-No Boys, as they cruised the camp looking for trouble.

They beat up those they felt were too cooperative with the administrators of the camp, and held noisy parades designed to impress everyone with how tough they were, and only served to increase the camp's tension. They particularly infuriated the loyals, because the behavior of the No-No Boys only helped to prove to the public that they all belonged in camps, and the newspapers seized on every occasion of disturbance in the camps to make all the internees look bad. And, as a result of the trouble they caused, the anger between the loyals and the No-No Boys constantly mounted, and it reached a fever pitch in September when nine thousand dissidents and "disloyals" from other camps were sent to Tule Lake. Because of the vast number shipped in, six thousand peaceful people had to move out to make room for them, and suddenly families who had survived Tanforan and then Tule Lake were asked to move again, and it caused untold grief as people were forced to leave friends, or even brothers and sisters. Some actually refused to leave, causing yet more problems in the camp, mainly due to their attitudes and overcrowding.

The Tanakas were afraid that they would be asked to leave too, because none of them were high security, and Takeo and Reiko didn't know if their family could survive another upheaval. They were used to it here, they had made friends, they both had decent jobs in the school and the infirmary. They didn't want to be shipped out to yet another camp even if conditions might have been a little more pleasant than they were at Tule Lake with so many dissidents and troublemakers around them. And in the end, by sheer luck, they weren't sent anywhere. But countless others were, and their life was one of constant good-byes and sorrow.

And once the new "disloyals" arrived, the camp's name was changed to Tule Lake Segregation Center. For purposes of containment and control, the government wanted all the high security risks in one place. The other internees in the camp had known it was coming, but it was even worse than they imagined. Now the camp had three thousand more people than it had been built for. There were well over eighty thousand in residence, and conditions grew noticeably worse. Everything was crowded and the lines for everything were longer than ever. There was never enough food or medicine. And inevitably, it meant more tension.

It was hard for Hiroko to believe they'd been there a year by then. It was an anniversary no one wanted to celebrate, and there was still no end in sight, although the war news kept right on coming. Mussolini was deposed in July, and Italy unconditionally surrendered after Labor Day, but the Germans were still there, as was Peter. He was now fighting in Italy, where the Allies were moving slowly north up the boot of Italy, trying to drive the Germans back to their homeland. There was still fighting in the villages and small towns, it was clearly rough going.

And in August, Admiral Yamamoto's plane was shot down by the Americans. He had masterminded Pearl Harbor, and it was a huge loss for the Japanese. They had printed it in the camp newspaper, and everyone had cheered when they read it. But even that didn't convince the camp authorities that they were real Americans and not Japanese sympathizers. The interned Japanese had few allies. So far, the only high-level officials who had officially told the President that they thought the internment camps were scandalous were Secretary of the Interior Harold Ickes and Attorney General Francis Biddle. But in spite of that, no one had made a single official move to free them.

The problems at Tule Lake only worsened as time went on: tempers were short, conditions were poor, and the disloyals did everything they could to agitate and exacerbate the problems.

And in October, the strikes began in earnest. The No-No Boys did all they could to convince everyone not to go to their jobs, or do anything to cooperate with the administration. Many of the older internees didn't want to get involved, but eventually it became too dangerous to defy the No-No Boys, and within weeks, the camp was crippled.

In November, the army finally took control of the entire camp at Tule Lake, and brought troops in to subdue them, and force them to go back to work. By then, five thousand people had demonstrated, and there were constant work strikes. A few of the administrators refused to allow their areas to come to a complete standstill, among them the Caucasian head of the infirmary. He refused to let his staff join the angry demonstrators. He needed them too badly, to care for the camp's sick and dying. But when the demonstrators became aware of his resistance, they stormed the infirmary and beat him until they almost killed him. His staff and co-workers, all of them Japanese, did all they could to protect him, and several of them were injured too in the process. It was an infamous incident, and martial law was finally declared in the camp on November thirteenth. There were no activities, no clubs, no dances, no kids hanging around anywhere. There was silence.

There was a curfew, and there were soldiers everywhere, enforcing the rules, and arresting anyone who didn't comply, or even looked ominous or unruly. There was a general work strike, and many of the old people were afraid to go out. The disloyals, as they were still officially called, were far too numerous in the camp, and had certainly made more than their fair share of trouble. And the rest of the camp was furious at them. The loyals had signed their oaths, they had sent off their sons to the army and the navy and the air force. There were stars in almost every window, and many had already died in the service of their country. And these other young people who were so angry at being there, that they now refused to acknowledge loyalty to anyone, were making everyone's lives a living hell. And the loyals felt they had no right to.

Their spirits reached an all-time low on Thanksgiving, when there was nothing to eat in the camp except baloney. And finally, the tides began to turn, as the loyals began to lose their tempers and physically threaten the No-No Boys. They'd had enough. The intimidation and the outrage and the violence had all gone too far, and for a time, the entire camp seemed to tremble on the brink of revolution.

But gradually, in December, things settled down and everyone's mood began to lighten. There were still a vast number of casualties in the infirmary, from fights and demonstrations. Tadashi and Hiroko and their co-workers were still shaken by the events of the night the infirmary had been stormed and the head of the hospital beaten by the No-No Boys. Tadashi had saved Hiroko and two other nurses from injury that night by shoving them into a closet and blocking the door. It was hours before he'd let them come out, and they had teased Tad about it afterward, but he wasn't going to let them get hurt. He'd have killed someone first, especially for Hiroko.

In fact, he had come toe-to-toe with one of Sally's friends that night, a boy named Jiro, whom her entire family disapproved of.

He was eighteen years old and a bright, good-looking boy from a respectable family, but since coming to the camps he had developed all the earmarks of a tough, unfeeling street kid. He had refused to sign the loyalty oath, although he was American born, and he was one of the most vocal of the young No-No's. He liked to march his battalion of No-No's in parade past Sally's house, and show off how tough they were, much to Takeo's horror and outrage. He had long since forbidden Sally to have anything to do with him, although the Tanakas knew and liked his parents. They had admitted that they could do nothing to control Jiro. But he and Sally had met through friends, and now and then they would sit and talk, and she was always impressed by how intelligent Jiro was, and how much sense he made when he wasn't marching, or shouting insults at one of the loyals, or fighting. He was a bright, witty boy but he behaved and looked like a juvenile delinquent.

"He's smart, Mom, and maybe he's right," she had

said once to Reiko defiantly, and it had won her a rare slap from her mother.

"Don't you ever let me hear you say that again!" Reiko had warned, trembling with fury. "Your brother is fighting for you, and for him. We're *Americans*! That boy, and the others like him, are all traitors." There had been no ambiguity in what Reiko said to her, but Sally still saw him on the sly sometimes. She wasn't in love with him, but she liked him, and in some ways it excited her to defy her parents.

He had taken part in the attack on the infirmary that night. Tadashi had seen him there, and he had approached Tad once and angrily called him an *inu*, and then as though in deference to the relationship he knew the Tanakas had with Tad, he ran away, and had been satisfied to overturn carts of instruments and bedpans. Hiroko saw him leave the building later on, and she had been incensed at his attitude and the destruction she saw him leave in his wake, but Sally had refused to listen to what Hiroko said when she told her younger cousin about it.

"He doesn't do things like that, he's too intelligent," Sally said, defending him, which only angered Hiroko further. Sally seemed to be growing more defiant by the hour, and her friends were more often than not the wrong kind now. It was something that worried all of them about her, particularly Reiko. She didn't know what to do with her—the camps were no place for a young girl, particularly Tule Lake, with so many young disloyals roaming around looking for trouble. The truly dangerous ones were in segregation of some kind, or even in prison, but there were many others whom the Tanakas did not like, and who hung around with the rest of the young people like Sally. And it was difficult not to be influenced by them, they were so persuasive in their complaints about how they had been ill-used and how America had betrayed them. And lately, Sally seemed far too willing to believe them.

Reiko talked to Tak about it, but there was little they could do. There were so many problems there, of health, of safety, of disappointment, of supply, of fear about the future. The only thing one could do to survive was live in the here and now, and do the best one could. For many of the internees, concentration on their families, and their friends, and even their jobs was a godsend. Working at the infirmary kept Hiroko from thinking of Peter incessantly. Though he was often on her mind, her days and nights were filled with Toyo, and the people she was helping.

She was working double shifts at the infirmary again long before Thanksgiving. And at nine months, Toyo was an adorable little terror and had just started walking.

Tadashi often came to their room to play with him, and bring him little things he made, and he was always polite to all of them, and he had a special gentleness with the children. As a child, he had often been tormented at school because of his leg, particularly in Japan, and it had made him especially compassionate about other people's sorrows. He had a nice sense of humor too, and Hiroko often teased him about how silly they had all looked when he pushed them into the closet to save them.

"I suppose I really should have locked it," he said thoughtfully, tossing Toyo up in the air with ease. In spite of the polio, he was young and strong and healthy, and very good-looking, Reiko always added.

"Never mind," Hiroko said, insisting that they were only friends. She was totally faithful to Peter, and the memory of their Buddhist wedding. But Tak and Reiko thought that Tadashi was a nice young man, and not by any means a negligible prospect. He was *kibei* after all, he had been born in the States, and studied in Japan. He knew her culture, her language, they were of the same race, and they would be equal in the face of any prejudice that came their way later on. Mixed marriages were not only illegal in California, Tak pointed out to her when they were discussing it one day, but they were extremely difficult, and potentially very dangerous for the children.

"Is that really what you think?" She had looked at her cousin sadly. "Is that what you think will happen to Toyo when his father comes back? That our love will be dangerous for him?" She looked shocked by what he was saying.

"Not your love," he said unhappily, "but the attitudes of those around you. Those attitudes have put us here. Look at this. Look at where you are. The people who believe these things, that we are different, that we are disloyal, that we are dangerous, will stop at nothing. And one day they will hurt your son, as they have hurt you. He won't be exempt, it won't end with us. You'll be better off with a man of your own kind, Hiroko, one who accepts you as you are, and even Toyo." She was horrified at what he was saying, not only the sorrow and sense of prejudice that seemed to have defeated him, but the fact that he didn't seem to think she should wait for Peter. Tadashi was there.

Why not marry him? The only problem was that, although they were friends, she didn't love him. She didn't want anyone except Peter.

Tadashi had asked her casually, several times, about what plans she had for "afterward," and what was going to happen to her and Toyo. She knew what he meant, and she was always guarded about what she said. She didn't discuss her plans with anyone, but she let him know nonetheless that as far as she was concerned, she was "taken."

She had talked to him about going back to Japan after Yuji died, to help her parents. But it was almost impossible to get back now, and she knew it was safer for her and Toyo in America. She knew she should stay in the States, and go back after the war was over, and all she could do was hope that her parents would be all right in the meantime.

The anniversary of Pearl Harbor came and went again with a somber mood, but at least no violence or problems. And when Christmas came that year, despite martial law, the authorities tried to encourage a more peaceful atmosphere. The curfew on special nights ended to allow them to have dances, and meetings of the friendship clubs. It was extraordinary how many positive groups there were in camp, all made up of people trying to overcome the grief and the fears and the problems. They were determined to make the best of a bad situation, and much of the time they succeeded.

There was even a Kabuki play Hiroko and Tami went to, and a Bunraku puppet show Tadashi took her to with Toyo. Hiroko and Tad played together in the symphony, and they went caroling, and despite all her efforts, she couldn't get Sally to join them.

"No. What do I care about Christmas?" Sally had spat at her, lying on her bed when Hiroko had asked her to go with her and Tadashi. "And why are you taking him anyway? If he's so crazy about you, why don't you get married?"

"I don't think that's any of your business," Hiroko said coldly. She was tired of her. Sally was rude to everyone. She fought with Tami all the time now, and argued with her mother till it drove them all to distraction. And no matter what Hiroko said, it set her off. The only human being she was ever civil to, and even loving, was Takeo, her father. She still idolized him, and Tak adored her.

"Just leave her," Reiko said, so Hiroko took Tami with her, and they had a lovely time singing "Silent Night" and "The First Noel," and all their favorite songs in the cold, crisp air of the mountains. Although Tule Lake was hot and dusty in the summer, it was freezing in the winter.

And in spite of where they were, and the inescapable restrictions, it was a lovely night, and afterward Tadashi came in to chat with them. Sally was sitting in a chair, sulking for a while. She watched him talking to her parents and Hiroko, and slipped quietly into their bedroom, but no one seemed to notice. He and Hiroko were too busy laughing about the dance the whole group from the infirmary had gone to the other night. The band had played "Don't Fence Me In," and even the soldiers who had monitored the dance didn't seem to get it. They had played a lot of other songs too, like "Harvest Moon," and "String of

Pearls," and "In the Mood," and many of the Glenn Miller arrangements.

Tadashi had only danced with her once, it was hard for him with his leg, but she had danced with her Uncle Tak, and one of the doctors she worked with. There weren't a lot of eligible young men left in camp, at least not nice ones, but she didn't care. She didn't want anyone except Peter, and anyone who knew her was aware that she was interested in being friends, but not dating.

She walked outside with Tad when he left that night, and they sat on the steps in the freezing cold for a minute, just talking about Christmas, and Santa Claus, and the things they had loved when they were kids. Tad had cut down a small Christmas tree for them, and they had made the decorations, but it wasn't quite the same as a "real" one, a big tree, with store-bought decorations.

"One day," Tadashi said with a warm smile, getting ready to leave her. "We'll have it all back again one day," he said, looking as though he believed it.

But in spite of Toyo's fascination with everything as he lurched everywhere, their Christmas was quieter this year. She hadn't seen her family for almost three years, her brother was dead, and now Ken was gone, and she hadn't heard from Peter since late November. Not hearing from him always frightened her, because she didn't know what it meant, if he was on the move, or injured, or worse. She knew that if something happened to him, it would take a long time for the news to reach her. He had put Tak on his list of people to be notified, but still he could have been dead for a month or two, before she knew it.

"Good night," Tadashi said, looking at her, as plumes of frost from their breath hung above their heads. "Merry Christmas," he said. Christmas Eve was the next day, and they would both be working. "See you tomorrow."

And when they met in the infirmary the following night, he handed her a tiny package. It was a small locket that he had carved out of wood for her, with her initials in it, on a gold chain his mother had saved from somewhere.

"Tad, it's beautiful," she said, handing him the scarf she had knitted him, wrapped in a small piece of red paper. He opened it and put it on immediately with a broad grin, and told her that he loved it. It was red and it looked well on him, and he pretended not to notice the mistakes she'd made. "I didn't win any prizes at the knitting club," she apologized and thanked him again for the locket. And then they both hurried away to work, and for the rest of the night they were busy.

He walked her home afterward and wished her a merry Christmas again, and she was pensive as she walked into their room and kissed the sleeping Toyo. Tad was a nice man, and she liked him, but she didn't want to encourage him. It wouldn't have been fair, no matter how good to her he'd been. But she convinced herself he understood that, and forgot about him until morning. Instead, she dreamed about Peter coming home to them, and Ken, and in the far, far distance, she thought she saw Yuji.

"Where did you get *that*?" Sally asked her the next day, and Hiroko glanced down to see what she meant, and remembered the locket Tad had made her.

"Tadashi gave it to me." She smiled pleasantly at Sally. She had knitted her a sweater too, and bought gloves for her from the Sears catalog. They all needed them so badly at Tule Lake. But Sally was suddenly furious again, and she made a comment about some girls going from one man to the other.

"What does that mean?" Hiroko asked her bluntly, hurt by what she'd said, and the obvious implications.

"You know what I mean," she said, looking angry, and sounding surly.

"Perhaps I do," Hiroko admitted to her, "but I do not like it. I do not go from one man to any other man. I have gone nowhere with Tadashi," she said correctly.

"I'll bet," Sally said, and left the room while Hiroko tried to control her temper. Sally was not only unkind, but rude, and she was barely civil to Tadashi when he came by to wish them all a merry Christmas a little while later. He brought them a watercolor his mother had made for them, and it was really lovely. It showed a summer sunset in the mountains.

"Sally is in a lovely mood," Tadashi said to her jokingly, and Hiroko groaned.

"I almost spanked her this morning," she admitted.

"Maybe you should. It would certainly surprise her." Hiroko laughed at the idea, and afterward they went for a long walk, and when they left, Reiko raised an eyebrow.

"Those walks of hers have a familiar ring," she teased Tak. "Should I be worried?" He smiled in answer.

"I think she's old enough to take care of herself, don't you?" And then he added more seriously, "He's a nice boy. I was telling her that the other day, but she didn't want to hear it. He's a much more reasonable choice for her than Peter."

"What makes you say that?" Reiko was surprised, and he told her all the same things he'd told Hiroko.

"You might be right, Tak. But she still loves Peter." Over the past months, she had said it repeatedly to Reiko.

"Maybe she can love Tad too," he said practically. "He's awfully good with Toyo." She was almost twenty-one years old, and she had a child. In some ways, it would be a lot better for her to get married. And there would be no objection to it from any quarter. Reiko had even met his mother and she had mentioned how much she liked Hiroko. But as Sally came through the room, and heard some of what they said, she slammed the door again to their bedroom.

"What's wrong with her?" Takeo asked, looking startled and then worried. He hoped she hadn't seen Jiro again. She always seemed to behave worse after she had seen him. But then he remembered having heard that Jiro had been put in segregation the week before, and Sally claimed he had a girlfriend.

Sally had been in a dreadful mood all week, and she seemed to be having a real vendetta against her cousin. Lately more than ever.

"Her worst problem is that she's sixteen," Reiko said in answer to Tak's question. She was almost seventeen, and growing up at Tule Lake was an unhappy time for her. Despite all their efforts to make life in camp livable, they all had to deal with constant deprivation. And in the young people's case, they missed all the frivolous things all their Caucasian friends still had, and their parents and older siblings had grown up with. She couldn't go to proms, or have pretty dresses or go to football games, or even movies, or even go to an ordinary school. She couldn't go anywhere or have anything. Just like the rest of them, she was in prison. She was cold all the time, wore ugly clothes, lived behind barbed wire, had too little medicine if she got sick, and most of the time, she was hungry.

"We'll have to send her away next summer," Tak said with the first real humor he'd shown in months. He was in a good mood over the holidays, and even took Reiko to a dance one of the bands organized for New Year's Eve, and they both agreed the music was terrific.

Hiroko had chosen to work that night, to give other people a chance to celebrate, since she didn't care and had no one to spend it with. And Tadashi had signed up to work with her.

They were both holding a sick child at midnight, and the poor kid was retching horribly with a bad case of influenza. Tadashi smiled at her over his head and mouthed the words "Happy New Year," and afterward, when the child was asleep again and everything was cleaned up, they laughed about how they had spent New Year's Eve.

"There's one to remember," he said, laughing. "When our children ask how we spent our first New Year's Eve, you can tell them that story." But she didn't look amused by what he had just said, she looked worried. No one else was around, and they sat down over two cups of coffee he'd made for them.

"Don't say that, Tad."

"Why not?" For once he was feeling brave with

her. Most of the time he was afraid to rock the boat. But just this once, he had decided to take his chances. "We all need a little hope in our lives to keep going. You're mine, Hiroko." It was the most honest thing he'd ever said to anyone, and no matter what she said, he didn't regret it.

"I don't want to be that," she said, equally honest with him. "You're a wonderful friend, Tad, but I can't give you more than that. I don't have it to give. It's someone else's."

"You're still that much in love with him?" They both knew about whom they were talking.

"I am," she said quietly, praying he was still alive. It had now been many weeks since his last letter.

"What if things are different when he gets back? What if he's changed, or you have? That happens, particularly at our age." He didn't know how old Peter was, but he assumed that he was somewhere in his twenties.

"I don't think that will happen."

"You're not even twenty-one, Hiroko. A lot must have happened to you before you came here. You came to this country, and five months later we were at war, you had to leave school, your cousins lost everything, and the next thing you know you're here. And now you have a baby. That's a whirlwind. How can you even begin to figure out what you're going to do from here?" And then he said something that really hurt her. "If you'd been that sure of him before, you'd have married him before Toyo happened. Or am I completely wrong?"

"You're not wrong," she said thoughtfully, wondering why she was even trying to explain it to him.

She owed him no explanations, but he had saved her child's life, and hers, and she suspected that he cared for her deeply. And in her own way, as a friend, she loved him. "I thought it was too complicated, and wrong. I wanted to go back to Japan and ask my father's permission first. And then the war came, and it was too late. I couldn't imagine running away out of state to get married. But . . . things happened anyway." She told him something then that he hadn't known before but shocked him deeply. "He doesn't know about Toyo."

"Are you serious? You never told him?" He couldn't imagine a situation where he wouldn't have wanted her to tell him. It was an enormous burden for her to have on only her own shoulders.

"I didn't think it was fair. I didn't want him to feel he had to come back, if he didn't want to."

"So you're not even sure of that?" He was surprised and pleased, things were better than he'd thought in some ways, worse in others.

"The only thing I'm sure of," she said softly, "is how much I love him."

"He's a lucky man," Tadashi said, looking at her, wishing that she was his, and he was Toyo's father. How lucky the guy was and he didn't even know it. "Maybe he doesn't deserve it," he said carefully.

"Yes, he does," she said, sounding absolutely certain.

He reached for her hand then, and looked at her. There was no other time or way to say it. "I love you," he said honestly. "I've been in love with you since the first day I saw you."

"I'm sorry." She shook her head sadly. "I can't

. . . I love you too, but not like that. . . . I can't . . ."

"What if he didn't exist?" He didn't want to say, "didn't come back," but they both knew what he meant, and Hiroko only looked at him, unable to answer.

"I don't know." She had said she loved him, and she did, as a friend, or even a brother.

"I can wait. We have a whole life ahead of us . . . hopefully not here." He smiled, aching to kiss her, but sure that he would have been wrong to try it, and he was right. It would have upset her.

"That's not very fair to you. I have no right to hang on to you, Tad. I'm not free to do that."

"I'm not asking for anything," he said fairly. "I'm satisfied just the way things are. We can play at the symphony together." She laughed, it sounded so ridiculously old-fashioned. They were leading such a crazy life here.

"You're a good sport," she said, using one of her favorite American expressions.

"You're beautiful, and I love you very much," he answered, and she blushed, but he was happy to see she was wearing his locket.

He walked her home that night, and they both seemed comfortable. They had reached an understanding. He was in love with her, and she loved him as a friend, and they were going to wait and see what happened. To have stopped seeing each other entirely when they weren't working would have been awkward for both of them, and would have deprived them both of a friendship they cherished. And then, although he had promised himself he wouldn't, he bent and kissed her lightly on the lips, and he moved away before she could even stop him. She hugged him afterward, and they stood there in the cold, wondering where life would take them. And then she told him she'd see him at work the next day and went inside. For the moment, it was all she had to offer.

But when she got up, one of the soldiers was outside talking to Tak, and she wondered if there was trouble. He looked very serious, and Tak kept nodding at him, and then the soldier left, and Tak didn't come inside, he just stood there. Aunt Rei had been watching him too, and after a minute she went outside and stood in the open doorway.

"What was that all about?" she asked, standing in the frigid air without a coat on, but Tak looked so strange and he was staring at her as though he wasn't quite sure who she was, or what she had asked him. "Tak? Are you all right, sweetheart?" She hurried down the two steps to him, and he stared at her, and nodded.

"Ken was killed in Italy," he said, looking at her vaguely. "They thought he was missing in action at first, but they found his body," he said, as though telling her about a package that had been delivered. "He's dead," he said, looking at her blankly as she stared at him in horror. "Ken. Ken, I mean. Ken's dead." He kept repeating Ken's name as though he didn't understand it, and by then Hiroko was watching them, and knew instinctively that something terrible had happened. She hurried down the steps to help her cousin. Takeo was turning this way and that, repeating himself as people in other houses watched him. His wife

couldn't even let herself cry, she was too frightened
and too worried about her husband.

"Come back inside, Tak, it's cold out here," she
said gently. But he made no move to follow. "Tak . . .
please . . ." There were tears swimming in her eyes,
she had heard what he'd said, but she couldn't react
until she took care of him. He had snapped when they
told him. "Darling, let's go inside." She and Hiroko
each put an arm around him and led him slowly back
up the stairs and into their tiny sitting room, and sat
him in a chair as they looked at each other.

"Ken's dead," he told them again. It was New
Year's Day, 1944, and Sally had just walked into the
room and heard him.

*"What?"* She screamed the word and Tami came
running, holding Toyo. It was a nightmare, but there
was no taking it back now. Sally was suddenly hysterical, and Hiroko went to deal with her while Reiko tried
to handle Takeo. And then suddenly Tami was crying
too, and Toyo, who saw them all crying and didn't
know what it meant, joined them.

Hiroko managed to shepherd all the children back
into the bedroom, and left Reiko talking quietly to
Takeo. Sally cried for an hour in Hiroko's arms, despite
her constant anger at her, and Tami sat on her other
side, holding her tightly. It was terrible news, and
Hiroko knew just how it felt. She had been devastated
when she lost Yuji the previous summer. And now
Ken. The war was taking a terrible toll on them, all
their fine young men, and in some cases their old ones.
There were so many men like Tak, shaken, bitter,
deeply ashamed of what had happened to them, when
in fact the shame was not really theirs, but they didn't

know that. They felt somehow that it was all their fault. And now Tak had snapped, but when Hiroko went back out to see how he was, he had returned to sanity again, and was sobbing in his wife's arms like a child. His firstborn was dead, his son, their baby. And the little table where his photograph in his uniform was kept looked more than ever like a shrine, only now to a dead hero.

Hiroko stayed home with them that day, and took care of the girls, and Reiko and Tak went to the Buddhist temple to see about arranging for a service. There would be no body returned to them. There was nothing they could hold or touch or kiss again. There were only memories, and the knowledge that he had served the country they all loved but had been betrayed by.

Tak looked a thousand years old when they returned from the temple, and Hiroko saw, as Reiko had, that he was having trouble breathing again. No one would have believed that he was fifty-two years old. He looked, and felt, ninety.

The service they had organized was the next day, for Kenji Jirohei Tanaka. He was eighteen years old, and no matter what one believed about the war, it was a terrible waste of youth and promise. Tadashi came to the temple with them, and he sat quietly between Hiroko and Sally. And for once, she wasn't angry at anyone. She was in despair, and afterward she clung to her father, keening for her brother. But he had no strength to share with anyone. He could barely leave the temple without Reiko's help, and seeing the condition he was in, Tadashi helped her. He was deeply sorry for them, and he even helped her put her husband to bed that night. Tak was in a terrible state. And it broke Hiroko's heart to see it.

The only thing that cheered her the next day was, finally, a letter from Peter.

He was alive, and well, and in Arezzo. But she couldn't even share the news with Tak. He was too distraught over Ken to be able to tolerate the news that someone else had survived their battles. Tadashi came back to see them that afternoon, and talked quietly to Hiroko outside. He didn't want to go in and bother anyone, and she admitted that Tak had stayed in bed all day and cried, but Reiko was with him. It was as though the loss of Ken was the last straw, and had broken him completely. He just couldn't take it. But there were other men in the camp who were just like him. They had lost sons, several of them in some cases, and businesses and homes and lives. And somehow they could no longer adjust to what had happened. They felt as though they could no longer face the world. They had been shamed too deeply.

Reiko was deeply upset about Ken too, but she couldn't even allow herself the luxury of time to think about it, and mourn, she was too busy taking care of Takeo. She didn't go to work all week, and everyone understood. Hiroko took some extra shifts for her. And two weeks later, Tak was better, but he still wasn't well. He looked tired and old and breathless, and Hiroko realized suddenly that his hair had been completely white for a while, and she hadn't even noticed.

Martial law in the camp ended completely in mid-January, and a committee of nonextremists were formed to control the No-No's. The committee called themselves the Nippon Patriotic Society, and the strikes ended almost immediately after the committee was established.

It appeared to be a peaceful time again, but not for the Tanakas. Sally was behaving worse than usual, in reaction to seeing her father falling apart, and Tami cried all the time, and Toyo had kept Hiroko up three nights in a row with new teeth he was getting. He was ten and a half months old and into everything. But even he didn't cheer Takeo. Tak no longer seemed to notice him at all. He was completely distracted.

Hiroko left him with Tak one afternoon when she went to work. Usually Sally came home to take care of him, but this time she didn't. And Takeo was at home, since he was still taking time off from teaching school because of Ken, and they were managing without him, though barely. With so many young people in the camp, they needed all their teachers, just as they needed all their doctors and nurses. But he wasn't well, and they'd agreed it would be better for him to spend a month at home to recover. As she left the house, Hiroko thought it might even do Tak good to have to take care of Toyo for a few minutes. It might take his mind off his sorrows. He'd been going to the temple every day, and lighting candles on the table where they kept Ken's picture.

"Sally will be home soon, Tak," she reminded him as she left for work, and hurried down the long, barren road to the infirmary. She saw Sally coming back from school on her way, and told her that her father was waiting for her with Toyo.

"I'll hurry," she said, not giving Hiroko an argument for once. She would do anything for her father.

And when Hiroko got to work she saw Reiko finishing up some papers.

"How is he?" she asked hurriedly, and Hiroko nodded. He wasn't great, but he was a little better. He had agreed to baby-sit for Toyo at least. That was something.

"I left the baby with him. I just saw Sally on her way home. I told her he was waiting."

Sally had gone home immediately, just as she had promised. She had hurried up the steps, and gone inside, and saw her father sitting in the chair, holding Toyo. Toyo was playing with a top he'd given him, which he'd made himself, and the little boy was chewing on it happily, as Tak slept peacefully. He had drifted off just after Hiroko left, and Sally smiled as she picked up the baby. And then she bent to kiss her father gently on the forehead, but as she did, his head fell backward. Although his eyes were closed, she knew instantly. And with Toyo still in her arms, she ran all the way to the infirmary to find her mother.

"It's Daddy," she gasped as soon as she got there, and Hiroko took the baby from her and handed him to Tadashi. "He's sick." But deep in her heart, she knew he wasn't. He wasn't sick at all when she left. He was gone, and she knew it, but she couldn't face it.

Reiko and Hiroko flew back down the road to him, with Sally right behind them, and Tadashi coming along as fast as he could, holding the baby. He put his own coat over him so he wouldn't catch cold, and when he got to the house, Reiko was working on Tak, but it was way too late, and she knew it. His heart had given out, and his spirit long before it. He couldn't hold on anymore. It was too much for him. And peacefully, without a murmur or a sound, or a good-bye, he had left them.

"Oh, Tak," Reiko said, sinking to her knees beside him. "Oh, Tak . . . please . . . don't leave me. . . ." It was so unfair, it would be so lonely without him. And they had just lost Ken. Without them, what did she have to live for? But she knew the answer to that, she had to go on for Tami and Sally. Her fate was not to be the luxury of giving up, or even dying. She had to keep going for them. She was forty years old, and a widow. And she knelt there, with her face in her hands, crying for the husband she had loved so much, and lost forever.

Hiroko put her arms around her and helped her up, as Sally stood sobbing, watching them, knowing she couldn't live without him.

"Daddy," she whispered as she cried, and Tad handed Toyo to his mother and took her gently in his arms. He just held her and let her cry, as Hiroko put a coat on Toyo and went outside to wait for Tami. It was only minutes before she came back from school, and Hiroko closed the door from the outside as soon as she arrived, and took her on a walk and told her as gently as she could about her father.

"Just like that?" She stared up at her cousin wide-eyed. "No one killed him or anything? But he wasn't old," she said, trying to understand it. It wasn't easy for any of them to accept, and she and Hiroko both cried as they walked along and talked about it. And when they got back, the others were waiting for them outside, and Tadashi was standing next to Sally. And as she looked at them, Hiroko understood something that she had never seen before. It explained everything, and she nodded.

Reiko went for a walk with the girls, while Tad and Hiroko went back to the hospital to get two pallbearers and a gurney for Takeo. They didn't want the children to see him carried out, but they had seen it before, with others. It was just too painful, with their own father. An hour later, he had been taken to the morgue, and Tadashi was back again. They all sat in the tiny living room that night, talking about him from time to time, but mostly stunned into silence.

Eventually, Hiroko went back to work with Tad. Reiko's shift was long over by then, and they walked slowly back to the hospital, talking about what had happened. He was so young to have died, but there were others like him who had been disheartened. And in many cases, particularly among the men, it had killed them. Despite their lack of physical strength, the women seemed stronger, and better able to withstand the disappointments.

"Poor Reiko," Tad said, with real emotion for her. His own father had died when he was young, and he knew how hard it had been on his mother. And then Hiroko said something odd under the circumstances, but they were so at ease with each other that she treated him like a brother.

"My cousin is in love with you," she said quietly, and he looked at her in horror.

"Reiko?"

"No, you idiot." She felt disgraceful for laughing, but she couldn't help it, and it relieved the agony of the moment. "Sally. I was watching her this afternoon, standing next to you. And I finally realized she's crazy about you. Maybe that's why she's been so mad at me. She thinks I'm trying to steal you." It certainly explained all the nasty comments about "going from one man to another."

"I think you're wrong," he said, looking embarrassed. He had noticed it too, and he had always liked her. But it had never occurred to him that she had a crush on him, or that he might pursue her. He had been far too involved in his feelings for Hiroko. And what she said now startled him, but it didn't displease him. But Sally was very young, she was only seventeen, and he was seven years older. It didn't seem like a suitable match to him, and he was sure Reiko wouldn't think so either.

"I just thought you should know," Hiroko said and he nodded, and they didn't mention it again, but she had wanted him to know it. She knew more than ever, especially since both Ken and Takeo had died, how precious life was, and how valuable every moment. And she knew too that she wouldn't have stopped loving Peter no matter what happened. It seemed particularly unfair to keep Tadashi hanging on for something that would never come. He was young, he had a right to more than someone else's crumbs, or someone else's wife and baby. It was time he started thinking of someone else. And she thought he would be perfect for Sally.

And that night, after she came home, Hiroko sat for a long time with Reiko, comforting her, letting her cry, listening to the memories and the broken dreams. And after that, she wrote a long letter to Peter. He and Tak had been such good friends that she knew the news would hit him hard, but she knew she had to tell him.

And it was a long time before she heard from Peter again, but when she did, he was devastated by the news of Tak's death. They had had his funeral by then, and laid him to rest in the graveyard that was already too full, with so many futile losses, people who might have been saved with better medicines, anesthetics, better living conditions. And perhaps a little hope might have saved them. Like Tak, who had just given up. He had just sat there and died, instead of surviving. It reminded her of the time Peter had said to her before she left, that she *had* to survive it, and she had promised.

Toyo's first birthday came six weeks later, and one of the nurses had made them a small cake in the infirmary kitchen. They gave it to him that night after work, and he dove into it with glee and made a total mess of himself while the women in his family watched him. Hiroko wished she could have taken photographs of him, but of course, there were no cameras. Tadashi had come to share the cake with him too, and he had made him a beautiful little wooden pull toy of a duck carrying an egg on his back, and Toyo loved it.

Tadashi seemed to have taken Hiroko's advice, and she knew that he had taken Sally out for several walks, and once he had taken her to his art class. But Sally was still in no mood to see anyone romantically. She was deeply upset about her father. But at least Tadashi was someone she could talk to. And ever since her father's death, she had been a lot warmer toward Hiroko.

In some ways, the tragedy of Tak's death had

brought them all closer. And the closeness lasted. If anything, it grew more so, through another long, hot, dusty summer. If the winters were hard, the summers were harder. And beyond the barbed wire that held them captive, the world was changing all around them. The Allies were winning. The British and Americans were dropping a maelstrom of bombs on Germany, with considerable success, the Americans had landed in Anzio, and the Russians had entered Poland, as MacArthur drove his forces through the Pacific Islands. In April, U.S. planes bombed Berlin for the first time and caused enormous damage. And in June, the Allies not only entered Rome, but they set foot on French soil, and headed inland from Normandy. And Peter was with them. He was in France by then, and Hiroko heard from him regularly until August. He had been in a town called Lessay with General Hodges, and they were moving on toward Paris. And the very last letter she had said they had made it, and Paris was the most beautiful city he'd ever seen, even now, and he wished that she could be there with him. But after that, she heard nothing. She had no idea what had happened.

Things in the camp were tense again that fall too. The Nippon Patriotic Society seemed to lose control of the No-No Boys, and extremists came out from underground again. And by October they were in the press constantly, with demonstrations, and reprisals. They were just as angry about their incarceration as they'd been before. Possibly even more so, and they were even more violent this time, and made a great deal of trouble. For those families who were loyal, like the Tanakas, and countless others, the unrest they caused was a constant source of terror and aggravation. The loyals did not want to be caught in the middle between the various factions. People got hurt, outside their homes and in strikes and demonstrations. And now that there were no men in the family to protect them, Reiko was always worried. And more and more lately, she was grateful for the time that Tadashi Watanabe spent with the family, and with Sally. He was a fine young man, and he did everything he could for them. It always made Hiroko smile when she saw them together. Since the summer, he and Sally had been inseparable, and it was the best thing for both of them. They both seemed to be thriving.

"Guess I was right, huh?" Hiroko teased him one day when they were working, and he tried to pretend he didn't know what she was talking about, but she wouldn't let him off the hook that easily. They really were like brother and sister, or at the very least, cousins.

"I don't know what you mean," he said vaguely, trying not to smile at her, but failing.

"Sure you don't, Tadashi-san." She loved to tease him. She sounded completely American now at times, and her English was almost perfect. "I mean Sally."

"I know what you meant. You sure aren't subtle." He looked at her, exasperated but amused. And he had long since understood how total her commitment was to Peter. He was grateful that she had been honest with him, and even more so that she had said something to him about Sally. She was young, and immature at times, but beneath it all was a sweet, gentle girl, who wanted the same kind of strong commitment her parents had shared. And in the months since her father had died she and Tadashi had fallen deeply in love. But it was too soon for them to get married because Sally was only seventeen and a half now. But his influence on her had been excellent. She had stopped hanging out with the No-No Boys, and her disruptive friends, and she had become once again the girl Reiko remembered.

Tadashi agreed to spend Thanksgiving with them that year.

It was going to be very painful for them, having lost both Ken and Tak since the last one. And Hiroko was nervous too. She still hadn't heard from Peter since he was in Paris in August.

"Maybe he ran off with a cute French girl," Tad teased, but realized that Hiroko was beyond humor. She hadn't said much about it, but she was deeply worried. Three months was a long time, and people were still getting killed in Europe. And the war in Japan wasn't over either. MacArthur had gone back to the Philippines in October.

But at least Thanksgiving Day was a day without news, bad or good. They existed as they often did, suspended in the isolated unreality of camp life. And this year at least they had turkey. They all laughed hollowly remembering the baloney dinner of the year before, and the ghastly strikes and demonstrations. But there wasn't much to laugh about. It seemed like it was going to go on forever. Franklin Roosevelt had just been reelected, and apparently had ignored everything Ickes and Biddle had told him. Or so it seemed until December.

Hiroko had been walking down the road from their "house," holding Toyo's hand, when two old men came running past her, shouting in Japanese. "It's over. . . . It's over. . . . We're free."

"The war?" she shouted after them in English.

"No," one of them shouted back. "The camp!" And then they were gone, and she went to find someone else she could ask. People were congregated everywhere, talking, and one of them was even talking to one of the soldiers. The guards were always there, watching them from the towers, and one forgot sometimes, but not for long, that they had guns pointed at them. For Hiroko, it had been one of the hardest things to get used to, but now she never even noticed.

But the soldier, in this case, was explaining that President Roosevelt had signed a decree and Major General Pratt, who had replaced De Witt, had issued Public Proclamation Number 21, which restored the rights of the evacuees to return to their homes or live wherever they wanted. And as of January second, there would be no such thing as contraband. They could have all the cameras and jewelry and weapons they wanted. But much more importantly, it meant they could go home now. The camps were being closed by the end of 1945. And the War Relocation Authority was urging everyone to leave as soon as feasible, which in many cases was more complicated than expected. But the headline was that the Japanese could leave the internment camps as soon as they wanted. And for Hiroko, because she had signed the loyalty oath, she would be free to go too, despite her alien status.

"Now?" she asked, unable to believe him. "This minute? If I wanted to, I could just walk out of here?"

"That's right, if you signed 'yes, yes,' " he said.

"It's finished." And then he looked at her strangely and asked her a question she couldn't answer. "Where will you go?" He had admired her for months. She was a lovely woman.

"I don't know," she said, looking startled. Where would she go? The war was still on, and she couldn't go back to Japan to her parents. And Peter wasn't home yet. She tried not to let herself think of the more than three months' silence, and that night she and Reiko talked about what they would do now. They had very little money saved up, and Tak's money, what there was of it, was in Peter's bank accounts, which they had no access to. He had given them papers acknowledging it, but without him, it would be almost impossible to get to. And as long as he was alive, which Hiroko prayed he was, his family couldn't get to it either. It was an awkward situation. And they had no other relatives in California. Reiko had a cousin in New York, she said, and another one in New Jersey. And that was it. Nowhere to go, no one to go home to.

After all this time, and wanting out so badly, there was nowhere to go. And everyone else was having the same problem. Their relatives were either in Japan, or all with them. A few of them had relatives in the East, and the War Relocation Authority was still willing to get them jobs in factories, but none of them wanted to just go East without knowing someone when they got there.

"What *are* we going to do?" Reiko asked seriously, as they pondered the problem. There was nothing left for them in Palo Alto.

"Why don't you write to your cousins in New York and New Jersey," Hiroko suggested. And when Reiko did, they wrote and told her they would love to have her. Her cousin in New Jersey was a nurse too and said that she was sure she could get Reiko a job. It all sounded so easy that it made her wonder why they hadn't gone there in the first place. But of course, by the time they'd understood they really needed to get out, they couldn't any longer. The "voluntary relocation" in the beginning had seemed so useless. Three years later, with all they knew and had experienced, it didn't seem quite so stupid.

And on December eighteenth, the Supreme Court decision in the *Endo* case was handed down, declaring that it was against the law to hold loyal citizens against their will. But the government already had, for two and a half years now. It was hard to take that back and say they were sorry. Most people had no idea how to put their lives back together. They had nowhere to go, and no way to get there, except for the twenty-five dollars the WRA was willing to give them for transportation. They all had the same problem as the Tanakas, or worse ones.

But the week before Christmas, Reiko and her children sat down and decided what to do. They were going to New Jersey, and of course they wanted Hiroko to come with them. She was quiet for two days while she thought about it seriously, and she noticed that Sally was subdued too. They all had decisions to make, and sad moments ahead of them. Having come together in shock and grief, they would all be leaving each other in loss and sorrow. But at least she was leaving with Toyo; he was her one great joy in life, her baby.

And finally, having thought about it carefully, she

sat down and talked seriously to Reiko. She was staying, not in the camp, but on the West Coast, if she
could find work there. She wasn't sure what she could
do. She had no degree, and although she had served as
a nurse's aide for two years, no hospital would hire her
without some training. She was going to have to look
for something more menial.

"But why won't you come with us?" Reiko looked
deeply upset when Hiroko told her.

"I want to stay here," she said quietly, "in case
Peter comes back here. But also, when the war is over,
I have to go back to Japan as soon as possible, to see
my parents." It had been four months since she'd
heard from Peter, and even she knew something must
have happened. She rarely spoke of it to anyone, but
she thought of him incessantly, and prayed that he was
still alive somewhere. She had to believe he was, not
only for her sake, but for Toyo's.

"If anything goes wrong, if you can't find work, or"
—Reiko didn't want to say the words *if Peter is killed*,
but she thought them—"whatever, I want you to come
to New Jersey. They'll be happy to take you, and once
I get a job, hopefully we can get a little apartment." All
she needed was one bedroom for herself and the girls,
and they could always make room for Hiroko and
Toyo.

"Thank you, Aunt Rei," she said softly, and the
two women embraced and held each other as they
cried. They had been through so much together. She
had come to spend a year, and learn lessons about life,
and she had learned so much more than she'd ever
dreamed in the three and a half years she'd been in the
States. Looking back at it, it seemed like a lifetime.

But the girls were devastated to hear she wasn't coming with them, and all through Christmas they tried to talk her into it. They weren't going until after New Year's. Some people had already left, but many refused to. Old people said they had nowhere to go, many of them had no relatives, and the camp was their only home now. And little by little, they were hearing horror stories from people who had left, about belongings that hadn't been kept or stored, automobiles that had disappeared from the federal reserve where they'd been kept, government warehouses that had been plundered. Most of the evacuees had lost all their belongings. And as they heard the first tales of it, Hiroko thought of Tami's dollhouse. At nearly twelve, she was too old for it now anyway, but it would have been a nice souvenir of her childhood. And Reiko wept again, thinking of all their photographs and mementos, which would have meant even more now, with Ken and Tak gone. Her wedding photographs were in there too, and all her photographs of Ken. It made her cry again realizing she had only one photograph of her son. The one that had been taken of him in his uniform, in Hawaii.

"Don't think of it," Hiroko said to her. But there was too much not to think of these days.

And on Christmas night, after he'd given her the tiny ring he'd made with a gold band he'd fashioned himself, and a tiny piece of turquoise he'd found in the nearby mountains, Tadashi sat down and had a serious talk with Sally. He wanted to know what she wanted to do with her future.

"What does that mean?" she asked, looking very young as he smiled at her. They had been "dating" for a year, ever since her father's death, and if he hadn't been twenty-five years old, he'd have called it "going steady."

"You mean like school?" she asked, confused and embarrassed, and unhappy to be leaving him. Her mind had been a jumble for weeks. She was happy they were about to be free, but she didn't want to leave Tadashi.

"I mean like us, not school." He smiled at her, and held her hand in his own. She was about to turn eighteen, and she had almost finished high school. She was a senior at the camp school, and she would graduate in New Jersey. "What do you want to do, Sally? Grow up and go to college in New Jersey?" She hadn't even thought of college yet. All any of them ever thought of was freedom.

"I don't know. I'm not sure I care about school that much," she said honestly. She was always honest with him. She could say anything to Tadashi. He was that kind of person, and she loved him. "I know my dad did, and my mom probably will again once we're out of here. I don't know what I want. . . . I just want . . ." Her eyes filled with tears as she looked at him, and weeks of terror and grief engulfed her. It brought it all back to her again, losing Ken, losing her dad, and now she was going to lose Tadashi. Why was it that she lost all the men in her life? That they all deserted her one way or the other? She could hardly breathe, she was in so much pain, thinking of leaving Tule Lake without him. "I just want to be with you," she said, crying as she finished her sentence, and he looked immensely relieved as she said it.

"So do I," he said soberly. She was young, but she

was old enough. Others had made their minds up at her age. "What do you think your mother would say if I ask her to come with you?" And then he gulped, and took another big step, which left her staring at him. "We could get married when we get there."

"Do you mean that?" She looked like a child at Christmas. Maybe she hadn't lost everything after all, and she threw her arms around his neck. He had been wonderful to her all year, and she had been reasonable and mature ever since she'd been with him. She thought her mother might just agree. And if she didn't, maybe he could come back later.

"I'd like to get married right away," he went on, "but I still want you to finish school," he said, sounding firm, and she giggled. "After you finish high school, we'll talk about what you want to do." But, by then, he hoped they'd be having a baby. They could wait till June at least, before they got started. But they had all lost so much of life in the past three years that he wanted it all now. A wife, and family, and babies, and decent meals, and warm clothes, and a real apartment with central heating. "I should be able to find work in New Jersey too. At least I hope so." He had a college degree, and unlike Hiroko, he also had training as a paramedic. "I'll talk to your mother," he promised.

And he did the next day. She was surprised at first. She thought Sally was still too young, but she had to agree with him that everything had accelerated in the camps, people grew up faster, people died young, just as Tak had. And now her little girl wanted to get married. But she was fond of Tad, and she thought he'd make Sally a good husband, and she agreed to let him go with them. And he had talked to his own mother that day about his plans, and she understood. She wanted to go to Ohio anyway, to stay with her sister. And she had no objection to him joining the Tanakas in New Jersey, or even marrying the elder daughter. At first she thought he meant Hiroko, and she hadn't been pleased. She didn't approve of Toyo, but she was happy when she heard it was Sally, and wished him well. And afterward, when they told the others, he and Sally were elated. The only one not going with them now was Hiroko. But she still insisted that she wanted to return to San Francisco.

"I can always go later," she promised again. But there was a sweet sadness to everything now, a bittersweet quality to the people they saw, the places they went. Every time Hiroko looked at something or saw someone, she remembered that soon she would never be seeing them again, and it made her weep and cling to Toyo. Soon he would be the only familiar face she saw, the only person she loved and who loved her. And he would never remember the place where he had been born, or the lessons they'd learned there.

On New Year's Day, they went to the temple and celebrated the anniversary of Takeo's death. And afterward, they went to his grave in the cemetery. Reiko hated leaving him there, and yet she couldn't take him with her, except in her heart, and her memories. They stood there for a long time, and the children left her alone with him, to say good-bye again. The ground around them was hard and frozen, just as it had been the year before when they buried him. And this time when they went back to their little rooms again, they started packing.

It only took two days. They gave away most of

their things. Much of it was useless to them. There was so little they wanted to save, the lion's share of the work was throwing away and sorting. Someone had found an old trunk somewhere, and Reiko packed the bulk of their things in it, and she and Hiroko packed yet another dollhouse to save for Tami, mostly as a souvenir this time, if she ever bothered to unpack it.

All of Hiroko's and Toyo's things fit into a single bag, the same one she had brought with her when she'd arrived. She had so little for him even now that it hardly took up any room in her suitcase. Reiko had given her two hundred dollars to tide her over until she got a job, and she had it in cash in her handbag. The cousins in New Jersey had sent them five hundred dollars to get them there, and told them they'd be happy to send more if they needed it. But all they needed were train tickets. They had decided to take the train to New Jersey, and they were leaving from Sacramento.

They were all leaving the next day. In the morning, Tad came with his things and helped them with the final packing. Reiko gave her small hibachi to the people next door. She had bought it from a family that had gone back to Japan at the beginning of their stay at Tule Lake, and there were some old toys she gave to another family down the road. The photograph of Ken was in her handbag, the memories of him in her heart, along with those of her husband.

And finally, after all of it, they stood looking around at the two small rooms they had lived in. The straw mattresses had been taken out, the steel cots were bare, the tatami mats Hiroko had made were gone, the cooking utensils passed along or thrown away. Their trunk and their bags stood in the road, the rooms behind them were empty.

"It's funny," Sally said, looking at her mother. "Now that it's happening, it seems so sad. I never thought I'd feel this way when we left here."

"It's hard leaving home . . . this was home for a while. . . ." For a long time, in her life. And they all felt the same way. Hiroko had cried when she said good-bye to the nurses in the infirmary, especially Sandra. Her baby had been born there, and despite the years of pain, there had been special moments. There had been humor and friends, and even music, and laughter behind the barbed wire, while the guards watched them.

"Ready to go?" Tad asked quietly. He'd already said good-bye to his mother, who had left for Ohio the day before. It was a sad good-bye, but he knew she wanted to be with her sister.

The War Relocation Authority had given them free train tickets to Sacramento and fifty dollars per family for expenses. After that, they were on their own. Tad and the Tanakas were taking the train. And Hiroko was taking a bus to San Francisco. Reiko was nervous about leaving her alone, but Hiroko insisted she'd be fine. She had absolutely no one in San Francisco, but she had promised again and again that if anything happened, if she couldn't get a job, she'd take a train to New Jersey before she ran out of money. She had their phone number and address and everything she needed to reach them.

One by one they picked up their bags, and Tad and Sally carried the small trunk between them. It was mostly filled with memories, and Reiko suspected she might never open it again, but still, she wanted to take it with her. It was full of odd little souvenirs of Tule Lake.

The bus was waiting for them at the gate, and there were others waiting there too. As always, the soldiers were standing sentry, but now it was more to keep the peace inside, than to keep anyone from leaving. They were more of a police force than prison guards, and they helped Hiroko put her bag on the bus, and then they shook hands with everyone and wished them luck. Oddly enough, neither side bore the other any malice. And now, whatever it had once been, good or bad, necessary or not, it was over. The subject was closed. It was January 1945, and soon Tule Lake, and Manzanar, and all the other camps like them would be nothing but memories, places to talk about and remember.

As the bus started up, Hiroko sat staring at the camp, engraving it on her memory, the barracks, the dust, the cold, the faces, the people she had loved, the children she had cared for, those who had died, and those who had moved on, never to be seen again, but always remembered.

Toyo sat on her lap, playing with her hair, and holding him close to her, she kissed him. One day she would tell him about it, the place where he was born, but he would never understand, he would never know. And as she looked at the other faces around her, she saw the same love, the same pain, the same agony slipping away from them after so long. And from somewhere behind her was a single voice speaking up in the silence, "We're free now." And with that, the bus drove away, and headed for Sacramento.

# Chapter 17

*F*OR HIROKO, leaving Tad and her cousins at the train was one of the hardest things she'd ever done. Everyone had cried copiously, and the emotions they hadn't been able to let go of when they left the camp came tumbling out of their pores now. Even Tad cried when he said good-bye to her, and she was still sobbing as the train pulled away and she and Toyo were waving.

She had kissed each one of them, and they had kissed her, and him, until they almost missed the train. And after they left, she thought she had never felt as empty. She felt drained as she walked the ten blocks to the bus station, carrying Toyo and her suitcase. A few people glanced at her, but no one seemed surprised to see a Japanese woman walking anywhere. There were no shouts of "Jap," and no unpleasantness, and yet the war wasn't over. She wondered what had happened while they'd been away, if everyone had forgotten or lost interest.

It was five o'clock by then, and she bought a sandwich for both of them before she got on the bus. At exactly five-thirty the bus left, right on schedule, and headed for San Francisco.

It was an uneventful ride, and Toyo slept most of the way, and as they came in over the Bay Bridge, Hiroko sat and stared at how beautiful the bridge was. It looked like diamonds strung across the bay. Everything looked so clean and so perfect. There was no barbed wire in sight, there were no guns, no one hurrying to their rooms, with newspaper in their coat because they were cold, to sleep on straw mattresses that scratched you all night. She couldn't even begin to imagine now what a real bed would be like, or even a comfortable futon. It made her smile, too, to realize that she had become so American over the past three and a half years since she'd come from Kyoto. It had been a hard way to become one.

She slept in a small hotel downtown that night, and thought about the others on the train. It was going to be a big adventure for them, and she smiled thinking of Tad and Sally. She was going to miss them all, but she still thought she had made the right decision.

She took Toyo to breakfast the next day, and afterward she looked for a phone booth. She was holding his hand, and flipping through the directory, and when she saw the familiar name, she started to tremble. Maybe she was wrong. She could go through an agency. She didn't have to do this, and yet she wanted to. Something told her that she had to.

Hiroko called, and asked for her, and she came on the line very quickly. She hadn't given her name, she just said "a friend from college," and whoever had answered went to get her.

"Yes?" a voice asked pleasantly.

"Anne?" Hiroko said as the phone trembled in her hand, and she tried to keep her voice normal, as she held Toyo with her other hand. But he was bored and started complaining. He was not yet two years old, and he didn't understand where they were, or where the others had gone. To him, it was all an incomprehensible adventure. He kept saying Tami's name, and Hiroko had explained to him that she was going on a train. But he didn't know what a train was.

"Yes, this is Anne," Anne Spencer said, sounding as aristocratic as ever. She was going back to school the next day. They were still on Christmas vacation. And she was graduating in June, but St. Andrew's seemed like a distant memory to Hiroko. "Who is this?"

"Hiroko," she said simply. "Hiroko Takashimaya." From St. Andrews and Tanforan . . . and Tule Lake . . . perhaps she had forgotten, but somehow Hiroko didn't believe it.

There was only a brief pause, and a small gasp.

"Your basket kept us going for days," Hiroko said sadly.

"Where are you?" Anne asked softly. It was hard to tell if she was glad she had called, or just startled.

"I got out of camp yesterday. My cousins went to New Jersey."

"And you, Hiroko?" she said gently. They had once been roommates, never friends. And yet twice she had come to tell her she was sorry. "Where are you?" she asked again.

"Here in San Francisco." Hiroko hesitated, and then looked down at Toyo to give her courage. "I need a job." It sounded so pathetic now that she had said it, and she was sorry she had called, but it was too late now. "I wondered if you know anyone . . . or even your parents, or friends . . . if you need a maid, or someone to clean house . . . really anything. . . . I've been working in the hospital for two years. I could take care of a child or an old person."

"Do you have my address?" Anne asked her bluntly, and she nodded, stunned into silence.

"It's in the phone book. Yes, I have it."

"Why don't you come right over. Take a cab, I'll pay for it." She wondered if Hiroko had decent clothes, or if she was hungry or had any money.

Hiroko left the phone booth and hailed a cab, but she paid for it herself, and was surprised to see Anne waiting for her outside. But Anne was even more surprised when she saw Toyo.

"Is he yours?" Anne asked in utter amazement, and Hiroko smiled as she nodded. While Anne had been playing tennis and learning French, and summering at Lake Tahoe, Hiroko had had a baby.

"Yes, he is," she said, looking down proudly at her son. "His name is Toyo."

Anne did not ask his last name, or if Hiroko was married. She suspected, looking at her, that that wasn't the case, and the dress Hiroko was wearing was not only ugly and too big for her, but it was threadbare and ancient.

"I spoke to my mother," she said as they stood on

the sidewalk on Upper Broadway. "She'll give you a job. I'm afraid it won't be a very fancy one. They need someone to help in the kitchen." She looked down at Toyo then, but she knew it wouldn't make a difference. "You can keep him with you when you work downstairs," she said, unlocking the door for her, and then she turned to her and asked if she was hungry. But Hiroko smiled and told her they'd had breakfast.

Anne took her right downstairs to see her room. It was small and clean and without frills of any kind, but it was far better than anything she'd seen in nearly three years, and she was grateful for the job, and when they were in the room that was to be hers, she told her.

"I cannot thank you enough for this, Anne. You owe me nothing."

"I thought what they did to you was wrong. It would have been better to send you home, if they didn't trust you. You, at least, were Japanese. But the others, the Americans, didn't belong there, and neither did you, really. What could you have done to them? You were no spy." The woman who had taken care of her as a child had died the year before at Manzanar, during an emergency operation. Anne thought of her as a beloved relative and Anne would never forgive them for taking her away and letting her die there. She was doing this for her, and the others. It was something she could do to make up for what had happened.

She explained that Hiroko would have to wear a black dress and a white lace apron and cap, with matching collar and cuffs, with black shoes and black stockings. But that didn't bother her either.

"What are you going to do after this?" Anne asked

her. She didn't imagine for a moment that this was going to be Hiroko's future. But the war was still on, her cousins were gone, and she couldn't go back to Japan yet.

"I'd like to stay here, with you, if I can, until I can go home again. My brother was killed, and I must go home to my parents." She didn't tell her that two of her cousins had died too, Ken and Tak. And she had no news of Peter. But Anne looked down at Toyo then, wondering.

"Will his father come back?" she asked cautiously, not quite sure of their arrangement. It was obvious that the child's father had been Caucasian. But Hiroko only looked at her with worried eyes. She wanted to ask her another favor.

"I need to find out if something has happened. I haven't heard from him since August. He's with the army, in France. But after they got to Paris, I heard nothing. I was wondering if, somehow . . . someone you know . . . maybe they can call someone and find out if anyone knows . . ." Anne understood and nodded.

"I'll ask my father."

The two women stood looking at each other then. It was an odd moment between two women who had never been friends, and yet she had just done everything possible for Hiroko, more than anyone else would have.

Hiroko left a few minutes later to get her things from the hotel, and then she came back in a cab again with Toyo. It was a handsome house, a large, imposing brick edifice, and one of the largest on Broadway. And as soon as she got back, she went to her room with

Toyo. She changed into her uniform, and holding Toyo's hand, she appeared in the kitchen. Everyone there was very pleasant to her, and they showed her what her responsibilities were, and two of the maids promised to help her with Toyo. The cook fell instantly in love with him, and gave him a big bowl of soup for lunch, and a chocolate eclair, which he thought was very exciting. For a child who had started out so big, he had grown quite thin from the inadequate food they had all had at the camp, and Hiroko was relieved to see him eating.

Anne came back downstairs and introduced Hiroko to her mother that afternoon. Mrs. Spencer was very beautiful, and very distinguished. She was wearing a beautiful gray wool suit, with a necklace of enormous pearls, and matching earrings. She was a woman of about fifty. Anne was the youngest of three daughters and a son. Mrs. Spencer wasn't warm, but she was extremely polite to Hiroko. She knew what her circumstances were, Anne had even told her about Toyo, and Margaret Spencer was as sorry for her as Anne was. She had told the entire staff to be kind to her, and feed them well. And the salary she offered her, Hiroko thought, was nothing less than staggering. She offered her three hundred dollars a month, which was more charity than wage, but she didn't mind it a bit. In ways no one could ever have measured, she had earned it, and she was going to need every penny if she was going to save enough money to return to Japan when the war finally ended. There was still no sign of Peter, and she had Toyo to support. She was deeply grateful for the high wages.

For Hiroko, once Anne had left, it was a little bit

like being Cinderella being there. Everyone was very kind, but they also knew that Hiroko had gone to school with Anne at St. Andrew's, and why she had left, and where she had been for the past three years. But no one ever asked her any questions. They showed her how to do her work, and let her be, and kept an eye on Toyo for her when she was busy. And Hiroko was always polite to everyone, and helpful; she worked hard and kept to herself. And on her days off, she took Toyo to the park, and she went to the Japanese tea garden she remembered visiting in Golden Gate Park with the Tanakas when she'd first arrived. It was run by a Chinese family now, and called the Oriental Tea Garden. There were lots of things to do with him, and she was reminded more than once of visits she had made to the city with her cousins.

Within a short time she heard from them. They were happy and well. Reiko was working at the hospital, both girls were in school, and on Valentine's Day, Sally and Tadashi got married. It was the day after she got their telegram, when Mr. Spencer finally had news for her from a friend in Washington. It had taken more than a month to get any information. And the news wasn't good. Hiroko trembled as she listened.

After Paris, they had moved on to Germany. And Peter had been missing in action since a skirmish near Antwerp. No one had seen him killed, and they had never recovered his body after the snipers moved on. But he hadn't turned up again either. It was impossible to say what had happened. Perhaps after the war they would find records of him, or find that he had been held prisoner by the Germans. But for now, all she knew was what she had known before, that he had vanished. His silence had been as ominous as she'd feared, possibly even more so.

She thanked Anne's father for getting the information for her, and silently went back to the kitchen to take care of Toyo.

"I feel sorry for her," Charles Spencer admitted to his wife after he'd told her. "Is she married to the boy's father?" he asked curiously.

"I'm not sure," his wife said cautiously. "I don't think so. Anne says she was awfully bright in school, one of the most outstanding students." In spite of herself, Anne's mother had come to genuinely like her, and could see why Anne cared about her.

"I don't suppose she'll want to go back," Charles said thoughtfully. One of their gardeners had gone to the camps as well, and Charles had had to move heaven and earth to get him out and sent to relatives in Wisconsin.

"Anne says she wants to go back to Japan to see her parents."

"Well, do what you can for her while she's here. To be honest with you, from what they said about her . . . er . . . friend . . . I think he's done for." They hadn't been able to prove he was dead beyond any doubt, but it sounded as though they were almost sure of it. It was one of those mysteries that wouldn't be solved until after the war, when they had all the information. But whatever actually happened, it didn't matter now. The man was gone. And the boy was without a father. It made Charles sorry for her all over again. But Hiroko was very happy there with the Spencers. She thought of Peter all the time, and despite what Anne's father had told her, she refused to be convinced that he was dead. Somehow, she just couldn't believe it.

And the war moved on without him. In February, the Allies destroyed Dresden, and in March, Manila fell to the Americans. Tokyo was being bombed relentlessly, along with other cities in Japan, killing eighty thousand and leaving more than a million people homeless. And Hiroko worried endlessly about her parents. She spoke to the Tanakas about it on the phone, and they were sympathetic about her concerns, but Hiroko's life seemed far from them now. She was constantly listening for news of the war, hoping to hear something about Peter or her parents. It was her only concern now.

In April, Roosevelt died, and Hitler committed suicide. And the following month the concentration camps were opened, much to everyone's horror. It made Tule Lake look like paradise in comparison, and she was embarrassed to have ever complained about whatever minor miseries they had suffered. Compared to the people who had suffered at the Nazis' hands, the Japanese had been extremely lucky in Tule Lake, and elsewhere.

And then at last, Germany surrendered in May. But Japan still fought on. And in June, they fought the bloody battle of Okinawa. It seemed as though the war in Japan would never end, and she would never be able to go home. But all she could do was wait, and a month after the war in Europe was over, she still had no news of Peter.

Charles Spencer kindly inquired again, but his status was still the same. Missing in action. But still, she refused to believe that she and Toyo had lost him forever.

And at the end of June, the Spencers moved to Lake Tahoe for the summer. At first they planned to leave her in town, and then they asked her to join them at their house on the lake, and as she thought of it, she realized it would be wonderful for Toyo.

Anne graduated from St. Andrew's just before they went, and Hiroko thought about her with a smile that morning. She had hardly seen her in months. She had rarely come home from school on weekends. Most of the time she either went away, or stayed for dances. And during holidays, she went to Santa Barbara or Palm Springs, or to New York to see her sister, who had had another baby. But whenever Hiroko did see Anne, though it was rare, she was always pleasant. They had an odd relationship, it was not friendship, and yet they both recognized that there was a bond between them.

And in Lake Tahoe, she was always surrounded by friends who came up to visit, especially for the weekend. They stayed with them, water-skied, played tennis, rode one of several speedboats. The others had had to be put away, as they needed their gas ration coupons for the drive back and forth to Tahoe.

It reminded Hiroko of when she had come to the lake with the Tanakas when she had first come from Japan. It had been four years, four years of war and agony throughout the world. And yet, here people were still playing tennis and driving speedboats. It was an odd feeling, watching them, and yet their giving up tennis or boats or having fun wouldn't have ended the war either.

Toyo particularly loved being there, and just as they were in town, the servants were extremely kind to him. And in Tahoe, Hiroko frequently served dinner, particularly when they had guests or dinner parties. And one night, one of the Spencers' guests asked how they had managed to keep her, indicating Hiroko.

"All ours went to Topaz, you know. Damn shame. Best servants we've ever had. What did you do, Charles?" He joked with him, but Charles did not look amused. "Did you hide her?"

"I believe she was in Tule Lake," Charles Spencer said stiffly. "She only came to us in January of this year. As I understand it, she went through a lot there." His words and his expression silenced the other man completely. But there were others who stared at her, who watched her, and who didn't hesitate to make comments.

"I don't know how you can keep her here, and eat dinner with her standing behind you," one of Margaret's friends said one day at lunch in Lake Tahoe. "When you think of what those people are doing to our boys over there, it ruins my appetite. Margaret, you must have a very strong stomach." Margaret Spencer did not respond, but as she glanced in Hiroko's direction, their eyes met, and then Hiroko quickly lowered hers. She had heard it all, and she understood. She had done penance to please people like her. In some ways, the Spencers were different from their friends. They had been appalled by the camps, and saddened when their employees had been sent away for internment. But there had been absolutely no way to stop it.

And at a dinner party, a friend of Charles had left their dinner table, because he had lost a son at Okinawa and he refused to be served by Hiroko. Hiroko had gone to her room quietly after that, and the Spencers let her go for her own sake. She had her own losses to think of too, Yuji, Ken, Peter, Tak. So many had been lost, there was so much sorrow and pain that needed to be healed now.

But in August, while the Allies divided up the Reich, the Americans finally got even at Hiroshima. It made everyone who had ever hated the Japanese, even for a single moment, feel vindicated, and yet again after the bombing at Nagasaki. At last, the war was over. And exactly four weeks later, the Japanese surrendered over Labor Day weekend. It was the Spencers' last weekend at Lake Tahoe before moving back to the city.

"What are you going to do now?" Anne asked her quietly. They were alone in the dining room the next morning.

"I'd like to go home when I can."

"I don't suppose things will settle down there for a while." Anne nodded at her, and Hiroko looked tired. She had been following the news for weeks. She was desperately worried about her parents. It seemed hard to believe anyone could have survived the endless bombings. And yet obviously some people had. She only prayed her parents were among them. And still there was no news from Peter. But she couldn't go in both directions. And she would have had no idea of how to find him in Europe.

"Your family has been very good to me," Hiroko said before she left the room again, not wanting to intrude on Anne's breakfast.

"You've been good to us too." She smiled at her. "How's Toyo?"

"Getting big and fat in the kitchen," Hiroko laughed. He was making up for lost time and a lot of bad food at Tule Lake. He was two and a half years old, and the darling of everyone in the Spencers' household.

Anne didn't ask if there had been news of his father. She knew there hadn't. And her father had said again that it was obvious Hiroko's friend was dead. It was a damn shame and he was sorry.

Hiroko waited another month, and went back to the city with them, and then she gave them her notice. Anne was moving to New York for a year, to be near her sister, and go to parties and meet people there. And Hiroko had learned that she could get passage on the U.S.S. *General W. P. Richardson* to Kobe in mid-October.

Even she had no illusions by then. She hadn't heard from Peter in fourteen months. And the war in Europe had been over for five of them. There simply wasn't any way they wouldn't have found him, if he were alive. And she admitted as much to Reiko when she called and told her she was leaving for Japan to see her parents.

"It's hard to believe we lost all three of them, isn't it? Ken, Tak . . . and Peter." And she had lost her brother too. It was so unfair. They had lost so much, and others had lost so little. She couldn't help thinking of the Spencers, even though they had been so kind to her. But they had scarcely noticed the war, except for the fact that it had improved some of their investments. Their son had been 4-F and had stayed home, their son-in-law had been kept in Washington during the entire war, and none of their daughters had lost husbands or even boyfriends. Anne had made her debut during the war, and she had graduated in June, right after Germany surrendered. All nice and neat and clean and simple. Maybe that was just the way life worked sometimes. There were those who paid, and those who didn't. And yet, in spite of that, Hiroko had to admit she liked them. The Spencers were good people, and they'd been wonderful to her and Toyo.

But Reiko was very worried about her going to Japan, especially alone with Toyo, but there was no one to go with her, or provide her escort.

"I'll be all right, Aunt Rei. The Americans are over there. Things will be fairly well controlled before I get there."

"Maybe less so than you think. Why don't you come here instead, and wait until you hear from your parents." But she had already tried to reach them, by telegram. It was impossible. Everyone had told her there was no way to contact anyone there. And she owed it to them to go to see them. It was time for her to go home now. They had their losses too, and despite the shock it might give them, she wanted them to see Toyo. He was their grandson and he might comfort them a little after losing her brother.

And when Sally got on the phone, she told Hiroko the news. She and Tad were expecting a baby.

"You didn't waste a minute," Hiroko said, and Sally laughed shyly, sounding very young and very happy.

"Neither did you," she dared from three thousand miles away, sounding like the old Sally that Hiroko knew and alternately loved and hated, but this time she laughed good-humoredly.

"I guess you're right."

But Sally's mother had already warned her not to ask Hiroko about Peter. The situation was hopeless.

She spoke to Tad and congratulated him too. The baby was due in April.

And the day before she left for Japan, she called them again, and this time she had a long, serious talk with Reiko. She was worried about what would happen to Hiroko in Japan, if things went wrong and there was no one there to help her.

"I'll go to the Americans and ask for help, I promise, Aunt Rei. Don't worry."

"And what if they won't help you? You're Japanese, you're not American." She was always on the wrong side somehow. To Hiroko it seemed ironic, but it terrified Reiko.

"I'll figure something out," she promised. "I'll be fine."

"You're too young to be going there alone," Reiko insisted.

"Aunt Rei, it's my home. I've got to go back now. I have to see my parents." Reiko didn't dare suggest to her that they might be gone too, but Hiroko was well aware of it. She needed to know what had happened, just as she did with Peter. But in his case she had to accept what she couldn't discover on her own. In their case, it was different. They had relatives and friends. She had had a life there and someone would know where her parents were.

"I want you to contact me as soon as you can," Reiko made Hiroko promise.

"I will. It must be a real mess over there though."

"I'm sure it is." The stories about Hiroshima were unbelievable, beyond awful. But Hiroko was going nowhere near there, or Reiko would have objected even harder.

And then, regretfully, she and her cousins said good-bye, and that night Hiroko packed their things in her small room, feeling sad as she did it. She really hated to leave the Spencers.

And in the morning, Anne's father surprised her. He handed her a thousand dollars in cash, as a bonus, in addition to her salary. To Hiroko, it was a fortune.

"You'll need it for the boy," he said kindly, and she accepted it, knowing he was right, and deeply grateful to him.

"You've done so much for us," she said, thanking him and his wife, and Anne insisted on taking her to the boat, with the driver.

"I can take a cab, Anne," Hiroko said, smiling at her. "You don't have to do that."

"I want to. Somehow, we missed the boat," she said, laughing at the pun. "Maybe if I'd been a little smarter then, or a little more worldly and grown-up, we'd have been friends. But I wasn't."

"You've done so much for me," Hiroko said, unable to imagine how much more it might have been if she'd added friendship. But she hadn't minded working for them. The job had been menial, but it had served a purpose, given her a home, and fed her and Toyo. That all made it worth doing, and the Spencers had always been extremely kind and pleasant, as had their servants.

She tried objecting again, but Anne insisted on

taking her to the ship with the chauffeur. The others all came out to say good-bye, and her parents waved from an upstairs window. And Toyo watched them all sadly as they drove away, with his belongings in the trunk of the Lincoln. He had no idea where they were going, and he was too young to understand it.

"We're going to Japan to find your grandparents," she had said to him, but he didn't know what that was yet.

And Anne looked at her with concern as they headed toward the Embarcadero. "Will you be all right there?"

"No worse than anywhere else I've been in the last four years." Her life had been an adventure for several years now.

"What will you do if you don't find them?" It was a cruel thing to ask, but she felt she had to.

"I'm not sure." Hiroko couldn't even imagine it. She still couldn't accept the idea that Peter was gone. She said she did to those who asked, mostly so they wouldn't argue with her, like Charles Spencer or Tadashi, but the truth was, she still didn't believe it. "I can't imagine that they're not there," she said to Anne. "When I think of Japan, I think of my parents. I *see* them," she said, closing her eyes, as though to demonstrate to her. And as she did, they reached the pier, and the car stopped slowly. "I'll find them," she said, reassuring herself as much as Anne. "I have to." She had no one else now, except Toyo.

"Come back, if you need to," Anne said, but they both knew she wouldn't do that. More than likely, if she did come back to the States, she would join her cousins in New Jersey. But she didn't want to be with them now either. They had their own lives. She had to find hers. And she wanted to go home. For Hiroko, it would complete an important circle.

She and Anne stood looking at each other for a long moment, with the ship behind them. Toyo was holding Hiroko's hand, and the chauffeur was watching their bags, ready to find a porter.

"You always seem to be there when I leave," Hiroko said, trying to find the words to thank her for all she'd done, but she couldn't.

"I wish I'd been there in the beginning," Anne said softly, and this time she took her in her arms and hugged her.

"Thank you," Hiroko said, with tears in her eyes, and when she pulled away from Anne, she saw that she was crying too.

"I hope you find them," Anne said hoarsely, and then turned to Toyo. "Be good, little man, take care of your mommy." She gave him a kiss, and then stood to look at Hiroko. "If you need me, call me . . . write to me . . . send a telegram . . . do something."

"I will." Hiroko smiled. "Take care of yourself, Anne." And she meant it.

"Be safe, Hiroko. Be careful. It will be dangerous over there." It was what Reiko and Tadashi had told her, and she knew they all were right. The entire country was in chaos. People would have moved mountains to get away from there just then, and instead, she was going. But she knew she had to.

"Thank you," Hiroko said, and squeezed her hand, and then she walked away with the chauffeur and waved, and so did Toyo.

He found a porter for her, and she went up the

gangplank holding Toyo's hand, waving at them. And a little while later, she found her cabin. It was small and spare, and it had a single porthole. At least they'd have air on the two-week trip. And she went back up on deck with him then, so Toyo could see the ship set sail and see all the excitement. There were, as always, balloons and music and a festive air, even though they weren't going to a happy place. But it was the first ship that had sailed for Japan since Pearl Harbor.

And as Hiroko looked down at the pier, holding him, she saw her, still standing there, still as beautiful as she had been the day she had first seen her, getting out of the limousine at St. Andrew's, and then discovered that they were roommates. She had thought they would be friends then, and for a time she had been wrong, but finally, she wasn't. Hiroko raised a hand and waved, and pointed her out to Toyo. And he waved and blew her a kiss and Hiroko and Anne laughed and waved harder.

"Good-bye," Anne called up to her as the ship pulled away slowly, and Toyo watched all of it with fascination.

"Thank you!" Hiroko mouthed again, and the two women waved at each other as the tugboats pulled them away from the dock.

They could not hear the words anymore. But she could still see her, standing there, waving, as the ship turned, and sailed slowly out through the harbor.

"Where are we going, Mama?" Toyo asked for the thousandth time that day as she set him down with a sad expression.

"Home," was all she answered this time. It was all they had left now.

# *Chapter 18*

$T$HE U.S.S. *General W. P. Richardson* took two
weeks and a day to sail across the Pacific Ocean.
And right on schedule, it docked in Kobe in the morning. It had seemed like an endless trip to her, and just
as they had when she came, they had bypassed Hawaii.
And she didn't mind it. Toyo had loved the trip, and
everyone had been wonderful to him. He was the only
child on the ship, and he had become everyone's play-
mate and mascot.

But on the morning they arrived, Hiroko was
oddly silent. It was a strange feeling for her, remembering what it had been like for her when she left, and
the terrifying symphony of emotions. She had ached at
leaving her parents, but she had gone so as not to
disappoint her father . . . just for a year, she said

. . . just one, he promised . . . and it had been almost four and a half, and so much had happened.

She watched the activity on the dock when they arrived, and listened silently to the dock workers, the birds, the people calling to each other and shouting. There was confusion in the port, and still the vestiges of wartime. But all over the pier she saw American soldiers, which even in her homeland she found oddly reassuring. She was no longer sure who were the enemies and who the friends. For four years, life had been too confusing.

She held Toyo's hand carefully as they got off, and she carried her own bags. There were taxis along the dock, and she asked one of them to take her to the train, and he asked her where she was going. When she said Kyoto, he offered to drive her there for fifty U.S. dollars. And given the state the country was in, the offer was appealing, and she accepted.

"How long have you been gone?" he asked as they drove along roads she had either never seen before, or no longer remembered. They were all in poor repair, and deeply rutted.

"More than four years." Four years and three months exactly.

"You're lucky," he said. "The war was hard here. It must have been good in the States." She couldn't explain to him about the camps, but he was probably right. It was probably worse here.

"How bad is it now?" she asked bluntly, holding tightly to Toyo. He was listening to them speak Japanese. He had heard plenty of it in the camps, but he had forgotten most of it in the past year. And Hiroko always spoke to him in English, so he didn't understand what they were saying.

"It's rough in places, terrible in others. Some places it's not so bad. Kyoto is so-so. There was some damage there, but none of the temples." It wasn't the temples she was worrying about, it was her parents. She had had no news of them at all, since the message about her brother's death, since Pearl Harbor. "The Americans are all over the place. You have to watch out for them. They think all Japanese women are geishas." She laughed at what he said, but just as he said, she noticed them everywhere, and many of them seemed to be eyeing the women. "Be careful," he said, warning her, and then they drove quietly through the countryside. It took him two hours to get to Kyoto. Normally, it should have been faster, but there were obstructions on the road, potholes, and a lot of traffic.

And her breath caught as she saw the familiar address. It looked as though nothing had changed. It was all so exactly the way she remembered that it felt like a dream, or a memory, to be there. She thanked the driver and paid him with money Charles Spencer had given her, and then holding Toyo's hand, she took her suitcase, and stood there.

"Do you want me to wait?" the driver asked kindly, but she shook her head, mesmerized by the house she had dreamed of a thousand times and longed for so often. The house she had grown up in.

"No, we're fine." She waved bravely, and he drove off, back to Kobe. And for a long time, she just stood there as Toyo watched her.

And then, carefully, she opened the gate. It squeaked exactly as it had before, and the grass around it looked a little overgrown, but nothing seemed destroyed or damaged, and as she walked slowly to the house, she rang the wind chimes. But nothing moved and no one answered. She walked closer and tapped on the shoji screens, but no one came, and she wondered if they were out. She had wanted to warn them she was coming, but there was still no way to reach them.

And cautiously, she opened the shojis, and what she saw took her breath away. Not one single thing had changed in their house. Even the scroll in the tokonoma was still there, placed exactly where it had been when she was a child, and her grandmother taught her how to arrange the flowers for it. And there were flowers there now, but they were dry and long since wilted. They had obviously gone away, for safety, somewhere.

"Who lives here, Mommy?"

"Your grandparents, Toyo. They will be very happy to see you."

"Who are they?"

"My mommy and daddy," she explained, and he looked intrigued, surprised that she had them.

She walked slowly around the house with him. Her mother's clothes were there, all their furniture and cooking utensils. There were several photographs of her, and of Yuji, and she stood staring at them, wanting to reach out and touch them. And then they walked out into the garden. She stopped at the little shrine, and bowed to it, and it felt odd to be doing it again. She hadn't bowed in so long now.

"What are you doing, Mommy?"

"Bowing to our shrine, to honor your grandparents." He had seen old people in the camps bow, but he had been too young to remember.

"Where are your mommy and daddy?" he asked with interest.

"I think they went away," she explained, and then slowly she walked next door to their neighbors' house. They were at home, and they looked very surprised to see her, and even more so to see Toyo. She bowed to them formally, and they told her that her parents had gone to the mountains for safety before the summer. They weren't sure where, but they thought to their old buraku near Ayabe.

It was the farming community where Hidemi was from originally, and it made perfect sense. They had probably been afraid that Kyoto would be bombed, to make an example of it, like Dresden. But she knew it would take them days to get to Ayabe. It was inaccessible normally, but with conditions such as they were, it would be nearly impossible. And then she decided to ask her neighbors if they had a car she could rent or borrow. They said they didn't, and suggested she take the train, which was a reasonable solution. And a little while later, she walked to the train station with Toyo. She took their suitcase, just in case, and she bought some fruit from a child selling apples on the way, and she and Toyo were happy to get them.

But then they told them there was no train till the next morning. She stopped with Toyo after that, and bought some food for them, and then they went back to her parents' house, and they moved into the second bedroom. It was the room where she had been born, and she remembered her father's story, about how she had been born there and not at the hospital because her mother was so stubborn. It made her smile, and she told Toyo that she had been born in that room, and that intrigued him. And that night, while he slept, she wandered from room to room, feeling the warmth of being near them.

There were soldiers patrolling the street outside, but they didn't bother them. And the next morning at seven, she and Toyo went to the train. And because of delays, and debris on the tracks that had to be removed, it took them fourteen hours to get to Ayabe. They didn't arrive until nine o'clock that night, and she had no idea where the house was. So she and Toyo curled up in the train station, under a small blanket she'd brought with them, but Toyo said he didn't like it.

"I don't either, sweetheart, but we can't find the house till tomorrow." And at dawn, she woke up, and got some food for him again from a street vendor, and then paid a man with a car to take them to her grand-parents' house out in the country. Her grandparents were long gone, but her mother had kept the house to go to in the summer.

And the man with the car took a thousand detours to get there. It took them well over an hour, and when they arrived, she could see why. The house, and a number like it, had been leveled.

"What happened?" she asked, looking horrified, and afraid that Toyo would be frightened. It looked as though the whole mountainside had caught fire, and it had. In August.

"A bomb," he said sadly. "There were a lot of them. Just before Hiroshima." There weren't even any neighbors to talk to about it, and he took her finally to a small Shinto shrine that she remembered going to once with her grandmother years before. And there was a priest there.

He looked at her like a ghost when she said who she was, and he shook his head. Yes, he knew her parents.

Did he know where they'd gone? He hesitated for a long time before he answered.

"To heaven, with their ancestors," he said, looking apologetic but holy. Both of her parents had apparently been killed in the bombing, along with several friends, some relatives, and all their neighbors. It had happened three months before. Three months before, they'd been alive, while she had been at Lake Tahoe, but there was no way she could have come then.

"I'm sorry," he said, and she gave him some money and walked back outside with Toyo, feeling dead inside. Everyone was gone. She had no one left. . . . Yuji, her parents . . . Ken . . . Takeo . . . even poor Peter . . . It wasn't fair. They were all such decent people.

"Where do you want to go now?" the man with the car asked her, and for a minute, she just stood there. There was nowhere to go. Except back to Kyoto. But after that, she had no idea. She had traveled four thousand miles to find no one, for nothing.

She got back in the car, and they drove slowly back to the train station, but there was no train for the next two days, and there was nowhere for them to stay in Ayabe, and now that she knew what had happened, she didn't want to. She just wanted to go home again, wherever that was. And sensing her mood, Toyo started to cry, and the driver looked unhappy.

In the end, Hiroko offered him a hundred dollars to take them back to Kyoto. He accepted gratefully, but the trip back was a nightmare. There were obstacles, and bombed-out areas, and detours, and dead animals on the road. There were soldiers and roadblocks, and people milling everywhere, some with nowhere to go, and some obviously crazy from what had happened to them. It took them almost two days to get back and she gave him another fifty dollars when he dropped them at the house in Kyoto. She brought him inside, and gave him some food and water, and then he went on his way again, and she and Toyo stood there, alone at last. And all Hiroko could think of was that they had come all this way for nothing.

"Where are they, Mommy?" he asked insistently. "They're still not here." He looked disappointed, but not as much as she was. She fought back tears as she explained it.

"They're not coming back, Toyo," she said sadly.

"Don't they want to see us?" He looked crestfallen.

"Very much," she said, as the tears spilled onto her cheeks, "but they had to go to heaven, to be with all the other people we love." But no matter how hard she tried, she couldn't bring herself to say "like your daddy." She just couldn't say it. But when he saw her face, he cried with her anyway. He hated it when his mother was unhappy. And she sat on the floor holding him as they both cried, and she heard a knock at the gate and wondered who it was. She hesitated, and then went out to see an M.P. at her parents' front gate. He said he was the new sentry for their street, and he wanted to know if they needed any assistance. He had

been told the house was empty, and he had seen her
and Toyo go into it, but she said they were fine, and
explained that it was the house of her parents.

He was a nice man, with kind eyes, and he handed
Toyo a chocolate bar, which delighted him, but Hiroko
was very cool with him. She remembered what everyone had said. They had all warned her about the
soldiers.

"Are you alone here?" he asked, looking at her
with interest. He was a handsome boy, with a Southern
drawl, but she didn't want any soldiers bothering
them. She wasn't sure what to answer.

"I . . . yes . . . no . . . my husband will be
back later."

The soldier glanced at Toyo then. It was easy to
figure out the rest. And here, the implications were
even worse than they were in San Francisco. It made it
look like she'd been sleeping with enemy soldiers.

"Let us know if there's anything we can do for you,
ma'am," he said, and for the next several days she and
Toyo hid in the house and the garden. She let the
neighbors know that they were back so they wouldn't
be frightened if they saw activity in the house, and she
told them what had happened to her parents, and they
were desolate for her. They even invited her and Toyo
to dinner. And the night they went, the sentry spotted
them again, and he came to chat with Toyo. He gave
him another chocolate bar, and Hiroko thanked him
coolly.

"You speak very good English. Where did you
learn?" he asked, trying to be friendly. She was one of
the prettiest women he'd seen, and he had not seen
her husband. He doubted there even was one.

"In California," she answered vaguely.

"You been there recently?" he asked, surprised.

"I just came back, last week," she said, hating to start a conversation with him. She just didn't want that. She had no idea what she and Toyo were going to do. She didn't know if they should stay here, or go back to the States. And even if she wanted to return to America, it seemed foolish to rush back right away. She had to decide what she wanted to do with her parents' house in Kyoto. And this would be no time to sell it. The sensible thing would be to stay here for a month or two, and then go back to the States, or maybe she had no reason to go there at all now. It was all a jumble in her head, but having soldiers at her gate was not going to make life any easier for her, if they stayed there. It was a complication she would have gone far to have avoided. But the man seemed to be crazy about Toyo.

"Were you there during the war?" the sentry asked, loath to move on and leave them.

"Yes, I was," she said, and thanked him for the chocolate again. Then she hurried into their garden and closed the gate, regretting that there was no lock there. She bowed hastily to their shrine, and went back into the house with Toyo.

He dropped by again once or twice in the next few days, and Hiroko never went to the gate, hoping to discourage him, and then she and Toyo went to Tokyo, to try to find some relatives of her father. But Hiroko learned rapidly that all their relatives were dead, and Tokyo was truly a disaster. The effects of the bombing were still sorely felt, and there were even more soldiers, most of them drunk, and all of them looking for women. And all Hiroko wanted to do was get back to the safety of her parents' house in Kyoto, which they did very quickly.

She had been in Japan for two weeks by then, and it was beginning to seem as though it was going to be too complicated to stay in Japan at all. She was both modern and independent now, but she was also wise enough to know that if she stayed in Japan alone with her son, she would be in too much danger. She already had the schedules of several ships returning to the United States, and there was one sailing on Christmas Day, and she was starting to think they should be on it.

And when she returned to her parents' house after their brief trip, her neighbors told her that a soldier had come by inquiring for her several times, and she told them that if he came back again, to just tell him that she had gone back to the States, or gone away, anything they wanted to tell him, and as she said it, she looked frightened. If it was the same sentry who was so interested in her, she sensed something ominous about his persistence, and it only served to confirm her feelings that they should go back to the States as soon as she could arrange it.

And late that evening, as Toyo slept on the futon in their room, she heard the chimes at the gate again, and didn't answer them. But the next day, Toyo was playing in the garden and heard them before she did. And just as he was, she was sure it was their friend with the chocolates. She ran out of the house, hoping to stop Toyo before he opened the gate, but it was too late. He was already talking to the soldier. And then she saw, as she approached, that it was a different one, and she called the boy to her. But he wouldn't come, and she saw that the man he was talking to was crouched down low with him, to talk to him better.

"Toyo!" she called insistently, but he didn't move, and she knew she would have to go and get him. But she hated these unnerving brushes with the Americans. She had seen the look in the sentry's eyes, and other soldiers like the ones she'd seen in Tokyo, and they frightened her. She didn't want any trouble. "Toyo!" she called again, and this time they both looked up at her, the same face twice, the two of them, as they held hands, and she stared at them. It was Peter. He was alive, and she had no idea how he'd found her. She just stood there and started to cry, and holding Toyo's hand, he came quickly toward her and without waiting for another moment or a sound from her, he kissed her.

She was trembling when he stopped, and she looked up at him, unable to believe he was back, and holding Toyo.

"Where were you?" she said, as though to a lost child who had finally returned to his parents.

"I was in a hospital in Germany for a while. . . . Before that, I was hiding in a pig sty. . . ." He grinned at her, looking like the boy he had been, and then he looked serious as he looked down at Toyo.

"Why didn't you tell me?" He looked so exactly the way she had remembered him, the way she had dreamed of him for three years since she'd last seen him.

She laughed through her tears. "I didn't want you to feel you had to come back if you didn't want to." It sounded so stupid now, but it seemed to have made sense at the time, and then she looked at him, confused again. "How did you get here?"

"The same way you did. I've been right behind you for weeks," he said with a look of exasperation as he pulled her into his arms with one hand and kept a grip on Toyo's hand with the other. He wasn't going to lose either of them again. He had come this far and he was sure of that much. "I went to my bank, and found you'd left a message there." And she had left another one at Stanford. "I got to the Spencers' the day after you left. I caught the next ship out, after I talked to Reiko. I had a hell of a time finding her, but the Spencers had her number." He had been an excellent detective. "She gave me the address here, but whenever I came, you were never here."

"We went to Ayabe right after we got here," she said, with huge, sad eyes. But she still couldn't believe that he was there, that he had survived, that he had come back to her, and all this way just to find her. "My parents were killed in an air raid."

He shook his head then, thinking of all they'd been through, all of them. Even poor Tak hadn't made it. "I came back a number of times, but you were never here. I kept asking the neighbors." And then she realized that he was the soldier the neighbors had mentioned.

"I thought you were the sentry, coming after us. . . . I think they're looking for geishas." She smiled at him.

"That wasn't what I had in mind," he said, devouring her with his eyes, remembering Tanforan, as they both did. "Or maybe it was," he said softly, and then

Toyo tugged at his hand just as Peter was about to kiss his mother.

"Do you have chocolates?" he asked, looking bored, and Peter shook his head.

"No, I don't. I'm sorry, Toyo."

"The other one did," he said with a look of annoyance, and Peter looked at Hiroko again, forgetting their son for just a moment.

"I'm sorry . . ." he said to her, "for everything . . . for all of it . . . for everything you had to go through . . . for my not being there with you . . . for not being there for him. . . ." He looked at Toyo. "For your parents. Hiroko, I'm so sorry. . . ." His eyes were filled with love and tenderness for her, his own miseries entirely forgotten. He was just so happy he had found her.

"*Shikata ga nai*," she said, and bowed low to him, reminding him of the phrase she had said to him before, so long ago, at Takeo's. It cannot be helped . . . *shikata ga nai*. . . . Perhaps not. But it had been so difficult for everyone and it had cost them so dearly.

"I love you," he said, as he took her in his arms and kissed her slowly, and then with all the longing that had filled him for three and a half years. It was hard to believe they had been apart for so long, and together for only moments before that. She remembered their time at Tanforan, the hours he had spent with her, talking to her, and their moments in the tall grass, hidden from everyone . . . the Buddhist priest who had "married" them in the brief ceremony that no one but they would ever honor. They had come through so much, and so far, and at last the days of shame and sorrow were over.

He smiled at her, and then looked down at their son, and even he could see how like him he was. And then Peter bowed low to her, as her father had done to Hidemi years before. And she bowed low to him and smiled, as he remembered her when they met, in her kimono.

"What are you doing, Mommy?" Toyo whispered.

"I am honoring your father," she said solemnly, as Peter took her hand, and then his, and they walked slowly into her parents' house. And she knew that somewhere they, and Ken, and Tak, and Yuji were watching. *"Arigato,"* she said softly, thanking Peter, and all of them, for all they had shared, as she closed the shoji screens gently behind her.

# About the Author

DANIELLE STEEL has been hailed as one of the world's most popular authors, with over 650 million copies of her novels sold. Her many international bestsellers include *In His Father's Footsteps*, *The Good Fight*, *The Cast*, *Accidental Heroes*, *Fall From Grace*, *Fairytale*, *Past Perfect*, *The Right Time*, *The Duchess*, *Against All Odds*, and other highly acclaimed novels. She is also the author of *His Bright Light*, the story of her son Nick Traina's life and death; *A Gift of Hope*, a memoir of her work with the homeless; *Pure Joy*, about the dogs she and her family have loved; and the children's books, *Pretty Minnie* in Paris and *Pretty Minnie in Hollywood*.

daniellesteel.com
Facebook.com/DanielleSteelOfficial
Twitter: @daniellesteel

On Sale in Hardcover
November 2018

#1 *New York Times* bestselling author
Danielle Steel tells the uplifting story of an ordinary
woman embracing an extraordinary adventure,
and the daring choice that transforms her world.

# Chapter One

WINONA FARMINGTON opened one eye and saw through the window the white wonderland she woke up to for most of the winter in Beecher, Michigan. It was a small town, almost two hours north of Detroit, with a population of ten thousand. Beecher's main claim to fame was that it had been hit by the tenth deadliest tornado in U.S. history in the 1950s, long before Winnie was born. Nothing much had happened there since.

The other side of her double bed was cold, which meant that Rob had gotten up at least an hour before, and left for the meat processing plant where he worked. She guessed even before she glanced out the window that he hadn't bothered to shovel after last night's snow. The house she lived in had been her mother's, and she owned it with her sister Marje. Marje was already married with kids when their mother died, and she and Erik owned their own house, so Winnie stayed in the family house and they agreed that if they ever sold it, they'd split the proceeds equally. But for now at least, Marje didn't need the money. Her husband owned a busy plumbing company, and the house was a good investment and bound to increase in value, so she'd never asked Winnie to sell it.

Rob stayed there with her almost every night. He had his own apartment, but rarely went there except when they had a fight, or if he stayed out too late and got too drunk when he went out with the boys, and didn't want to hear Winnie complain about it the next morning. The rest of the time he slept at Winnie's, did no repairs, felt no great attachment to the place, and only helped her with something minor when she asked him. He kept some clothes in her closet, but nothing too personal.

Winnie had once escaped Beecher to attend the University of Michigan in Ann Arbor, and had loved it for the three years she'd been there. She had big dreams then, and wanted to work in publishing in New York after she graduated. She'd even visited the city a couple of times with her roommates and loved it, but then her mother got sick at the end of junior year, and by the end of the summer, it looked as if she only had a few months to live. Winnie didn't want to miss being with her mother for her final days. They'd always been close, particularly after Marje moved out when she graduated from high school when Winnie was eight. She had her mother to herself from then on, and their time together was precious. Her mother had shared with her a love of reading, the delight of Jane Austen, the Brontë sisters, and her favorite authors.

Winnie took the first semester of senior year off to be with her. But she was no better by Christmas, and Winnie took spring semester off as well to nurse her. It had been hard to come home to a small, quiet town, where nothing ever happened, after the excitement of the university. Coming back to Beecher was like returning to her childhood, and her whole focus was on her mother. She had no life of her own. Her friends had married right out of high school, or gone to Detroit to find better jobs than they could find in Beecher. A few had gone to college, but not many. Some even had babies by then, and Winnie suddenly had nothing in common with them. She was busy with her mother's care.

It was never spoken, but Marje simply assumed that Winnie would care for their mother. She had a husband and a child by then and made it clear she had no time. Winnie was single, still in college, and Marje saw no reason why Winnie's plans couldn't be deferred, and her dreams put on the back burner. Winnie was the obvious choice of caretaker, and she didn't want to let her mother down. She had always given up so much for them. And Winnie didn't want to abandon her mother in her final months. She loved her and wanted to spend as much time with her as she could.

Miraculously, and despite the doctors' dire predictions, her mother had hung on for seven years, and even rallied several times, but never long enough for Winnie to leave again. She fought a noble battle, and finally died when Winnie was twenty-seven. By then it seemed too late to go back to college. She had a job, a house, a life, and New York and her dreams seemed as if they were on another planet by then. She was working as a cashier at a restaurant, and got a better job at the local printing company after that. She met Rob four months after her mother died, and the time had drifted by like a river from then on, carrying her along with it. And she didn't need a college degree for the job she had. Her own natural organizational skills were enough.

It was hard to believe she and Rob had been dating for eleven years. She wasn't madly in love with him, but he was familiar and comfortable. They never talked about marriage or the future, they lived in the present, had dinner together on most nights, went to the movies, bowling with friends sometimes. It wasn't what she really wanted, but there was no one else more interesting around, and suddenly she slipped from twenty-seven to twenty-nine, then turned thirty at dinner one evening with Marje, Erik, and Rob. Then just as quickly she was thirty-two and then thirty-five. They'd been together for ten years when she turned thirty-seven. And now she was thirty-eight and couldn't figure out where the years had gone. Eleven of them, with Marje reminding her constantly that she needed to get married and start having kids before it was too late. She conveniently forgot that seven of those years were spent taking care of their mother, while Marje claimed she was too busy to help. Winnie wasn't angry about it, but it was a fact of her life. She had sacrificed a big chunk of time, which she'd never get back.

She couldn't see herself having kids with Rob either, and he wasn't eager for kids or marriage. He was thirty-nine, and most of his friends were getting divorced after fifteen and twenty years of marriage. Her sister Marje and Erik had a good marriage and seemed happy enough. She knew her sister had had at least one affair, maybe two, which Marje had never admitted to, but Beecher was small, people talked, and Winnie had guessed. She didn't know if Erik knew or not. He was a good breadwinner and a terrific father who coached Little League for their two boys. Winnie couldn't imagine Rob doing that. He had nieces and nephews of his own who didn't interest him much, and he referred to all of them as the "rug rats."

Winnie had read in *Cosmopolitan* magazine once that women couldn't afford dead-end relationships after the age of twenty-eight, or they ran the risk of getting stuck in them. The magazine had warned that you turn forty before you know it. Her mom had always cautioned her to try to find the right man and settle down before the bloom was off the rose. She wasn't there yet, but she was getting close, with a man who didn't set her heart on fire, took her for granted most of the time, and never told her he loved her. It wasn't exactly a dead-end relationship, it was more of an open-ended one that just kept limping forward through the years without arriving anywhere. She wondered if he would marry her if she made a fuss about it, but she didn't because she wasn't sure how she felt about it herself. It was a no-frills relationship: a box of candy on Valentine's Day if he remembered, and he almost always forgot her birthday but would take her out to dinner a few days later. She couldn't see the point of getting married, unless they wanted kids, and they didn't. She wasn't ready to have babies, she wanted to figure out what she envisioned for her future first.

"Well, you'd better figure it out pretty damn soon," her sister scolded her. "Or you'll wake up one day and be forty-five or fifty, and it'll be too late, for kids anyway. It happens faster than you think." Marje was ten years older than Winnie.

"I'm only thirty-eight," Winnie reminded her.

"Yeah, and it seems like just last week you were twenty-eight. You won't be young forever, Win." Marje always liked reminding Winnie that she was getting older, it made her feel more comfortable about being middle-aged herself. It had taken Marje and Erik a long time to get pregnant, and their boys were now fourteen and seventeen.

They were good kids, who had no ambition to leave Beecher. Erik expected both of them to come to work with him at his plumbing company someday, and neither of them objected. They already worked there after school. The company was a good moneymaker, and neither boy was planning to go to college since their parents hadn't. Winnie's three years at Michigan, as an English major with a creative writing minor, were considered an aberration for her family. She'd gone to college before her nephews were even born, so she wasn't an example they could relate to, and she had done nothing special with her life.

She kept herself busy with the things she loved to do. She still read voraciously and was first on the list at the library for every bestseller that came out. Her mother had been the town librarian and instilled in her a love of books. She wrote short stories from time to time, and had done well in her writing classes in college. And when her mother had gotten too sick to continue working, Winnie had taken over one of her favorite duties. She read stories to children every Saturday morning. It was a volunteer job and she loved it. Her mother had been "The Story Lady" to the local children, and Winnie happily stepped into her shoes. She had done it to help her mother at first, who didn't want to disappoint the children who expected her to be there on Saturdays. It gave Winnie a chance to share the gifts her mother had given her with the children. She introduced them to "The Red Shoes," *Charlotte's Web*, *Stuart Little*, *The Little Prince*, and *The Secret Garden*, *Little Women*, and Nancy Drew to the slightly older girls. The children loved her and she got to read her favorite childhood books again. She had a gift with them, like her mother had, although she didn't think so. Marje always said the books had bored her, while Winnie devoured them, much to their mother's delight. Every Saturday morning, Winnie spent two hours at the library, and was "The Story Lady," carrying on her mother's tradition and following in her footsteps. It was Winnie's only contact with kids, other than her two nephews, who were as uninterested in books as their mother.

Winnie's other passion had always been horses, ever since she was a little girl. She'd had a chance to ride at a friend's father's farm, and had had a few lessons. She was a decent rider and her friend's father said she was a natural. She liked to ride, but what she liked best was watching them. She had an instinctive sense for what a horse seemed to be thinking or feeling. She had walked into the corral once where they were keeping a horse that had been mistreated before they bought him. No one had been able to ride him, he was wild-eyed and terrified, bucked off anyone who rode him, and kicked anyone who came near. The farmhands said he was hopeless and they were planning to sell him again, or worse. Winnie felt so sorry for the horse that she let herself into the corral where he stood alone. She spoke softly to him, as he eyed her in terror but didn't move. He let her stroke him, and pawed the ground next to her, as one of the farm hands watched, afraid to call out to her to stand back, stunned by what she was doing.

In time, Winnie was able to ride him, bareback with only a bridle. They called her "the horse whisperer" after that. She had a talent for taming abused horses, and people in Beecher knew it, and called on her once in a while to help them out. As far as they were concerned, she had a gift. She didn't get a chance to use it often, but it was there. It was as if she could get into a horse's mind and still its fears. They trusted her, and calmed down whenever she was there.

*       *       *

Winnie peeled off her flannel pajamas and got into the shower. She had a long, lean body, in contrast to Rob's heavyset frame with a paunch. He liked drinking beer when he came home from work. Marje had put on weight, and was a different body type from Winnie, who had always been tall and slim. Winnie had dark hair, pale blue eyes, and creamy skin. With better clothes and somewhere to wear them, she would have been pretty. Their mother had been, though she had let herself go once she was widowed at thirty-three. Her husband had died in a hunting accident. Marje remembered him slightly, Winnie didn't. Marje looked more like him, sturdy and rugged, with a tendency to put on weight after she had her kids. She envied Winnie's slim figure, but ate too much of what she cooked for her family to lose the weight she'd gained. She'd been the prom queen in high school, but looked ten years older than she was while Winnie looked younger than her age. Winnie had never been a prom queen and didn't care. She was always lost in the books she read.

While drying her hair, Winnie looked out the window again, trying to assess how long it would take her to shovel the driveway. She did it nearly every day since there was new snow almost every night this time of year. Rob could have, before he left for work, but never did. When she asked him to, he reminded her that it wasn't his house and that was why he parked his truck in the street, and suggested she do the same.

She made a bowl of instant oatmeal and had a cup of coffee, bundled up in her parka and snow boots, grabbed the shovel from the garage, put on gloves, and went to work on the driveway. It took her half an hour to get the snow pushed aside and packed down enough to drive over it in her SUV, but she was only ten minutes late when she got to the printing company where she worked as the production manager. She kept all the big projects organized and on track. She had exceptional organizational skills, and thanks to her, they met all their deadlines. It wasn't a creative job, but vital for the smooth running of the business, and she did it well.

Hamm Winslow, her boss, came out of his office and glared at her. She hated the job, and her boss, but it was decent money. He owned the printing company where she had worked for the last ten years, and her best friend, Barb, worked there too. She had a more menial job than Winnie, but was good with layouts, and very visual.

"Nice of you to come in before lunchtime," he said snidely. He always had something unpleasant to say, and had no respect for his employees, or anyone for that matter. He was a miserable person.

"Sorry, my driveway was iced up," she said blandly.

"Whose isn't? You expected to wake up in Hawaii, maybe? Get up earlier, don't come in here late again. Got it?" He was even nastier to the women who worked for him than the men, and he got away with it.

"Sorry." He was always angry and complaining about something. Nothing was ever done fast enough or well enough for him, and he took pleasure in pointing out publicly the mistakes they made. "He's in a great mood," Winnie commented under her breath as she slipped into her seat at the desk next to Barb's. They'd gone to middle school and high school together, and Barb had gone to junior college and got her AA degree, which didn't seem to make much difference. She'd been dating Pete for four years, they'd gotten engaged a few months before, and were planning to get married next summer. Her future husband was a dentist and a nice guy. She spent all her spare time now planning the wedding. They were going to have the reception at the local hotel. Barb wanted to work in his office after they were married and quit the job she had, which would leave Winnie to face the ogre alone. She wasn't looking forward to it.

"Somebody screwed up a big order for the bank," Barb whispered to her. "You should have heard him yelling ten minutes ago."

"Glad I missed that," Winnie whispered back, shot a smile at Barb, and turned on her computer. It felt just like high school, and middle school before that, when they sat next to each other in class. Barb opened a drawer and pointed to three bridal magazines in it and Winnie laughed.

"I'm throwing the bouquet at you, you know. You'd better be ready to catch it," Barb said, smiling.

"I'll be sure to duck," Winnie said, checking on an order she had on her screen. It wasn't ready yet, and they were getting close to deadline. She was going to get on the production department about it immediately. Hamm never realized how vital her services were to him, or never showed it if he did. He never praised her or thanked her.

"Rob is a great guy, you should marry him. It's time, Win," Barb said as a follow-up to her comment about the bouquet.

"Who says?" she said, looking unconcerned.

"We're getting old!"

"At thirty-eight? You sound like my sister. She got married right out of high school. Thank God we didn't do that. She could be a grandmother by now, for God's sake. Now there's a scary thought."

"*You'll* be old enough to be one by the time you start having kids, if you don't hurry up." There was nothing else to do in Beecher except marry, have kids, go bowling, and play softball in the summer. She didn't say it, but Winnie wanted more than that, much more. Barb had been engaged once before, after years of dating the same guy, and it hadn't worked out. He'd cheated on her constantly. Now she was ready to settle down, and in a hurry to have babies. Winnie wasn't. "Who are you waiting for? Bradley Cooper? Send him a map. You've got everything you need right now." That wasn't how Winnie saw it, but she didn't say it. She didn't know what she wanted, but she knew this wasn't it, working for Hamm Winslow for the rest of her life. And she wasn't sure Rob was it either. After eleven years, she knew things weren't going to get any better than they were now. Their relationship was lackluster at best, but not bad enough to walk away from either. It wasn't exciting, or romantic. Rob said only women, and men with low testosterone, were romantic and liked all that mushy crap. That was one way to look at it. She didn't expect him to throw roses at her feet, but a little more attention might be nice. Like shoveling the driveway for her once in a while, so she wouldn't be late for work and didn't have to start the day cold and tired. He could have done at least that for her, particularly since he slept there most nights. He bought groceries for them occasionally, which he thought was a big deal. He always said she owned the house after all, and she wasn't paying rent, so she could afford to pay for her own food.

Both women got busy at work then, Winnie went to push the production department. At the end of the day, Barb turned to her with a question.

"How about dinner at my place tonight? Pete is going to a dental conference in Detroit."

"I'm having dinner at my sister's," Winnie said with a sigh.

"That should be fun. Not."

"Yeah, but she makes a big fuss about it when I don't see her for a while. She claims the boys miss me. I know they don't. They don't even talk to me when I'm there. I wouldn't have at their age either."

"Have a good time," Barb said with a smirk, and they both left work and got in their cars. It was already dark, bitter cold, and the roads were icy. But it was only two miles to Marje and Erik's house and Winnie was a careful driver. She let herself in the back door when she got there, and the boys, Jimmy and Adam, were watching TV in the basement playroom. You could hear it all the way up to the front door. And as usual, the house was a mess. No one ever cared. Marje's strong suit was not keeping house, and she made no apology for it. Erik was used to it and didn't seem to see it.

She found Marje in the kitchen, getting dinner ready. It was pot roast, which seemed like a hearty meal for a cold night. Her sister was a good cook, and her family were all big eaters. Winnie wasn't, but it smelled good anyway. Marje was lucky, she hadn't had a job in years. She was a stay-at-home mom, thanks to Erik's business, and she got a new car every two years. She drove a Cadillac Escalade, which was a lot nicer than Winnie's six-year-old SUV.

"How was work?" Marje asked, as she checked on the pot roast and smiled at Winnie. They were very different, but there was a sisterly bond between them. Marje blamed their mother for encouraging Winnie to be a dreamer. Marje had made fun of her when Winnie had written a paper once in high school about why Mr. Darcy from *Pride and Prejudice* was her favorite hero of all time and she wanted to marry a man like him. Winnie loved stories from another century, preferably set in England, which her sister thought was ridiculous. Marje loved watching reality shows, and still never read a book. Their mother had given up trying to encourage Marje to read in her teens, and shared her love of books with her younger daughter.

"Work was okay," Winnie answered. "Hamm is such a jerk. He's not happy unless he's beating someone up and humiliating them in front of everyone else. It gets pretty old." But they both knew the money was good, and Winnie had seniority now. She didn't want to start over somewhere else, which was part of what kept her with Rob too. What if she never met anyone and never had another date? It was easier to stick with "the devil she knew," at work and with Rob.

They talked for a few minutes about Erik and the kids while Winnie set the table and Marje slid into her favorite subject.

"So what's happening with you and Rob?"

"Nothing. Don't start that, please. We both go to work, he comes over at night, we fall asleep, and go back to work the next day."

"Sounds very exotic," Marje said, "and a lot like marriage. You've had a lot of years of practice. You might as well just do it one of these days."

"Why are you so hot for me to get married?" It always annoyed her. It was the only thing they ever talked about.

"I don't want your life to pass you by. Trust me, at your age it starts to fly. I don't want you to miss it."

"I'm not missing anything. I'm happy."

"Really? You don't like your job, your boss is a horse's ass, you're not crazy about your boyfriend, and what else is there in your life?"

"What's in your life?" Winnie volleyed back. "Erik and the kids. That's no more exciting than mine."

"It suits me," Marje said, and Winnie knew it did. "You've always been such a dreamer, I'm just afraid you're going to dream your life away, waiting for some kind of magic to happen. There's no magic, Winnie. This is all we get." It sounded sad to Winnie.

"You mean I don't get to be Cinderella when I grow up? Mom always said I could be anything I wanted to be. That's why I went to college and wanted a job in New York." It would have been so much more than what she had here.

"Well, that didn't happen, so you've got to work with what you've got. 'Bloom where you're planted,' as they say." That was very philosophical for Marje, and Winnie smiled.

"Very profound. Don't I look like I'm blooming?" she teased her sister. She knew Marje meant well, or thought she did, although she could be a pain in the neck at times. And there was a wide chasm between them. They were so different and always had been. That hadn't changed.

"Actually," Marje said, narrowing her eyes to study her, "you look depressed. Why don't you get highlights or something, or change your hair color? Rob might like it." It was always about Rob and what might make him propose. Marje had dyed blond hair with three inches of dark roots. Winnie's was her natural dark brown, almost black, color. Their mother used to say she looked like Snow White.

"He likes me the way I am," Winnie argued. "And I'm not depressed. I accept my life as it is." But she thought about what she'd said again on the way home. Did she accept her life? Had she made her peace with it? Did she still want more? Did she have a right to it? She was no longer sure. Dinner at her sister's had been the way it always was, always the same conversation between the adults, about work or the kids, brief chaos when the boys joined them at the table, and then Winnie went home to her empty house. Rob was bowling with friends that night.

She turned on the lights when she got home and sat in front of the fireplace in the living room for a few minutes. She remembered when she used to sit there with her mother, in the last years of her life, talking about the books they read, and the dreams the stories spawned. She still thought she was going back to college in those days, but they never talked about that because it would only happen after her mother was dead. And then she didn't go back anyway.

She heard the front door open behind her and turned to see Rob walk in and shake the snow off his boots. He was a big, burly guy with lumberjack looks, and didn't talk a lot. His family was originally from Norway, and there was a raw, hearty look to him. She had expected him to come home later, he usually did.

"You're home early." She smiled at him. "I just got home from Marje and Erik's."

He went to get a beer, popped it open and took a sip, and sat down on the couch next to her, the can in his hand. "Everyone was tired tonight, and two of the guys were sick. We called it a night early, and went to Murphy's Bar for a while." She could smell it on his breath. He wasn't an alcoholic, but he drank a lot. He said it was the Scandinavian in him. Her brother-in-law Erik drank just as much. Most of the women she knew didn't. "What are you doing in here?" He looked around the room they never sat in. They either sat in the kitchen or her bedroom. There was an old-lady quality to the living room. She hadn't changed anything since her mother died. It was full of her mother's things, and some antiques she'd inherited from her mother. Winnie kept the room as a shrine to her.

"I was just thinking of my mom when I got home, and the books we used to read. At the end, I used to read aloud to her. *Rebecca*, it was her favorite." She didn't know why she was telling Rob, she knew he didn't care. Just the thought of reading a book put him to sleep.

"That sounds maudlin," he said matter-of-factly, chugged his beer, and got up. "I'm beat. I'm going to bed."

She turned off the lights and followed him upstairs. He turned on the TV in her bedroom, dropped his clothes on the floor, and climbed into bed while she took a shower, in case he wanted to make love. Their sex life was pretty good, despite his lack of romantic sensibilities. He was great in bed when he was in the right mood. It had been part of the glue that held them for the last eleven years, the strongest thing between them.

She started talking to him when she got out of the shower, and he didn't answer. She walked into the bedroom, and he was sound asleep on his back, snoring loudly. The beers on his bowling night had caught up with him. She looked at him for a moment, put on her pajamas, and tiptoed downstairs to her mother's bookcase. She knew exactly where the book was, and she hadn't read it in years. *Jane Eyre*. She ran back upstairs with it and got into bed, smiling as she held it. It was like a visit with her mother, and a trip back in time, as she opened the familiar book. The pages were yellowed, and it felt like meeting up with old friends as she began reading, and Rob continued to snore next to her. She knew that when she woke up in the morning, he'd be gone again, and he wouldn't have shoveled the driveway for her if it snowed during the night. Nothing was ever going to change. But as she read the book her mother had given her as a young girl, nothing around her mattered, and her real life faded away.